"**W**e've
we
ton

kissed Leda's soft mouth gently.

No tongue, of course, Leda noted silently to herself. We both have to go to work now, no time for noogies; that's the morning excuse. And at night— it's late, she's tired, and we have to get up early, she says. But I'll do you if you want me to, she'll say, if you need me to!

Leda suddenly felt an overwhelming urge to pull Chrys to her roughly, to open her lover's mouth wide with her own and probe deeply with her tongue that soft, warm cavern; to feed passionately and hungrily from her mouth. What she wanted most was to rip off Chrys's conservative clothes and run her fingernails over every inch of that soft, lotioned, and perfumed skin until it reddened with anger at her roughness, at her cruelty; wanted more than anything at this moment to force her lover down on the cold kitchen floor and bite her wickedly all over, then tie her, naked, to the table and fuck her with wild abandon, with all the heat that burned beneath Leda's skin; let out the desperate, aching need that boiled beneath the surface of Leda's calm exterior, the need to make her woman scream with desire and pleasure, to let loose the groans and grunts and cries of wild animal passion under Leda's fevered command....

Also by Aarona Griffin:

*Passage & Other Stories*

# LEDA

**&**

# THE HOUSE OF SPIRITS

## AARONA GRIFFIN

ROSEBUD

First Rosebud Edition 1997

First Printing November 1997

ISBN 1-56333-585-9

Manufactured in the United States of America
Published by Masquerade Books, Inc.
801 Second Avenue
New York, N.Y. 10017

leda

# 1.

"Don't you ever just get sick of everything, sometimes? I mean, what is the purpose of all this? Fuck, I just get so tired of this whole damn city and the blank faces on these streets, the money hustle, the patheticness of this whole race, and nobody wins, now do they? I get so fucking frustrated. So much fucking attitude in this fucking community. What a fucked life, I swear. I feel like I'm twenty-nine going on sixty. Good-bye youth. Wherever the hell it went, I'll never know."

Leda took a long breath and thrust her hands deep into the front pockets of her jeans, resting her chin on the stiff collar of her brown bomber jacket. Her short almost-black hair was moussed into a myriad of soft spikes and her small round glasses reflected the street-lights and the headlights of cars that passed as she and her lover walked down Market Street. It was a cool, crisp San Francisco night, a little after eight o'clock, and they were on their way to the video store to rent a video.

It was Chrys's idea. Leda couldn't get excited about anything tonight. Her answer had been, "What the hell, why not escape into the illusion of living. Makes the reality of our own lack of life a little easier to take, right?"

"I'll take that as a yes," Chrys'd answered, and they'd hopped into the car and come on down to the video store.

Chrys sighed and looked in shop windows or watched the people as they passed. She was used to this sort of rambling from Leda, but the last few weeks had been just a little more intense than usual.

"You know, you're sort of like a volcano," Chrys said.

"How's that?" Leda returned, a little defensive.

"Just when I think you're only simmering over the state of the world and your boring life, as usual, you build up into this incredible pitch and I'm never sure if you're going to just blow and wipe out all living things in a thousand-mile radius or just go back to simmering again." She chuckled quietly, pleased with her analogy.

"That's cute, sweetheart," Leda said sarcastically. "At least I'm exotic, then, right? One-of-a-kind." Leda smiled curtly at Chrys, then shook her head a little and said, under her breath, "Yeah, and dangerous...watch out, you never know what might set me off, babe."

Chrys heard this last addition but knew better than to respond; she'd lived with Leda nearly a decade, and although there had been growth and changes in both of them over the years, Leda's basic personality seemed to stay pretty much the same. Or at least Chrys had thought so, until just recently. Leda seemed to be changing almost daily, and this round of discontentment seemed to be for real, not just a passing fancy.

Change wasn't something Chrys liked a lot of. She preferred consistency; a sturdy foundation that one could count on; calm and certainty and a steady pace.

She had some tiny inkling that this steady pace was about to drive Leda crazy.

"C'mon, let's just get a movie and have a nice, relaxing evening, okay? Can we do that?" Chrys asked, her voice a little edgy, irritated. "No fighting, no bitching, just for tonight, all right? Then you can start all over tomorrow, refreshed."

The light changed and they crossed the street.

"Fine, Chrys, whatever you want," Leda answered flatly as they entered the store.

But somewhere deep inside Leda, there was a bomb ticking, about to explode, a dark little tremor that was about to break out into a full-fledged earthquake; she could feel it beneath her skin, pushing at the confines of her body and the present state of her life.

This couldn't be it, just couldn't be what she'd been put here for: this mundane existence, five-day work week and video rentals on the weekends.

This nice little marriage was strangling her. She sometimes felt like screaming at all hours of the night, couldn't sleep, and had nightmares or twisted dreams like little trips through mazes she couldn't get out of.

Leda wasn't sure she could sit through one more stupid, mindless, family entertainment new release. She was sick of viewing other people's lives; it was time to have one of her own—the kind of life she really wanted —before she became another casualty of caution.

Leda loved Chrys, more than anyone she'd ever been with before. But something had to be done before she self-destructed and the whole damn relationship went up in flames.

Flames, yes, that was what she needed: heat and passion and a little danger, a little of the unknown, the wild, intensity she'd left behind with her youth.

Maybe she hadn't lost her youth at all, Leda thought, but just her daring spirit and the hunger for a good challenge. Yes. All she really needed was someone to give her a good challenge like she hadn't had in years. Yeah. And it was time to start looking for it.

Because something had to give.

Something big.

## 2.

The gateway to her new search came in the form of a flyer stapled to a pole on Market Street. She saw it on the way to work Monday morning and tore it off, taking it with her. At lunch break she went for a little walk and read it again.

FIRE AND FLESH—A PLAY SPACE FOR WOMEN WITH DISCRIMINATING NEEDS. COMPLETE DUNGEONS, MAZES, DIFFERENT SETS FOR CREATIVE SCENES, AND OUR VERY OWN ONE-OF-A-KIND JUNGLE WILDERNESS, COMPLETE WITH A WORKING WATERFALL AND STREAM. NO ANIMALS ALLOWED, UNLESS HUMAN EQUIVALENTS. CALL FOR INFORMATION. WE DO NOT KEEP LISTS, COMPLETELY ANONYMOUS MEMBERSHIP.

And a phone number at the bottom with an area code outside of the city. She'd have to drive to get there. They only had one car between the two of them and she and Chrys never seemed to go anywhere separately, especially overnight. How would she get the car, and what would she say about why she wouldn't be back until the morning?

Leda knew she'd have to really dig for this one and make it as believable as possible. It would take a lot of planning, and energy, and what would she wear? All her gear was outdated and old and she hadn't bought a leather item in years. And her body...well, Christ, marriage'll soften up any young body. But what the hell. She'd put her ego aside and go for the thrill.

Besides, Chrys thought she was a knockout still. Of course, that was a biased opinion. But just because she hadn't cruised in almost ten years didn't mean she couldn't whip herself into some sort of decent shape.

*Go for the guts, girl. Before you lose everything.*

Quickly, before she changed her mind, she walked briskly to a phone booth on the corner and dialed the number.

"Thank you for calling the Flesh Line. If you haven't come before, you'll come like you never have before! Join us on Friday and Saturday nights," the recording told her, "from 8:00 P.M. to 6:00 A.M., doors open from 8:00 P.M. to 11:00. P.M. No one allowed in after 11:00 P.M. so get your ass in gear and be on time or you won't get your share. Leave your name and phone number at the tone for a reservation and a call-back with the location. First time membership is twenty-five dollars at the door, and members with cards and ID are fifteen dollars. No one under twenty-one allowed."

A dyke with blonde hair dressed in office drag walked by Leda as she tried to look nonchalant, listening to a recording for some hot sex club out in the broad daylight of a fall afternoon in the financial district. She nodded at the woman, who—surprise, surprise —nodded back amiably as a way of hello, a subtle confirmation of a sisterhood of sorts. Leda turned and watched the woman walk away down the sidewalk, feeling her skin flush with arousal, her heart pounding as she dared to envision this stranger naked and sweaty and moaning under the covers...Leda hadn't touched another woman, other than Chrys, in years.

"This is an exclusive club," the recording continued, snapping Leda out of her hot reverie as if to chastise her for letting her mind wander. "You show up, you play. You don't want to play, it's ten dollars to sit in the viewing room behind the one-way glass. Only a designated area of the club is open for viewing and all participants are aware you'll be watching."

Leda's pussy throbbed. This was something she never told anyone, this little thrill she had for watching! But she only got to watch once, and Chrys almost died of embarrassment as Leda stuck to her request that Chrys play with herself—bring herself to orgasm while Leda watched—a bright light shining on Chrys's face to increase the bad-girl quality of the deed.

Chrys had told Leda that night before falling asleep what a wicked woman she was. It felt to Leda like the first true thing Chrys had said about her in a long time. But she was sure Chrys had no idea of the depth of that truth; not in a really bad way, but a good sort of wicked. Leda would never push Chrys against her will for her own satisfaction—unfortunately. There was no room for force, power, domination, or submission in their bed, their home, their nice little marriage.

So ten bucks wasn't all that much money, and it wouldn't kill their marriage now, would it? Leda was dying to let loose, couldn't hold back any longer; she could feel the danger in trying to hold on to this questionable control.

A brisk wind blew down the street and she turned her back against it, listening for more information, more temptations.

"If that's your thang, well, feel free to touch your thang on into the morning while being entertained. Designated areas for harder players and padded rooms for sound allowance are available. Come push the limits of your desire."

Leda's mind went wild with images and possibilities.

"Free tour and initiation lessons for first-time Fire and Flesh virgins—of course, we'll keep your preferences in mind. See you there, if you dare."

In the background Leda could hear the sounds of sex and whips and groans and grunts of pleasure. This lingered on the line until a beep sounded.

Leda stood with the receiver against her ear for a moment, seeing nothing but an orgy in her head of a thousand wildly passionate women all seeking release and each other in a sweating, throbbing mass of sexual hunger. She wanted to be a part of it, to rule over a small part of this passion. A small part, yes, to begin with.

"Uh, Leda, 555-4260," she said awkwardly, the numbers of her work phone tumbling out of her mouth and into the receiver, then quickly hung up. She hoped they wouldn't say who was calling.

Her heart thudded in her chest and she tried smoothly, inconspicuously to pull her underwear out from the crack of her ass, the moist lips of her sex drawing them in uncomfortably under her jeans as she hung up the phone. No one seemed to notice. Leda's face was flushed and her nipples throbbed at attention under her crisp white shirt. She had an urge to pop open her front-clasp bra and expose her tits to the world while hollering at the top of her lungs, "Oh, take me, sweet devil desire!"

Instead, she lowered her head and cleared her throat, taking off her glasses and wiping away the condensation with a handkerchief retrieved from her pocket. She dabbed at the moisture on her forehead and took a long slow breath to calm herself, waiting for the wild passion in her eyes to subside so she could face the financial district and the reality of her workday once again.

She had to go. No doubt about it.

Leda would have a plan and an excuse by Friday, and be on her way by 9:00 P.M. sharp.

# 3.

Thursday night, late, the phone rang. One of the lumps under the heavy comforter moved, groaning, and turning over in the bed. The other, Leda, remained perfectly still in a decent imitation of a comfortable sleeping position, holding her breath, wide awake, heart pounding.

The phone was on Chrys's side of the bed, so she usually picked it up. She hated being woken up from a deep sleep, especially after a certain time of the night after which she could never get back to sleep. It was after midnight. Leda said a little silent prayer that Chrys would wake up.

Sure enough, by the third ring Chrys's sandy head emerged from the blankets, hair tousled, eyes still shut. With a little groan she reached out for the receiver on

17

the bedside table, pulling some of the covers with her.

"Hullo?" she said into it, her voice heavy with sleep. "Yeah, no, hi Martha, it's okay, we were just sleeping… no problem. What time is it?"

Leda listened, trying not to shake the bed with her pounding heart.

"Mmm hmm. Mmm hmmm," Chrys mumbled into the receiver, resting her head on the edge of the bed as she hung off it a little so the phone wouldn't fall off the bedside table.

"Oh, jeez, I'm sorry to hear that, is she okay? Mmmm. Well, sure. Of course. Well, I mean, actually I can't tomorrow night, I'm having a business meeting here. No, wait, don't worry, let me ask Leda, I'm sure she won't mind. No, no problem. Really. Hang on, let me see if she's awake."

Chrys, eyes still closed, rolled over onto her back, the receiver still in one hand outstretched toward the phone, the other hand kind of landing with a flop on Leda's covered figure.

"Leda, sweetheart, telephone—wake up, it's Martha. She needs you to stay over and baby-sit the kids tomorrow. Her mother's sick and needs help tomorrow night, something about her sister can't do it and Rachel's out of town until Saturday. Okay? I said you wouldn't mind, do you mind?"

Leda cleared her throat, concentrating on sounding groggy. "No, I don't mind. I didn't really have any plans for tomorrow night anyway. Tell her I'm sorry to hear that, and of course I will."

Chrys's limp arm lifted off Leda and she sort of rolled back over toward the receiver, hanging off the bed again.

"Martha, it's fine, she said she'll be there, don't worry." There was the whispery sound of a voice saying something on the other end of the line. Leda froze, wondering if Martha would really come through or not.

"Okay, I'll tell her. Kiss the baby for me and don't worry, everything will be okay. G'night, Martha."

There was a sleepy pause and then Chrys reached out and put the receiver back in the cradle with a clatter.

"She said to tell you you two can discuss the big payoff of this huge debt later. She's such a nut. It's really no big deal," Chrys sighed, turning over and settling back under the covers.

"No, no big deal," Leda said as casually as possible. "I don't mind. I know she'd do the same for me, I mean us, if we needed her."

There was a muffled agreement from beneath the comforter and then deep breathing. It was always incredible to Leda how Chrys could just turn over and fall right back to sleep without any readjustment or preparation time, just boom and she was out again—if it wasn't that particular hour of the night.

*Yeeeesuh!* Leda crowed to herself. How simple it was! Of course, she wouldn't be cheating on Chrys, just watching. Just taking some space like she deserved, just like anyone. After all, she wasn't a prisoner, just married. And of course there was a difference, wasn't there?

She drifted off into a light sleep filled with wet tongues and shining lips, wet slits between open legs, bidding her come in, come in, we've been waiting for you....

# 4.

Friday dawned clear and cold. Leda and Chrys sucked down some coffee and toast together, standing at the counter in the kitchen, both running late.

Leda wore her usual work attire: white shirt rolled up at the sleeves, jeans (black today), boots. Since it was always cold in their house, Chrys already had on her long coat over her slacks and blouse and sensible shoes. Her long sandy hair was swept back in a French twist. Leda always admired how she could make such nice designs with it, but today she could hardly look at Chrys straight on. She knew that face by heart anyway, eyes closed. And even after all these years, Leda had to admit Chrys was still a knockout.

Yes, true. But in a very reserved way, a way she hadn't been when they'd first met. Years ago. When Leda had been young and bold and free…

"Listen," Leda said, interrupting her internal ragging and clearing her throat. "I think I'll just leave straight from work for Martha's house, that way I'll beat the five o'clock rush out of the city and make sure I'm there by the time Martha has to split, okay?"

That way she'd be able to hang out till it was time to get dressed and go. She could just grab something from the deli and eat it at work. Everyone usually left by five o'clock, but she sometimes stayed late, so most likely no one would suspect anything or be around—she hoped.

"Oh," Chrys said, surprised, looking up from buttering her second piece of toast, her face a little pouty. "That means we won't see each other at all until tomorrow night then. I was expecting to at least see you between coming home from work and going back out to Martha's."

Oh.

"Oh, yeah, I know, me too. But there's so much to finish up at work today before the weekend and you know how the traffic is anytime after 3:00 P.M. on a Friday. She wanted me to get there just after dinner so she could leave right away, and that's around six-thirty or so."

"Well, seven o'clock anyway," Chrys added.

"Yeah. But why come all the way here for fifteen minutes just to go back out to the bridge?"

Leda chewed her toast, her deep blue eyes full of as much logic and innocence as she could muster, not knowing what else to say, if anything. She could feel Chrys's brain working, but she knew she was only feeling sad that they wouldn't be together. She would never suspect anything; they'd really been together too long for that kind of melodrama.

*This* kind of melodrama, Leda thought.

Chrys looked thoughtfully at Leda, then finished her toast and coffee and turned to the sink to rinse her cup.

"Yeah, you're right, sweetie. I was just being selfish, hoping to steal a last kiss before you flew away for the night and left me to our cold bed alone without you. It's been so long since we've slept apart, can you believe how long?"

Leda considered the question, almost letting escape her initial reaction which would have been something on the lines of: *Yes! Forever! A lifetime! A life sentence! A purgatory's worth of time and suffocation!*

But that wasn't even particularly true in all respects: The love was still there and she didn't necessarily want to leave what they'd built together. It's just that things had changed, stagnated, like their life together had shrunk and left no room for her bigger...wilder...needs. Yeah, needs. Sweetness and cuddles and happy home had begun to grate on her.

Still, she wasn't doing anything wrong, nothing to ruin what they'd built, either. And wouldn't be, she reminded herself, suddenly fighting off a huge wave of guilt as she looked at Chrys's tender nostalgic face. Leda swallowed and did her best to sound sad about the apart thing, too.

"Long time," she said, nodding and smiling what she hoped appeared as a sane and loving smile. She was beginning to wonder, herself, about the sane part.

Chrys moved toward her and took Leda's coffee mug out of her hands, then wrapped her arms around Leda's neck.

"We've been through a lot you and I, haven't we?" she said sweetly. "I'll miss you tonight, punkin." And she leaned in and kissed Leda's soft mouth gently.

No tongue, of course, Leda noted silently to herself. We both have to go to work now, no time for noogies; that's the morning excuse. And at night—it's late, she's tired, and we have to get up early, she says. But I'll do you if you want me to, she'll say, if you need me to!

Leda suddenly felt an overwhelming urge to pull Chrys to her roughly, to open her lover's mouth wide with her own and probe deeply with her tongue that soft, warm cavern; to feed passionately and hungrily from her mouth. What she wanted most was to rip off Chrys's conservative clothes and run her fingernails over every inch of that soft, lotioned, and perfumed skin until it reddened with anger at her roughness, at her cruelty; wanted more than anything at this moment to force her lover down on the cold kitchen floor and bite her wickedly all over, then tie her, naked, to the table and fuck her with wild abandon, with all the heat that burned beneath Leda's skin; let out the desperate, aching need that boiled beneath the surface of Leda's calm exterior, the need to make her woman scream with desire and pleasure, to let loose the groans and grunts and cries of wild animal passion under Leda's fevered command....

*Whooooaaa!* her internal voice warned, flashing little exploding lights before her now alarmingly lust-filled eyes. Leda quickly pecked a final moment to the soft little kiss, pulling away as if suddenly realizing how late it was, her face slightly flushed. Chrys, surprised, looked at her and smiled, thinking the rush of passion a natural desire between them and looking flattered.

"Wish we had more time," Chrys said seductively, like a kitten.

Leda looked up only long enough to see Chrys's coy, beaming face, relieved to see how Chrys had taken her response. Then Leda looked quickly down at her watch, feeling certain Chrys could read her nasty thoughts, and that somehow she would know they were leading her elsewhere....

*Know what?* she asked to herself. *I'm not doing anything wrong!*

But still, she'd been on edge now for the last couple of days and these episodes were becoming a common occurrence, she was beginning to notice; these earth-shattering adrenaline rushes complete with Technicolor images of naked women and a stereo sensurround soundtrack of moans and whispers. And Leda was concerned that she was beginning to experience little flashes of anger, almost hatred toward Chrys, for reasons she couldn't yet pinpoint. After all, they'd discussed this many times: The Compromise. Chrys had been very clear years ago that bondage and SM weren't really her style. And Leda would never have dreamed of forcing Chrys....

Well, maybe dreamed of it, but...

"Ho, it's late, my sweet," Leda said, pointing to her wristwatch. "Caroline will be here to pick you up any minute and I still have to gas up the car on the way in. Have to be off." She pecked a good-bye kiss on Chrys's forehead.

"I'll miss you tonight, but I'll call you after the kid is down and sleeping, okay? Around eight o'clock or so. Your meeting should be over by then. Have a good day today."

And with that, she moved briskly out of the kitchen to the front door, where she reached into the closet for her old worn leather jacket. She hadn't worn it in years, but it still fit—she'd tried it on last night while Chrys was in the shower. Luckily, leather never really went out of style, and even the cut of it had come back in in the last year or so.

With a quick wave to Chrys who was now standing between the kitchen and the living room, Leda went to open the front door.

"Wait, Lee, where's your overnight bag? Aren't you bringing anything with you? Like your toothbrush? Or your glasses?"

Leda jumped and froze, then quickly turned back and looked at Chrys. "Oh, I already put it in the car this morning, all packed up and ready to go. I knew I'd probably be running late as usual. And I'm wearing my contacts today. Thanks for reminding me, though! *Ciao* honey!"

And she finally managed to escape into the crisp fall morning.

Chrys watched the door close behind Leda. Somewhere in her subconscious a note was made that this was the first time in years she'd seen Leda take her leather jacket to work. In fact, the first time in years she'd worn it at all, after talking about selling it for as long. Instead, what she heard straight out in her head was a sigh, and the pushing aside of any further thoughts about Leda; mental notes of her workday ahead and what not to forget to take to with her to the office, and all the other menial tasks the habitual brain attends to, forcing its way onto center stage.

And then there was a honking outside and Caroline and her car pool had arrived to pick up Chrys, right on time as usual.

# 5.

The whole damn day dragged out as if it were a scorching hot summer afternoon in the deep south; in actuality it was another crisp, nippy day in San Francisco. But Leda was sure the clock was keeping time for some other galaxy, it was moving so excruciatingly slow.

By the time Leda slipped out to grab a sandwich for dinner, the early fall sun was setting and the city lights were humming with electricity, preparing for the long party night ahead.

Leda suddenly felt horribly guilty.

Yes, the major emotion Leda could certainly pinpoint if asked to do so at any particular moment of this day was guilt. Straight out and neon bright. But running a close second was a shy streak, mixed heavily with a strangely familiar awkward rush of almost adolescent excitement; the kind of sexual energy that had propelled her wildly through her teens and shot her out like a bullet into the world and into her twenties. She'd ridden that wave all the way through, right into Chrys's lovin' arms.

And there she'd landed.

Stalled out, really.

Well, not at first, she certainly couldn't say that. Fire was what they created and what kept her alive. But this smoldering that it had turned into didn't do it. A pilot light, for God's sake, could not do it. And sure, yeah, with age and maturity, the happy, horny bunnies were supposed to turn into sleeker versions of other, perhaps rather farmish animals.

But, no, not Leda. She wasn't built for that. There was a hum that kept her up at night now that would not let her rest until she sated this hunger that was beginning to devour her mind like an obsession.

*And my sanity, too!* she mused nervously, unable to eat much of her sandwich, her stomach a meeting of nerve endings. *Okay, okay, let's do it. Get dressed, phone home like a good ET and get out of here already. Be bold. No guts, no glory, chickie. Let's gooooo!*

And with that, she wrapped up the remains of her sandwich and slipped into the office bathroom. It was a largish space with a good mirror and lighting for checking out appearances. Leda locked the door and dropped her workout bag onto one side of the counter that flanked the sink; she'd slipped in her old pair of cuffs just in case—a highly optimistic move—and her favorite pair of ankle restraints, which she hadn't used in years, but was dying to. Chrys had dabbled in it—the bondage, the idea of scenes—but she felt like it made sex too much work, too complicated, too much energy required. Chrys liked to kiss a little, rub their bodies together, and kiss some more, then go straight for the big O.

Too much energy to put a little creativity into it, a little challenge, a little danger, a little planning?

Wow. How had Leda landed in a house with someone who felt that way? How could anyone really feel that way? What could be more important than pushing the intimacy envelope, pushing your limits with someone you love? Too much energy? Christ!

But Leda could feel the energy in her own now semi-naked body beating through her like she was sixteen again, a just-ripening fruit bursting from the vine, hungering for what she didn't know; hungering for the unexplored, the unexperienced. She felt like that silly, sex-hungry young woman again, only this time with not quite the same cockiness she'd had before.

But who knew what might resurface from the ruins of time? Like the familiarity of getting back on a motorcycle after years of not riding, Leda knew the feel of the power and pleasure and pain, and the sweet thrill of a seduction well conducted.

In the mirror, she snapped open her front-clasp bra

and watched her well-rounded tits tumble out, watched her hands run over their smooth creamy surface, making the pink nipples hard and puckered. Then she bent over and reached into her bag, withdrawing a leather item that proved to be a vest with a tie-up front that, as she slipped her arms through and began to lace up the front, she found left much cleavage and temptation to the eye. That was the plan, and why she'd bought it just yesterday on her lunch break, especially for the occasion of her, well, rebirth of sorts.

But, of course, she wouldn't do anything stupid, wasn't going to "cheat." No.

*No*, she thought, running her hand down her lightly sloping belly. She scowled at the roundness and sucked in her stomach, turning a little sideways to see if it still worked or if it'd gone too far. She relaxed, deciding she was still somewhat in control of her body at least, and that sucking it in looked better. Not that she was trying to impress anyone. But what she saw was better than she'd hoped.

"No," she whispered aloud into the tiled room as her hand slid down to her blue cotton panties, which she slipped down over her downy thighs and stepped out of, tossing them into the bag and reaching down to retrieve a new pair: black, thong-style. She stepped into them and watched in the mirror as she pulled the black fabric slowly up her firm legs, flexing the muscles of her thighs, then bending her knees and doing a little squat to push her crotch down onto the soft, shiny fabric more quickly as if she couldn't wait for it to make contact with her already moist lips. Her clit was already awake, the satin of the panties exciting it, just at the thought of what might be tonight.

"Oh, no, stop, don't...," she moaned into the mirror playfully as the G-string slid up between her legs, ever so slightly into the slit of her sex and up the crack of her ass as she pulled them up harder, her clit pulsing lightly as she rode the panties for just the briefest second, wetting them like a tease.

A wicked little chuckle escaped from deep in her throat as she studied her reflection in the mirror now: light face flushed pink with anticipation and smiling slightly, blue eyes clear and direct and ready to face off with...well, you know, just in case someone might accept her challenge. Her full tits bound against her chest and tightly laced together left cleavage for days, the shadows between her globes tempting where a tongue might seek out the shade, to wet it, to taste her skin or a drop of fresh sweat, and down to her belly button and the high waist of her shiny black G-string.

The face in the mirror changed expression, one nicely arched eyebrow rising over long dark eyelashes, the head tipping to the side a little and her mouth puckering into a funny pooched smile of doubt. Her cheeks were rosy.

*Now come on, Leda girl, that isn't really what you're going for, not really, right?* she asked herself silently. *Just to watch, just to see, be around it, be inside the scene and feel the power, to remind me who I was, and what remains of me today. That's all. Right?*

She ran a hand over her short black spikes, perking them up, and smiled widely, leaning into the mirror and checking her teeth, running a finger over them. She decided to brush with the toothbrush and paste she'd brought, then did a quick once-over of her cleanliness status. She'd showered this morning and had an easy day. But for good measure, and for no good reason but to feed the wild streak that was beginning to raise its mischievous head again, she did a little wash-up of the most important parts, then surveyed the final product in the mirror.

She felt old and nervous and embarrassed—but only for a minute. Because the sparks she saw flying in those eyes in the mirror reminded her of what lay in waiting, hibernating for too long, but by no means dead and gone. The season, her season, was beginning to change. She could see the energy lighting up her face and body with a new life-force, a new pulse that ached for release. Her cheeks and lips glowed pink and fresh.

Quickly, glancing at her watch to catch the time (9:00 P.M.), she slipped into a fresh pair of black Levi's, a black subtly studded belt, and a white loose sweatshirt to wear on the way over. Lastly, she pulled on her boots, the ones with the soles and heels that really made a force on the ground, that announced her arrival with a deep, solid, powerful stride and made her feel like she could go anywhere, do anything. No other decorations, symbols, signs of any kind except her body—ready and able—and a few choice whips from days before Chrys; whips she'd been practicing with in the odd moments she stole alone in the house. So rusty, so much to relearn, and to learn…

Suddenly still, considering her reflection in the mirror, a twinkle of a dare in her eyes, at the last minute Leda re-opened her bag and slipped her hand back inside. As she withdrew it, a semi-hard fleshy dick and black harness was in her grasp. If the mood was right and called for it, she'd be prepared to pack. That was all. Just pack. Just for the fun of it.

Right.

Content with the finished product, and doggedly accepting whatever imperfections usually irked her in the past, she opened the bathroom door, turned off the light, and headed back toward the front to make that call home to Chrys—let her know the baby had gone down just fine.

# 6.

Leda switched on the overhead light in the car as she drove down the dark stretch of freeway.

"Shit," she muttered, glancing down at the directions she'd scribbled haphazardly onto the sheet of paper in her hand. "I'll just get fucking lost and that'll be the end of my big night on the town, shit. 'Take the Wellerby exit off the 580 just past Novato,' it says, but I still haven't seen that goddamned exit and I passed Novato already. Shit fucking shit!"

Directions had never been Leda's forte, and especially as nervous as she was, the whole process just seemed way out of her control. But she'd be dammed if she'd submit to her poor sense of direction tonight. Leda floored the gas pedal and zoomed down the freeway towards the next exit sign. And just when she was about to a) turn around or b) get off the freeway and ask for fucking directions, the next sign announced WELLERBY EXIT 1-1/2 MILES. And she was on her way.

The street was empty of shoppers at this hour, though it was a cozy, shop-packed street. A few stores glowed with safety lights left on inside, but none were open.

"One fifty-eight, 160," she read off, slowing down to catch the numbers better. The address was 168 South Court Street.

"One sixty-four, 166…"

She spotted a tough-looking woman in leather on the sidewalk approaching the only lit store on the long block, with a red and purple neon sign flashing, UNDER-WORLD RAILROAD STATION in the window.

*Well,* she said to herself, *you found it.*

Leda's heart raced as she suddenly felt incredibly shy, and all her usual judgements and imperfections blasted up like a tidal wave. She slowed down and checked out the women walking toward the storefront. There were women of all kinds, it appeared, and in various types of dress: some bedecked with chains, wearing their power tools and in-your-face attitude for all to see; others covered with nondescript coats or jackets, or clothed simply, the true nature of their intention for the night ahead concealed completely.

A combination of both appealed to Leda, and she was grateful to see that not everyone had the perfect leather chic of the highest price and fashion. Maybe she wouldn't stick out as much as she thought.

Maybe.

Her heart beat high up in her throat. What the hell was she doing? What would Chrys think? *You don't belong here!*

*Yes,* a little voice inside her head said, *yes, you do. Come in and see. Come in to see it all and find out.*

The voice was so strong it seemed to have its own body separate from her own with hands that slid over her sex and stroked it alive, creating a force a thousand times more powerful than any uncertainty or shyness.

It had been so long—this scene, the play.

She continued past the Station and a large, tall woman in leather motioned Leda into a dirt parking lot. She turned in, listening to the tires crunch over the ground as she pulled up beside a blue sports car and killed the engine.

Last minute check: keys, cash, ID, just-in-case items in her smaller bag to take in. Leda inhaled a deep breath, blood pumping through her veins, and held it for a moment, trying to steady herself, then let it out with a huff.

*Come on,* her body told her, *don't fight the rush, just go with it.*

And with a burst of adrenaline—and no more escape plans—Leda was up and out of the car, swinging the door shut, checking the lock, then turning and walking with the others toward the open door of the Underworld Railroad Station.

# 7.

Inside the store, Leda waited in line to pay her entrance fee—ten dollars like the phone recording said, confirmed by a hand-scrawled sign that announced $25 NEW MEMBERS, $15 MEMBERS, $10 VIEWING ONLY.

When it was Leda's turn, she slipped her ten-dollar bill up onto the counter. The woman at the register glanced at it and didn't ask for specifics, just snagged the bill from the counter. She was a mousy-looking creature who reminded Leda of the woman in *Rocky*—his girlfriend—complete with cat-eye glasses and retro clothing on her young face and body. She gave Leda a blue ticket and told her to wait with the group forming near the back of the store.

Leda thanked her and moved away from the counter. Out of the corner of her eye, Leda noticed a couple of toughly dressed women eyeing her as she stood back, tucking away her ID. She looked up and nodded a solemn cool-dyke hello, receiving similar stone-faced nods back. It made her want to laugh, how serious public sex had become. But Leda had to admit it was part of the thrill: the tough facade that maybe or maybe not hid a softer core.

She hoped not too soft.

"This way," a woman's voice announced to the small group that had already paid and was waiting.

Leda turned to find another woman dressed like a store clerk standing near her, motioning her and a few others to follow her to the back of the store. Leda obediently followed the woman silently, the guide not bothering to look back, just moving briskly toward a heavy black curtain ahead. With a sweep of her hand, they were beyond it and standing in front of a large red door. Two burly women flanked the door and looked the group over. "Have a successful night," the guide said, sort of nodding a good evening to everyone. Then she turned away and moved back toward the front of the store through the black curtain. Leda watched her go.

"Ticket," one of the guards said.

Leda turned back to the matter at hand, taking in her surroundings. Both guards wore security uniforms, she noted with pleasure. Leda smiled to herself; she loved females in uniforms. She might just like the place after all.

Leda handed her ticket to the husky-voiced guard and waited. "Voyeurs on the left," the guard said, motioning for Leda to put out her arm, then securing a narrow blue plastic band around Leda's wrist. "Stay to the left of the brass rail and follow the red carpet around to the door that says VIEWING ROOM. Hope you see what you've come for."

The woman paused.

Leda looked at her hard, not liking her attitude and knowing the irritation was showing in her eyes. The uniformed dyke's serious tough face held Leda's gaze for a moment then broke into a nice smile.

"Because if you do see something that appeals to you, you can pay the difference at the window to the right just as you go through the door. Save your stub. No need to watch what you'd rather have."

She winked at Leda.

Leda blushed and nodded.

*Wow, women have changed in the cruise scene,* she mused to herself, remembering throngs of dykes holding up the walls at the bars, all too passively conditioned to take a lead, much less have the nerve to ask each other to dance or even say hello most of the time.

"Maybe I'll see you inside," Leda offered, noting the woman's beautiful, well-carved features and strong jawline beneath short, slicked-back hair. She loved a strong jaw and well-formed mouth; the husky body filling out the guard uniform didn't hurt the picture any either.

The woman chuckled as Leda openly looked her over, nodding and offering a corner of her mouth in a sort of smile at Leda—more like a smirk—but her eyes sparkled with interest.

Leda smiled a little herself, thanking the guard and walking through the archway as the door was held open for her briefly, then shut snugly behind her.

A throbbing beat escaped through a heavy black curtain to her right. A brass railing came straight out from the wall in front of her, separating the short path to the black curtain and one that led off to the left—the red carpeted path to the Viewing Room.

Leda glanced to her right at the window the guard had mentioned. A punked-out, collared woman looked out at her and smiled. The small group of women that had been led in with her moved her further into the room as they walked though the door behind her. Leda looked back at them: one was collared and on a leash held by another woman who was masked, gloved, and decked almost completely in leather. The collared woman was blindfolded, her hands secured behind her. Her round, full globes could be easily viewed through her sheer white T-shirt, nipples hard and pushing at the fabric. She wore black chaps with see-through white underwear, possibly of the same fabric as the T-shirt, and was barefoot—the ultimate reminder of submission in a public place.

The others in the group were similarly dressed, though one couple wore simple jeans, shirts, and boots. One woman, tall, with long legs and arms and a fiery head of red hair, sported a latex bodysuit and spiked heels. It was, all in all, a kaleidoscope of flavors, and Leda watched with lust in her eyes as they all moved past her, handed in their tickets, and disappeared through the thick black curtain.

"Not much more to enter the palace," the woman in the booth said over the beat of the music.

She had been watching Leda. Leda watched her exhale a cloud of smoke that swirled around the woman's head as she smiled devilishly at Leda.

"You're a virgin, I see," she continued, surveying the merchandise. "Virgins are the most fun to play with cuz you all are so scared and nervous. Ha!" She giggled a high-pitched, grating giggle like Columbia from *The Rocky Horror Picture Show,* thoroughly amused with her own words.

"Go on in, doll. I'll page a trainer for you." She paused. "Too bad I'm working the box all night," she added with a raise of her eyebrows, and reached for a little phone that sat next to her. "Go on," she whispered, shooing Leda in with one hand. "Have fun."

Leda watched the girl for another moment, fighting back the urge to slap the little impudent punk. Instead, she ignored the woman's urgings and turned away from her, making her way up the red carpet to the door that announced VIEWING ROOM. The energy was building inside Leda, she could feel it: a mixture of anger, irritation, and passion far too long suppressed. She reached out and the handle turned in her hand.

Leda found herself in a darkened room, but to her right was the wildest scene she'd ever laid eyes on: the den Leda had been hungering for. Comfortable-looking couches and chairs filled the long, rectangular room, all facing the one-way window that stretched the length of it to her right. Soft moans here and there aroused Leda's senses.

As her eyes adjusted, she moved into the room. Three small neon signs lit up the floor. She moved along and read each one. The first said INTERESTED—SINGLES; the second, PRIVATE PARTIES; the third, INTERESTED—COUPLES. Leda stopped at the INTERESTED—COUPLES sign, standing as nonchalantly as possible behind a long couch where, in front and to the right of it, two leather-clad women had tied an almost naked third to a heavy-looking wooden-legged ottoman, forcing her to keep her eyes on the scenes beyond the glass as one parted her legs from behind, busily inserting a long, wicked-looking dildo into the woman's ass. The other woman was securing a gag around the tied woman's head, smothering her groans and cries as she was penetrated rudely, Leda watching as the metal dildo slid deeply into the woman's exposed asshole.

"Silence," the woman securing the gag whispered harshly into the submissive's ear, and the moans and cries were stifled. The woman at the rear was now unbuttoning her pants and pulling out a long, thick, firm, packing dick with her free hand as she continued to drive the metal dildo into the submissive's puckered ass. The other woman finished securing the gag and moved quickly to assist the obvious top, slipping a black condom over the huge phallus and slathering on a little lube.

"Only a little," the top said very quietly, "let her work for it."

"Yes, sir," the woman responded, moving back.

The top pulled the painfully long metal dildo all the way out from the bottom's ass, then poised it once again against the tight hole, gripping it tightly, pushing very slowly, harder and harder until the woman's muscles finally yielded again. The gagged woman groaned as the dildo slid in a quarter of the way, the top not letting her have it all.

"C'mon," the top whispered in command. "Sit back on it and take it, slut, you know you want it."

The bound woman whimpered, obeying the top and pushing her hips and ass back against the probing metal rod. But the top wouldn't let her have more than a quarter of it, pulling back as the woman pushed, whimpering now in frustration. The top smiled and nodded at the third woman who applied more lube. Then the top withdrew the metal rod until only the tip remained inside that sweet ass and, with her other hand, she poised her monster-sized strapped-on cock at the woman's now desperately squirming cunt and, all at once, plowed both tools deep into the woman's body, stuffing her ass and pussy full to bursting.

A heavy groan was forced from the woman's throat,

but Leda was impressed at her control behind the gag. The top's hips began to thrust the long appendage into the obviously tight cave, making subtle smacking noises as it dove deep, then withdrew, sometimes in time with the one in the bottom's ass, sometimes not.

The third woman pinched and played with the tied woman's tits and nipples, sucking and tweaking them as they hung over the edge of the ottoman, every once in a while slipping a hand down between the woman's legs to just barely tease at her swollen clit.

Leda knew these moments well, from before. It all seemed to come back naturally, like riding a bike, and her body flared with desire and energy as she stood watching, wanting to witness the final explosion. The threesome seemed to like performing. The bound woman's anguished cries of pleasure bashed up against the gag, almost escaping fully into the room where others were busy taking care of themselves, each other, watching the activities on the other side of the viewing glass in the main playroom, or, like Leda, watching the threesome but too shy to indulge themselves to climax.

Leda watched as the butch top worked herself into a frenzy, her hips pumping desperately into the slave. The third woman took control of the metal dildo now, giving complete freedom for the top to fuck the submissive hard and deep, concentrating. The top pulled back on the bound woman's long hair and her pet groaned. With an awkward twist, her body filled to capacity, the bound woman managed to turn with the top's demanding tug, far enough to meet the top's hungry mouth that licked and gently bit the woman's parted lips around the gag. Then the top let her go, stood up fully, and plunged the tool deeply into the woman's ass before she could take a full breath. The sound of the bottom's groan escaped around the gag with the force of her breath.

Leda wanted more than anything at that moment to undo the gag and steal a long kiss from the bottom's open mouth, suck at the passion that was obviously threatening to explode her; Leda could tell by the way the woman's body shook and shivered and her chest rose and fell like an athlete's as the two other women probed into the deepest parts of her, the third woman's hand teasing her clit every now and then, but with no release.

Still, she wasn't really Leda's type. And besides, the moment passed and the top was fucking the woman harder and faster now, the third woman following the top's lead, increasing the speed in the woman's ass, diving in deep with the metal rod and out and slamming back in. Like two trains racing toward each other, the fucker and the fuckee panted and beat against each other, swollen hungry cunt to thick woman's cock, blasting out the pleasure with the assistance of the third woman who fucked the bottom's open ass with the slippery metal dildo, now sliding her hand down between her own legs.

"Don't you dare!" the top managed to command breathlessly through tight jaws, and the third woman withdrew her hand obediently, fucking the bound woman's ass even harder in her frustration, seemingly entranced by the slippery dildos pumping in and out with a fury.

The top exploded then against the base of the strap-on, grunting audibly but catching her hissing cries between her teeth, controlling her voice in the relative quiet of the viewing room. She forced the tool in harder and deeper and faster, releasing an explosion of lust into the bottom's slick shining body as she gripped the voluptuous hips in her hands, bouncing the woman toward her, then away, in deep, then out to aim again and shove her hips forward.

The top's face was a tangle of concentrated pleasure in the dim light as she continued fucking the woman, more slowly now, but staying deep inside the woman's cunt, directing the third woman to do the same with the metal dildo, keeping her pet completely full: ass, pussy, and mouth.

The bottom let out a desperate whimper, followed by a muffled, but audible "please."

"No way," the top said, "no come for you until after midnight; until after we've used you to our satisfaction." And she pinched the woman's ass hard, then slapped it approvingly.

"Good job, pet," she crooned.

Feeling suddenly self-conscious now that the energy was shifting, Leda looked away toward the glass window that spanned the entire front wall. She moved quietly down the middle aisle with her bag over her shoulder and took a seat in the front row, away from the other women in the viewing room. She noticed singles here and there and some couples—no one seemed to be paying any attention to the specified areas of the room. That was a good sign, she decided, and would have worried if perverts actually followed instructions without question.

She sat for a moment, leaning back in the chair and looking through the one-way glass window, rubbing her hand over her crotch to calm the fire a little. What to do now? Leda's cunt ached and she knew she couldn't just go home after a brief peep into the place. Maybe it was a mistake being here; maybe she shouldn't have done this. Oh, but Leda could feel the longing in her to just fall into the place, slip into the sensations of the night that breathed around her, and forget the danger of drowning. *Oh, what the hell,* she thought. *Just relax, watch for a little while. Whatever.*

Then it hit her—like a Mack truck straight at her in tandem with a whiptailed crack of lightning the size of the state of Texas. It was like she reached right in—right through the glass, through the wall, through Leda's clothes—blasted like a breathlessly quick fuse burning and crackling across an invisible line that jumped the distance between Leda and a dark-haired, Hispanic soft-butch, completely obliterating everything else, electrifying Leda in her seat.

"Ohhh man," Leda whispered slowly, sitting forward to get a better look, resting her elbows on her open knees.

The view before her was a display of naked and semi-naked women of all body types and sizes, some bound to hooks in the walls or hanging from chains that dangled from the ceiling as they took the sting of a whip from a masked woman or opened their legs wide to the slippery fingers of another. Others were lying together on long soft mats in somewhat separate areas— but open to the view of those behind the glass—their naked bodies entangled and moving together in passionate, undulating motion. One of these woman slid down over the one beneath her and slowly parted the woman's legs, opening her own mouth to slide her long tongue out and up along the sweet opening, tasting her. The woman on the bottom closed her eyes and reached her hands up above her head, lost in the sensation. Music purred and beat its way through the room like the heartbeat of passion. Leda could hear the music even through the glass.

She took in the entire scene with a single sweep of her gaze. What had been an exciting view only a moment before, now paled into an uninteresting shade of gray as all color and light and depth and intensity seemed to spark to life only in the middle of Leda's view, in the form of the dark-haired beauty who stood against a wall, drinking something from a cup and taking in everything around her, cool, carefully laid-back, but open, too. Her face was not set or hard, but easy, casual, sure.

Leda could hardly breathe. Her heart pounded in her

chest and between her legs. She groaned deep in her throat without thinking. There was something about this one, a combination of so many things that turned Leda on like crazy. She watched the woman move around the huge room, casually checking out the action. Her walk was an endearing combination of butch-jock and cool-grrrl; Leda liked her immediately.

The woman wore a man's undershirt maybe one size too small, clinging to her athletic chest, diving down sexy low over the sides of the curve of her tits, around her definitely toned shoulders and arms, olive-skinned and a little shiny, like maybe she'd oiled up a little.

*Oiled,* Leda thought. *Mmmmm.*

The woman's dark tumble of wavy hair framed a high-cheekboned face with a somewhat full mouth and beautifully shaped nose. Her eyes appeared dark, a little deep-set from what Leda could make out; she leaned in closer to the glass for a better look. The woman's leather pants hugged the curve of her hips and the swell of what appeared to be well-shaped thighs. Everything below her hips was partially in shadow, but she wore what appeared from Leda's view to be heavy black boots.

The icing on the cake Leda saw when the woman turned to put her cup on a tray nearby: a rainbow array of hankies peeking out from a back pocket on the "top" side, flowering out in a little bud from her snug pocket. Leda smiled and chuckled out loud, letting her head fall back for a minute in her amusement—no one wore hankies in their pockets anymore except gay men, and mostly older ones at that. But Leda liked them, liked the signals they allowed. She tried to make out the color to get the full message, but the woman turned back around before she could squint it into view.

Leda watched her for another minute, just making sure that no one like a girlfriend returned with a fresh drink or had just been in the bathroom or something. No one showed. A few minutes passed. The woman remained by herself, alone but not aloof, and definitely putting off an air of possible interest.

Leda flushed with desire and uncertainty. *Oh, Christ, I haven't approached a woman in years!* she thought. *What if she thinks I'm a putz? I doubt I'm her type, I doubt she'd even consider someone as uncool as...*

*Hold it,* her mind said. *You were only going to watch, remember? You're a married woman with a devoted partner. Besides you're too old for this kind of thing and...*

"Oh, shut up," she grumbled aloud under her breath, eyes fixed on the woman on the other side of the glass. And with that final word, she lifted her bag from the floor and headed up the aisle, past the make-out couples and out through the Viewing Room door, closing it quietly behind her.

# 8.

In the entrance hall again, Leda walked right up to the ticket counter without letting herself begin to think. The collared punky woman smiled a sly amused smile.

"Saw something you liked, huh?" she asked.

Leda just sort of "mmm"ed a little and· pulled out her money. The woman took it. "Wrist."

Leda put her wrist on the counter and the woman snipped off the blue band with a little pair of sharp scissors. Then she secured a narrow black plastic band in its place and handed Leda a ticket.

"This is to check your bag and whatever else you want to check so you can do your thang. There's no smoking in the playrooms, only in the Fire Room, which is in the back."

She paused.

"Oh, and here's a little gift from me, cuz I can tell you don't do this too often."

She handed Leda a third ticket with ONE FREE DRINK printed on it. Leda looked up and met her grinning, squinty-eyed face.

"Thanks," Leda said. "And no, I don't, but is it that obvious?"

"Well," the woman replied, "you just don't have an attitude that precedes you and you're way too cute to be on your own if you were a regular."

She winked at Leda, who smiled and felt her cheeks redden.

"Oh," she said surprised, suddenly shy. Then, catching herself, she added, "Then you must not be a regular either."

That worked wonders and the punky woman laughed a twinkly bubbly high-pitched laugh that Leda could live with for maybe a minute. But Leda nodded, thanked her kindly, and moved toward the curtain, hoping she was walking a composed, confident walk; certain her legs would give out at any second.

The other side of the curtain offered a dim rectangular room with a long counter to Leda's right. *First, the bag*, she thought, trying to remain calm enough to think in some semblance of a logical sequence. A cute woman with a crew cut and just about everything on her face pierced stood at the counter. She wore a chopped-up white T-shirt with big black letters across the front that said BOY. Leda handed her the bag and ticket.

"Oh, and this," she said quickly, remembering that she was still wearing the white sweatshirt. Leda wondered why anyone would think she looked cute in a baggy sweatshirt, but felt grateful for the little motor-revving compliments she'd received on the way in.

Almost nauseous with nerves—quickly being replaced by anticipation and a hunger she hadn't felt in years—Leda turned to check out the rest of the room. A long table of munchies and drinks was laid out across from her. The cost was reasonable, she noted, not totally bar prices. *Fair enough,* she decided.

"Need to see your band," the check clerk said.

Leda turned back and held out her wrist. Ms. Boy wrapped a small label with Leda's ticket number on it around her plastic wrist band.

"Just show the band when you need to get to your stuff," she told Leda.

"Thanks. Will you take care of me personally?" Leda asked in a friendly voice, offering an open smile, feeling her old bold and flirty self returning with surprising force.

"Depends," the woman said, not adding any explanation or attempting to be friendly back.

"Mmm," Leda returned, disappointed. "Well, then I'll just have to take my chances now, won't I?"

She turned away, slipping a hand indiscreetly into her vest to position her tits just right behind the snug leather and ties. She ran a hand through her spiky hair.

*Asshole,* she thought.

That too-cool-for-you and stonier-than-stone attitude had kept Leda away from the parties and clubs for years. *Why did so many SM players, especially tops, have to be such fucking arrogant unfriendly jerks?* she grumbled to herself. It didn't have to be this way.

"I'm worth it," Ms. Boy said behind her, many beats behind Leda.

Leda turned back. The woman didn't crack a smile, but her dark eyes weren't so stony as they'd been and they looked straight at Leda.

"Why is that?" Leda asked, perturbed and mulling over the wonders a fuck in the ass would probably do this chick, but also completely willing and hoping to be proved wrong about her judgement.

"Ask around, anyone can tell you," Ms. Boy said with a great deal of narcissistic drama, no hint of a sense of humor.

Leda lost interest.

"Yeah, I'll do that," she said, disappointed again, hoping the rest of the party wouldn't be filled with this woman's kindred spirits. She moved away from the counter and picked up a soda at the munchie table with her drink ticket, taking a sip and deciding on the next step. She took a breath, then let it out, sucked in her stomach a little for good measure, and moved toward the archway into the main room.

The music in the main room was loud, a bass beat pounding the floor and walls. The lighting was electric hurricane lamps mounted on the walls behind textured gold glass, like an old dungeon, maybe in a castle. The air was warm, inviting disrobing. The night was already in full swing as an old Marianne Faithfull tune rocked the place, the sound of whips cracking against flesh, women's voices raised in cries of delicious pain and pleasure mixing into an ambrosia for the ears. Leda sighed, grinning a little on the outside and hugely on the inside, wanting to whoop and holler "I'm back!"

Instead, she sipped her drink shyly and watched a tall, spiked-heel-wearing, latex-bound and corsetted woman clothespinning an intricate design onto the flesh of a completely naked tall blonde butch whose small tits disappeared into a fan of clothespins. The butch's arms extended out as she stood secured to a black lacquered cross. The look on her face was pure bliss as her body was transformed into human art. Every now and then the Mistress raised her latexed knee to the butch's exposed crotch and rubbed against her, her mouth moving in words that Leda couldn't hear over the music, then reaching out to bite the flesh around the clothespins on various parts of her pet's body. The butch woman howled with pain when she did this, especially at the most tender spots. A small crowd had assembled, watching the scene, but more women were playing than watching, Leda noted, and most of those observing seemed completely ready to play if the opportunity presented itself.

Yes. The Opportunity.

Leda's eyes scanned the large room but didn't locate

the woman she'd seen through the glass. An attendant stood beside her for a moment, collecting cups.

"Can you tell me how to get to the room that the Viewing Room looks into?" Leda asked.

The attendant looked up and checked her out.

"Nice vest," she said approvingly, her own tits barely covered by extra-wide purple and black suspenders that hooked to snug Levi's. Her ATTENDANT badge was pinned to one of the suspenders just below one tit. She flipped her long brown hair back out of her face with a quick whip of her head as she turned to point out the direction to Leda.

"Through the maze, that way," the attendant offered, smiling.

"Thank you," Leda replied. "I just love your outfit," she added, her eyes taking in the smooth curve of the swell of the woman's ample chest, only the nipples and very center stretch seductively obscured from view by the suspenders, her long locks of shining hair falling around them. The woman's stomach was flat and tight, Leda noted appreciatively, and she wore her jeans low on her hips with one button open so the top of the wide band of her men's style underwear showed. She looked young, early twenties maybe. Leda liked the way she carried herself with confidence, obviously comfortable in her body.

"Very sexy," she noted.

The attendant flashed her a brilliant open smile.

"Nice of you to say so," she answered. "Let me know if you need anything; I'll be around."

Leda nodded, downed the rest of her drink, and quickly added her cup to the woman's growing pile of empties. She smiled a thank-you to the woman, who nodded, lifted her tray, and disappeared into the ever-growing crowd.

Cries of submission and the thwack! of a paddle came from one corner of the room as the music changed, a faster tempo, mixing with women's voices, talking, moaning, screaming, obeying. Leda hurried in the direction the attendant had pointed out.

She walked through an archway and found herself in a sort of hallway. The music pulsed through here, too, from speakers set in the walls, and as before, she could hear the sounds of women's voices now wafting through the corridor.

Leda walked in further, stopping for a moment to check out a group of four or five young women. They were engaged in what appeared to be an intense and complicated sexual orgy in a deep, wide-mattressed alcove set into the wall of the maze—one of many, she discovered later, after first watching the group for a while, hidden in a shadow across from them. A single dim light shone rose-tinted light over the women's entangled bodies. Leda smiled. *A sort of sexual dinner party,* she thought, watching them feed on each other hungrily, the heated moans and cries of women's pleasure escaping, seductive, the arching of their bodies like a dance: mouths seeking out mouths, hair pulled back by a strong hand, another kiss taken with force and pleasure, mouths seeking out lips—upper, lower—faces disappearing between open welcoming legs, a mixture of shades of skin and textures of whatever clothing remained, like a painting. Fists and fingers and dildos pumped with the beat of the music. The women were oblivious to everything but each other.

Leda felt her body urge her on with a vengeance. She hadn't felt this kind of aching desire in a long, long time. *What could I have been thinking—only watching, my ass!* she mused silently, smiling, face flushed with excitement. She moved as quickly as possible deeper into the maze, turning left, then right, right again and into a long tunnel, hoping at any minute to arrive at her destination.

No such luck.

Halfway through the tunnel, a room opened up to her left. Leda peered in. Inside, a woman, naked except for a black leather harness, was hanging upside-down, suspended from the ceiling, her feet held fast in heavy shackles attached to a thick metal spreader bar that opened her thighs wide. The woman's arms were bound together and hung to the floor, her backside to the door and to Leda who, again, hid in the shadows. The woman's long brown hair rested on the ground as she hung there and her voice was muffled as she moaned and made sounds of pleasure, punctuated by cries of ecstatic pain.

Between the woman's open legs was the intensely into-it face of a beautiful Asian woman, her long shiny black hair pulled back from her face as she ate out the suspended female with gusto. She stood in front of the hanging woman, facing Leda's direction. Leda peeked in a little further and noticed that there were quite a few observers: the corners of the room were dim but she could make out many shadows filling them. Of course she had read the signs as she'd entered the club announcing the entire club as open space for all women with only the areas marked PRIVATE STALLS reserved for private interactions, *sans* voyeurs. That worked out well and Leda had yet to run into the aforementioned private areas. But it could still be an awkward situation without at least a few other watchers joining in.

In this room that was not a problem.

Leda quietly slipped inside and moved carefully along the wall to a free spot in the shadows. The air smelled like something was burning, maybe coals, though the room was well ventilated and not too stuffy. From her new side angle, Leda could see that the Asian woman's hands were tied behind her back, her lower body fully clothed from the waist down, upper body nude, small breasts topped by hard nipples. Leda could also see that a flaming red-haired woman was the source of the suspended slave's pain-filled cries. As the first woman flicked and sucked the slave's clit, digging her tongue deep into the warm slit that was obviously easily accessed between such widely parted legs, the second woman was busy inserting shiny needles into what seemed to be random areas of the slave's flesh, but just a few, and only every so often, critically timed, it seemed.

The inverted woman's breathing was quickening and Leda could see her asscheeks tightening in a slow rhythm as the woman between her legs worked her into a frenzy, punctuated by the flashes of intense pain as the needles dove in and out the other side, held in place by her body's own flesh. It was like a carefully crafted orchestral piece, the woman's moans and cries and groans the product of their labors, the sweet results of their skillful interpretation.

As Leda watched, sitting among the others doing the same—a pressure-filled silence emanating from the attentive crowd (some with their hands shoved into their pants, she noted)—the hanging woman's body suddenly tensed, bound hands curling into fists, the Asian woman's concentration like a laser beam on her clit now. It was obvious she was nearly ready to come. Just then, the redhead—who wore leather chaps in an intense shade of deep blue, a matching leather bra top, and heavy black boots—suddenly stopped her needle ministrations and turned to reach for something that was blocked from Leda's view by a woman who sat in front of her. But she could see absolutely fine when the red-haired woman marched around to the suspended woman's naked buttocks, brandishing a long black rod whose tip glowed bright red-orange like embers, molten.

*Oh my God, fucking shit, girl!* Leda said silently to herself, a barely audible hush of sound escaping from her open lips, jaw dropped, eyes blinking in disbelief. Her ears registered someone closing the heavy door just as the woman arrived at her destination behind the hanged woman. Leda watched, mesmerized, as the red-haired woman concentrated on the exact moment, poised, as the Asian woman worked the brown-haired woman's clit. And as her voice rose in a deep groan that built into a high cry of pleasure, quickly sweeping up the scale in intensity as the orgasm blasted through her, the red-haired woman, in a single smooth motion, placed the burning rod against the smooth flesh of the hanging woman's ass.

What happened then, no gag could suppress.

The scream of agony that thundered out from the core of the inverted woman's body was like nothing Leda had ever heard. The room rang and shook with it; the tunnel, she was sure, filled with the pulverizing force of it, the sound destined to reach every ear in the place. And as quickly as it began, it was over. Though the woman's screams continued beyond this, the branding ended. The rod swiftly disengaged from the flesh and some sort of ice set-up was applied to the area— something else, too, that Leda couldn't make out. Two other women materialized at the red-haired woman's side and there was a bustle of activity. Leda watched as the Asian woman's hands were now freed by another Asian woman with shorter hair and a petite, sinewy, tough body. They fell into each other, one feeding off the slave's juices that lingered on the other woman's lips.

She had obviously done well, and now it was her turn for the payoff.

The woman still hanging was limp, no energy left in her body but her breath still hard and labored, a constant low moan escaping. The needles remained embedded in her skin. Leda could only imagine the intensity of the sensations, how the sting of the needles probably was not even noticeable now against the burn of her branded asscheek. And although she was curious to see what the brand looked like, the hot, dim room—which now smelled of hot metal and seared flesh—suddenly felt small and stifling. Leda quickly slipped between the onlookers, along the wall, and out the door.

Tunnel. She was still in the tunnel; she had forgotten. Which way? Leda picked a direction randomly (to the left), somewhat lost now, and moved ahead. At the end of it, she made another left, and a little further down, a right, running into other women in various stages of undress going at it in alcoves and dead-end corners into which she stumbled, trying to get through to the other side, her state of mind bordering on pissed-off now.

*This could be funny if I wasn't so damned desperate!* Leda thought, her mind focused like lightning on the picture in her head of the woman she had seen through the glass of the Viewing Room. "Damn," she said aloud as she met up with another dead-end. "I don't fucking believe this!"

"Trying to get through to the Viewing Room play-room?" a friendly voice asked. Leda turned toward it, surprised. The maze was very dim, lit only by hurricane lamps every few feet and other lights in the alcoves.

"Yes, actually," she said. "I didn't really expect this to be such a fucking challenge of a maze! I mean, what's their point?" she added, chuckling, "Trying to keep us *away* from each other?"

"I know, I think they may have overdone it this time," the woman agreed. She was sitting on a high barstool-type chair in the corner of a 90 degree right turn in the maze. A lamp above her illuminated short curly hair, pale skin, and Victorian clothing: a well-endowed chest pushed up almost cruelly, beautifully, in a fine-boned green corset. Leda could see the edges of the woman's pink areola, nipples about ready to pop out and greet her. A black ribbon was tied around the woman's long neck, and her lips shone with glossy lipstick. Leda smiled.

"You look great," she said, knowing the work it took to dress up like that and enjoying the end product.

"Thank you," the woman returned appreciatively, "I could live in clothes like these."

Leda nodded her approval, eyebrows raising.

"Actually, although I may seem just a pretty doll on display," she said to Leda, winking, "I'm here to help people out who get stuck in the maze, especially available women seeking out partners—and I think that might qualify you to receive my services?"

The woman shifted on her stool, opening her legs wide, which had been crossed demurely, hooking the high heels of her turn-of-the-century laced-up boots onto the rung of the chair. She wore what appeared to be red satin underwear above stockinged legs, black garters outlining creamy fair skin. Leda had walked toward her as she'd started chatting, and now stood almost directly in front of the woman: a key position to appreciate the full impact of her display. Leda couldn't help but notice the soft curls of pubic hair escaping around the edge of the narrow band of satin between her open thighs.

*Ah, women*, Leda sighed to herself. She was crazy about the female form, had partaken of the sharing of this on many occasions with many women along the way—before Chrys. Yeah, true. Before…

…Chrys.

…*especially single women seeking out partners…*

The woman's words echoed in Leda's mind for a moment. How could she explain? She couldn't. Why should she have to? Did it matter? Why incriminate herself? Everyone deserved a day off from marriage once in a while for God's sake.

*Uh huh*, her internal voice ragged. *And if it was on the other shoe, this cheating?*

Cheating? Nah. Just looking.

*Yeah, right*, came the voice again.

Well, whatever it was by now, she'd come much too far to turn back. The maze had surrounded her and all she could do now would be to graciously take and follow the directions bestowed upon her from the wise lips of this intriguing lady, until Leda found her way through it. To the other side. Yes.

"Don't be too shy to ask for what you see if you like something you see here tonight," the woman half-whispered in an intimate sexy voice, sending a kiss out to Leda with her shiny ruby red lips. "Just go down this passage and make two immediate lefts, and an immediate right. You're out."

"Left left right," Leda repeated.

"Yep. And by the way, you can always just go through the tunnel that connects the two rooms; the one you just came from and the Viewing Room playroom. It's the only other doorway that leads out of the playroom on this side."

"You're kidding me! I asked an attendant how to get to the room you can see from the Viewing Room and she told me through the fucking maze!"

"Wearing suspenders and not much else?" the Victorian woman asked.

"Uh huh," Leda confirmed.

The woman chuckled. "She just loves to play with party virgins, it's in her blood. But you'll catch on fast, I can tell. Oh, and in case you didn't know, the notorious Jungle Room—complete with foliage and water to play in—is down in the basement. The elevator is over by the bathrooms which are located in the passageway between the Viewing Room playroom and the dance area on the other side of it, that way."

She pointed.

"Got all that?" The woman smiled a fabulously mischievous Cheshire cat sort of grin, showing a fine set of pearly teeth, leaning forward with her elbows on her open knees.

"I got the left left right part, and the general idea of the rest," Leda answered. "I thank you again, madam."

Leda made her best turn-of-the-century gentlemanly bow to the lady in the chair, taking the opportunity to glance down and check that the ties on her vest were holding her tits in. Then she returned to a vertical position. And seeing the woman's playful state, Leda boldly ran her hands over the woman's creamy open thighs and stockings. The woman on the chair purred, eyelids lowering a bit, and blew Leda another kiss.

"Ooo, too bad I'm working," she sighed. "You have the greatest tits." The woman shook her pretty head disappointedly. "Ah, but do let me know if you don't find what you're looking for in there."

Leda confirmed that she would keep that in mind and smiled as the woman on the chair waved a flittery-fingered good-bye. Then Leda moved down the passage, making an immediate left, as instructed, intent on the final escape.

But suddenly a scene flashed by her peripheral vision and she did a stop-in-your-tracks double take, backtracking a few steps to check it out. There was something so intimate and intensely connected about the two women playing, and both were striking. This was too compelling to pass by without checking it out.

A large high alcove with a single round pillar in the middle of it and a chair with arms that sat off to one side was the location for their tryst, or whatever it was. An adorable dyke boy, slim and dressed only in very packed men's white cotton briefs that barely held the hard-on, was standing in front of the pillar with his/her hands tied back around it. A voluptuous honey-brown-haired, stretchy black-cat-suited femme in high Mistress gear (which included the sleek low-cut cat suit, black excruciatingly high spiked heel boots up to her thighs, and a mask that covered her eyes—though they sparkled through, the whites visible even at the distance from which Leda observed) was securing the boy—rope circle by rope circle—to the pillar. There was something about the energy between them as the cat-suited woman circled the pillar, moving her sexy, curvaceous, long-legged body in a teasing way as the boy's eyes remained riveted to her form, except for a quick glance up at Leda in the doorway. Leda didn't notice the boy's gaze on her, focusing instead on the fact that with each revolution, the woman in the catsuit removed some small part of her outfit. The first that Leda noticed missing were two circles of stretch fabric that had covered the tips of the femme's full pushed-up tits. Removed, the pieces left the tips pointing out, begging for a mouth to do them good, the nipples hardening as the rope gradually encircled her boy, binding him/her snugly and totally to the pillar.

The femme wrapped the rough-looking rope across the boy's lightly muscled, small-breasted chest in a cross pattern, then began on the boy's neck. Carefully, with what appeared to be great love, patience, and an obvious attention to detail, the femme mixed two types of ropes in the process of securing the boy's sweet neck. She punctuated her designs with intricate knots and even bound the boy's head, around his forehead and chin.

"If I had a gun," the femme said, her voice full of intense sincerity, "I would put it against your head and lead you out into the deepest space of your fear, my love. Yes, I would do that for you."

The boy gazed out at the femme with large blue long-lashed eyes that could have been an advertisement for hunger—but McDonald's wouldn't have a clue how to satisfy this customer…

Leda smiled at the thought.

The dyke boy's mouth was open, loose, tongue darting out to moisten nicely shaped lips.

"But we'll see how good you are here, today," the femme continued. "I want to show off my mummified sex slave." She bent down to finish off the knots that secured the boy's legs and ankles. Leda could imagine, by the appearance of it, that the rope was an itchy one, rough. She smiled at the thought of that, too. The boy certainly didn't seem to be having a miserable time of it with the rope; far to the contrary, actually.

As the femme finished her boy's feet, she rose, this time reaching down to swiftly remove a panel of the shiny, stretchy black cat-suit fabric that had covered her crotch. Now the woman's slit was exposed to her boy's view. Leda could tell this because, from her point of view behind the woman, the missing fabric also left the woman's crack halfway exposed up her ass.

*And a fine ass it is, too,* Leda noticed. *An ass you'd want to bite and grab a handful of just because you couldn't help it.* The woman checked her handiwork: her boy was quite bound at every level of his body and the pattern was intricately balanced, little space left between each revolution of rope, perfect lines crossing the boy's body from forehead, chin, neck, down to his toes. Not much flesh showed through between the ropes: just the boy's underpants and hard-on beneath the cotton fabric, and the boy's eyes and nose, a slit for the mouth, just the outline of his femininely soft lips.

Leda watched, enthralled, as the femme woman completed her inspection and, seemingly satisfied, stepped back and reached for the chair, pulling it up close. Beside her boy sat a red play bag. The femme reached inside it and removed a long rubber dildo with a wide flat base. She very adeptly and quite swiftly rolled a condom up the length of the toy. Then, standing right in front of her bound boy, she moved the dildo up to her exposed crotch and, standing strong on her spiked heels with her legs apart, slid the head of it into her cunt. She moaned, staring straight into the eyes of her boy, who stared back, eyes flashing down to the dildo below his lover's open thighs and back to the woman's face. Then the femme slipped the wet-tipped dildo back out and up to her boy's face.

"Can you smell me?" she asked the boy. "See what you do to me? Wanna taste?"

She ran the shining tip of the dildo up to the boy's mouth and in a flash his tongue was out, pushing between two ropes to grab a taste of the woman's obviously exquisite nectar. Leda could see that's how the dyke-boy felt: absolutely crazy about the woman and her juices now on the boy's tongue.

After allowing a quick lick of the wet tip, the femme quickly removed the dildo from the boy's reach.

"Oh, what you do to me with that tongue. I can't wait, my love, I can't control myself." And with that she stepped over to the chair, pulled it right in front of her "mummified" boy, and placed the very long dildo's wide base onto the chair.

"Because of you, because of what you do to me, I don't need any lube, just my honey to make it slippery enough to go in." The femme straddled the chair. Because the back of it was partly open, Leda could see the femme's open cuntlips from behind as she leaned over, positioning the dildo at her shining entrance, legs wide apart. Then she sat down, sliding the length of the dildo into her pussy, filling her own body. Then she sat back, hooking her longish legs up over either low arm of the chair. This position opened her sex wide, Leda could partially see—she had changed spots for a better view. The femme's nipples were hard and held out and aloft by the strong fabric from which her cat suit was made. The femme was a display of womanly virtues, and now she was using her obviously strong legs to raise and lower herself up and down on the stiff rubber dick.

Leda looked up at the boy's face. He was entranced, moans and groans escaping from a mouth that was only allowed partially to open, jaw held in place as it was by the ropes. Those eyes said a million things, and one of the strongest themes, Leda could see clearly, was love. The power of their connection awed her and she watched somewhat dumbly from just beyond the entrance to the alcove.

For a brief moment, Leda thought about Chrys and herself, trying, suddenly desperately, to find in her heart and mind and cunt that sort of connection to her partner. She couldn't. Leda shivered just a little and forced the thought from her mind, focusing on the scene before her.

The femme woman continued to ride the long dildo on the chair, the muscles in her thighs flexing in a rhythm, steadily increasing in speed and adding one hand to play with her clit. Leda moved over as far as possible to check out the action, careful to stay in the shadows, as before. It was hard to see everything from where she stood, but the femme's voice drove home the action. It rose and fell with increasingly intense moans and whispers of "oh yes, mmm, I just can't control myself around you, love, I can't; it's just too much, ooo, yeah, see how deep it is in me, filling me up inside, fucking my cunt because I just can't wait. I'm sorry, but…ah…"

The woman was now raising her strong hips and arching back against the back of the chair, pushing her pelvis up toward her lover and plowing back down onto the fine large rubber tool. Her hand on her clit worked feverishly and the woman's head fell back, then forward, her breath growing ragged, the words trailing off until she bucked against her hand and threw herself hard down onto the long phallus that Leda could hear make a little smacking sound as she rammed it inside her, bucking and riding and releasing her orgasm into the room along with a husky cry of pleasure.

The boy on the pillar was beside himself. Sweat trickled down his face and the moans increased in intensity. The woman on the chair laid her head back against the back of the chair, pulling out the dildo slowly, her crimson cunt open wide to her boy.

"Can you see, my sweet boy, what you do to me?" she said between ragged breaths. "See how swollen and wet I am? It's because I need you and only you. I just can't…" She took a long breath, "…I can't control myself around you. But you've been so good, so good, yes. I might just have to release you from your briefs, see what you have in store there, what you need, my sweet boy.…"

But the woman stayed where she was, the two eye-to-eye, a million words and messages moving silently between them. Leda suddenly felt like she was intruding in a too intimate moment not meant for strangers' eyes, regardless of the club policy. As inconspicuously as possible, she crossed the entranceway and moved out into the tunnel.

"Thanks for participating," she heard the femme call out sweetly.

Stunned, Leda realized the line was meant for her. She stopped cold for a moment, frozen in the realization that she hadn't been so invisible after all. Not only that, but it seemed like they had approved of her stopping by.

*Cool,* she thought. *Very cool.*

Very, very hot crotch, however, and Leda quickly tried to recall the words of her director. She made another left—moving hurriedly toward the maze exit, wherever it might be, and toward the object of her hopeful desire—then a quick right.

# 9.

Instead of leading out into a room as the woman in the tunnel had promised, the right turn took Leda into a wide hall. Directly across from her—and across a small sea of women milling about—were two doors that said RESTROOM on them. Leda thought for a moment. There was something near the restrooms that the woman had told her about. Was it the Viewing Room room? Her head swam. The whole damn place seemed suddenly not to fit; she couldn't get her bearings, not even where the front door of the club was situated from here, and she couldn't recall the specifics of what the Victorian woman had said.

"Shit," she swore aloud. Exasperated, Leda turned

right and moved through the loose crowd. On her left was an elevator and a group of women waiting for it. The light above the door flashed on and the doors opened. A few females—some in wet bathing suits or wrapped in towels, and some just plain wet and naked or semi-naked, breasts bare and hair slicked back away from a variety of beautiful faces—disembarked from the elevator.

"C'mon, let's get something to eat," a white woman in a light blue towel wrapped only around her narrow hips, said to a few others beside her.

Leda watched them go off to her left, heading toward the archway that opened into a room on the opposite end of the hall, back past the restrooms. She considered following them as she made a quick search of the faces in the hall for the one burned in her mind from the Viewing Room. But before she could decide, the group in front of the elevators moved in a mass through the open doors and Leda was being pushed in by more women from behind. She found herself on board, doors closing; the packed-in group descended.

A dark-haired, petite woman on Leda's right glanced over at her, checking out Leda's attire. Leda watched her looking, the woman's gaze eventually making its way up to Leda's amused face. The woman smiled a little and nodded.

"Nice vest," she said.

"Thanks," Leda returned, glancing down at the woman's attire. With a start, she realized she was standing next to an almost buck-naked gorgeous female, naked except for a slick black G-string that sat high on her slim hips, small, tight buns exposed, legs smoothly shaved and bare except for heavy black boots that went just below her knees, her upper body covered only in a black shorty tank top made out of a very, very, open-weave, lightweight net fabric. The woman's perky tits peeked through, as tan as the rest of her.

"You've got guts," Leda said with a smile. The woman laughed a sparkly laugh, her slightly slanted, very long-lashed eyes creasing with pleasure.

"That's a nice way of putting it," she said. "My girl-friend just calls me a tease."

"Lucky woman," Leda offered.

On the woman's other side, a woman with a pretty face on which sat a slightly turned-up nose leaned over to see who she was talking to. Her face, framed by shiny gold hair, was curious, shy. Leda smiled and waved a little. The woman smiled back, blushed, moved back out of Leda's view, and giggled to the woman next to Leda. Leda smiled openly and chuckled, amused at their youthful goofiness.

"This is *not* my girlfriend," the dark-haired woman next to her said, rolling her eyes and smiling as she pointed to her blushing, still-giggling friend. Leda nodded her understanding, preoccupied with thinking about the three of them getting naked together; what this petite beauty would like done to her, or to do; what she was into, or would be willing to try. But cute and femme wasn't really what Leda was into tonight. Still, the thought lingered in her head: removing the young woman's net shirt and kissing those incredible tits. Leda's own nipples throbbed behind the soft leather that held them.

She sighed just as the elevator doors opened. Everyone moved out, fanning off in different directions. The shy woman looked back over her shoulder, still smiling, and waved a little good-bye to Leda. Her friend in the G-string and net shirt who had been beside Leda slapped her playfully on the shoulder as if to tell her to stop being such a pain. But Leda didn't mind the flirt. She took a breath and shook her head, feeling hot in her jeans, smoldering even. But she hadn't brought anything else to walk around in, since of course she was just going to watch.

*So, you don't have to walk around in anything!* a voice in her head countered. *Just that cute girly G-string you chose!*

*Oh, yeah, right, like I'm really going to do that,* she said back. *Yeah, right, sure.*

Instead, she focused on the crowd milling about and the absolutely stunning scenery: real palm trees, high ceiling painted like a midnight blue sky with shiny stars all across it, blinking, the lighting soft like moonlight, but as bright as a full-moon night. Dripping wet women were everywhere and the sound of water rushing, splashing, and Caribbean-style music moved around Leda. The smell of food was here, too, though Leda couldn't quite tell what kind of food was cooking. She scanned the scene and noticed a few cabanas, one larger than the others with tables outside. Closer to where she stood, a very tan topless woman in just a grass skirt and arm bracelets was standing at a fruit stand laden with exotic fruits and plastic cups of fruit salad. It was a popular place.

Women sat at little round wooden tables placed around the stand, eating and feeding each other fruit. One couple passed fruit to each other with kisses, mouths lingering with each bite as they sat side-by-side at the corner of a table. During one fruit-passing kiss, Leda watched them linger and one of the women—who was tall, with a strong squarish jaw and short bleached hair—moved in closer to her partner, her mouth working the kiss, hands reaching for her partner's pink tits, which were bare. She caressed them, then moved back up to the woman's smooth cheek as they kissed furiously. The other woman—also somewhat tall, her head shaved and tattooed with an intricate design on one side, ears pierced all the way up with thick silver hoops—ended the kiss and smiled languidly, the ring in her nose catching the light, striking dark eyes heavy with passion. She reached for the bleached-haired woman's chair, pulling it in as close as it would go as the woman stood up to allow it, face intense on her lover's mouth throughout the exchange.

Obediently she sat back down, hands remaining on her partner's naked thigh. Leda watched the two of them feed each other for another moment, then Leda turned and moved into the crowd a way, but glanced back. She noticed from this angle that the two women wore only towels around their waists and Leda smiled as she watched the white-haired woman trying mischievously to get her hands up under the other woman's towel, moving up her thighs playfully as her partner pretended to bat her hands away. The tension between them was riveting. Leda's own cunt ached, trapped as it was in her too-stifling black jeans.

Quickly, and in a huff of frustration, she turned and moved further into the huge warehouse-sized space, searching for the woman she'd seen from the Viewing Room. No way she'd still be where Leda had last seen her; it felt as though hours had passed since then. But no trace of her here. Leda's eyes wandered up the incredibly high walls and saw a huge waterfall on the far end to her left, tumbling down over a high ledge of rocks and down, down, into the wide constructed river. At the top of the ledge where the water shot out over the rocks, a naked woman stood perched to one side. She stepped to the edge, balanced herself with her arms, lowered them, concentrating still, then pushed off in a swan dive, hitting the water with hardly a ripple.

Leda was impressed. She joined in as women all along the "bank" of the river hooted and clapped. Many women, she noticed, were paired up, or in a group already. She strolled down the walkway by the riverside, watching the women swimming or lying on the strip of sandy shore. There was also a strip of island in the middle of the wide river. The sound of exotic birds and wind in the trees mixed with the Caribbean-flavored dance music that pumped through the Jungle Room and Leda closed her eyes for a minute, appreciating the lush soundtrack that transformed this place—along with the incredible scenery—into an exotic island of sexual fantasy.

Leda took a long breath and opened her eyes, distracted by a crowd of women's voices whooping and hollering from across the river. Her eyes were drawn to the island in the middle of the river where a bonfire circled by large stones was in full flame. Huge multicolored spotlights were focused on the strip of island and they were moving now, like searchlights. Women of all types and sizes were dancing and moving, performing for those on the shore. Some wore grass skirts and bathing suits and moved together in an impersonation of a Hawaiian sort of dance; some just wore grass skirts and nothing else, also trying to follow along with the first group. Others wore only men's boxers or a G-string, with their hair—short, long, or in-between—slicked back, faces shining. One butch woman danced with another butch and their packed dildos—not so packed anymore in their loose boxer shorts—bounced and danced right along with them, making their boxers pooch out, the tips of the dildos appearing, then disappearing.

Leda laughed out loud and shook her head as the

two women danced and raised their beers in a whoop and holler of celebratory enthusiasm. Their cheer was infectious and pretty soon all the women on the island were dancing and whooping and raising their beers or various other drinks in a toast, too. It was like an all-female Carnivale without the distraction of ogling men.

"Yay women!" Leda whooped, swept up in the growing tide of revelry. Someone next to her added, "Amen sister!"

Leda turned, smiling, and met the wide, pretty smile of a dreadlocked African-American woman dressed in a striking skirt and bathing suit—type top of eye-catching multicolored fabrics. She was sipping a large fruity drink and bobbing with the rhythm of the music.

"Ain't that the truth!" she said, sort of to Leda.

"Definitely!" Leda replied. The woman looked her over briefly.

"You need a drink," she asked after a moment. "Can I buy you one?"

Leda was tempted, but reminded herself that if she stuck around much longer, she might not find the woman she'd come in for, not for the rest of the night probably. The thought panicked her some in an odd way, since of course she didn't even know the woman she was pining after. She felt like Cinderella at the ball: *Hurry before the clock strikes midnight and you're sent back to your old self, old world, old stuck place!* There was just something so seductive about the woman she'd seen through the window. In some strange way the attraction was incredibly intense, as though she'd known the woman a long, long time; just hadn't been able to get close to her before, intimately. But tonight there was a possibility. Tonight, everything was possible. Leda just couldn't give up yet. First she had to finish her search.

"Thanks so much for the offer, I'd love to hang with you a while. But I'm looking for someone," Leda explained. The woman smiled and nodded as she continued to bob to the music. Her body was beautiful, breasts crisscrossed with the colorful cloth, ample hips moving with the music.

"I hope you find her," the woman said, raising her drink in a toast to Leda. "Have fun. Come back if you don't find her." She smiled.

"Thanks, I will," Leda said, and the woman moved on down the path that ran along the river.

*I'll definitely be back if that happens,* Leda thought to herself.

Reggae music followed her back to the elevators, which opened before she had a chance to touch the up arrow button. Another crowd of women in various states of undress moved out of the elevator, some already caught up in the reggae beat. Leda slipped into the elevator as the last woman disembarked. A couple of other women got on with her and she hit the up button, taking the calm moment to check out her hair, teeth, face, in the shiny metal panel that housed the elevator buttons. She also watched the two women making out madly behind her. One wore a collar and the other woman was holding it tight as she pressed against her, kissing her furiously and deeply. The sound of her leather pants as she moved caught Leda's attention and she felt a shiver of disappointment that she'd never put aside enough money to buy some of her own, luxury that they were.

But oh, so worth it.

When the elevator doors opened, she was back in the hallway. Leda got off and looked both ways. A brighter light was coming from the room to her right at the end of the hall so she turned that way, remembering that the light seemed pretty bright in the room she had been watching from the Viewing Room. She moved quickly down the dim hallway, past the bathrooms where a line was forming, hoping that at last she'd be in the right place at the right time tonight.

Leda walked through the archway and entered a large room, the one she recognized from the Viewing Room! It was much brighter in this room than in the passage from which she'd just emerged and Leda squinted, waiting a minute for her eyes to adjust.

After a moment, she checked out the wall where the windows were, behind which she knew other women watched the goings-on in this room. By the way the lights were set up, all you could see were mirrors mostly, or the effects of mirrors. If you didn't know they were there, you might miss the fact that this was a room to be watched in.

*I definitely wouldn't want to do anything in here,* Leda thought, stepping up and onto a low platform to move out of the way as women filed past her. But then who had actually been watching in the Viewing Room other than her? It was hard to tell. And besides, more people were showing up by the minute; it might be full of women up there by now. Leda squinted up, trying to see the Viewing Room through the mirrored glass.

Suddenly she felt someone's gaze on her. She looked out of the corner of her eye, for some reason too shy to turn around and look. Her body tingled and her mouth went dry. She forced herself at least to turn her head a little to get a better view out of the corner of her eye.

And there she was. And close by: the soft butch she had seen from the Viewing Room.

The woman seemed to be watching Leda before Leda had a chance to do it first. Leda smiled inside, but out of nervousness, didn't smile outwardly, keeping a carefully cool exterior, trying not to show that she had noticed the woman's gaze. She tried doggedly to stay relaxed, but her hand went up and ran itself nervously through her spiky hair, seemingly of its own accord. The music pumped through this room, too, but the lighting was brighter than even the other main room she'd been in, obviously for better viewing. Still, the lighting wasn't harsh, some dramatic accents to it coming mostly from colored lights and hurricane lamps, and spotlights illuminating equipment and certain scene areas of the playroom.

Leda tried to turn nonchalantly toward the woman whose eyes she could feel on her body so intensely even from this distance. *Stay cool, calm,* she thought, *don't do anything stupid.* But as she turned and took a few steps as if she were just casually moving a little further into the room, she found herself accidentally stepping right into the beam of a bright white spotlight, looking straight into it and temporarily blinded by the hot light. Leda raised her hand to shield her eyes, then turned away from the blaze, blinking, making a disgusted face as the cameras of her eyes played back the image again and again.

*Oh, that was very very very cool,* she commented disgustedly to herself, her pulse racing now, feeling just like the awkward novice she'd been when she'd first stepped into the world of women, sex, and SM play years ago. It was like some terrible embarrassing flash-back.

She groaned.

But as the image of the lights dissipated, she worked up the guts to turn back and look. The spot where the woman had been standing was empty; she was gone.

"Shit," Leda mumbled under her breath.

Suddenly all the white spotlights in the room started to roam, making big sweeping circles like a police helicopter as the music changed into a pounding dance tune with a wailing female vocalist. Leda noticed as she glanced around that she was standing in a scene space (hence, the spotlight). A wooden wall just behind her was equipped with heavy hooks all the way up at different heights, chains hanging from the ceiling, which was low here, the area constructed like a sort of cage with metal barrel-shaped doors that were swung wide open. Leda pulled on one and saw that they would meet in the center with a metal rod that slid into a little cylinder to secure them. In the same scene area was a black leather vault-style horse, heavily padded, and a large wooden step stool.

*A world of possibilities*, Leda thought, a fire in her eyes and streaking through her overheated body. She could feel the wetness of the fabric of her underwear that clung to her mound, the heat most intense between her legs.

"Lots of possibilities in this room," a sexy tenor voice said from behind her, making her jump a little.

Leda turned and there before her was the object of her desire, the one woman she knew could make her do things she really shouldn't.

But, oh, man, she wanted to.

"That's just what I was thinking," Leda said, the sides of her mouth creeping up into a slight smile, the surprise still on her face, blue eyes sparkling at the brown ones eyeing her coolly, but with great interest and friendly enough.

*Wow. Wow, wow, wow!* Leda thought stupidly, struck dumb for the moment and uncertain how to proceed.

The soft tan of the woman's skin and the obvious

strength of her toned arms; the way she stood so confidently and seductively in her body; her legs which were actually much longer up close, incredibly shaped; her thick dark hair which had been pulled back loosely in a low ponytail, away from a beautiful face—all of this served only to absolutely transfix Leda where she stood, unable to move or speak, much less breathe.

The overwhelming shyness that Leda hated so much threatened to wipe out any attempt at boldness. She noted this internally with disgust, but couldn't change it for the moment. There was something about this woman, as though she'd been wanting her for a lifetime. Luckily, all was not lost.

"Would you be interested in joining me in trying out some of this great equipment?" the woman asked. "My name is Michelle, but I go by Mikki or Mik most of the time."

Leda almost choked with excitement, still feeling self-conscious but more confident by the minute. Mikki was eyeing her with great approval and a hunger in her eyes that seemed to match what Leda felt. Leda suddenly realized that her composure was beginning to loosen, that the words TAKE ME! were probably actually visible to the eye in big flashing letters across her whole nervous face.

"Leda," she answered, "my name is Leda. And yes, oh, yes, I would love to."

She tried to sound casual about the whole thing, but she could hear her own voice too sincere, too emphatic, and she couldn't take her eyes away from Mikki's. It was like falling into a deep chocolate sea and she was high already from the sugar rush.

*Yes, I would love to give you my body and my passion and drink madly from your mouth and take you and open you and open wide for you and scream for you and be your dog, oh mama mama mama...*

Leda felt relief that the only empaths she knew of only showed up on *Star Trek* and she blushed at her own thoughts, her obvious ravenous hunger, so starved as she was for what turned her on.

"Great, what are you into?" Mikki asked intimately, moving in closer.

Leda felt suddenly overwhelmed by everything she'd just seen and heard and this woman in front of her, and she moved in as if pushed by a tidal wave of passion, almost against Mikki's hot body, no words for the desire she felt, just action. She boldly slipped one hand around and held one of Mikki's leather-clad asscheeks, turning her a little until Leda could see the hankies in the pocket of Mikki's obviously custom-made pants. They fit like a glove on her firm ass.

"Sixty-nine is good..." Leda said in agreement, speaking to Mikki's butt and flipping through the tails of colored hankies with her fingertip: robin's egg blue, gray...

"...but I don't know you well enough for that yet," Leda continued. "A good beating by a strong but caring hand with a little torture and a lot of challenge is my taste. Yeah. Do you switch with the fisting or just top?"

Leda took a breath and looked back up, slowly, travelling over the impossible perfection of Mikki's thighs, ass, waist, small but ample tits, smooth round shoulders covered with creamy brown flesh, soft neck, beautiful high-cheekboned face. The face was smiling and a laugh was escaping through that incredible open mouth.

"Well, great!" Mikki laughed. "We must be meant for each other, destined to meet!" Her laugh was mellow and friendly, but there was serious passion in those eyes. She didn't pull away either. "Like I've been waiting all night for you to get here or something," she added.

Leda's gaze matched Mik's intensity and suddenly there wasn't room for any thoughts of Chrys or other considerations that had appeared before her as she'd first wrapped her arm around this new woman. There was just Mik, and their bodies together: tits, hips, thighs almost touching, and the rippled subtle flexing of the muscles in Mik's arms as she looked down slightly to gaze at the parted lips of Leda's mouth.

"Yeah," Leda whispered, definitely feeling an odd familiarity and uncharacteristic boldness.

"What about kissing?" Mikki asked in a quiet voice, her breath touching Leda's cheek as she spoke.

"Kissing is good," Leda whispered back. "Before we play, though, are you negative?"

"I am," Mik confirmed. "You?"

"Yep."

"No lies," the woman insisted.

"No lies," Leda agreed.

"And kisses are good?"

"Can be very very good," Leda replied.

The two women were now close against each other. Leda felt the rest of the club fade away. And to her surprise, without further ado, Mik leaned down into a deep kiss that seemed electrified with the energy between them, transferring back and forth in a frantic current and waking up every cell in Leda's body. Mikki's hands found Leda's hips and held them, but only tentatively, not overly intimate or aggressive, the passion escaping instead in their kiss, bonding them.

Leda's tongue found Mik's and they battled hungrily for command, Mik ultimately winning and orchestrating the ending of the kiss with the control of a good leader, top, commander...lover, Master...

"Mmh," Leda said through a fog of passion, eyes lingering on Mikki's lips. "You taste good. And you won."

"Right back at you. Yeah, I did. You consent to it?" Mik whispered hoarsely, studying Leda's face, her eyes a wash of hunger, too, but smoldering, not wild untamed flames like Leda's.

Leda realized she meant for playing together, that whoever won control of the kiss won control of the scene...or maybe the night, if she was lucky. Leda wished she'd known, but liked it, too, that she didn't—and lost.

"Yeah," Leda answered thoughtfully. "For Round One. Do you switch for anything?"

"Not much," Mikki said honestly. "But, you never know."

Her knee had found its way, subtly, up between Leda's legs, ever so slightly parting them, the ball of her booted foot still resting on the ground. Leda was delighted: someone more aggressive than herself! Although she often would get shy in groups, Leda wasn't, in general, especially once she got to know someone. In fact, when faced with another similarly strong character, she usually bristled and faced off with the person, not actually meaning to, just instinctively.

But tonight she fed on this woman's aggressiveness, glad for it and shocked by her own passive behavior when faced with someone maybe even more strong-willed than herself. There was something about Mik that turned her upside down, lowered her guard. It had been ages since she'd bottomed but she was surprised to see she hadn't lost the feel of it, the behavior and hunger for it.

"You like sex with your pain and torture?" Mik asked, obvious hope in her voice.

Leda smiled, pleased with Mik's upfront communication style and courage.

"I do," she said. "You practice safe sex?"

"I don't like it, but I do," she replied. "You?"

"Yeah, don't like it either, though."

"Then safe sex it is."

"Cool," Leda agreed.

"Do you like to get fucked by a woman who's just gotta have you?" Mik asked fearlessly, smiling.

Leda's cunt ached at the sound of the words and it

answered for her with a throbbing beat she wondered if Mik could feel with her leg still up gently between Leda's thighs.

"Oh yeah," she said, running her hands over the outside of Mik's arms, admiring them, envisioning their strength when in use.

She looked up. "And I pack a mean fuck myself," she offered. "You up to the competition?"

*Ah, there she is*, Leda thought. The cocky butch inside her stood up to face off with Mik for a moment.

Mikki laughed her great amused laugh again. There wasn't a hint of anything but pleasure and amusement in it.

"I'm up for the possibility and challenge if you trust me to lead this one first…to, well, satisfaction."

Leda felt stupid for admitting it to herself and with a complete stranger, but she could feel it in everything about this woman that she could trust her, would trust her, maybe with her life if they committed to play that hard.

Well, maybe.

But definitely something special, and something that woke up a place in Leda that had no problem being the collar bearer.

"I don't know why, but I do trust you," Leda said. She felt a whimper of desire in her throat, the clothes on her body suddenly overwhelmingly constraining.

"Shall we start here and make our way up to the padded room for further testing?" Mikki asked, still gathering information but with a great deal of taste and flair—and sexiness, Leda noted. Practiced. Almost slick.

"You come here often?" Leda asked, leaning back, checking her out. "You know everything about this club?"

Mikki looked surprised, then chuckled. "Not *too* often, but yeah, I know the place. Never had an experience like this, though; I'm usually playing early on in the night, but like I said, guess I was waiting for you."

Her eyes sparkled and she seemed as surprised and dumbfounded as Leda. "Have you been here before?"

"No, my first time," Leda answered honestly. "But I learn fast. And I've been to other play parties."

Mikki nodded.

"Didn't think I've seen you here before. What other places do you like to frequent?"

"Oh, I haven't been…out…for a long time. I mean out to the sex clubs. I'm, well, really out of practice, you might say. Almost…," she considered the right wording, "…virginal." Leda said this a little shyly, surprised at her own honesty.

"You don't seem it," Mik said brightly, leaning in toward her, her eyes studying Leda's face.

"Well, almost virginal." Leda's eyes twinkled with mischief. "Uh huh," Mik pressed.

Leda was having fun with their banter. She loved it, in fact.

"You wanna show me the, uh, ropes here tonight since I'm such a, well, you know?"

"Oh, I do," Mik answered almost earnestly, no smile on her face now.

Leda's body hummed. "Well, now we've both said 'I do,'" she whispered, smiling. "So I guess we're, like, committed." Leda paused for a moment, feeling her body in this space, connecting with this woman. "Okay, I submit to you, Mikki," she said with finality. "To…satisfaction."

She couldn't *believe* she was saying this, how right and natural it felt to say such dramatic, but absolutely true words. Her life with Chrys felt far away, disconnected, and what opened up inside her like a bulb in the spring after a long cold season was a shedding of her usual control as the aggressor, the caretaker, the controller, the negotiator, the compromiser. This was something else, somehow truer than what she'd been doing for way, way, too long.

Leda watched Mik's face light up as she spoke the words of submission to her.

"And if you rip off my clothes, I won't beg you to stop either," Leda whispered like a challenge, leaning in toward Mik's ear to say it, her breath lingering.

"Oh, man, you make me wanna do it all at once, nice and nasty and cruel and kind," Mik hoarsely whispered back. She couldn't help but grasp Leda's hips hard, then move her hands around and grip Leda's ass in both strong palms, moving her hips in against Leda's and pulling her in.

Leda smiled and her breathing got a little ragged. She

chuckled with pleasure down deep in her throat and pretended to resist.

"No, oh please, no, stop..." Then the chuckle escaped and she blurted out, "Oh *fuck!* where have you been all my life, woman?" Leda realized with horror that she asked this only half jokingly, but they both broke into all-out laughter. Leda couldn't help herself, though, pact or no pact, she had to have another one, couldn't wait suddenly. They had contracted, in a way, and she'd submitted to the passive role. But without thinking, Leda pushed in and took a kiss from Mik's surprised mouth without asking, interrupting their laughter. Those muscular arms wrapped around her then, Leda feeling the heat and pulse of Mikki's active body; active, hard... *yeah...hard...really hard.*

Leda was totally and completely shocked to feel a hard-on under Mik's pants and almost hooted and laughed out loud at how she'd picked a kindred packer; amazed even more at how hungry her body was for just such a pleasure, even without the promise of a switch. She was glad her own toys were in her bag tonight. In fact, if Leda hadn't been sober, she was sure she'd have jumped right into Mik's arms and wrapped her legs right around those strong gorgeous hips.

Leda didn't want to relinquish it, but somehow Mik took it without question—the control of the kiss—and ended it before Leda would have liked.

"What have you got on under those jeans?" Mik asked.

This caught Leda a little by surprise as she embarrassedly remembered what she was wearing.

"Um, you know, underwear...well, a thong sort of thang actually..."

Leda grimaced at her babbling and at her Victoria's Secret ultra-femme possibly-humiliatingly-so underwear choice. Really, she hadn't dressed thinking of actually playing. Well, mostly not.

But Mikki smiled, apparently not noticing her babbling, and actually seeming perfectly pleased with Leda's response.

"Oooo, girly lingerie, mmm, I love it. You're a surprise a minute! I like that."

Leda watched the smile fade and the commander slip in. An attendant passed by. "'Scuse me," Mik called out. The attendant turned, looked at Mik, and came back.

"Yeah, babe," the woman said in a friendly voice from behind a leather cat mask. Leda couldn't hear what Mik was saying to the woman, but she saw money change hands. The attendant turned and moved quickly away, her body language saying that she was definitely on a mission.

Mik turned back to her.

"So I don't think I'd wanna rip off your nice jeans, but there's definitely too much clothing between us. I'll take it from here if you don't mind," Mik told her, rather than asked. She commanded Leda gently and surely. To Leda, it felt completely natural and she slipped into the scene with absolute commitment and anticipation, surprised, but too caught up to be amazed.

"Yes, Mik," she said.

Mik smiled, a wicked and mischievous glint in her eyes, and obvious pleasure. She nodded her approval.

"Good girl," she said. "Let's begin."

# 10.

Mik undid the ties on Leda's vest, her body moving with the beat of the trancelike music that filled the place as she undressed Leda. Rather than undoing the ties and slipping the vest up over Leda's head, Mik lingered, running her thumbs over Leda's hard buds and tweaking them lightly, squeezing her tits, and teasing Leda, who had been instructed to keep her hands at her sides. Then Mik pulled the cord completely out of the vest with a long tug, and the vest fell open, exposing Leda's chest, belly, waist. "Take it off," Mik told her.

Leda removed the vest and stood naked from the waist up.

"Off with the boots."

Leda squatted down and attended to her boots, setting them aside.

"Good girl. Well done—so far." Mik's eyes were playful, the edge of her mouth just barely turned up in a suggestion of a smile.

Leda blushed at the pride and pleasure she felt, how much she liked the approving words; pleasing Mik. She felt free with her body and her desires as she hadn't felt for years. It was like a rebirth into the sensation of her passion; into the ultimate exchange between two passionately attracted women.

Passionately attracted—that was the key. A key that had been missing in her life for how long now? The feel of it here, so strong, almost brought tears to her eyes, the intensity of it—but not quite.

Mik was in front of Leda, opening the zipper of Leda's jeans, slipping her strong hand inside just a little way, feeling Leda's heat, the muscles in her arms flexing and rippling as she maneuvered.

"Mmmmm, so hot, Leda, so wet. I think I'll have to teach you some control, girl. Yeah, a little control."

And with that she removed her hand and pulled Leda's jeans down hard, all at once, exposing her thong-covered mound. Leda stepped obediently out of her pants as Mik instructed. Mik set the pants aside with the vest and swung the horse into the center of the stage area—the middle of the cage if the doors were swung shut. At this moment, they were not. Mik moved the wide rectangular step stool in front of the horse, then glanced around.

Leda glanced around, too, suddenly remembering what room they were in; that she hadn't left the Viewing Room playroom.

*Oh, Lord,* she swore silently, *don't let anyone I know be watching tonight...* But the thought passed right out of her mind at the harsh sound of Mik's voice.

"I didn't give you permission to avert your eyes!" Mik barked.

Leda quickly looked back at her, attempting to stand taller, proud but quite naked except for her thong. She wanted to reach back and tug it out of the crack of her ass, but knew better. Mikki seemed to read her mind, but Leda had actually unconsciously moved her hand toward doing the deed, then stopped as she remembered her place.

"Bet those sexy fucking panties are driving you crazy, way up between your ass where they shouldn't be...." Mik smiled. "Bet you wish I would let you give them a good yank...."

The smile was wicked and wonderful and made Leda's cunt swell, which only worsened the panty situation.

"Yes," Leda said a little too emphatically.

"Yes, ma'am, when you answer."

"Yes, ma'am," Leda corrected obediently.

"Since we're strangers," Mik told her, "and it's our first time together..." Mik felt the throbbing of her sex as she envisioned fucking Leda. "...I'll let you choose the safe word this time. I prefer to have one, I hope you do."

"Yes, ma'am," Leda answered, thinking. "Justice."

"Justice. Okay, justice it is. You can prove there exists such a thing; I highly doubt it. I can't wait to test-drive you, see how far you go before you use it." She smiled her cruel smile again. "Approach the horse, Leda."

Leda moved forward and stood in front of the horse, facing it, as Mik stepped aside. Just then the attendant returned with a large black bag in hand. Out of the corner of her eye, Leda watched Mik take it from the woman. She thanked her and barely missed a beat, swinging the bag up onto the horse in front of Leda.

"I have a test or two for you, my slave, before I enter your body and fill you up and let you fly out into oblivion. First you take what I give you here, with these."

Mik opened her bag and withdrew three different whips: a cat, a rather soft-looking short whip, and a large, heavy-looking, beautifully crafted, thick long-tailed whip.

"But first I'll have to secure you because you might not stay still for me and that wouldn't do." She pulled out narrow shackles and chains with clips, which she secured to four hooks on the horse.

Just the words of what Mik was going to do to her melted Leda where she stood. Every inch of her was seduced into absolute submission. The sound of the metal clips as they closed around the hooks made her whimper just barely audibly. Mikki adjusted the height of the horse to a satisfactory level, then instructed Leda to lean over. She did. Mik took her wrists, shackled them, and secured each to a short chain that had been added to the hooks. Then, from behind, with her heavy boots she parted Leda's legs to a satisfactory width apart, shackled them, and secured each to chains that met at either side of the base of the horse.

"Tug," Mik said.

Leda tugged at each binding. They didn't give, and the length of the chain didn't allow any play so her legs were forced to remain open. The cool leather of the horse chilled Leda's skin as she bent over it, her tits squished in against it, resting there. Then Mik's hand reached into the crack of her ass and graciously pulled the thong free.

"Thank you, ma'am," Leda said sincerely.

"Yes, you learn fast. You will thank me for everything I give you. After each gift I give you. Understand?"

"Yes, ma'am."

And with that she pulled Leda's panties down around her ankles and left them there. Leda was appalled, feeling the rush of embarrassment at standing there with her panties down around her ankles, especially such froofy ones as these. She swallowed hard, hoping her pride would stay put.

The sound of a whip behind her caught her attention. The huge playroom was warm, especially their little area, and smelled of incense and sex. Leda listened as the music changed, one song melting into the next, following the bass beat. A single scream broke through the tapestry of the music like punctuation and the music carried it away. Leda shivered, but not with cold. Here she was: naked, bottoming to a strong-armed, obviously skilled top she didn't know. What if she had wussed out over the years; what if she couldn't take what turned her on anymore?

*Take it, girl,* she told herself, *you can do it. Go with it, ride it, ride with her, connect with it. You haven't forgotten how to take it, all the way.*

And then there was a strong hand rubbing Leda's back, kneading her muscles briefly, relaxing her; then caressing her sides, her ass, pushing through under her arms to grasp her tits and squeeze them gently, knead them, excite them. They continued up her back to her neck, where Leda's head hung down over the horse as she leaned over it. Mik's hands grabbed a handful of Leda's hair and pulled Leda's head back gently but with purpose. Lips caressed her right ear.

"I know you can take it," Mikki whispered passionately, straight into her soul. "Make me proud; show me your strength."

Leda felt a rush of adrenaline, everything melting into a desire to please, to be pleased. And as she relaxed into Mik's words—head returning to its original spot, looking out at the wall behind the horse, torso bent over, arms braced against the padded leather, wrists shackled to the heavy hooks—she could feel the floor beneath her, feet firm on parted, shackled legs, as steady as the whispered words.

And just as she slipped into a quieter place, guard

down for just a moment, Mikki moved back away from her, and the whipping began. Light, rhythmic thwacks, lightly at first, with the soft-tailed shorter whip landed as an introduction against Leda's bare back. The music was a perfect rhythm for accompaniment and Mik was alive with the beat of the scene, her arm strong, body full of energy, completely tuned in to Leda and to the rhythm between them.

Behind Leda, Mik smiled, her eyes blazing with a mixture of sadistic pleasure and excitement as she discovered the landscape of Leda's naked body with the whip, landing here, there, watching for a reaction to each new spot, laying the foundation as they warmed up together.

"I will tell you when to thank me and I will expect you to, each and every time I say so, understood?"

Mik spoke to Leda as she continued the light whipping, slowly increasing the intensity, the tempo.

"Yes, ma'am," Leda answered, feeling her skin light up with each contact, the wetness of her cunt, the heat, even with her legs wide.

Mikki could see it, too, the silky wetness of Leda's sex between her open legs, asscheeks presented to her for her pleasure. She used it as a gauge, carefully watching the muscles of Leda's body and her ass, her cunt, watching all of it as the intensity of the whipping increased.

Leda breathed into it, anticipating each point of contact landing with purpose on her back, thwack! against her shoulders, ass, thighs, and back up to begin again. Leda's body was alive with concentration and sensation.

The softness of the short whip was replaced by a harder, stinging connection as the intensity of the blows increased, coming faster, more edgy. Leda wanted to turn and look at her delicious tormentor, but couldn't. Instead, she envisioned those arms in her mind, muscles flexed as Mik raised the whip in preparation, her whole body behind each blow. Leda could feel the electricity between them, the concentration. But most of all now she could feel the pain as Mik carefully orchestrated the scene to the next level.

*Yes!* Leda wanted to cry out, unable to contain herself. *Oh, God, yes!* Her voice pushed at her chest, her throat, wanting to release itself into the humid warm air of the playroom. But it wasn't allowed. She hadn't been given permission even to speak. Leda breathed carefully: *control, control,* she repeated silently to herself.

But then Mikki gave her a gift, just as she said we would. There was a brief pause, then Mik commanded: "Thank me! Thank me loud so I can hear you. I'll count for you."

"One!" Mik cried out, and Leda felt the first blow from the long, heavy-gauge whip as it smacked into her ass.

"Thank you!" she cried out almost automatically, her entire body flushing with pleasure and pain and determination. The tails were not wide, but thick and mean— the way she liked them best.

"Two!" Mik said as the whip flew into the air, then came straight down onto Leda's upper back.

"Thank you!" she cried again, feeling her skin burn with the whip's bite. Mik's arms were indeed strong, and Leda braced herself, wanting to take it, to please her, to prove herself not only to Mikki, but to herself.

*Breathe, breathe…,* Leda reminded herself.

"Three!" Mik hollered.

"Thank you," she half grunted.

"I can't hear you, speak up!" Mik told her loudly. "Four!"

"Thank you!" Leda hollered. "Ahh shiiit!"

"Just thank you, slave, that's all I want to hear from you!" came the command.

Mik and Leda continued this way, in a steady rhythm of pain, up to twenty-three, twenty-four… And on the twenty-fifth blow, Leda let out a curse and a holler and gripped the horse, her legs unsteady beneath her, breathing hard, sweat stinging her eyes and flying off the tips of her spiky hair as she momentarily shook her head as if to shake off the pressurized pain that burned on her skin.

"Good girl," Mik said with great care and kindness as she stopped the whipping, approaching Leda from behind and kissing her angry skin, the light welts that stood up in a fury. She inspected her work: no skin broken, just a little tormented.

"Good girl," Mikki said over and over, lightly stroking Leda's waist with one hand, then down over her reddened ass, flat soft palm against it, then slipping down further between Leda's shaky legs from behind, palm against the heat of Leda's pussy, fingers lightly stroking her hard clit, playing in the wetness of Leda's swollen lips as they opened to Mik's touch.

"Oh, yes, oh, please, please," Leda breathed, unable to remain silent, her body on fire, the incredible rush of pleasure temporarily obliterating the rage of her skin, the echoing pain. Sweat stung the angry places on her back and ass, on her thighs. But all of it disappeared at the touch of Mikki's fingers on her sex, her clit hardening and straining for the woman's touch. Leda's empty cunt throbbed with longing she hadn't felt in what seemed a lifetime.

"Do you wanna be fucked?" Mik asked her in a husky voice. "Or should I make you wait?"

A desperate groan was all Leda could offer, unable to see or think behind the veil of her hunger, lost in the sweet wickedness of pain and heady pleasure.

"Maybe I should pin your tits and mask you, make you wait...."

*How cruel you are*, Leda thought, almost smiling. She didn't know Mik well enough to know if the woman really would make her wait or not, and the not knowing was the worst—and best—of all.

"Please," Leda begged as Mik continued to stroke her sex, her clit, but not fast enough or hard enough. And still Leda remained empty, aching with need, on the edge of being downright irritable.

"What do you want?" Mik asked in a hoarse, excited voice, watching Leda squirm. "Ask me nicely."

"Please, ma'am, please fuck me, please…" She could hardly catch her breath. "Touch me harder."

"Oooo, you didn't say please on that second one," Mik countered. "Hmmm."

"Please!" Leda begged, trying doggedly to press her cunt against Mikki's too-gentle hand. But the hand moved with her, making her beg, remaining lightly against her, with just the hint, the suggestion of contact.

Behind Leda, Mik smiled, feeling the incredible wetness of Leda's swollen, ready cunt. "But you're not allowed to come yet," Mik admonished. "Too soon. Uh uh."

Leda groaned loudly, a whimper mixed in with it, pulling at the chains that held her hands, frustrated, unable to do anything about this last word, this denial of release.

"Thank me for the discipline, for my skilled training of you," Mik directed.

Leda couldn't do that. No way. She couldn't thank Mik for denying her, not after bringing her to such a wild state of hunger, her clit feeling every breeze that passed between her spread and shackled legs. Leda remained defiantly silent.

"Thank me," Mik said again, an order this time.

Leda was enraged, almost out of control at the audacity of this woman's denial of her basic needs after Leda had taken her pain so well. She teetered at the edge of losing her temper, of forgetting her place and falling into the flames that entranced her, provoked her, controlled her.

But she didn't. Leda wasn't quite that gone yet.

This she realized as the braided cat-o'-nine-tails cruelly

met the already raw skin of her ass when the required words did not obediently emerge from her mouth as ordered.

"Thank you!" Leda cried out, the words bursting from her lips, surprised into submission and obedience.

"Again!" Mik ordered as the cat whipped through the air and down again on the other cheek like jagged teeth biting into her tender flesh.

"Thank you!" Leda hollered again, sweat dripping down her face, the pain intense, stars flashing before her unfocused eyes.

"One more gift to you for your insolence," Mik said.

The cat crashed down across Leda's ass once more and this time Leda screamed out her thanks with enthusiasm, and desperation, the cry of a wild animal cornered by a predator, caught.

*"Thank you!"*

The sound blasted from her throat with emphatic force, the blow sending spikes of pain exploding outward like fireworks from her center and out her limbs, exploding her alive. Blood pounded through Leda's veins and in her head, blocking out the music, this place, the crowd, everything, her life force travelling at light speed through her entire body, only to be magnetized into a single point at the apex of her thighs, filling her clit to bursting.

"Good girl," Mik offered flatly. "Next time I trust you'll follow orders. Am I right?"

"Yes, ma'am," Leda answered automatically, her

breathing ragged, vision cloudy with the distraction of her throbbing clit.

Mik approached Leda once again, but this time she dropped the whips into her bag as she passed it, moving around to the opposite side of the horse. She studied Leda, looking hard at her, gauging her next move, assessing the situation, determining if maybe she had been too hard on her new pet. But it was apparent that Leda was getting off on the whole orchestration, even though the obviousness of this was temporarily lost in an entertaining rage of indignation.

Mik smiled approvingly, her face beaming with enjoyment at the frustration she was causing, the pleasure of her power to control, to choose to cause either pain or pleasure at will.

"You take it well," she said gently to Leda.

Leda leaned heavily against the horse, head hanging down, the sweat on her chest gleaming as it pooled slightly between her cleavage, dripping onto and slippery against the leather of the horse beneath her. Droplets of sweat fell in a slow rhythm off the tips of Leda's soft, spiky hair as she breathed, lost in her body's sensations and the rush of willing herself to go the distance with this woman; to give it all up to her.

As the throbbing in her cunt subsided a little and the flaming skin of her buttcheeks began to cool, Leda found she could focus on her surroundings again. She lifted her head, which felt heavy.

There in front of her eyes was smooth naked olive

skin above leather pants, the top button open seductively at the waist, the muscles of Mik's naked stomach easily visible beneath her skin, the indentation of her navel beckoning Leda's tongue—but too far away to reach. Leda raised her head higher, her eyes taking in the shapely curves of Mikki's waist, firm chest—not too small, but not large—sloping slightly down and up again at the tips, soft brown-pink nipples hard at attention. Mik's arms rested at her sides, the veins sticking out on her right bicep and forearm, even in a relaxed state, from the effort of her attentions. Leda's eyes travelled up again to smooth, round, muscular shoulders, then rested again on Mikki's inviting chest and lingered there, hungry for a taste.

Leda couldn't quite force her head up any further above the beautiful view, although she knew Mik's face was to die for, too. But, oh, her body was beyond Leda's fantasies, so much of what took her breath away. Chrys's body was nice, too, but not like this. Chrys's was very soft and sort of passively feminine, pretty and pink, waiting to be approached, touched, seduced—rather than aggressively sexy in a smooth, taut, tough way like Mik's.

Both were nice, though, each with their own distinct advantages. But tonight Leda didn't want nice or soft or passively feminine. She wanted what stood before her.

Mikki watched Leda's hungry, appreciative eyes. She stepped closer, leaning forward and down slightly to line up one of her tits with Leda's mouth.

Out of her mind with passion, Leda opened her mouth at the first touch of Mik's nipple against the flesh of her lips and sucked in the hard bud, running her tongue around the soft skin and flicking the tip again and again, sucking and loving it. It felt to Leda as though a lifetime had passed since she'd been with another woman, tasted the sweet flesh of anyone's body except Chrys's. And at this moment, that life with Chrys felt light-years away. Only this moment existed, the taste and texture of Mikki's sweet tit in her mouth, the after-effects of the woman's ministrations still lingering on Leda's marked flesh. Leda moaned with pleasure, forgetting her tied wrists that kept her restrained as she instinctively tried to reach up, to hold and stroke Mik's body. Finding the restraints denying her access, she sucked harder in frustration, the passion growing once again to an overwhelming pitch.

"Good girl," Mik whispered to her intimately, "no biting now. Yeah, like that. Mmm. Good."

Leda looked up at Mik's face then and saw the excitement in her eyes as Leda sucked and teased her hard nipple. Then Mik slipped gently out of Leda's mouth and moved the other tit to Leda's lips, running it against them first, not allowing her to have it yet, feeling the smoothness of Leda's mouth.

Leda opened wider, waiting, gauging, then closed suddenly on the hard bud as it passed, catching it and sucking it hard, licking the smooth surface around it. Desperately wishing for freedom of motion, Leda nonetheless obediently took what she was given, believing her longing for more to be well hidden. But with every taste of Mik's flesh, the heat between her legs became almost unbearably insistent and Leda, sensing the danger of this growing tide of frustration, had to gather all her strength, fight like a warrior against the urge to bite and cause pain to her tormentor, her goddess, the one who both denied and fed her.

On the receiving end, Mik watched Leda battle for control, then smiled slightly, closing her eyes, enjoying the sensations, blocking out the ones she would not allow until later. "Mmmm, yes, very good," she praised.

After a moment, Mik slid her breast out of Leda's warm moist mouth, then leaned in and kissed her deeply. They sought out each other's tongues and played with them as if they were clits, hard-ons, the key to the climax. Both women breathed heavily, completely, into each other and the music dancing around them, the scene—contact. The spotlights swirled around the play space, moving over them repeatedly as the beat fed them.

Mik took Leda's face in her hands as they kissed, leaning in against the horse, on the opposite side, grinding in just a little against it, feeling the dildo in her pants push back against her, anticipating the moment when there would be no horse between them, no leather containing her; just the force of her body, her muscles, the thrust of her hips opening the sweet passageway into Leda's hot body.

"Mmmm yes," she moaned into Leda's open mouth as she ended the kiss. "Shall we move on?" she whispered hoarsely.

Leda looked into her eyes. How could she do it, deny her like this, and herself? Was Leda the only one crazy with wanting? Suddenly Leda was struck with consideration of a potentially serious problem: Maybe Mik didn't feel the same way Leda did, about the fucking part. Maybe the tease was going to be everything and enough for her. It didn't really appear that way, but...shit!

*Maybe it's the Great Spirit of Chastity and Monogamy telling you to save it for Chrys,* her head said loudly.

*Oh shut UP!* she angrily told the nagging voice, silently but with great force. *Don't even try and take me there.*

And to her surprise, her head was silent.

Beyond it, the music blasted into another tune that turned sort of dreamy, otherworldly, seductive. The spotlights stood still, but tiny lights flashed and whirled from a myriad of slowly turning disco-type balls and light fixtures that hung from the somewhat high ceilings beyond the low-ceilinged area of their particular play space. Leda temporarily floated out of her body and away with the entrancing music.

When she returned after a moment, her eyes refocusing, Mikki was removing the chains that secured Leda's wrists to the horse, then unhooked the clips at her ankles. Leda stood up straight, stretching her stiff back, feeling the ache of her skin. Without thinking, she started to undo the buckles of the shackles on her wrists; now that the chains no longer held her, of course she wouldn't need these.

"Oh, hell no," Mik said, grabbing her wrist with great force. "Don't even think about removing these, ever. My job. And I say they stay on."

She resecured the buckle, turning Leda back around to the horse, pushing her hard against it. Then she came in close, up behind Leda, placing her entire body—naked torso and leather-clad hips—up against Leda's naked backside. Mik's firm tits teased against Leda's back as she pressed in against her, hips and packed woman-cock pumping seductively against Leda's bare, welted ass.

"Damn, you look good enough to take right now and I do so want to. Mmm…shit…," she whispered.

Mik lost herself momentarily in the nasty hunger that could easily bring things to a quick finish if she let it. She moaned into Leda's short dark hair. There was nothing she liked more than to fuck a good hot woman who wanted her bad, like Leda did. And the energy between the two of them was beyond anything she'd experienced, by far. Anticipation pushed at Mik's control, her mind filling with ideas of how Leda would be with Mikki inside her, deep inside her and rockin' and rollin' as only two women can, as long as they want it, until they've both had enough. Would she scream? Would she swear and cry out? Would she call out Mik's name and beg her for more, open wider for her?

Christ, it was tempting.

"But...," Mik said aloud, unable to stop the rhythm of her hips as they continued to pump with the bass heavy, slow-ridin' R&B beat blasting through the playroom and finding its way into their scene.

Beneath her, Leda held her breath, eyes closed as every part of her concentrated on the meeting places of their bodies; the two moving together, her body opening to Mikki's thrusts, the hardness of the packed dildo now so obviously apparent against Leda's bare sensitive ass and thighs.

She wanted it so bad, she couldn't believe it. The sensation of aching and hunger was unlike anything Leda had ever experienced. Though Chrys had been nice enough to try to fuck Leda with a strap-on once or twice, it didn't work. Chrys giggled and was obviously uncomfortable.

And fist-fucking was way out of the question.

Leda realized at that incredible moment of high-pitched passion that she had given up a lot to be with Chrys. She couldn't remember the last time she had been taken to the edge, blasted out of her skin with a little cruelty; overtaken and controlled by the friction and motion and thrust of an able woman. No one had ever really taken her, not where she ached to go, beyond all control and with a wicked hunger.

Not the way that she was sure that Mikki could... would. She was taking her there already. Spellbound. That's how Leda felt: spellbound with anticipation, curiosity...and hope. She groaned with excitement and frustration as Mik pumped against her through the animal skin, wanting so bad, trying somehow to *will* Mik's tool free of the leather that held it captive; the leather that rubbed against Leda with the heat of Mik's incredibly warm and alive body behind it, the electric energy of her humming right into Leda as she ran her hands down and up Leda's sides, sliding them over Leda's arms as Leda braced herself against the horse. Mik's tits against her back felt delicious, firm and soft and moist with sweat. Leda tried harder, with all her might, her mind, to will the fabric between them to melt away like a miracle, obliterate the only barrier between the thrust of Mik's incredible thighs and hips, and Leda's heated cunt.

*Please give it to me*, she wanted to beg, *please fuck me, take me, blast me wide open*. But she knew better now. Disobedience, though it had its place, was not the route to pleasure here. Instead, Leda listened intently as Mik spoke, hanging on her every word.

"I have other plans for you, dear Leda," Mik continued, raising her head from its nuzzled place in the thickness of Leda's hair. "I want to decorate your soft bare skin with wax on the table in the padded room and warm you up until you're steaming and can't stand it."

*I can't stand it* NOW! Leda wanted to cry out, to whimper.

Mik kissed Leda's neck, bit it playfully but with a sting of purpose, almost breaking the skin. Leda drew in her breath, shutting her eyes tight. Mikki changed sides, sucking hard on her soft skin almost to pain, stopping just before Leda felt the need to holler. She breathed hard, her heart beating through her entire body, barely drowned out by the music and Mik's mesmerizing voice as she continued.

"Then I'm going to take you on your hands and knees, my slave, take you hard and wild and with nasty intentions—the same as yours—with no mercy." Mik's breath was ragged, her words heavy with passion. "I wanna hear you scream, Leda. I wanna hear you beg me for more. And I won't let you come, not until I say so."

She paused to bite the top of Leda's shoulder, then kiss it. Pain, then sweetness... Mik smiled to herself, a knowing smiling that seemed to say aloud that tonight, yes tonight she would get what she wanted, exactly what she wanted. She spoke in an intense, breathy whisper into Leda's ear, a word or two tumbling out full force in a sort of gravelly moan every now and then, the dam pressing against Mik's control, too.

"Then I'll flip you over, girl, tie you up in the sling and slip my lubed and hungry fist into your hole and fill you up to bursting; fuck you until you can't stand it, until I feel gracious enough to work your clit into a frenzy. And then, when I'm good and ready, and you can't hold it anymore, maybe I'll let you come, explode your body with pleasure. Maybe. If I feel like it. If you're real good."

Mik's voice got progressively more husky and intense

as she described her plans to Leda, punctuating with hungry kisses, bites, taking Leda's hair in her hands and pulling her head to the left to get a better patch of her neck and suck it again like a creature of the night. Leda half wondered if Mik really *wanted* to sink those teeth into her soft neck, Mik's passion was so intense as if for blood, meeting Leda's passion breath for breath. Leda melted, panting under the rain of Mik's erotic words in her ear, her tough affections, telling Leda what was in store—her so-tasteful way, Leda noted, of offering the chance to use the safe word if any of the above went beyond her zone, her agreement.

None of it did, though Leda had never played with wax before. The opportunity excited and aroused her: a chance to test her threshold and her courage. And Mik's sweet fist a challenge, too. Could Leda take it? After all this time? She'd be damned if she'd be denied the chance to try.

*Yes,* was all she heard in her mind, *yes yes, all of it, everything you've got...*

Mikki was quiet for a moment, letting her words sink in. Her hands explored Leda's body as she leaned in against her from behind, her hands slinking around Leda's waist, around to her pelvis, strong hands pressing in a diamond shape around Leda's mound, the very tops of her thighs, around her pubic hair, as if framing the object of her desire. Contact, of course, would be denied until Mikki decided otherwise.

Leda held her breath for a moment, feeling Mik's

fingers so close, so close to her clit, to the moist opening of her sex. She would have done almost anything to get that touch, to win that caress tonight, Leda realized. She knew that the trust and openness she felt toward this woman seemed ridiculous and naive on the one hand. But on the other hand, it made perfect sense because she felt as though she had known Mik for years, a sense of intense familiarity and almost joyousness at connecting—more like reconnecting—with her; as though they'd known each other all their lives, just as Mikki had said.

"Shall we proceed?" Mik asked suddenly in a voice full of anticipation, bringing Leda back to the moment. Leda wanted to tell her everything, share everything.

"Yes, yes, please, yes, ma'am," Leda stuttered, the words tumbling over themselves as she fumbled with her words, trying to form the right phrase, flustered. *Oh God fucking heavenly shit yes yes and yes!* she really wanted to holler. Instead, she said it all with her eyes as Mik turned her around. Face-to-face, Mik smiled in return, her eyes mirroring Leda's sentiments exactly.

"Then let us move on," she said.

# 11.

After wiping down the horse, Mik passed Leda a bottle of cool water that had been set beside the far end of the horse. Leda took it gratefully and drank, her sweaty palms cooling as they circled the chilled bottle. She handed it back to Mik, who drank, then moved toward the bag to put it away. Leda reached for her clothes which had been carefully folded and laid on a towel on the floor beside the near end of the horse.

"Uh uh," Mik said gently.

Leda turned, her eyes a question, then a thought, then a guess: *Oh, she's going to dress me herself.* This quickly metamorphosed into a sort of wide-eyed edge-of-panic shock of realization as she watched Mikki fold

127

her clothes with care and slip them into the toy bag after first withdrawing a simple black dog-type collar and a leash.

Leda automatically shook her head, standing naked beside the horse, her pale skin flushed all-over rosy with arousal—and now, embarrassment—punctuated by the dark-haired triangle of her mound, and the wildish, now somewhat disheveled hair on her head, sweaty tendrils moist around her pretty face. Being bare as a babe while they played—kind of stowed away in this special play area where only people in passing looked and few bothered to stop and really watch—that was one thing. Being paraded around butt naked and barefooted, much less collared and shackled and led by a fucking leash—that was an altogether *other* thing; way beyond her comfort, and pride, zone.

Leda continued to shake her head, her entire face a collage of resistance and rebellion. At this moment, hers were the eyes of a very stubborn woman.

Mik finished packing Leda's clothes in the bag and turned back easily with the collar and leash. To her surprise, she met up with a completely different face than she'd seen just a minute before.

"What's this?" she asked, surprised.

Leda couldn't stop shaking her head; it was the only way she could resist speaking out directly and risking further punishment. The head shaking she had no control over; words she could somehow force behind the barrier of her carefully, tightly shut mouth.

"Is that a 'no,' or are you simply shaking the sweat from your eyes?" Mik asked, dark, beautifully arched eyebrows raised in a question. But her voice sounded more as though she was telling Leda that she meant the latter, giving her a chance to avoid punishment.

Leda continued to shake her head, though much slower now and not quite so adamantly. She just couldn't stop.

*No, no, dammit, not fucking naked through a fucking crowded club of more or less dressed people, collared and shackled like a good submissive—no dammit! I'm not fucking twenty-something years old, you know, or part of the ultra-fit fitness jockette force or a true bottom! Why would she want to display me? What the fuck is the point here?*

Leda's thoughts collided with each other in an explosive case of almost panic, worried not only about being naked to the world after God knows how many years of having only one woman seeing her naked—and then only when she wanted her to—and the even more disturbing ego fuck of being paraded around like a domesticated dog!

Mik noted a real streak of panic there in Leda's eyes and softened a little.

"You can wear your boots," she said, smiling a sort of pooched-out lips smile, almost a smirk, full of mischief but not mean. She approached Leda, who stood absolutely still, frozen in the same spot she'd been in since Mik had rudely interrupted her attempt to cover herself.

*Oh, like boots will make me feel dressed and covered,* Leda muttered silently to herself.

Mik studied her, seeing the mixture of feelings and questions. "You're beautiful," she said to Leda matter-of-factly. "I want to show you off."

"Oh, yeah, right," Leda couldn't help but mumble, though quietly.

"Yeah, *right,*" Mik said, a little force in her voice, a little edge. "And if I say so, it's true," she added. "And I think you're fucking hot, babe, so just wipe that rebellious look off your puss and face up to your place in life at this moment: at my command. My word goes, what I think is true. And don't you forget that."

Mik looked at Leda for a moment, waiting for Leda to look up at her. Leda didn't, remaining stubborn. Mik retrieved Leda's boots from beside the play bag, approaching Leda's feet where the ankle shackles were still in place.

"Hm, y'know these boots, well, they just won't fit over the ankle restraints," Mik said then. "Oh, bummer."

Mik's voice was a study in concern and surprise. She shook her head the way Leda had and sighed, rising from her bent-over position and putting the boots back by the play bag, turning quickly back to Leda. The collar was around Leda's slim neck then before Leda could even think of protesting further.

"Besides, if you cut yourself down, you cut me down, too. And you wouldn't want to do that now, would you, especially in your position?"

Mik was shaking her head again, just back and forth, once each way in answer to her own question.

This irritated Leda, who was seething, having had even the small comfort of her promised boots denied her, losing her grip on being a good submissive, since of course she was not. Images of a howlingly painful beating flashed before her eyes but she grabbed a breath, getting ready to speak her mind anyway, and good.

"No, I wouldn't recommend it," Mik said, placing a finger against Leda's opening mouth. "Uh uh. Because, y'see, I wouldn't pick an ugly fuck," she said. "And you were wrong to fight me. End of discussion." She winked then, adding an open smile after her crude comment, her face intimately close and radiating with the connection between them even at this moment. The smell of her skin, of her fresh sweat, filled Leda's senses. And suddenly she couldn't see anything but that face, and then nothing but the muscles in Mik's tan arms as they completed their work securing the collar and leash. Any opportunity to speak had passed, and the urge to get angry passed with it.

Mik looked Leda straight in the eye as she finished securing her, pulling Leda's gaze back up with the power of her own. "Truth or dare," Mikki said, boring her sincere passion, at once both gentle and cruel, straight into Leda's mind, the core of her body's center. Mik didn't wait for an answer, of course. There wouldn't be one. That was the whole rush of it.

Leda could feel her own wetness slippery between

her bare thighs as she was forced by the leash that tugged at her to take a horrifying step away from the safety of the horse and the platform and the conceal-ment of the carefully constructed hideaway space. She blushed a deep intense scarlet red and could hardly breathe as she reluctantly stepped off the platform.

*Oh fuck oh fuck oh fuck oh fuck oh fuck oh fuck!* she screamed to herself, almost frantic with embarrass-ment, her heart pounding, thudding in her chest and in her cunt. She realized she was both horrified—definitely —and excited beyond belief. Humiliation, in this instance, did have some sort of long-term payoff, she realized, if only she didn't run into anyone she knew.... Leda raised her stubborn chin just a little higher above her pink pearl nakedness, above round breasts with puck-ered nipples at attention, the curve of her waist flowing into the smooth counter curve of her hips and down slim legs that threatened to give out if she didn't abso-lutely and completely concentrate.

In front of her, Mik leaned down and swung the toy bag up onto one strong shoulder, not bothering to put her shirt back on, Leda noted, the woman's beautiful shoulders, chest, and torso gleaming with sweat and sexy as hell. That vision worked like a lure and, concen-trating only on the strong, muscular back before her, on her desire for it, Leda followed Mik away from the cozy space and out into the crowded walkway.

The club had filled up since Leda had last walked—fully clothed—through the walkways and passageways and open rooms. Sturdy carpet ran down the middle of all the main walkways and Leda was glad, after crossing the cement floor to get to it, that Mik stayed on this since the painted cement floors were cold. The hint of incense mixed with the powerful scent of female bodies, of sex and sweat and a variety of oils, lubes, and perfumes. It was a heady mixture that wafted around Mik and Leda, but somehow did not penetrate the intense connection between them.

Mik had arranged the leash so that she held only a short length of it free, forcing Leda to follow so closely behind her, their energy seemed to act like a magnetic force between them; no leash was needed really, and Leda was sure Mik was aware of this. Every once in a while, as Mik led Leda through what Leda noted was a suddenly very interested crowd, Mikki would have to stop short, maneuvering through the crowd. And at those moments, Leda would suddenly find herself pushed up close against Mik's back, her firm tits pressing against the woman's smooth skin, the soft waves of Mikki's lightly pulled-back hair soft against Leda's cheek. Mik would pull Leda in closer, tighter, then wrap a hand around Leda' torso, or ass if she could reach it, and pull her in. Leda would lean her face, her cheek, against the moist skin of Mik's shoulder, maybe kiss it for an instant, lightly bite it rebelliously, just a little, before the crowd would thin and they would move again, two women as one.

Leda watched as Mik led her under a high archway

and into a dimly lit short hallway where another archway waited at the other end, the door on that end open. A rapturous cry of pain met Leda's ears. She looked around the hall: It looked almost castlelike with the high arches, the walls seemingly made of stone or painted that way, and a medieval-type lamp hanging from the ceiling shining a yellowish light. Leda stayed close behind Mik as the crowd in the hall was moving in both directions, bodies brushing close as they passed, some pushing her forward, eventually in through the second archway.

Leda felt the sting of embarrassment keenly as strangers passed her as she stood naked, collared, and shackled, obedient. Their clothing rubbed against her warm skin, or their own naked female flesh against her own, as they passed. Leda tried inconspicuously to move in tighter against Mikki, to shield herself from stranger's eyes in this compromised position.

*One stranger was enough to begin with…*, she thought to herself, fighting the pride that threatened to obliterate her chances of satisfaction. If it didn't come soon, she wasn't so sure she could keep her mouth shut and her rebellious spirit from speaking up much longer.

The crowd thinned out then and Leda saw that a door actually was closing behind them—had been opened, or kept open, by the crowd in front of them and now closed of its own accord as she stepped out of its way, barely avoiding it. She instinctively covered her chest, pulling away from the people and room around her, at the same time catching Mik looking back at her disapprovingly, shaking her head. Leda scowled a little, but lowered her arms. She looked hard at Mik, frustrated by this game now. But Mikki winked at her and grinned her disarming grin, eyes bright...and coaxing...and so fucking sexy....

She had a way of demolishing Leda's resolve.

Mik turned away then and led Leda into and across the room.

"It's free," she said, passing the comment to Leda over one shoulder. Her voice was filled with anticipation; serious, intense.

Leda followed Mik's gaze. On the far side of the room was a rather cruel-looking table: flat, obviously padded but cold appearing, with many hooks sticking out of it. Leda's body responded with little electric flashes over her skin, down her legs, anticipating, too. There seemed to be someone on it, but not actually engaged. It was a strange mixture of everyday and danger, the table and the person casually sitting on it. The entire room, itself, was like a scene from a movie, a sort of erotic horror flick, Leda thought.

Mik stood still about halfway to the table. The crowd that had been milling about dissipated some, the women either leaving the room or finding a place, and Leda had a better view of the huge dim space. The room was round with a high domed ceiling and when Leda craned her head back and looked up into the dome, it was like midnight sky between the slats of the dome, lit with a sort of cobalt blue background. Incredible.

The sound here was odd, flat, sort of muffled in an unnatural way. There was a great deal of sound being made—she could plainly hear women's voices raised in a release of pent-up control, moaning, begging for more, for mercy, graciously thanking a mistress for her kind tortures. Oh, yes, the sounds matched—or rather should have matched—the smorgasbord of smells that filled the room: sex and lube and oils, sweat, and the scent of female heat. (This last one drove Leda crazy: there was a scent that only a woman had, a woman aroused and hungry for another. The room was filled with it.) But the flattened sound continued around her and Leda looked closer, turning to look in all directions, pivoting on her spot, returning to face her partner after her little survey. Here, in this room, the walls were heavily padded—she could plainly see it—like thick quilting.

*Like a nut house. Like a torture chamber. Like a…*

Leda's internal voice and wild imagination picked up speed, racing in front of her nervous heartbeat and threatening to break her courageous streak as she felt lightheaded and cut off from all the interaction in the room and from the woman at the end of the leash, the dog leash, the…

Mik turned and ran a hand over one of Leda's exposed tits, cupping it and caressing the tip. A shiver of pleasure passed through Leda's body, mixed as it was with a tinge of irritation at being taken in hand with no warning. But, of course, the pleasure beat out the rebellion, riveting her attention back on the scene before her.

that incredible mouth, turned up slightly at one corner, the deep brown of Mik's intense eyes, the curve of her cheekbones, waves of black hair still pulled back, but framing her face slightly as some of them escaped.

Shit, Leda couldn't believe this was real. Mikki's presence and attention brought Leda back from her edgy place, though, and Leda took a calming breath.

"Come on, woman, I have plans for you," Mik said, all business and concentration now. The obvious hunger in her eyes drove Leda to want to do anything she asked of her, anything at all, just to see her satisfied, pleased. It felt surreal, this place, the atmosphere fueled by the eerie music wafting through the huge high-ceilinged room, the dim lighting, the scenes taking place all around. It was as if at any moment Leda would wake up and it would all be a dream.

But when she felt the rough tug of the leash on the collar around her smooth throat, Leda's body came alive along with the continuing realization that this was indeed real; the tingling and throbbing in her cunt and along her naked thighs announced it almost rudely, like a nasty hand had taken hold of her for now and forever. And nothing would ever be the same from here on out. Leda tried to focus on the moment as she was led further into the room toward the far wall. She noticed, as she and Mik approached the table, that the woman sitting on it was fully clothed, obviously trying to go unnoticed as she nonchalantly watched a scene taking place on some nearby equipment. Leda followed the young woman's gaze and smiled at the potpourri of females of all types and tones participating together. This club definitely had an excellent mixture which was hard, if not impossible, to find these days.

"Excuse me, we'd like to use this," Mik said in her firm but patient, sort of soft-butchy tenor voice. Leda tried to stay hidden behind Mik, but, appalled, she felt a strong tug on the leash and Leda was forced to stand in her full nakedness beside Mik, right in front of the woman who looked up, startled, then. A sheepish look crossed her face, her cheeks flushing pink with embarrassment. Her body language said *shy and inexperienced* in neon letters as she quickly jumped up off the table, looking at the two women and trying not to stare at Leda's naked body. Leda watched the woman's eyes quickly travel down the landscape of her nude form and she tried to stand taller, with pride, gamely trying to cover up the acute discomfort of her embarrassment.

"Wow, you two make a nice couple," the woman said, her voice sort of Valley-girlish and youthful, overly enthusiastic. Her blue eyes were wide open, oval face framed by long shiny blonde hair. When Mikki didn't say anything—sort of ignoring the young woman, having already let go of Leda's leash and retrieving items from the bag, including a spray bottle which she began spraying the table with, wiping it down carefully, briskly setting up—Leda couldn't help but smile at the young woman, even thanking her politely because it was obvious the comment was sincere.

The woman's youthful innocence and lack of party and equipment etiquette (like not being on it unless you're playing on it) made Leda think of the first few times she had played and didn't know the rules. The women who ran the parties had been full of attitude then, especially the most toppish tops who said it all with a disdainful attitude and cold eyes, easily disgusted with what they curtly called "party pussies." Leda didn't want to convey the same coolness or disapproval to this woman who seemed genuinely excited to be here. She would learn the rules soon enough. Leda knew that just getting here was the hard part, but that feeling comfortable at the beginning was important, too. So, she was nice to her, thinking that would be enough and the woman would go away.

But she didn't. Instead she dumbly continued to grin at Leda, obviously having decided to stand right there and just watch. At close range. Right beside the damn table.

*Nope, that won't work, too close, crossing the rude border,* Leda thought to the girl. And Leda's face must've said it all because the woman sort of said "Oh," waved awkwardly and moved quickly away from them, hopefully to watch more discreetly some other goings-on, Leda thought.

Leda watched the girl go for a moment, her eyes pausing on the way back on a very cool scene of a small group of women doing an intense piercing session, the pretty petite figure of the piercee stretched across a thick black-netted canvas on the wall that looked like a fishing net, needles pierced in close, intricate designs down her arms, chest, tits, belly, legs. Her breathing was ragged and she huffed every now and then, letting out thin howling cries that spiraled up toward the dome above them when a new needle would pierce her already heavily punctured skin. A third woman was in the process of finalizing the masterpiece by connecting the needles with shiny-looking gold cord that caught the spotlights on the scene.

"Come here, Leda," Mik said, carefully punctuating each word.

It was the second time: Leda hadn't heard the first call. But the tone in Mik's voice announced that she had definitely missed something. Leda turned quickly and saw that Mik had readied the table while Leda had been daydreaming. She stood at the far end of it, at the head by the wall, across from where Leda stood at its foot. In Mikki's hand was a white candle, as yet unlit. She had pulled back her thick wavy hair more tightly and her beautiful face caught the light from above in a startlingly dramatic beauty. She stood with her still leather-clad legs apart, boots firm on the floor, strong and ready to work. Leda's eyes rested on the swell of her olive-pink tits and the tight pattern of her stomach. The muscles of her arms were pronounced shadows in the dramatic overhead light.

Leda moved quickly around the table and stood beside it, sensing the tension.

"Up on the table," Mik instructed.

Leda did as she was told, catching, out of the corner of her eye, more women entering the room, some walking around, some watching. A few were making their way toward her, now sprawled on the table. Mik instructed Leda to lie down on her back with her feet facing into the room. And when the shackles were attached to short chains, and the chains to the hooks in the table, Leda's creamy thighs were parted ever so slightly, opening her sex to those who wished to view it, on display like a science project.

She couldn't help it, couldn't stand it—the words erupted from her mouth: "Please, Mik, uh ma'am, can you face me the other way, please, possibly, if you could possibly agree to this, just this one thing, maybe?"

Surprised, Leda watched as Mik actually considered her question for a moment, studying Leda's face (which was near panic-stricken). Silently and quickly, Mik undid the clips, motioning for Leda to swivel around, then re-fastened them on the hooks at the wall side of the table, Leda's arms up over her head and, again, thighs open—much wider this time.

*Oh yes yes yes, thank you, thank you oh great and kind mistress, thank you thank you...* Leda repeated her gratefulness like a mantra in her head, though she didn't speak a word. She hadn't realized she wasn't breathing and took a long breath of relief. Even the wide angle of her open legs didn't matter in comparison.

"Now that I have accommodated you, girl, you owe

me," Mik said roughly. But she smiled a little, as if acknowledging the importance of the last request but keeping track, as well. And with that, Mik touched the flame of a clear lighter to the tip of the white candle. It took a moment, then the candle wick flickered to life.

"This is special wax, it shouldn't burn you…too much. I didn't choose the coolest one. I don't think you deserve that now." Mik said.

Leda noted that the woman's tone of voice had changed since she had granted Leda's wish for accommodation. There was a deep concentration and intensity that drew Leda in. Serious pain—she was definitely preparing Leda for serious pain. Leda could sense it. And Leda welcomed it, preparing herself mentally for as long as the session would last, determined to please this woman and to get the big payoff for her damn good behavior and courage in the face of this…serious pain

*And I shall give you serious passion, then, my friend,* Leda thought. She would will herself to win.

An electronic beat mixed with a strange sort of pipe organ music, dramatic and dark. Leda's mind followed its trail as she heard Mikki repeat the safe word—a reminder—and the first drop of white wax fell in its molten form through the air as if in slow motion, landing on the soft flesh of Leda's stomach with a momentary sizzle and sting.

Leda sucked in her breath and her stomach, her arms automatically trying to push the heat away. But they were bound to the hooks on the table, same as her ankles, the collar remaining secured around her neck as well.

"I would blindfold you, but I want you to see it. Watch as I decorate your body, wrap it up in the heat of this...mmm...," Mik drew out the "m" sound, letting another drop of hot wax fall onto her sweet and willing victim. "...mmmelting passion. Think of it as my excitement, my desire for you, on you, igniting you. The more you take, the more I'll have to give you, sweet Leda."

Again, as before at the horse during the whipping, Leda was entranced by Mik's low, sexy voice speaking intimately as the pain began, reminding her of the pleasure to come, the promise of release. As the wax began to cover small areas of her belly, Leda began to grow more accustomed to the sensation of the heat, the sting, the unbearable moments before it cooled. She relaxed some, beginning to enjoy the challenge, the feel of it.

Mikki watched her closely, gauging the pace. Slowly, she began to move the candle up toward the sensitive flesh of Leda's nicely-endowed chest, the pink skin flushed with arousal, nipples hardening as Mik let her other hand slip down between Leda's parted legs. She lingered there for a moment, fingertips ever so gently caressing Leda's brown pubic hair, the soft flesh of her groin, sliding down to stroke, with the lightest of touches, Leda's swelling clit.

"Oohhhh...," Leda moaned, closing her eyes, then cried out as a stinging drop of hot wax landed on her left nipple just as Mik's fingers grazed the sensitive tip of her re-awakening clit. Leda arched her back slightly with the subtle wave of pleasure crashing against the very much unsubtle pain. The wax dropped more quickly now, decorating first her left tit, then her right.

"No, uhhh! Shit!" she cried out, but not loudly, as the pain increased, the pace picking up, the heat now covering areas of flesh that she knew were turning feverishly pink in defiance, tortured under the momentary burn and sizzle of pain. Mik allowed Leda's voice to release itself, and in some strange way, Leda felt her body wanting even more, daring Mik to go further; with each increase in the level of pain, there seemed to be a corresponding increase in her desire for more challenge, the heat of the fire making her hungry for the flames.

"More?" Mik asked, almost on cue, in tune with the shifts of energy and intensity.

Leda looked up through a veil of sensation from her place on the table, arms overhead, legs opening further. She couldn't help but let a smile cross her face. Her hands were in fists; she hadn't noticed until there was a pause in the rhythm of the scene and the throbbing in her palms surfaced, fingernails digging into her flesh. She liked the pain of it.

"Yes," Leda answered hoarsely.

"Ask me nicely."

"Please, ma'am, more. More," Leda asked breathlessly.

"More what?" Mikki asked, teasing her.

"More…wax…more…pain…on my…please…" Leda couldn't finish the question or form a complete thought.

Her words were abstract art forms hanging in the air between them. Just saying the words was distracting, that and watching as the buds on Mikki's tits hardened, her beautiful body flushed with excitement and responding, too.

"On your…?" Mik asked, not giving an inch.

Leda couldn't speak, couldn't force any words out of her mouth. Mik had begun to drop a path of hot scalding wax down the middle of Leda's chest, over her belly, filling Leda's belly button with four or five drops, the heat pooling up painfully. Leda squirmed in her bindings, breathing hard and squinting her eyes shut, concentrating on control.

"You can cry out all you want; I do want you to give me the payoff for what I'm doing to you. Let me hear it, let me hear you scream, Leda. Tell me how good I am," Mik added, and chuckled a wicked little chuckle, low and deep in her throat.

The wax path was continuing now down over Leda's right hip, carefully drip-dripping down onto her right thigh, sizzling and cooling like the ebb and flow of an ocean of stinging heat. Instinctively, the muscles in her thigh twitched, flexed as Leda pulled on the chain that held her leg still, unable to escape the pain.

"Ah, shit—mmmm, fuck!" she swore with each splash of wax. "I'll tell you: you're a cruel motherfucker! My my…tormentor and I—dammit!—I want you, yes, yes I do…you do it so—aah!—so well! I want more—mmm—please!"

Leda spoke in sections, between sizzling crashes of molten wax on sensitive skin, squirming on the now slippery table as her sweat worked like lube, vinyl against naked skin, on fire with the heat of the wax and the heat of her passion as Leda arched on the table and pulled on her bindings, moving both away and into the pain.

A small crowd had been attracted by Leda's cries and swearing and now watched from nearby. Every now and then Leda could sense them. A couple of the women seemed to know Mikki; Leda had heard them mentioning her name, but in a warped sort of soundtrack that mixed with the haunting music and the sound of Mik's voice when she would talk dirty to Leda, talk her through the scene now and then. Mik didn't seem to notice anyone beyond the two of them, this table, the exchange taking place between them like an electrical current, laser beams connecting two life forms with one sexual heart.

Leda suddenly let out a loud howl of pain into the high dome—ceilinged room as the first drop of wax landed on her tender left inner thigh, after Mik had coated the tops of both legs. Leda's cries fell flat, too, against the padded walls, not returning to roam the room as in the other play space. It made her want—no, need—to scream louder, to holler her angry pain louder and louder into this room that would not give it back to her, give her voice back to her and satisfy her rage. For a moment, Leda had a fleeting insight of how it must feel to be in a padded room in a mental hospital: how tempting it would be just to scream and scream since the room would deny the satisfaction of real sound, no hearty return of each vocal investment, but more of a mockery.

Leda felt that it made absolute sense just about now: the urge to scream as loud as her lungs could accommodate. Mik didn't let up, but kept the pace brisk as if being fed by Leda's screams and cries. The wax ignited the soft flesh of her inner thighs, but after as long as they had been in the scene now, Leda was on another plane, rising and flying straight into the fire and loving it. She opened her thighs, exposing her mound and the lips of her sex, begging without words.

"What do you want, pet?" Mik asked, her voice husky with passion. "Do you want this?"

Leda almost lost her mind, overcome with the incredible rush of sensation that blasted through her as Mik bent her head and let her tongue graze Leda's hard little clit, flicking it for a moment, the heat of her breath lingering on the skin of Leda's open cunt.

"Oh God oh God oh God, yes...," Leda whispered, her eyes closing as she arched gently into the woman's sweet mouth. "Oh fuck...," Leda half whimpered the words, then sucked in a long breath, the pleasure so intense it was almost overwhelming after having been denied her this long.

And then it passed: Mik's tongue left the nest of her sex and the pleasure lingered but dissipated far too quickly. Before Leda could whimper in protest, an amazing blast of heat and pain crashed onto her skin, just beside her open cuntlips, on the smooth, hairless flesh of her groin.

"Aaaaahahhhh!"

The scream left her body of its own accord, an animal cry of pain, pleasure, determination, loss of control. Leda opened her legs wider, her knees facing out as if they were attached to pulleys that were slowly forcing them apart in opposing directions. But it was her passion, her hunger now that ruled her body, forced her legs open wide, wanting more.

Mik answered Leda's desire and another hot splash of wax fell on the other side of her sex, dripping just for the briefest of moments down the side of her mound and down to where her asscheeks met, cushioning her heated body as she lay on her back on the table. Two or three more stinging liquid fireballs fell on either side of Leda's slit, close enough to rage the sensation right into the core of her body. Leda's cries became a mixture of fury, pain, and incredible pleasure—some other level having been achieved that would drive her to the edges of torture with ease.

"Yes, oh God!" she cried, welcoming each blast. Leda's face was a blaze of emotion as she burned.

Mik watched Leda with passion and care and concentration in her eyes; took in the slippery shine of Leda's open cunt, shiny slick with desire. She saw the woman beneath her on the table diving deep into the flames of the fire Mik had lit for her, dared her to play in, and she was pleased. More than pleased. Absolutely fucking positively pleased and fucking hot for this chick and beside herself with having found someone to match her intensity. She could see that Leda was beyond sensibleness now, willing herself into the outer limits of control and in whatever direction Mik would take her.

But Mik didn't want to wear this passionate woman out before they both got what they most wanted.

Leda panted on the table, letting her knees fall back into a neutral position as she realized the wax would not come again, that Mik was holding back. Leda's cunt ached with wanting, pulsing and beating with a heartbeat that thundered through her everywhere at once. Her body felt as if it had been dipped in a vat of wax and she was encased in it, the heat inside of her threatening to explode the trap of her wax coating. She breathed deeply and opened her eyes. In sections, Mik began peeling the cool wax, lifting it gently off of Leda's angry pink skin, causing Leda to ache from even the brief contact of removal.

But that, too, had its pleasure.

Leda imagined being reborn as if from a wax womb, transformed as if emerging from a white wax cave or eggshell, and she felt freed with each new section of wax removed; freed from all that had trapped her passion, sectioned it off away from her and denied her expression and this passionate life; freed her into the arms of this fucking incredible woman. Leda's cunt throbbed with the beat of her heart and irritation began to creep up around the edges of her control. Too long denied the deed and she always got pissy, couldn't help it. And yes, she'd fallen into a pattern of pissy in the last few months.

*Yeah, that tells ya something, doesn't it?* she thought wryly, thinking of so many long nights of wanting and now, here, wanting more than anything at this moment to get it on hot and nasty with this woman that somehow played her passion like an intricate improvisation; one that was beginning to grate on her nerves, this dependency on someone else's willingness, or unwillingness, to orchestrate the moves she so desperately wanted.

Mik carefully peeled away Leda's second skin—the ghostly armor, the memory of pain—leaving Leda's body rosy, alive with color. She leaned down and took one of Leda's tits in her mouth then, running her tongue over the heated, ever-so-slightly inflamed skin, gently sucking it and tweaking the hard nipple to a point.

Beneath Mik's tongue, her voice returned to Leda's mind then like a taunt, a tease, the passionate words she had hoarsely whispered to Leda, promises: "Then I'll slip my lubed and hungry fist into your hole, fill you up to bursting; fuck you until you can't stand it...."

Leda groaned. This gentle sucking was too nice, too prolonged. Maybe Mik didn't have it for her. Maybe she couldn't go there with Leda, didn't really want to fuck. Maybe...

At her tit, Mik took the groan as a sign of pleasure,

not frustration, and she ran her thumb lightly over Leda's other nipple, both now paying strict attention as she commanded, pink from the wax play. Mik leaned over Leda from the side of the table, twisting, facing the middle of the room and the largish group of women that stood watching. But her focus remained on Leda, every shiver, every sigh, reading Leda's eyes, listening to her body's story. Then suddenly out of nowhere, while Leda's gaze was trapped by Mik's, eyes riveted to Mik's darkening, intense face, Leda felt an aching pinch on one nipple as tiny teeth dug into the fragile flesh and clamped on tighter than a mad dog's jaws on a human arm. Leda closed her eyes and fell into the pain of it, surprised, delighted, but remaining controlled this time.

"Ooow," she said, barely a whisper as she sucked in her breath, the pain slowly dissipating out in waves like concentric rings in a pond. She couldn't help it, her body just naturally pulled away as she lay on the table. She forgot Mik's arm was under her torso, holding her up just a little off the table, and felt it holding her fast now, completely at Mik's command—trapped.

Leda opened her eyes. Mik was smiling, enjoying the rush of pain that crisscrossed Leda's surprised face. Then she slapped Leda lightly across one cheek, a little playful but purposeful wake-up cuff on her momentarily stunned face.

"Hey, I didn't say you could talk," Mik said in response to Leda's whispered expression of pain. "Ask me for the other one, nicely."

Leda couldn't get the words out, her face flushed with insolent rage.

*Smack!* And this time harder, on the other cheek. Leda's head turned with the impact, though her body remained trapped in Mik's ever-stronger hold. Leda let her head stay turned away as it was for a moment, feeling the precious sting, eyes closed in concentration. She breathed, open-mouthed, and licked her lips once over with her tongue.

"Please," Leda managed to squeeze out through clenched teeth. And in went the teeth of the other clamp on her tender nipple, holding on fast and sending shivers of red-hot sensation through Leda's now ultra-sensitive body.

Leda smiled, sweat gleaming on her face. It was good. Very good.

"I wanna give you something else, Leda, a little something to hold on to. I expect you not to lose them on the walk we're about to take, because if you do, you may live to regret it."

Mik was doing it again, leaning in close to Leda's ear and whispery-hissing the words in her sexy-as-hell voice, at the same time tweaking one of the nipple clamps, which Leda could see now were shiny gold metal. Her body hummed and howled. She tried to see what it was Mik had to give her, to hold on to. But she never did get to see it.

With the hand that was not holding Leda, Mik parted Leda's creamy legs a little wider, then ran a fingernail a little cruelly up her inner thigh, almost breaking the soft skin, stopping just short of Leda's pussy. Leda hissed like a snake at Mik, watching as the woman reached somewhere for something. That something was cold metal and round and it made tinkly bell-like sounds. It was pushing at the entrance to Leda's cunt now, insisting on entrance, the chilly metal a shock against the incredibly warm, moist heat of her aroused cunt, the muscles tight against the cold of it but interested in the visitor.

Leda moaned and arched slightly, uncontrollably, in Mik's arms, shocked by the cold and yet too wet and slick with her own juices to resist the inquiring item. Besides, the chains that held her ankles did not allow her legs to close in any amount that would make a difference. Like a mouth sucking in a shiny cool jawbreaker, Leda's cunt opened for Mik as the pressure increased and the small but oversized globe slid inside her, the muscles of her pussy opening to receive it, then closing around it.

Leda knew it was dangerous, slipping loose balls into one's cunt, but it was heaven, and big. The ball was too large to go anywhere unretrievable; and inside now anyway, warming up fast.

Mik's fingers lingered momentarily over Leda's swollen clit and slit as Leda lay bound and stretched full-length, naked, legs spread. Leda drew in her breath and closed her eyes, every nerve focused on the meeting point of the woman's fingertips and the tip of her clit.

She could feel the hardness of the ball in her cunt as she clenched the muscles of her pussy around it, her muscles shivering with anticipation of more, easily moving toward a climax.

"Open up, slave," Mik said in a low, intimate voice next to Leda's ear. Then, with an edge she added, "You want more, you want it harder, I got it for you, babe."

Leda suddenly felt the people around her and flushed with embarrassment at the idea that they might be able to see what Mik was doing as she lay there with her legs wide open, though away from them. But the sweet pressure of another, somewhat larger metal ball at the lips of her cunt forced Leda into an edgy desperate place of longing that blocked out the room, the play space. Mik slid the second ball around in the slickness of Leda's slippery lubricant, wetting it, teasing her. Leda moaned under Mik's ministrations, the woman's throaty chuckle sifting through the veil of her passion. She couldn't resist, a slave to the hunger, to the rhythm of the ball sliding along her slit, the hunger for the rhythm of this woman's passion.

Mik focused completely on Leda's cunt, pressing against her tight muscles, sliding the ball just barely in, then out of her again. Until, with a gentle push of force, she slid the second ball, with a slight suction, past the strong muscles of Leda's gate and into the moist heat of her sex, joining the other. Leda could feel the throbbing and pulsing of her cunt all around the metal balls as they massaged and teased her sugar walls.

"Now you hold on to those, Leda girl, because I'll expect them to be returned at the conclusion of our journey. You hear me?" Mik asked, outlining Leda's slit lazily with one finger as she spoke, then travelling around, over her hard clit and down between wide-open legs to tease at Leda's asshole.

"Oh, yes, ma'am," Leda moaned back as she felt the shiver of sensation at her ass, a slight whimper in her voice. She raised her hips ever so slightly up against Mik's probing finger, wondering—mixed with both fear and longing—if Mik had yet another hollow metal singing ball to thrust up her asshole, as well. But logic told her that it would be too impossible to remove one such as the two in her twat. And besides, Mik was reaching out and unlocking the clips at Leda's ankles now, the strong, sure touch of Mik's hand on the outside of her thighs easing them together.

"You hold on to my gifts; it's an honor," Mik commanded.

Leda nodded, concentrating and pressing her thighs together. Mik ran one hand through the dark brown curls on Leda's mound.

"Mmm mm," Mik responded approvingly.

Leda could see that she wished to linger there, now, not wait. And Leda wanted her to, more than anything.

"Yes," she breathed, as if to create a subliminal message that would get her the orgasm she could almost taste it was so close, and would take so very little assistance to reach. But there was more to come, before she would be allowed to come. The orgasm would have to beat against the strength of her will for a little longer. Leda could see this in Mik's body language: She was ready to move on. Leda turned her full attention to holding on as tightly as possible to Mikki's "gifts."

Mik stood and reached up to undo the clips at the head of the table; all four of Leda's limbs were now free, though still shackled. Slowly, Leda brought her arms down from over her head. Her shoulders ached, but ached so good. She smiled. Mik caught her smile and smiled back, a little wicked smile, deep brown eyes flashing an enticing mixture of joyousness and sadistic distraction, dark eyebrows up slightly.

"We're not done yet," she said, face flushed with barely contained passion, with Mik's particularly serious brand of passion.

"No," Leda responded, that single word hanging between them like a dare, as if one of them might pluck it out of the air and, by flinging it aside, blast open the doors of control that kept the order in place, the tension and denial in place between them, until the entire symphony was completed in all its glory.

This denial and anticipation filled the space around the two women. And though the air was warm and she did not feel cold, Leda watched Mik take out a long black cloak from the large toy bag that sat by the table, felt Mik wrap it around her naked, marked form, Leda's skin pink and warm, the clamps bouncing a little on her hanging globes as Mik commanded Leda to stand.

She managed it, just barely keeping the cloak wrapped around her and her legs tight together. Leda shyly faced Mik, her back to the center of the room.

"No, face the middle of the room, slave," Mik said in her most commanding voice.

Without even considering disobeying, Leda turned, face-to-face with the group of voyeurs who had been watching, who knew for how long? Hit with the impact of their presence, she stood a little taller after just a beat of adjustment, looked right at them, proud, and her open gaze made some of them uncomfortable. The ranks thinned. Leda took a breath and steadied herself on shaky legs, concentrating (but trying not to show it) on retaining the two hollow but somewhat heavy metal balls that nested in her cunt, trying to keep in check the obvious crazed passion that she knew flooded her face and body like neon.

Mik handed Leda a bottle of some sort of sparkling juice and she drank appreciatively, feeling her head clear as the sweetness fed her. She studied the feel of the balls in her cunt as she stood drinking. They really were not heavy, she decided, but they were definitely slippery with her lube. Leda wondered if she would be able to walk at all and tightened the muscles of her sex more securely around them for good measure. She chuckled quietly, remembering in amusement all those hours of practicing the pussy-muscle-tightening-flexing exercises that young women told each other would make your man crazy with desire for you. The thought seemed completely hilarious here, deep in the pleasures of dyke sex, thrilled as she was to be free of the straight constraints, preferring constraints of a different kind. She could have it all: intense scenes, beautiful kisses, and the thrill of a woman's soft, incredible body, plus an endlessly long wild fuck from a good woman—without the spurting come-shot that men seemed to think women required. She almost choked on her drink just thinking about it but chuckled again instead. To each her own.

Her thoughts were momentarily broken by an especially bold woman in the remaining voyeur contingent. From the middle of the room, a short red-haired dyke in snazzy manly dress—a sort of gangster suit complete with tie and tails—ran her tongue over her teeth at Leda, then stuck a finger in her mouth to suck, her tongue following the finger out to lick the tip. Leda followed the woman's just-sucked-finger down to the woman's crotch where she proceeded to grab a very long dildo packed into her loose, sexy, old-time gangster pants. Leda's eyes followed, too, as the woman's hand went back up to her mouth and the mouth blew her a kiss, releasing it with her hand in the air. Then the woman mouthed very clearly, "That's what you need, huh?" and her eyebrows went up seductively.

*Whoa!* Leda thought. *Whoa baby! Shit girl!*

But Leda didn't blush—it was true!

*Fuck yeah. Better believe it.*

And just for the hell of it, Leda blew her a kiss back,

raising her own eyebrows in response and smiling with amusement. The woman laughed and grinned, nodding her approval.

Then Mik was taking the now half-empty bottle from Leda, and they were leaving the table, Leda led by Mik's firm hand on the small of her cloak-covered back; led through the domed room, leaving the voyeurs and the woman with the wet finger, wild tongue, and impossibly long dong behind. Leda noticed out of the corner of her eye that the woman and Mik made eye contact, none too friendly either.

Leda wanted to laugh out loud, but her giddy sense of humor was absorbed in a vacuum of concentration: The metal balls now rested at the mouth of the tight den of her pussy and Leda minced a little as she walked. Luckily the cloak was almost floor-length and covered her efforts quite nicely. She was, as always, grateful for the nice touches of Mik's quirky sweet courtesies.

They continued out through a door opposite the one through which they had entered. Leda remained shackled, but arms were free to hold the cloak around herself. She ran a hand absently through her wild spikes, sure they were just a mess now, and God only knew what her face looked like.

But it was all fine. Everything was fine. And everything would remain fine.

As long as the balls didn't drop.

*Small, minced steps, tight twat, strong thighs. Breathe.*

*Breathe. Tight, strong...* Leda repeated the instructions silently to herself like a unit leader to a group of grunts. *And I got the balls to fit the pants!* she mused silently, suppressing a chuckle, nervousness and the ache for an orgasm creating a dizzy rush that shivered through her naked body, making her feel stoned, a little punch-drunk. But the balls in her cunt, the pressure of their spheres against her wet, warm walls, again returned her to the moment as she felt the muscles relax, just for a moment, as her mind wandered. Danger snapped her to attention and she seemed to bump into it like a wall. Quickly, she regained her composure.

The two of them—Leda led by the leash, Mik leading in front—moved through the arched doorway and into a hall.

"C'mon, Leda girl. You're going to love this," Mik said.

Leda's body flushed with anticipation, feeling amazingly suspended in a continuous state of arousal. Yes, yes, she was sure she would love it. Whatever it was.

# 12.

The room the two women entered next was not padded, Leda noted. Rough, unfinished wooden walls surrounded them on all four sides. Hard to tell if it was decorative, or if the room really was this rustic and unfinished. Stark white light bulbs hung from the wood-covered ceiling, but they couldn't have been brighter than maybe sixty watts from what Leda could tell. Mik tugged at the leash, trying to get Leda to hurry up, but there was no way Leda could move any faster without losing the metal balls; too slippery, the passage-way between her legs. Her concentration become somewhat desperate, as she realized that the balls would not be too large to slip out. Apparently they were not as large as they had felt when first introduced to her hungry body.

"Hurry up, slave, or I'll remove your cloak and make you walk without it," Mik said harshly.

Yes, after all it was the cloak that gave Leda privacy to tweak her body as needed to retain the gifts; it gave her an edge on Mik's demand—and the odds of receiving her ultimate fulfillment.

Leda tried to increase her speed, but she accomplished little as far as actual acceleration. It was hopeless; no way she could stay in control with longer steps or a quicker stride. In a flash, Mik whirled around then, impatient, and whisked the cloak from Leda's grasp, removing it completely from her person. Evidently what Leda had attempted in response to the demand had not been enough to please her mistress.

Leda swallowed hard, glancing around the room as she stood naked. A few women turned and watched from the shadows. The room was full of heavy leather players in full regalia: mostly stone butches dressed in leather drag or uniforms, butches on butches. A handful of femme dominatrixes worked on other femmes or nondescript androgynous women, or in a group with a variety of types, some switching. Whips thwacked and groans and cries filled the space, but only at intervals—except for one corner where a woman was tied to a thick stake that jutted out from the floor, her tits smushed into it as she faced the stake, arms tied high overhead to hooks in the stake; an obviously uncomfortable position. A woman with a thick blonde braid was beating her methodically and at quite a pace, alternating between a crop and a paddle all over the woman's body. The slave's voice was a constant solo of animal sounds that pierced the musical soundtrack feeding erotic energy into the room.

Leda watched, enthralled at the intensity and the degree of concentration apparent on both women's flushed, sweating faces. The woman at the stake screamed as the beatings intensified; it was obvious that they had been at this for some time. The edge in the slave's voice was that of a heavily tested subject.

"Yes, Mistress, more…please, I don't deserve your… kindness!" she managed to say between ragged breaths, as commanded. And then an angry holler followed on impact and a groan.

The blonde was just switching to a long mean-looking braided whip with a thick handle when Leda felt Mik's hands slide up between her legs. Leda realized she had relaxed a moment, watching the two women, and quickly tightened her exposed cunt around the metal balls. Mik's hands surprised her as they contacted the naked flesh of her mound, insistent.

Leda turned her head toward Mik but remained still, barely breathing; Mik was standing facing Leda from the side, one hand slipping down to Leda's cunt from the front, the other down between her bare asscheeks. The room was dim between splashes of harsh light from the bare bulbs and Leda could not see who all was in it, though her eyes flitted about the room nervously as Mik invaded her, parting Leda's legs—trying to, against Leda's strong thigh muscles that resisted of their own accord. The music in this room was muted and intense, vocals with screaming singers, weird synth sounds, laid-back drums beating at the speed of a heartbeat.

Leda could feel herself being easy—too easy—lost in a flash to Mik's fingers running over her ass, dabbling at the moist lips of her sex. Leda ever so slowly was losing her grip on the metal spheres, her cunt flowering open to receive Mik's promising touches, melting into the release of her muscles.

Mik chuckled, low and wicked.

"No, not here," she said in a husky voice, again removing her hands.

Leda, with all her concentration, flexed the muscles of her sex around the balls and brought her legs quickly back together.

"What?" she asked as if through a haze.

"Over here," Mik said, moving away from Leda.

Leda blinked her eyes clear and slowly followed Mik, hardly able to breath. The contact of Mik's insistent fingers on the sensitive flesh between legs remained like the sizzle of lightning on a target caught unaware, and she moaned a little. Leda was getting irritable again, she could feel it crackling through her. tired, frustrated, pushed too far, waiting too long. Her eyes narrowed and Leda's feisty spirit fought her sexual hunger, making a war zone inside her. She tried to calm herself, but what was the point?

*Let it rip*, she thought, *what the hell.*

When Mik arrived at her destination, Leda following behind, Leda took in the four rough wooden stakes that were sunk into the wooden floor beneath Mik's boots (and Leda's bare feet). A heavy leather sling hung, waiting, between them.

"Just what I need," Leda said, smirking, feeling disgusted, lost on a wave of attitude and impatience, and forgetting the deal altogether. She didn't notice that Mik was watching her, one ear cocked toward Leda as she mumbled.

"Up here," Mik demanded, indicating a low wooden table.

Leda took a step towards it, realizing she had forgotten to pay attention to the balls before doing so. They shifted, but with all her might she caught them, forcing her thighs tight together again, thinking hers must be the strongest fucking pussy in town by now. A smile flickered like the quick pass of a spotlight over her face, then faded, leaving an expression of urgent concentration. But before she could move again, Mik was beside her, irritated. Leda stood with her thighs stuck together as if glued, her face in an obvious quandary.

"Hurry it up!" Mik commanded, making Leda's motion decision for her and yanking her roughly by one arm away from the spot where she stood. And when that wasn't enough, Mik wrapped her arms roughly around Leda's middle, lifting her off the floor and up onto the long hardwood table next to the sling. Then she was forcing Leda's legs apart into an open stance.

Leda grunted, partly from controlling her anger, partly from the pain of her gut getting squished by Mik's painfully strong arms and partly in a panic of trying to retain the "gifts." Mik's eyes were intently watching Leda's exposed cunt, admiring the tiny, slightly wet curls around the barely closed lips of her sex. Leda strained to hang on to the balls, her face full of the stubborn fight of the battle, growing pinker by the minute, hands in front of herself for balance, wrists still shackled.

Mik forced Leda's feet apart wider still, the muscles in her arms flexing, winning against those of Leda's cunt and shaky thighs. Instinctively, Leda tried to reach down with her hands to help stop the balls from slipping out of her sex and onto the hard wooden table on which she stood. Suddenly a short quirt was slapped against Leda's hands, smacking them away with a sharp stinging *thwack!*

Leda's hands retreated. She looked up, shocked. Mik stood holding the quirt dangling in one strong fist.

"Wider!" Mik commanded, eyes transfixed on the woman before her, daring her to disobey.

Leda paused, her face an intricate web of emotions that seemed somehow to please Mik, who let just the edge of the corner of her gorgeous mouth turn up in an amused, excited smile. They faced off for a moment, Mik waiting just long enough to let Leda take a breath. Then, *smack!* on Leda's right ankle, and *smack!* on her left one, repeating once more on each side. The sting was unlike any Leda had ever felt, the skin of her bony ankles sensitive and virgin to the whip's wicked edges, the sting of contact completely unexpected—making her barely able to resist the urge to move her feet in a dance of avoidance, as if a shotgun were shooting at her feet. Instead, she obediently opened her legs just a hint wider, giving in somewhat, instinctively moving to avoid the pain but in a direction that would please her Mistress. The expression on her face, however, remained rebellious, set, a struggle of anger, pride, and pain.

"Wider," Mik shot at her in a hoarse voice, looking up at her captive from under lowered eyebrows as she stood on the ground before Leda, her beautiful face an incredible display of strength, a little violence in her eyes, a nasty edge.

Leda considered the demand, knowing the next step would do in her control. It wasn't possible to open her legs that wide and still hold on. The sounds of sex and sadistic play continued around them, but it all melted away in the moment of decision. Who would win? The air crackled with their energy, both women strong and unbending as the hardest steel, and yet...

"Damn," Leda whispered, eyes fierce with pride and frustration. She held her breath and stepped her legs wide apart. The weight of the balls in the slippery river of her juices made an urgent struggle for release. Sweat dripped down the sides of Leda's face.

"Now relax," Mik demanded, not noticing that a small scattered group of women had begun watching intently from the shadows behind her. The energy intensified because of their presence, the music a snake hissing out the demands and the challenges, the breaking rebellion.

Leda stood stiffly, chest out, stomach tight, hands in fists in the shackles that held them in front of her, just below her belly button. Leda's control—her muscular control—was her only saving grace, she knew. Relax, and her cunt would open for them, release the metal balls. She was too hungry for a good fuck and her cunt betrayed her ravenous state. The first ball slipped from between her strong, wide-open legs and landed with a firm metal-on-wood sound, rolling quickly toward the edge. Mik's hand was there in a flash and it rolled off onto her open palm.

Mik raised the ball to her face and sniffed it.

"Good girl," she said. "Now give me the other one."

The second ball slipped down the passageway of Leda's throbbing cunt and this time Leda could feel the blossoming of the slippery flesh. This ball fell through the air, but was caught mid-air in the cradle of Mik's strong hand. Mik sniffed this one, too, then wickedly and with great drama, slid her tongue out, licking Leda's honey off of the warm metal sphere in long strokes, then sucking the ball with her smooth lips around it, eyes dancing with excitement, lids heavy with desire. Leda's body hungered for the contact of that insistent tongue and mouth as if she'd wanted this chick for years and years, and it felt that way, like forever; like a fucking lifetime of waiting!

Leda watched Mik watching her face, heard the low chuckle of pleasure deep in Mik's throat, and Leda knew that everything she was thinking—the longing and the desperate need—all of it was displayed like blinding neon in their brutally honest passion play of negotiation; all of it was magnified a hundred times all over Leda's flushed face. It was the one control Leda had yet to master.

Mik slipped the shining metal ball from her mouth, dropping it into her palm, side-by-side with the first sticky one, then ran her tongue over her lips and let a smile flicker across her beautiful face, eyes boring into Leda's. Then she broke away for a moment, leaning over briefly to drop the slick balls into a velvet bag, tying it, then laying this and the quirt inside the big black play bag. Then she lifted the bag by the handles and slid it onto one bare tan shoulder, muscles flexing as she moved. Surprising Leda completely, Mik moved forward and grabbed Leda around the legs, catching her off balance and forcing her to lean over Mik's shoulder like a cavewoman's prize after a good hunt.

"Come on, girl, I get to take you now, you're all mine!" she playfully roared into the room, ending with a laugh of delight as the thrill and the rush of the night washed over her.

Lying across Mik's shoulders, Leda had to hang her shackled hands down Mik's back and they bounced as Mik moved away from the table. A few of the wild leather dykes in the room had responded to Mik's roar with replies of their own: "Shit yeah!" and "Hell yes, mama!" and "Go for it!" and "Watch out, girl!" and wolf whistles in support of what was about to take place.

But before Leda could get in a position to raise her head and check out who was in the room, Mik was laying her down on her back in the black leather sling that connected to the ceiling with heavy-duty silver chains, each wrapped around the other in a pattern of bondage and discipline that would hold Leda's naked body in a firm grip. In a flash, Mik had Leda's wrist shackles apart, then each attached to the chains at the top on either side of Leda's head. She did the same with Leda's ankles—still-smarting ankles—and secured them to the chains at the other end which faced the large room. The scene continued.

"Want me?" Mik asked, her face bright with excitement as she leaned in from the side, running her smooth hands over Leda's vulnerable body, lightly with her fingernails over Leda's round tits, tense belly, a tease of a stroke over Leda's sex, up her sensitive thighs as Leda's legs opened wider from just the suggestion.

"You better want me because you're going to have me, all of me, as much as I want to give you because you're a slut, you know it. Sex-starved, want it all. Don't you, Leda? Don't you want it all?" Mik teased, playing her with words, taunting Leda.

"Yes," was all Leda could answer, her body on fire, responding to Mik's words, to the curve and swell of Mik's naked torso, the beautiful cheekbones of her face, strong shoulders, firm tits with hard buds that Leda fucking ached to suck again, to suck and bite and flick with her tongue. And those hands, those strong hands that were slipping on black rubber gloves with gauntlets now. Leda groaned, imagining what those gloved hands might do to her, and yes, fucking yes, she wanted it all!

"I was gonna fuck you with my hard dyke dick, Leda, but I think you need more than I've got to give you, faster than my hips could pump into your incredibly beautiful cunt that needs the very best, mmm hmm." Her voice was intense, low, almost a whisper, as she slathered lube all over her right gloved hand and wrist.

"I'm gonna take you now, Leda, fill you up completely because that's what I wanna do, I just have to do it now. See what you do to me? See what you make me do?"

Leda was breathing in ragged excited breaths, her head spinning from the wild pumping of her heart in her chest as she lay with her body open wide for all the women to see. She could see them watching, could even hear one dyke say quietly, but insistently, "Fuck her, yeah, she needs a good fuck, you can see she's a bratty one…"

"You stay with me now, Leda girl, only with me…" Leda's mind reconnected with Mik's voice as Mik leaned in between Leda's open legs, eyes riveted on Leda's face, keeping Leda with her. Leda clutched the chains with her hands. Mik slipped two fingers into Leda's open cunt; they slipped in easily and Leda's eyes closed for a moment as she felt Mik enter her body, clutching Mik's fingers with her still-capable muscles.

"Oh God," she whispered, "yes..."

Mik let Leda speak, slipping a third finger into her forgiving cunt, slowly pumping into Leda's body that seemed to feed itself to her, as if each were feeding the other in the exchange. As Mik began slowly to fuck her, Leda breathed hard, feeling the sweat pooling along her back. The smell of sex surrounded them, the sweet smell of fresh lube mixing with her own juices and Mik's sweating body close to hers at last, leaning in with her shoulder as she slid a fourth finger into Leda's willing body.

"Yeah, oh yeah, I can take it, give it to me, Mik, give me what you've got...," Leda whispered hoarsely, insistently, not a command, but an impassioned plea, dare, hope. Leda's clit was pounding with the pressure of a much-needed climax, aching to move toward it with the sure touch of Mik's tongue, of her touch on Leda's clit. Leda moved her hips hard into Mik's hand that was slowly sliding in and out of her pussy, seducing her open, open...

"Oh yes, oh fuck me, oohhh yeah...," Leda groaned as Mik squeezed more lube into her now barely exposed palm, four fingers inside Leda already, covering her thumb and all the rest with a thick coat of lube. And as soon as that was done, Mik looked up at Leda's face and their eyes met. *Ready?* Mik's eyes asked. *Oh please,* Leda's answered. And with a long, strong, slippery thrust, Mik's thumb tucking in tight as she felt Leda's muscles relax, inviting her in, she slid her fist into Leda's cunt, filling it completely.

"Oh, yeah, oh fuck yeah, aahhhh…," Leda moaned, lost in a waterfall of pleasure and sensation that thrilled through her body. She wanted to cry, to scream, to howl with the incredible pleasure that was like a smorgasbord of food and drink after an eternity lost in the desert somewhere. But her words barely escaped her mouth, so controlled had she become. She took Mik's fist and held it, warmed it, welcomed it into the deepest recesses of her hot, tight hole.

Mik began slowly to pump her fist into Leda's cunt, leaning in to listen to Leda's words, feeling the woman's need for a release of sound. Just then the music segued into a new song and for some reason Mik noticed it: "Wicked," by an artist whose name she couldn't recall at the moment. She loved the song. The lyrics slithered through the room and into Mik's ears.

"I wanna be in her while you're in me, and then the three of us will truly see the light…ooohhh wicked, that's how I feel tonight…"

Mik's face lit up, her eyebrows rising, and she turned her head, still pumping into Leda's sweet body, her own cunt slick with excitement, pressing her clit against the firm flesh of the dildo in her jeans as she worked her fist deep in Leda's body. With her head, she motioned for a woman watching nearby to come forward. The woman nodded and approached her.

"Grab the vibrator that's in my bag there, would you mind?" she asked in a whisper. The woman kneeled down and withdrew the vibrator, then looked up as Mik whispered something else to her. The woman smiled—at least that's all Leda saw when she looked down to try and see what was going on: a woman in a neat blue cop suit, hair slicked back away from a strong, attractive face beneath the cop cap, a smile creeping across it now, a mischievous one. *The best kind,* Leda thought.

The woman disappeared from Leda's view again, then reappeared at Leda's side. Caught off guard, Leda self-consciously saw herself as she must appear from the woman's view: laid out buck naked, tits jiggling as the black leather sling rocked with their sex, her hands gripping the chains as if for dear life, knees rudely wide and accepting all of Mik's strong, sweet fist, breathing hard, hair wild, certain her face was flushed and exposing...

But Mik was moving faster now and Leda was shiny with sweat, completely at Mik's mercy, out of control and unable to stop the moans and groans and small cries that escaped from her lips as her body was filled and pumping with the pleasure of Mik's strong arm and fist. It didn't matter who was joining the party at that moment; Leda could hardly see through the crimson pleasure that draped across her view, blocking out events around her. She felt isolated in her own intense sensation, her body a vehicle in flames, Mik's ministrations creating a vacuum that sucked her deeper and deeper still into their trancelike sex. The blood in her veins blasted through her body, crashing through at double speed, every drop making its way to her swelling cunt and engorged clit as it pounded out a path toward ecstasy.

The cop held a magic wand in one black leather—gloved hand. Leda had watched her lean in and had tried to hear what Mik had said to her just a minute ago, but was unsuccessful. The woman didn't say a word now, but switched on the vibrator with a whir of the little motor. Leda didn't notice: She and Mik were connected like one life form, connected by fist to cunt, eye to eye, rockin' and rollin' together as Mik's body rippled with the workings of the muscles in her shoulders, chest, arms, biceps tight, triceps flexing…. Leda had watched Mik's incredible body from the beginning and now the image hung in her mind as she closed her eyes under the tidal wave of sensation. She could see Mik even with her eyes closed, connected by heat and desire, by their minds….

"… so go on and light your cigarette, but only after the feelin' is gone…cuz me I guarantee I can make you last 'til dawn, yeah that long…ooohhh wicked, that's how I feel tonight…," the singer sang.

The music found its way into Leda's mind, too, and she smiled slightly, the appropriateness of the lyric almost too perfect. But any thoughts other than the pleasure and desperation she felt as her body was worked into a frenzy quickly passed, dissipated in the moist heat around the three women. The pounding beat of the music mixed with the rhythm of Mik's fist as it thrust and fucked Leda again and again.

Mik's eyes were like lasers on Leda's face as she worked the woman; Leda could feel her watching and, with great effort, raised the heavy lids of her eyes that were filled with a million intense pleasures, wanting to watch Mik fucking her, to see the wild rush of their sex in her eyes. And she did—saw everything as their eyes met. Leda gripped the chains tighter. Mik quickened the pace, pumping faster as she watched Leda's belly tighten, the woman's eyes glaze over, the muscles of her cunt flickering with zaps of electrical pleasure that lit around Mik's fist as Leda's cunt muscles tightened their hold.

But even this deep into it, Leda could still feel the embarrassment of her position, and doggedly she tried not to make a lot of noise, feeling keenly aware of the need for control, here in a public place, with a woman she hardly knew beside her. But the pressure of this wanting, this aching for release—for a fucking wild, raucous, unbridled release—was more than she could handle. It had been too long and too long a night, teased and played like a puppet right into this woman's able hands....

So when the cop ever so unobtrusively slipped the

round head of the vibrator down onto Leda's throbbing clit, Leda lost control completely and cried out with a deep groan that rose to a wail, and then to words: "Yes, oh fuck!" The vibrator summoned all the blood in Leda's body to the one fine point at the tip of her clit. The throbbing of her cunt around Mik's hand as the woman fucked her madly grew and expanded, one pressure front building over another. The vibrator hummed and seduced her pleasure until the force inside Leda became desperate, beyond desperate, a massive balloon inside her blowing up to inhuman proportions, trying to force its way out through the one point on the swollen tip of her throbbing clit.

Leda couldn't feel the metal then as the chains that she gripped dug into her soft hands, knuckles turning white as she shut her eyes tight and threw her head back, holding her breath as the pressure broke out in a million crashing pieces, blasting through her and out out out with a wailing cry and scream and holler of sweet release—out through her open mouth and into the wooden dungeon. She arched into the hands of the two women and bucked again and again as her clit exploded, her cunt gripping Mik's fist in a death grip of orgasm, clamping and releasing over and over, then pushing, forcing, rocketing it out from her pounding body.

"Ohhhh, God, yes, aaaahhhhhhhh…!" she screamed. But the cop kept the vibrator at its home base, electrifying Leda's clit in a continuous wave until the pleasure turned almost to pain, so extended was Leda's clit, her entire body an intricate highway of rushing blood and electrified nerve endings.

"No, please, no more, stop, ah shiiiit!" she said hoarsely.

Leda bucked again and again, breathing hard, arching her naked body, narrow rib cage rising and falling, nipples hard buds on tits thrust high into the air, lungs filling again, then holding as she gritted her teeth against the barrage, her body tensed in response to the continuous now over-stimulation. She couldn't breath for the overwhelming sensation. And as the experience peeked—and she was sure she'd have to scream to make it stop since she was powerless to do so any other way—like a drowning person, Leda made a decision just to let go, to fall into the powerlessness rather than try to escape it. She wasn't altogether sure she had any other choice at this point.

But the change in attitude caused a change in her body. Like a miracle, her clit seemed to recede, step back and take a breather beneath its hood; still feeling the vibration but cloaked from it. But really her clit was just reloading, gathering up the blazing tips of nerves from all corners of her sweating, shining body and building the pressure once again.

Leda concentrated, tried to resist but barely able to pull in enough air to stop the spinning in her head. She opened her eyes and met those of the uniformed woman head-on. The cop looked out at Leda from under her low-slung cap and dark eyebrows. A wicked smile curled the corners of the woman's thin-lipped mouth. Her eyes were light gray with intense points of black in the middle, rimmed with a thin line of black that made them appear incredibly light, almost colorless; strange.

*A weird open place you could fall into,* Leda thought, sweat stinging her eyes as she blinked, suddenly feeling the impact of this stranger's stare, harsh and ravenous; eyes that would not accept a bargain, a deal, a plea, to be sure. Leda suddenly wished she could pull her legs closed against this woman, feeling too exposed for those eyes. Her discomfort began to grow, but still the hum of the vibrator continued, pulling her attention back to the point of contact. Though she tried, Leda could not coerce her clit away from its hungry journey back to the vibrator's touch—to the woman's touch, then, too, and who knew what else.

Was this what Mik wanted to do with her? Hand her off to someone else? *Maybe this wasn't such a good idea after all,* Leda thought.

"No, stop," Leda whispered to the woman, for the first time that night almost imploring in her tone of voice, on the edge of using the safe word just to stop this uncomfortable game. It must have been apparent, because Mik's familiar intimate tones filled her world then.

"Don't worry, Leda girl," Mik was whispering into Leda's ear, having approached from the side, fist no longer sunk deep in Leda's body, and now leaning in, running her long fingers through Leda's short wild hair.

She kissed Leda's forehead with incredibly soft, firm, warm lips, moving behind Leda to the back of the sling. Leda sighed, immediately slipping back into the trance of Mik's voice and passion, unable to find the track her thoughts had been following only seconds before.

"She has strict orders, this one," Mik said in her husky whisper. "Only my hands on you, that's the rule. She only has one job and I told her to stay on you, not to give in, no matter how you begged. You see, I'm in charge here, don't worry my slave. Just relax, relax into the pleasure." Her tongue slowly ran a path over the curve of Leda's ear, arousing Leda with her hot breath.

"I know it's there, coming around again; let it come, I can see it coming, see the flush just under your skin. Your tits are so hard, slave, your hungry muscles seeking out that touch, you know it's true. You want it, don't you?" Mikki asked.

Leda didn't respond. Mik waited.

"Talk to me, Leda, tell me you do, want it," Mik said, entwining her fingers in Leda's brown locks and giving them a tug. Leda sucked in her breath.

"Open your eyes and tell me you want it, you want more, whatever I have to give you. Tell me you want everything I want to give you," Mik commanded now, though her voice never rose a decibel, just increased in intensity.

"Yes, yes, I want it," Leda almost whimpered, a fly in the web, the same web, again; over and over. She just wasn't learning, she knew it. But there was something that lured her to this woman's game, beyond what she wanted and into what she didn't even know she wanted, until after.

Oh, but she did want it.

"I do want you, what you have to give me," Leda admitted out loud, her breath ragged, body still tense but slowly melting into the sound of Mik's seductive words, body humming like the sound of the vibrator still on her clit.

"Good. And, oh, I do have something for you. And I just know you can go further than this. I have faith in you, Leda girl. Faith."

Mikki's hands slid over Leda's face then, the woman standing, still, at the crown of Leda's head, an ungloved finger on her left hand sliding across Leda's open mouth, outlining her lips. And Leda was hungry again, the familiar sound of Mik's voice blocking out the outside attendant busy at her clit, creating safety in an atmosphere of danger, her body willing in Mik's able hands. She felt drugged by her own desire and the energy that their scene brought to the room; a connection with this woman that she had never felt with anyone before.

Not even Chrys.

*Whatever*, Leda thought, too gone on a ride for deep thoughts at the moment; just the edges of them flicking at her every now and then, like the impossibly sharp tip of a knife on new flesh, not really drawing blood but stinging.

She sighed and shivered as Mik ran her open palms down over Leda's tits, running light circles over the hard tips. The gentleness was exquisitely unbearable and Leda squirmed under Mik's touch. Then the hands were travelling down to Leda's tense belly, Mikki's beautiful torso and tits momentarily bending down over her captive, almost close enough for Leda to nip at, or flick her tongue out for a taste. But before she could consider either, the hands doubled back with a vengeance, finger-nails dragging an "I still mean business" path back up across Leda's belly and up to her chest where fingers squeezed and twisted her nipples painfully.

Leda groaned, though she really wanted to scream out her pain. She did not, but she could not control her instinct to pull her body back away from the pain, wonderful as it was. A sudden slap, meant more to get her attention than to cause real pain, reminded Leda of who was in charge.

"Stay still," Mik commanded, "don't move until I tell you to." And then the hands were gone, leaving her tits throbbing in their wake, her clit humming with the vibrator's insistent contact, though it moved over her mound every now and then, and down over her wet open lips, then back to its target.

Leda's eyes darted, following Mik as the woman moved around the sling at a slow pace. Mik leaned down and momentarily disappeared; Leda knew the play bag was there, but what Mik was doing in it remained unknown to her. Leda's ears strained to distinguish any clues as to what was going on below her rudely open legs. The soft flesh of her thighs left her exposed, feet still held captive by the sling, and she blushed profusely as her eyes travelled down to the light brown hair on her mound which was now half covered by the large white head of a vibrator, actually an extension of the pale hand with neatly trimmed nails which gripped it. Caught off guard, Leda moaned as the woman moved the head of the vibrator over her sex, calling her back, hitting a spot that sparked her entire body back to life.

"Oh, shit," she whimpered, not wanting to respond to this woman, but only to Mik. But she couldn't help it, her hot sweaty ass seemed to lift off the leather sling of its own accord. Out of the corner of her eye, she saw the cop smile. Like a tangible blow, Leda felt the humiliation blast into her and she hated it, hated the woman. But still the pleasure continued at her clit, commanding her body and too much of her mind. She tried to breathe through it, but it was too much. The cop's hand teased her, moving the vibrator over and around her now attentive clit. Again, her hips rose of their own accord and Leda moaned.

The moan quickly turned into a cry of surprise as Leda felt a pressure against her ass. Her eyes flew open, afraid the cop had overstepped her bounds. But it wasn't the cop. She turned to see that Mik stood tall between her legs, obviously on a step of some sort because the wickedly long dick that hung between her strong naked thighs was dressed with a shining condom and poised at Leda's exposed asshole, ready to make its way into her world.

And before Leda could take another breath or tense up, Mik slid the head of the long dildo into Leda's relaxed ass, plunging the tool in with one long steady thrust of her hips. And in a flash, Mik's hips were flush against Leda's asscheeks, hands holding onto Leda's legs as they hung, parted, on either side of her.

Leda cried out then. Swore and screamed into the room as her ass was filled to the bursting point with Mik's long, hard rod. The vibrator continued its dance. Leda opened her eyes and looked out through a haze at Mik standing, face wild with desire, between her open legs, face intensely concentrated on the tool plunging into Leda's pink asshole. And like a volcano kept simmering for way too long, Mik was explosive with her passion. After two brief, but kind, slower, easier thrusts, Leda tried hard to keep her eyes open to watch Mik's incredible body as it finally got what it wanted. But far too quickly, the rhythmic thrusting increased in speed, Mik plunging into Leda's open body harder and harder with each re-entry. Mik leaned into Leda, holding both of Leda's ankles in her strong grip, her face a wild display of hunger, intention, and lust.

Leda was on fire, her ass was on fire, her clit, too. Her body pounded as the women both took her hungrily, feeding her own ravenous appetite as they ate her alive. The electricity of their sex fried Leda's body as she climbed again toward climax, eyes threatening to close. But she didn't want to miss this. Mik was incredible, her skin shining with sweat and the muscles in her stomach rippling as she thrust and pulled out, thrust and pulled out, faster and faster now. The contact of the base of the dildo against Mik's female form was a vision that filled Leda's imagination. Her mouth watered just thinking about Mikki's pussy beneath the hard dyke cock that blasted away inside her ass, crashing the passion into her faster and faster now.

Mik grunted and growled as the pressure of her approaching orgasm shimmered over her flushed skin, pressing against her control. Leda couldn't help it then, but closed her eyes as the vibrator doggedly began to coax an orgasm from her pulsing clit, a million points of sensation flaming to life inside her. Mik fucked her in the ass, launching into her again and again like a rocket, slamming into Leda's forgiving flesh, boring her out like a hot metal rod, taking all of her in its wake. And as Mik plunged deeply, Leda raised her hips and gave herself to Mik, and to the cop's insistent command of the vibrator that opened the tiny doorway that Leda's orgasm now blasted through, all valves open for the floodwaters this time, no holding back.

Leda screamed into the room, thrashing her throat with her animal cries. At the sound of Leda's orgasm, Mik blew, too, pumping madly into the woman and crying out in a guttural cry of release, "Yes! Yes! Fuck, oh, uhn!" Mik groaned and forced her strong hips in tight against Leda, thrusting the tool in just as deep as it would go with tiny thrusts just to get it in a little more, if possible, her clit flush against Leda's ass.

Leda felt her orgasm take hold deep in her gut, felt it grip her very soul and fill it with a rush of energy that expanded out and away, at last, soaring and bursting out through the tip of her clit and this time, this time she took Mik with her, the sound of their voices echoing off the walls.

# Epilogue

Mik, Leda, and the cop—whose name turned out to be Bobbie—sat at a small round table in the jungle eating exotic fruit salad from clear plastic cups.

"God, I'd swear I'm stoned, this shit tastes so fucking good!" Leda said in amazement, keeping her voice low but enthusiastic. She sat wrapped in a big white towel, one edge tucked into the wrap to keep it closed.

Mik looked at her. Leda's face was flushed a soft pink from the night's events and a cool dip she'd taken in the river as Mik had sat on the shore, legs leather-clad once again, but dangling her bare feet in the cool water while she talked with Bobbie, who crouched, fully clothed, beside her. Mik liked the look of Leda's hair like this:

slicked back away from her face and glistening under the lights.

"You really look different without your hair all spiked out," Mik noted out loud.

Leda looked at her. She didn't know what to say to Mik's comment and "oh" didn't even seem like a fair choice. So she didn't say anything. But their eyes met and stayed that way for a long minute.

Bobbie the cop tossed her own empty fruit cup into a wastebasket nearby and ran her tongue over her lips. The woman was still in full cop regalia, which got her plenty of attention from interested bottoms that seemed to be sort of passing by in a pretty regular pattern or hovering like flies over an especially sweet find.

"Well, ladies," Bobbie said, pushing up from her chair where she had been sitting next to Mik, "the night is still young and I have yet to find me a woman worthy of me taking off my uniform."

Both Leda and Mik broke their gaze and craned their necks to look up at Bobbie with indignant looks on their faces.

"Thought that would get your attention!" A wry smile creased her usually reserved face. "But, hey, no offense intended. You know this was a...special situation." She winked at them. Mik leaned back in her chair, then reached out and swatted Bobbie's butt as she moved slowly by.

"Oh, you go get your fillies, Bobbie. Don't you dare let all that sexy uniform and preparation go to waste!" Mik grinned at her friend. "And thanks for the favor; I owe you one." Both women grinned then.

"Yes, you do. I'll talk to you soon, Mik," Bobbie added through her smile. "Pleasure meeting you, Leda. We'll have to explore this further sometime."

Leda couldn't see Bobbie's eyes behind her sunglasses, which had yet to leave the woman's face, but she nodded her head in response, smiling. *Sure, what the hell,* Leda thought good-naturedly.

Bobbie moved off into the milling crowd of half-naked and naked women. Reggae strains seemed to feed her movements as she moved away from Leda and Mik toward the river's edge, dancing a little as she went. A small crowd of naked dancers on the island in the middle of the river started a round of whoops that moved like a wave through the crowd across from the island, along the shore, to the women seated at the small umbrella'd tables and those hiding in the foliage, doin' the nasty or making out or just hiding out together. The waterfall continued its endless cascade. And what a night it was.

Leda sighed, putting aside her empty cup and leaning in on her elbows. Mik leaned in, too. Leda smiled at her.

"Thanks," she said, "for a really incredible night."

"My pleasure," Mik replied. "You're fun to play with, bold. You really trusted me and you hardly know me. Pretty awesome."

"I know, damn, that's the weirdest thing!" Leda agreed.

"I don't know what it is, but there's something. I just…"

Leda looked up, words not forming into complete sentences. And there was Mikki, long dark wavy hair down at last, loose and beautiful around her glorious face, creamy olive skin and high cheekbones, brown eyes bright with intelligence and a continuous sparkle of mischief. Without thinking, Leda leaned in on a rush of passion and kissed Mik's soft mouth, her eyes closing as Mik kissed her back. It was like a connection of pure matter; you couldn't see it, but it was there, tangible between them as they lingered in the connection.

The kiss ended. They opened their eyes and looked at each other.

"Mmm," Leda said.

Mik pooched out her lips a little and nodded her agreement, eyes resting on where her mouth had just been. Leda pulled her gaze away and panned the jungle room, trying to get herself together.

"It's pretty late," Leda said with regret.

"Got somewhere you have to be?" Mik asked, sitting back in her chair, opening her legs noticeably. She'd unpacked her leathers, that is, stowed the dildo in her play bag, leaving her pants fitting a bit looser. Now all Leda could think about was Mik's bare snatch under the thin layer of leather. Leda knew it was close to 5:00 A.M. because the club had called one more hour to closing: there was no alcohol served after 2:00 A.M., but the club stayed open until 6:00 A.M. for playing, swimming, eating, or drinking non-alcoholic beverages.

Leda considered Mik's question.

"Well, yes and no. I've been babysitting tonight," she said with a grin.

"Oh," Mik answered, almost a question, understanding appearing on her face. Then she added mischievously, "And was I a good baby?"

"Oh, man, the best," Leda said emphatically, smiling. "I think my discipline was lax, though."

"Mmm. Then maybe I'll see you here again sometime for another shot; sometime soon," Mik said, "real soon."

"Yeah," Leda answered, "definitely." What else could she say? She meant it, wanted it. Everything was changing tonight, opening up possibilities she hadn't considered for years that made her blood pump with passion and enthusiasm. She felt revived after a long, long sleep.

There was a pause as the two women sat side by side, not wanting the night to end, but both a little unsure of how to proceed.

"You're one helluva good lover," Leda said, wanting to make sure Mik knew just what a great night this had been, how grateful she was for it.

"Thank you," Mik said. "I do my best. Nice woman to make lo…um, play with," Mik added, her brows furrowing for a moment, then her face returning to a smile. "Well," she said, rising from her chair. "C'mon then, I'll go help you change, then walk you to your car." She winked at the offer to help Leda change.

"Aren't you leaving yet?" Leda asked.

"Yeah, soon, why? You need a ride home? A place to stay for the night maybe? A place to move into, someone to spend the rest of your life with?" She smiled that open smile that just seemed to glow with charm and chuckled at herself. "I got a place with room to spare, at least for one more anyway."

"Damn, Mikki, you are hard to resist. And I don't really want to resist, but I...I got a few things to figure out first. Can I hold on to that offer and get back to you on it? Maybe call you?"

Mik's business card appeared between her fingers like a magician's trick. "Call me anytime. I'm not in the phone book, so hang on tight to this. No phone at your place?" she asked.

"No, not really," Leda answered, embarrassed, looking down for a moment. When she looked back up she said, "But I promise, if you really want me to, that I will give this one some good hard thought."

"Agreed," Mik smiled seriously. "Take your time. But don't forget lonely ol' me here at the sex camp for girls pining away for my perfect partner. If you know what I mean."

"Oh, I do, I do," Leda said, smiling.

Mik leaned in and kissed Leda on the cheek. "I'll be thinking of you," Mik said. Leda wanted to reach out and hold that beautiful face in her hands and kiss it for hours. But she had other obligations that she cared about as well. And some hard decisions to make. She sat there, head close to Mik's after the kiss.

"Well, c'mon then," Mik said, reaching for Leda's hand. "Let's get you dressed and outta here."

The two women rose from their chairs, tossed their garbage in the can. Leda didn't take Mik's hand, but stood equal beside her, not willing to play the femme. Mik smiled and nodded. Together they headed toward the archway back to the elevators, talking easily, shoulders almost touching as they moved through the crowd to the changing room.

# the house of spirits

# 1. Arrival

It was late. The moon was high and almost full in the sky above the large, looming figure of the old plantation-style house. Though most of the house was dark, light warmed the interior behind two windows upstairs on the second floor; windows that faced the large, overgrown backyard where an old greenhouse sat in the middle of a weed-filled overgrown lawn, casting eerie shadows in glistening patterns across the expanse. The shadows stretched and disappeared into the forest beyond. The perimeter of the huge yard that completely encircled the white two-story house, front, sides, and back, seemed to act as a barrier against the encroaching trees that flourished just beyond it.

At the front of the house, a long, wide driveway led out from a separate two-car garage that sat beside the main house, the driveway curving around and down a slight incline to meet up at its end with a narrow two-lane road—the only way to and from the house. On the front lawn—now the home to dead grass, weeds, and wildflowers—a decaying old wooden sign hung from a rusty metal post, the fading words FOR SALE now crossed out by a bright white sticker that announced SOLD in bold black letters.

The sign creaked on its rusty hinges as a slight wind blew down the long country road, up the driveway, and around the house, finding its way in after many years through the open back windows of the large upstairs master bedroom. Inside, Lydia Ryder, a tan, dark-haired woman of thirty-one years, sat on a rug on the hardwood floor in the middle of the room, unpacking boxes by candlelight. Mellow rock played from a little cassette deck on the bedside table behind her, one of the few pieces of furniture situated in its proper place by the bed. Moonlight flooded the burgundy comforter that covered the large bed, and the gauzy white curtain that graced the nearby window billowed in a large arc, letting in the warm curious breeze. Lydia looked up nervously as the candles flickered around her, sending wild shadows through the room.

"Ho, it's late," she sighed, running her hands through her long hair as she turned toward the moonlit window. "I think I'm spooking myself with fatigue. Bedtime, old girl. I'll finish this in the morning."

The glow of the candles reflected in Lydia's silky hair and made her tan cheeks rosy. She spoke to herself in the empty room, made somewhat cozy by the candlelight and soft music despite its large size and the many boxes that filled it. She had found some long-stemmed wildflowers growing in the front yard when she'd arrived earlier in the day and a bunch of them now bloomed brightly in an old glass jar on the bedside table beside the cassette player, the flowers the only living things in the old house, besides herself. The arrangement of the bed, beside table, flowers, and candles along the wall adjacent to the open windows made for a cozy central spot, showcasing the potential of the space once she got settled. The glass in the French-style windows was old and bent the moonlight in patterns as it hit the hardwood floor.

Begrudgingly, Lydia pushed herself up from the floor, brushing off her baggy workout pants and cropped T-shirt, a strip of toned tan stomach showing between the two.

"Well," she sighed, "I had big dreams for getting at least this room unpacked tonight, but…"

She yawned and stretched her arms high overhead, leaning left, right, then arching back, hands on her lower back, letting out a long relaxing breath. Her cropped T rode up as she stretched, the drawstring of her cotton workout pants loosening with the motion, riding low on her hips, held up by the curve of her hipbones. The soft line of her pubic hair peeked out at the edge of the drawstring waistband. She rolled her head in slow circles a few times, took a few long inhalations, letting them out slowly, then looked around the room.

"This is going to be so great," she said with as much enthusiasm as she could muster this late at night and after such a long moving day. "I can't believe it's all mine."

Lydia grinned a sleepy, contented grin, hiking up her pants and tightening the drawstring absently. Then she turned, and using her long legs and arms to their maximum benefit, started shoving aside the boxes that had yet to be opened, making a path from the bed to the door that led from the bedroom and out into the open hall, which was lined by an elegant wood railing. It wasn't so much a hall, really, as a walkway; a carpeted walkway that looked down onto the living room below and circled the entire second floor like a balcony.

Once a path was made, Lydia picked up a large suitcase from among the boxes on the floor and heaved it up onto the bed; the mattress bounced a little under the weight of it. With a loud click, she released the two latches and opened the suitcase. The familiarity of her personal things flooded her with a calm sense of normality and consistency, making her more at ease her first night alone in her new home, in a new town, miles away from the city she'd lived in most of her life.

"Big change," she said aloud, staring into the suitcase. "But like Mr. Elton John says, 'Change is gonna do me good.' Just remember that."

Even in the strange uneasiness of the big old house

and the odd country people who ran the markets and post office and other small shops in the main part of the town—all four blocks of it—Lydia was certain this was the right move. The fresh air, the privacy, the lull of the crickets and resonant hoots of the night owls, all of it filled her with a sense of rightness somehow.

"It's what I've always wanted," she reminded herself. "And if there aren't any lesbians in this little town, well, so be it. I'll live a hermit's life for a while, what the hell."

She sighed.

"Then I'll have all the time in the world to paint and read and relax, at least until what's left of the nest egg runs out."

She shook her head and smiled, envisioning herself as a hermit—she who hadn't lived alone, ever, and had mostly bounced from one lover to the next, caught up in the drama of lesbian nightlife.

"I can do this," she said aloud to the creaking house, the whispery wind, and the night creatures outside the windows. "You know, I have always wanted my own place," she said as if speaking directly to the house itself. "And in this case, I've got this huge, beautiful—well, run-down, yes—but incredible house! I can use my hands and fix you up right, make this place my own. Fill you with my paintings…"

Her voice took on a dreamy quality as she felt the reality of making a lifetime dream come true at last, all the possibility right here.

Outside, there was a stirring of some creature in the

weeds of the backyard. It was a foreign sound to Lydia's city ears, and it caught her attention over the lull of the quiet music still playing on the stereo. "Hm, maybe getting a dog would be a good idea," she mumbled to herself, "and a cat or two for rodent control."

Lydia glanced at her watch; both hands pointed straight up to the full moon hanging high up in the night sky above the roof of the house. The thought crossed her mind that from now on she could stay up as late as she wanted, reading in bed or whatever—with all the damn lights on if she pleased! Play music until all hours of the morning! A wave of excitement ran through her tired body and she smiled, nodding her approval.

Then she sat down on the bed next to the suitcase; the contents inside had been neatly packed and organized. As Lydia unhooked the straps that secured her clothes, her eye was caught by a partially crumpled photograph that had been stuffed into one corner. She reached down and retrieved it, brushing it flat with one hand. The porcelain face of a strikingly beautiful woman with light gray-green eyes looked out from the photograph, her wide, painted mouth in a happy smile, eyes shining beneath a mane of bright, rust-colored hair. Large, glittery green rhinestone earrings dangled from both ears, catching little stars of light from the flash. She wore a smart forest green blazer and cream-colored silky blouse—the perfect picture except for the deep veinlike creases in the crumpled paper that seemed to crisscross her out like shattered glass.

Lydia breathed a long sigh and the corners of her lovely mouth turned down for the first time since her arrival, eyebrows furrowing as she studied the photograph for a moment. The emptiness of the house, the wide-open country night, seemed to move in on her ever so slightly. She shook her head, anger crossing her face like a shadow, and crumpled up the photograph again, throwing it into a dark corner of the room beyond the candlelight's reach.

Another breeze wafted in through the window, stronger than the others, and extinguished a couple of the candles nearest the window. The room grew darker.

"For chrissake," she said aloud, "the one thing I was really counting on was electricity. I mean, I can wait till tomorrow to take a shower or just take a cold one; it's warm enough that I don't need the gas heat, but lights would have been fucking nice my first night here! Just a little *electricity*, that's all I asked for!"

Anger caused her shoulders to rise and tense, making her reach for the back of her neck and rub it—an old habit. Catching herself, she laughed suddenly.

"She's not even here, just a picture of her, and look at me! Back to the tension pit! But I am free, m'dear, free as the birds out in those woods back there. So what if it's all I've got!" The house echoed her words. The creases in her forehead relaxed and her mouth drew up into a little smile then.

It *was* a crazy situation, what she'd done: sinking all her investment money into the big old house and leaving behind everyone and everything she'd ever known. And way out here, in the middle of nowhere, she didn't even have any lights! To top it all off, the female singer's voice on the tape she'd been playing was getting strangely deeper as the batteries began to wear out. Lydia clicked off the tape deck. The silence surrounded her. The house seemed to pull her in without much light and no sound to separate her from it. She shivered—though not from cold on such a warm summer night—and sighed at the way her first night had turned out. But she was too tired to worry about any of it right now.

Lydia stood up and hauled the suitcase down onto the floor, grabbed her toothbrush and an oversized nightshirt out of it. Then she headed into the master bathroom that adjoined the bedroom, bringing one of the two still-lit candles to light her way, the flame illuminating the bathroom in an eerie flickering glow. Lydia felt herself moving much more quickly than usual, peeing and brushing her teeth without lingering, cutting her rituals short. She stepped out of her baggy drawstring pants and T-shirt, and slipped into her big nightshirt. Taking the candle once again, she moved back into the bedroom.

The restless motions of the wind continuing danced through the trees and across the fields into the bedroom.

"Yes, I locked the front door," Lydia assured herself, "and there's no electricity, so there are no lights to turn off." She looked around, moved along the path she'd made between the boxes and peeked out into the hall, feeling odd and very small in the huge, unfamiliar house. The house had been cleaned before she moved in and the movers had placed all the furniture and boxes in the rooms she'd requested. But Lydia didn't have all that much at the moment and four of the six bedrooms remained empty, the living room sparsely furnished, and the dining room empty until she could get out and buy a new table. It really was a ridiculous purchase for one person, this huge house.

"Oh, Cheri baby," she said aloud, "if you could see me now you'd shit your pants—say I've pissed away my hard-earned cash."

But the truth was the house had been incredibly, downright ridiculously cheap, and escrow had closed in record time—before Lydia had been able to talk herself, logically, out of her love for the place. And before she knew it, *boom!* it was hers! She couldn't imagine why the house was so cheap. It had been on the market a long time, she'd been told, but when asked what was wrong with the place, the realtor couldn't come up with anything. Oh, it needed a little repair and maybe new paint, but the plumbing, the heating system, the roof, the foundation, the basic frame, everything was in great shape, if a little stiff or rusty from lack of use.

Lydia walked out into the hall and peered out over the railing. The bright moonlight was streaming in through the tall windows in the living room below. The doors to the other rooms were open as she'd left them: one room to her left, two along the wall to her right, the railing continuing around in a square, making a left and then another left where two more rooms faced her across the open space. The staircase led down from the final side of the square to her left in a smooth, elegant curve that grew wider at the bottom. Beautiful antique light fixtures curved out from the walls between the rooms, a variety of earlier-era lampshades topping them, except for one that looked straight out of the sixties. Lydia looked forward to seeing all of them lit tomorrow when the electricity was finally turned on.

She sighed, looking down at her modern furniture, which looked so out of place in the living room below. The place was built just before the turn of the century, the realtor had told her, but its heyday began in the twenties and it all but insisted on those styles of furnishings, it seemed. Lydia had inquired what kind of heyday that might have been, but the woman just said, "Oh, it was a big social club, I think, something like that." Then she'd quickly changed the subject.

Yawning, Lydia wrapped her arms around herself, wiggling her toes in the thick mauve carpet runner running down the middle of the smooth hardwood floor. Content now that all was fine in the house, she turned back to the bedroom. The candles were shimmying in the light breeze from the window, but they stayed lit. She padded quietly across the floor, around the bed, and over to the window, looking out into the silvery, moonlit night. Smiling sleepily, she pulled one of the windows in (they opened like miniature French doors) and locked it shut. The other she left open a few inches, able to sleep now with a window open as she liked, since she was sleeping alone. Having endured year after year of stale, stuffy air during her partnered days, this action—leaving the window open now, to sleep in a room of her own as she liked it—was like a bit of paradise; as if by opening the window she were opening herself to the cool, fresh breeze of the night and new endless possibilities.

After blowing out all but two of the candles and placing the two lit ones on the bedside table, Lydia pulled back the heavy comforter and slipped in between the cool sheets. She plumped the two pillows a little, took a last scan around the room, then leaned over the nightstand and blew out the remaining candles.

The night sounds wafted in through the open window as she snuggled under the blankets, strange but somehow familiar, even comforting after the sirens and traffic and carrying on-of the busy city nights. A bird called from a far-off tree branch and Lydia sighed contentedly, exhausted. In no time at all she dozed off, a warm breeze lazily billowing the sheer white curtain that covered the window beside the big four-poster bed that had come with the house (what Lydia had considered a lucky break since Cheri had ended up with the bed). The starlit country sky beyond the window was alive with moonlight. Shadows shimmered through the room, moving like phantom hands over the bed, caressing Lydia, calling to her with silent longing as she drifted off into a heavy sleep.

## 2. The Party

In a large evergreen tree that sat near the side of the house there was a rustle of foliage and wings. A bird rose suddenly from the uppermost shelter of thick pine needles, lifting off into the blue-black sky. It flew up over the dark silhouette of the house, the bird itself now a silhouette as it moved across the brilliant glowing figure of the moon and disappeared into the night.

On the ground below, pine needles shimmered down in a light rain from where the bird had disturbed the branch of the tree, the greenish brown needles blanketing the grass near the side of the house. Music and laughter escaped through the partially open windows. Inside, behind heavy black-and-red velvet curtains, candles and dimmed chandeliers burned in the large living and dining rooms. Two women—one a bleached blonde with a trendy bob cut, dressed in blue cuffed bell-bottomed hip-huggers and a chiffon leopard-print blouse tied at the waist; the other a tall, dark-haired slender vision in a sheer red halter top and red satin pants—locked arms as they laughed, leaning against the back of one of the couches in the living room, leaning in to kiss each other with hungry mouths, exploring with their tongues, then sealing the kiss with soft lips pressed tightly against each other.

The blonde laughed and whooped out a holler of excitement as the two women raised their champagne glasses in a toast. Her partner joined in. Wild Roaring Twenties music filled the room, the source of it a huge black grand piano where two women in flapper dresses played madly together, fingers flying over the keys, manipulating the notes with precision and speed. Around the piano were a medley of women, some with arms draped over each other, some scantily clad, others handsomely bedecked in full trouser suits with hats, scarves, and spit-shined black shoes. The variety of costumes spanned a hundred years of fashion.

The women around the piano sang and drank from long-stemmed champagne glasses, creating a raucous round of song and laughter. Just behind them, an especially stunning woman wearing an elegant trouser suit with a long coat and cap, scarf meticulously arranged at her neck, took a drag off a cigarette in a long-stemmed gold cigarette holder. As the smoke curled up around her face, her dark eyes took in every detail, landing momentarily on the two women groping each other across the room and drinking from opposing champagne glasses. She watched them stand upright with great effort, draping their arms over each other's shoulders for support—the brunette's long elegant fingers dangling greedily over the blonde's ample cleavage. Then the two women made their way unsteadily toward the staircase and the private rooms above.

"Maxine," the tall woman called over the raucous singing and music. "I'd recommend you check with Grace before you seduce Miss Sadie into your den of pleasures."

Maxine looked up, brushing her dark curls out of her eyes with the back of the hand that held the champagne glass, beautiful blue eyes full of passion, lids heavy from the buzz of alcohol. She studied the source of the words for a moment, then smiled a little crooked smile.

"Why, Miss Grey, you know I wouldn't seduce an unknowing child into my room without first checking with her daddy, now would I?"

Maxine's overacted Southern drawl was like syrup as she replied, pulling Sadie closer to her, wrapping her arm around the woman's neck playfully. In Maxine's hold, Sadie laughed and pinched Maxine's ass through the woman's satin hip-huggers. Then she raised her other hand, negotiating the last of the champagne from her glass into her hot pink–painted mouth.

"Don't say I didn't warn you, doll," Miss Grey called back, smiling wryly, cigarette and holder held out at a jaunty angle, the smoke at its tip swirling and rising around the powerful figure as the women at the piano ripped into a wild rendition of the Charleston Rag.

Moving her small party once again toward the staircase, Maxine raised her glass in a toast to Miss Grey as she passed into the dining room and out of Miss Grey's sight. They passed a wide, very long dining table draped in a crisp white cloth that stretched almost the full length of the large room. Two glittery chandeliers glowed brightly above it, illuminating a feast of foods.

One woman, at the far end of the table from where Maxine and Sadie now stood, momentarily taking in the sights, was sitting backwards in a carved wooden high-backed chair. She was naked but for her laced-up high-heeled ankle boots, thigh-high silk stockings, garters, and panties, small perky breasts jutting out, nipples up against the wooden back of the chair. Her hands were tied securely behind her with shiny rope, feet secured to the legs of the chair as she sat up straight, looking out over the top of the back of the chair, obediently opening her soft round mouth to take in a piece of cake. The cake was held aloft just out of her reach by a trim redhead in a fancy 1930s chiffon party dress complete with puffy sleeves. The woman's hair was rolled and pressed in a delicate design on her head. She opened her own painted mouth just a hint as she teased the bound woman on the chair.

"Ask me nicely, Jane," she said in a soft but demanding voice, "or I'll have to get Miss Randall to increase your bindings until you know your place."

"Please, Miss Sarah, please may I have some cake?" Jane asked demurely from her perch on the chair. Her eyes were heavily accentuated with charcoal black eyeliner and sparkly gray eyeshadow, lips a deep red, cheeks rosy with blush, the make-up overdone, garish.

Next to Miss Sarah, across from Jane, stood a handsome woman in black pressed trousers, crisp white shirt, and a matching smoking jacket. From her neck hung a monocle on a black ribbon. She turned her head to look at Miss Sarah after Jane's pathetic attempt at good behavior. Miss Sarah stood demurely in her fluffy dress and shook her head in disappointment.

"Well Miss Randall, I'm afraid our little doll has yet to master the sounds of complete humility. I fear the cake will have to wait."

And with that, she withdrew the silver fork that held the cake and, instead, ate it herself.

"Mmm, quite lovely. Yes, marvelous in fact. Oh, just the best cake I've ever had the pleasure of tasting." Her eyes sparkled as she chewed and swallowed. "Of course, cake is nice, but I'm so in the mood for even more pleasurable…tastes," she added, light eyes connecting with Jane's large, dark, round ones.

So engrossed was Miss Sarah in meeting Jane's eyes that she was caught completely unaware when a slight, angular young woman in Little Lord Fauntleroy dress crawled right up to her on hands and knees, lifted the puffy frills of the edges of Miss Sarah's party dress, and crawled under.

Miss Sarah let out a cry of surprise as the woman's hands quickly made their way up the smooth inside of Miss Sarah's thighs, caressing her sex through the thin silk of Miss Sarah's panties—the modern silk panties that Kenya had given to her just last night as a gift. (Under Kenya's detailed instructions, Miss Sarah had, tonight, as promised, worn only the silk panties and nothing else beneath her party frock.) She blushed furiously as the mouth of the woman beneath her skirt (Mimi, she discovered, when Carol called out the woman's name frantically upon discovering where Mimi had got off to) made contact with her barely covered mound. Still, her eyes closed for a moment under the intense rush of pleasure. Mimi's hands were quick as they caressed Miss Sarah's incredibly smooth thighs, uncharacteristically free of stockings tonight, and her tongue darted out to flick at Miss Sarah's quickly hardening clit now pressing at the sheer silk fabric of the panties.

Miss Sarah moaned.

Out loud.

Her eyes flew open as she realized she'd actually made a sound, the echoes of it escaping into the crowded room. Her astonished eyes were met directly by Jane's bright, excited ones. Immediately, Miss Sarah stepped back away from Mimi's grasp and busy tongue, pushing the woman away. Mimi tumbled out from beneath Miss Sarah's frilly skirt, the buckles of her shoes shining as she fell onto her butt, the bow in her hair askew as she smiled a mischievous and delighted smile.

"Mmm, Miss Sarah, my my but you have no stockings on at all tonight and, why, nothing more than a slip of silk across your wet slippery, mmmm, sweet pussy."

Well, that did everyone in and the whoops and laughter rang through the dining room, women from the living room crowding in to see what all the commotion was about. Carol, light brown hair bouncing with the fury of her movement, quickly grabbed Mimi by the collar of her jacket and yanked her up off the floor in a strong pull.

"Mimi, you little shit, I'm supposed to be watching you, you idiot! If a lesson is what you want, I'll give you one!"

Carol's voice was strong, but ever so slightly laced with a ripple of amusement.

"Oh, Carol," Mimi said laughing, "it's all in fun, you know."

Carol cut her a look, but her eyes showed a hint of approval in them in relation to Sarah the Untouchable, the better-than-thou princess. She was a tough cookie to play a joke on, or even get next to. Carol wasn't sure if it was brilliant or asinine of Mimi. And her uncertainly irritated her even more. She tugged on Mimi and led her away from the dining table.

Getting dragged along behind Carol, Mimi turned and blew kisses to the women still laughing and watching her go, the bow in Mimi's white blonde hair slipping even further as Carol dragged her off. Carol glanced back at Mimi.

"You're twenty-five, not twelve," she chastised angrily. "Maybe it's *my* responsibility to get you past your idiotic adolescence. I told you to stay put; you didn't. I told you to stop; you wouldn't. Elan put in you in *my* charge, mine! *You* chose to ignore my commands!"

"Oh, you're a harmless one with that little bark of yours," Mimi countered nonchalantly. "Now be a sport and help me with my bow," she added, walking easily beside Carol without Carol's urging.

"I'll show you harmless, you little slut!" Carol said, turning toward Mimi and blasting her with the venom of her words as they continued walking. "You think I *like* babysitting you? The adult baby of the house? Well, I've got news for you!"

Stunned at Carol's intensity, Mimi turned her head and looked hard at Carol.

"I've never seen you like this, just relax. Don't bend yourself all out of shape," Mimi said, distractedly fixing the bow on her head and rolling her eyes at Carol.

Carol stopped in her tracks and grabbed Mimi by the shoulders. Mimi didn't see the stinging slap coming and when it landed, her head snapped to the side with the force of it. She reached up to guard and comfort her cheek, face stunned.

"I've got news for you: I've had *enough* of this shit!" Carol hissed. "You're in my charge for another two hours and I intend to knock a little sense into that spoiled brat head of yours!"

The handcuffs seemed to fly out of Carol's back pocket and wrap themselves around Mimi's wrists before she could even consider pulling them away. They went on tightly, Mimi's pale wrists going pink almost immediately, though they were not tight enough to cut off her circulation. Just enough to drive the point home.

"Ow! They're too tight, take them off me this minute, Carol! Off off off!" Mimi cried, angry now. "This is not funny!"

"No," Carol smirked, "it isn't. Not at all. And we've only just begun."

Carol yanked Mimi by her handcuffed wrists then and dragged her down the hallway to the cellar door and down the long flight of wooden steps.

"No, Carol, I don't want to play with you, dammit! Let me go! I'm going to tell Elan!" Mimi shrieked then.

Carol turned, her face close to Mimi's furious distraught face. "Go ahead," she said, everything about her challenging Mimi's helplessness. "You have no power over me, Mimi. Surprise surprise. Your mommy's not here and you're on *my* time now."

She turned and flicked on a switch and the dark cellar was transformed into an eerily lit dungeon full of shadows, equipment of many kinds standing ready nearby.

"*Stop it, Carol!*" Mimi ordered. "*This instant!*"

"That's enough of you, I have heard enough for one lifetime," Carol mumbled, shaking her head.

She grabbed a long black scarf off a nearby table and turned and stuffed it into Mimi's mouth, wrapping the ends around tightly and tying them behind the woman's head. Mimi fought her, but Carol was ready with every countermove.

"I have waited a long time for this," Carol informed her roughly, smiling with satisfaction as she pushed Mimi face-front up to a large metal cross. Mimi cried out through the gag and shook her head wildly.

"I'm sorry, I can't hear you. So I'm certain no one else can," Carol said sweetly, lifting the woman's handcuffed hands and securing them to a hook on the middle of the cross, slipping them easily into place. Next were Mimi's ankles, secured with quick-latch restraints that attached to the wooden floor, forcing her legs into a wide stance, but not excessively. Of course, this took a while as Mimi kicked like a mule against Carol's hands, but Carol won, face flushed with effort and excitement.

"Ha! I win!" she crowed, smiling triumphantly, obviously enjoying herself.

Mimi's shoes were yanked off next, though Mimi grabbed mightily with her toes trying to hang on. Again, Carol won. She threw the shoes aside with gusto.

"I win again!" she crowed. Mimi was beside herself with frustration and rage. The place shook with it, her energy rippling like an ocean through the air. Carol approached her, coming in close behind the woman.

"D'you like this?" she hissed, pulling Mimi's head back by her meticulously coiffed hair with a little tug. "I know you do, you slut." Carol yanked the bow out of Mimi's hair then, throwing it to the floor. Mimi had quit screaming and yelling by now.

Carol turned away and stepped over to the wooden table where the gag had been. Gingerly and with great decorum, she lifted a pair of glistening silver scissors off it, eyes shining as she surveyed their exquisite sharpness. She turned back and approached her captive.

"I would advise you at this time to stand very, very, *very* still. I'm afraid I don't have the steadiest hand, so..." Carol's voice trailed off.

Mimi craned her neck to see what Carol was up to. Her eyes grew round as saucers and she started her muffled yelling again through the gag as Carol moved up behind her, opening and closing the jaws of the shiny scissors.

"Bet you're wondering what I'm about to cut, to slice open," Carol said, playing with the words, enjoying her moment.

Mimi's head turned this way and that, trying to see what Carol was going to do. To her horror, she watched Carol kneel behind her, between Mimi's open, stockinged legs, and slide the impossibly sharp tip of one blade carefully into the fabric, pulling it out from Mimi's calf to do it. She made a slit just behind Mimi's left ankle, then did the same to her right. Mimi shrieked as Carol smiled up at her smugly and slid one of the cold metal blades into the left slit. Then she began methodically opening and closing the jaws, slicing the stockings and sliding up the inside of Mimi's calf, up to the inside of her knee. When she reached Mimi's knickers, Carol just pushed the blades through, cutting the fabric up the inside of Mimi's sweet thighs, and up and up. The tips of the scissors were dangerously close now to Mimi's crotch, Carol's hand and the scissors half hidden up underneath her hip-length jacket.

"Hold still," Carol whispered, "or you might lose something you'd rather keep."

Mimi held very very still, holding her breath, facing into the cross. The chilly tip of the scissors slid up against the side of her mound and Mimi almost jumped but willed herself still, only just barely. Carol chuckled.

"Ooo, almost gotcha," she said. "Now that would have been a fine sight."

Then the scissors changed their angle and closed on the crotch of Mimi's stockings, the tip up under her black satin panties, slicing right through. Mimi whimpered.

"Ooo, I just love the sound effects, it's like the score of a really great movie. Go on," she urged. Mimi was, of course, immediately, stubbornly, furiously silent.

Excited by the vision of so much flesh emerging before her eyes, Carol slid the blades around Mimi's buns and slit the fabric right up the crack of her ass, exposing two smooth, inviting cheeks. Mimi began whimpering again uncontrollably.

"Yes, there you go, there's that movie score. Damn, I

see why Elan keeps you as a pet," Carol said in honest admiration. "I've never seen such perfect, unblemished cheeks in all my life. The absolute perfect canvas." She sighed and shook her head. "And I do intend to have some of that."

Standing then and moving without thinking, Carol positioned the scissor blades at the base of Mimi's expensive jacket where it settled at her waist and, with a whoop of adrenaline rush, slit the jacket in two, straight up the back to the collar, breaking right through. All Mimi wore underneath the jacket was a black front-clasp bra. With a quick bite of the scissors, the bra was history, hanging limply from the woman's shoulders.

Mimi was shaking, gripping the longish handcuff chain in her fists.

"God, I love this, I really love this," Carol announced. She surveyed the smooth creamy flesh of Mimi's neck, back, waist, ass, thighs, calves. All of the woman's backside was exposed for her viewing pleasure. Reaching out both hands, face amazed at the action, Carol ran her hands down over Mimi's skin, over the curve of her narrow waist, resting both palms on the woman's buttocks, firm in her hands. Carol closed her eyes then and slid one hand down between those incredible asscheeks, fingers caressing the soft hair of Mimi's pussy from behind, bending slightly to touch the moist flesh of Mimi's slit and graze the round bud of her clit. Mimi pulled in her breath, and Carol felt a shiver when she touched her sex.

"You're a little slippery there, Mimi. Are you liking

this? I think so," she said, sliding her other hand around Mimi's body, inside what remained of her clothes. She caressed Mimi's smooth, firm belly, reaching down, caressing with the palm of her hand, fingers travelling over Mimi's pubic hair, both hands almost meeting as Carol reached for her from behind and in front, hands meeting at her sex.

"Now all you have to do is sit on my hands like I'm a swing. Come on and ride me, girl. I know you want to."

Mimi's sweet wetness obligingly moistened Carol's hand and, as a tease, she began to play lightly with Mimi's clit. She felt the woman's legs buckle ever so slightly, glancing up to watch Mimi's hands reassert their grip on the chains.

"Mmm hmm…," Carol coaxed. "You want more, don't you?" she asked. Mimi whimpered again. "That's all you have to give me?" Carol probed, her hands matching her tone of voice and increasing their business on Mimi's pussy, clit growing hard beneath her fingers, the flesh of Mimi's delicate pink slit becoming plump, obviously against the woman's will.

"Well, that's a pathetic display. So I'll just have to *make* you give me what I want to hear," Carol said, as if issuing a verdict, the words harsh, cold. And with that, she removed her hands, slid them free of Mimi's body.

Mimi let her breath out. She turned her head as far as she could, craning her neck to get a good view of what Carol was up to now. She could feel her mouth getting dry, but between her open legs a river was awakening. Her exposed ass presented itself boldly to Carol and Mimi could feel the arch in her back begin, feel her body take the asking position. She blushed, furious with herself, growling into the gag and shaking herself in frustration. She wanted out of this disgraceful position; but her face held a look of interest now, too.

Carol caught the look as she turned, standing at the table. "Good girl, be the animal you are," she said, smiling. "It's a start anyway. Now it's time you proved yourself to me, since no one else in this place has the guts to break you. But I do, Mimi. *I* have the guts. And you deserve it, you pampered pathetic excuse for a sex kitten. Prove your worth, Mimi. Show me you deserve that place next to Elan. That place that used to be mine!"

The whip in Carol's hand seemed to grow straight out of her fist then. She flung it through the air and Mimi watched, horrified, her eyes seeming to register its flight in slow motion as it approached its target. And when it landed squarely on the flesh of her back with a firm, convincing smack, Mimi could have sworn that her scream came out in slow motion, too, filling the room in a circling, building sweep of emotion.

"Oh, yes!" Carol chortled. "Music to my ears. More, Mimi, give me more! That's it!"

Carol wielded the whip again and watched with pleasure as Mimi squirmed and jumped, her smooth perfect skin now growing crimson in places, beginning to burn, Carol was sure. She knew the feel of the whip, but highly doubted that Mimi had ever felt its bite. Before now.

"Prove to me you're worth your weight in a good fuck," Carol called out as she beat her prey carefully, methodically, watching for signs of overuse. Mimi hung on and took it, prepared herself each time, body shivering. The woman's hands gripped the chains and she arched her back, laying her head back, too, after a few intense passes. Carol watched, enthralled, as Mimi squirmed and danced, as if in pleasure.

Yes. Pleasure.

After the tenth crack of the whip, Carol all but whispered, "You love this," wonder in her voice. The gears in her brain all seemed to fall into place. She stopped the beating and approached Mimi, grabbing a clump of Mimi's fine blonde hair and tugging it back, looking down into the woman's face.

"You want this," she both stated and asked. "You set me up to want to do this to you. Didn't you? Answer me!" Carol demanded, her body pulsing with adrenaline and effort from her ministrations.

She freed the woman's head from her grip and undid the gag.

"Go on, tell me," she ordered.

In answer, Mimi turned her head to where Carol was standing beside her and a little behind, the woman taller than she by a few inches. Face flushed, she stood on her toes a bit to reach her and pressed her lips against Carol's, tasting Carol's mouth, asking, explaining with her passion. Carol kissed her back wildly, crazy with need, beyond the surprise of the truth she'd discovered. And she thought she had been so bold, so cruel, breaking rules and norms.

*Fuck it all,* she thought, and in a blaze of desire, Carol tugged off her boots, using the opposing foot to accomplish this without interrupting the feeding frenzy of ravenous mouths. Then she reached down and unzipped her slacks, letting them slide to the floor and stepping out of them. Between her strong legs was a hard-on fit for a queen, the dildo amazingly close to her own skin tone, long and firm. The harness she wore was skin tone, as well. But Mimi, still caught in their kiss, missed the show, even the part when Carol pulled her shirt up over her head, moved her head away from Mimi's for a second and removed it; she was naked now. Breaking away from Mimi's hot mouth, Carol moved up behind her, close.

What Mimi didn't miss was the cool contact of the head of the dildo at her own maidenhead, pushing in from behind, up between her widely parted legs, up toward the center of her hungry body. Her back arched unashamedly into the asking position, her ass sticking out as she leaned against the cool strong metal structure.

Mimi's breathing was excited now, matching Carol's. With a strong hand and a firm thrust of her hips, Carol positioned her long tool, playing the tip in the river of Mimi's pussy for a fleeting moment, teasing at her entrance—and teasing herself. Overcome with the hunger, with a groan of satisfaction Carol penetrated Mimi from behind, bending her knees to get up and underneath the woman just right. Mimi assisted her, moving her body into the best position for complete fulfillment. And Carol obliged her willingly.

When Mimi's cunt could take no more, Carol played inside her, plunging in and out, deeper every time, making the woman's body yield to her a bit more with every thrust. Mimi moaned, her body heated.

"Take all of it, Mimi. Show me you're worth my efforts. Open to me, and let me come inside you," Carol whispered in Mimi's ear, her head higher than Mimi's, but close by. Carol wrapped both hands around Mimi's waist now, holding on tight as she fucked the woman, opening her to Carol's wishes. Then she leaned in and her hands slipped around, cupping Mimi's incredible breasts, the hard tips pressing into her palms, insistent.

Their bodies moved together, both women's eyes shut tight in concentration, Mimi pressed up against the metal cross, hands gripping the chains that held them captive to its side. She rode Carol with a passion, making sure to press her ass in tight against Carol's body, working the woman's clit hidden beneath the harness. This motion drove Carol crazy and she fucked Mimi hard and fast, her strong hips giving it to Mimi as the woman cried out her pleasure, Mimi's voice filling the room. Carol's rapid breathing and impassioned voice urged Mimi on.

"Yes, oh yeah, that's my girl! So deep, you're taking me so deep inside you. So wet, you're gonna make me have to blast you, have to fuck you hard," Carol said in a voice heavy with desire and sensation. She increased her speed then, Mimi riding her back as hard and fast as Carol was giving it to her, sucking her in, body pounding, close to the edge.

"Like this, hard and fast like this, Mimi!" Carol continued as their pace increased, both women sweating and shining from their efforts. "You got it, you got all of me inside you, in and out of you, yeah…c'mon, take me all the way, Mimi. Let me fuck you hard enough to come inside you."

"Yes! All the way!" Mimi screamed into the room, her pale body shimmering with sweat as she took it all, crying out in pleasure as Carol fucked her hard, harder, with all the force of an incredible passion that had consumed Carol for months, ever since she had been assigned the task of "assisting" (aka babysitting) Mimi. She had hated the woman, and then the hatred had slowly twisted and transformed into a fascination. An obsession. And then a raging fury of hunger.

She fed off Mimi now like a wild animal on its prey, completely aware that Mimi, too, was feeding off her, as well. It was the perfect buffet. Carol smiled, feeling her body pounding with the oncoming wave of an orgasm that threatened to blow her body apart.

"Yes, Mimi, take it, take it, girl!" Carol was holding on tight to Mimi now, pressing the woman's body into the cross, forcing Mimi to stand strong, firm.

Mimi did, took it all and more; took everything Carol had to give and was stronger than Carol had imagined. They fucked long and hard and as Carol held her breath, on the edge as she thrust and thrust again,

Mimi's body, too, was a fireworks display of sensation. Carol came with a vengeance then, her long tool lost inside Mimi's wet, sweating body, tight muscles pulling and manipulating Carol's dick, and her clit behind it. Carol groaned and cried out as the orgasm ripped through her body, all sensation shooting out through her clit and into the woman she held so tightly.

She could feel that Mimi was ready, too.

"Touch yourself, Mimi, c'mon, touch yourself while I fill you up," Carol's voice was urgent, insistent. "C'mon, don't be shy, I won't tell! Touch it, bring yourself off for me!"

Mimi reached down then, needing, her body a storm of pulsing, pounding sensation. As her fingers touched the sensitive tip of her swollen clit, she felt for just the right spot, the right pressure. And as Carol continued to fuck her, feeling her own aftershocks, Mimi blasted through to the other side and screamed as she came, hard and strong and with all her body's might.

The sweat between them was a slippery second skin that bound them together as one, breasts to back, hot and pulsing with life; hanging together on the cross, on each other, every last bit of energy, emotion, spent.

"God, I owe you one," Mimi whispered, breathing hard.

"Yeah," Carol said from behind her. "I guess you do."

## 3. Maxine and Sadie

Meanwhile, back in the dining room, left in Mimi and Carol's wake, Maxine and Sadie were barely able to breathe they were laughing so hard. Maxine grabbed a half-full bottle of champagne from the table and held it in the same hand as her champagne glass, then scooped up a handful of fresh strawberries in the other, causing Sadie to have to lean in with her, trapped as she was under Maxine's arm. Then Maxine turned and whispered hotly into Sadie's creamy ear: "Sadie, my dear, that is only the beginning of what I wanna do with *you* tonight. Slip up inside your slinky pants and slide my tongue around your underpants until I find the prize."

Sadie purred in response, rubbing her ear up against

Maxine's soft mouth as she spoke. The two of them turned as one away from the table and the festive crowd of rowdy women now fanning out across the floor after Mimi's entertaining display. Miss Sarah had regained her composure and walked with head held high straight out of the room and down the hall, leaving Miss Randall to tend to poor meek Jane, still bound to the chair. Jane was earnestly asking Miss Randall to please release her as Miss Sarah was obviously done with her. Her reasons were many and quite creative, sending Sadie and Maxine into another round of laughter as they moved ever forward and out of the room.

At last, they made it to the stairs and dizzily negotiated their way up the steps to the walkway balcony above. At a lamp that wore a psychedelic shade made of thin, multicolored paper, Maxine turned the handle of the nearest door and pushed it open. The two women disappeared, the door closing behind them.

Once on the other side, the women's hot breath mixed in the passing of passion as they kissed, leaning against the closed door. A black light lit the room dimly, casting them in blue highlights.

"Grace is gonna kill you," Sadie murmured as their ravenous kisses turned to soft pecks, tongues darting out to discover the sensitive skin of beautifully formed mouths, glistening.

"Mm, but won't we have fun before she does," Maxine murmured back, her tongue diving into the soft, wet cavern of Sadie's welcoming mouth. Sadie sucked

Maxine's tongue and teased it, her chest rising and falling as the need between her legs grew and expanded.

It was Sadie this time who urged Maxine further into the room, stumbling at intervals as they approached Maxine's huge king-sized waterbed. In the process, Maxine lost her grip on the now-empty champagne glass she had been holding, but managed to save the still half-full bottle. The glass broke as it hit the shag carpet, but it didn't shatter. Sadie roared with laughter, tossing her own glass over her shoulder, reveling in the crash of it as it shattered against the psychedelic painted wall. Maxine laughed, too, eyes somewhat glazed with passion and inebriation. Sadie grinned and reached into her own blouse between her breasts, retrieving a thin white hand-rolled cigarette.

"Let's get high," she said, face pink with excitement. Maxine threw her a lighter from the bedside table and Sadie bounced herself onto the bed, sliding into the middle of it, riding the rolling waves that rippled across it, back and forth. She inhaled deeply, holding the smoke, savoring it, her face full with the pleasure of it as she closed her eyes, concentrating. With eyes still closed, she held out the joint for Maxine. Since Sadie's arm didn't reach much further than where she now was lying in the middle of the big bed, Maxine was forced to crawl aboard, too. She did this with enthusiastic gusto and Sadie exhaled with a surprised cough and laugh as her body was bounced and tumbled wildly from the force of Maxine's mount. She rode the waves, eyes closed, getting higher by the minute. She opened her red-rimmed eyes as the joint disappeared from her grasp, watched as Maxine's incredible mouth sucked daintily at the joint, inhaling deeply, letting a little smoke escape, curling up in front of her half-open eyes.

"Pass it back to me," Sadie said, pushing Maxine back onto the bed and opening her mouth to cover Maxine's, to steal away the sweet smoke that hid in her mouth. Maxine opened and gave the smoke to her.

"Do it again," Sadie whispered seductively after she exhaled it. The two women were close, their bodies almost touching, teasing, concentrating intently as if passing the breath of life between them.

Maxine took another long, deep drag off the joint. She looked out at Sadie who was leaning in close now, opening that sweet mouth, asking her to share. Carefully, Maxine made a puckered small circle with her mouth and blew a steady narrow stream of smoke into Sadie's mouth. Sadie trapped it and inhaled, too, eyes glazing over as her lips stretched into a wide Cheshire cat grin. A chuckle bubbled up from deep in her throat as she released the smoke, her beautiful eyes a little glazed, interested.

Maxine was on her then, laying the woman on her back, opening the buttons of her blouse. Sadie's body rose to meet Maxine's hands, offering her firm tits to Maxine, as if on a platter, pushed up by the smooth black silk of her bra. Maxine leaned in and kissed the soft tops, tongue seeking out the sensual curves, sneaking in along the edges of Sadie's low-cut bra to tease the tender flesh, flick the edge of Sadie's nipple. Maxine grinned with pleasure as both buds grew to attention under her ministrations, pushing at the fabric. Sadie arched her back, sighing, pressing her chest into Maxine's face.

"Yeah," she whispered. "That's it, flow with me, flow with me, baby."

Maxine unhooked the black bra, freeing Sadie's full display. Her tits tumbled out, hard-tipped and fucking incredible. This last observation Maxine said aloud in an intense whisper and Sadie smiled with pleasure, breathing heavily as they moved with the waves of the waterbed. Maxine sucked and nipped and squeezed Sadie's tits, pressing them together, burying her face in them, flicking the tips with her tongue. Then, on her knees, she pressed one red satin—covered leg up and in between Sadie's legs, forcing them to open to her. Maxine moaned as she felt Sadie's heat through the fabric of the woman's jeans, her knee up against Sadie's hot crotch.

"Oh, you want me, I can feel it. Don't you? Want me more than anything right now, huh?" Maxine asked, lost in the heat, the anticipation of naked flesh—Sadie's to be precise. She imagined it soft and smooth, as soft as the sweet blonde hair that would mark the spot where Maxine ached to go.

"Mmm, I do want you," Sadie said shamelessly, an ache in her voice. She took a long drag on the joint she'd been holding, then propped herself up on one elbow and offered it to Maxine. Both women took a couple more puffs, smiling, feeding off each other's gaze. Then Sadie stamped out the butt in an ashtray on the bedside table and, to illustrate the depth of her desire, she lay back on the bed, reached down, and yanked down the zipper of her jeans, raising her ass off the rippling bed and pushing the jeans down over her hips, panties and all.

Maxine groaned with pleasure, quickly assisting Sadie the rest of the way, pants flying through the air and onto the carpet below. Sadie lay naked on the soft comforter on the bed, legs open, blonde curls marking the opening of her beautiful body, the soft curve of her waist leading up to the round gracefulness of her breasts. She massaged them, using the tips of her thumbs to tease her own nipples, eyes boring into Maxine's as the woman's gaze met hers.

"Fuck me with your tongue, with your fingers, with everything you've got," she said to Maxine, Sadie's energy reaching out to seduce the woman.

Maxine smiled. She didn't need any seducing; it was all she wanted to do tonight. Do Sadie. Maxine chuckled.

"Take off your shirt," Sadie instructed, a little bossy from below.

"You take it off," Maxine countered, smiling through a foggy stoned haze of desire. Then she laid her long, curvaceous body full out on Sadie's nakedness, moaning as she felt the woman's heat, her curves beneath Maxine's own.

"Oh, man, you feel so good, Sadie," Maxine murmured. But Sadie was busy with her arms around Maxine, unfastening the straps of her halter top. She was good, and the flimsy piece of material fell away from Maxine's torso in record time. Maxine let it stay there between them momentarily as her mouth found its way to Sadie's and they kissed hungrily. Sadie whimpered and pressed her hips into Maxine's. The dark-haired woman recipro- cated, thrusting gently, passionately against Sadie, their bodies undulating waves, matching the flow of the waterbed, the flow of the passion between them.

Sadie's head was spinning and she could feel the blood rushing through her body. Her clit throbbed with longing and in a rush of desire, she ran her fingernails down over Maxine's smooth, strong back. Maxine cried out, but Sadie's nails did not draw blood. Instead, light welts rose on Maxine's skin, feeling, under the influence of good weed, like a trail of fire down her back.

"Oh, you wicked woman," Maxine growled, her biting kisses becoming more aggressive, rougher, hands knead- ing, manipulating Sadie's body. Rudely, Maxine pressed Sadie's legs wide apart and bent her head to deliver painful little bites along the inside of Sadie's soft thighs. Sadie shivered and cried out, a wide grin stretching across her face. She opened her legs as wide as they would go for Maxine, begging with her body.

Maxine's mouth was on her then, licking and suck- ing the slippery, moist skin of her slit, teasing the woman. Again and again her soft lips passed ever so lightly over Sadie's swollen clit, only to lower her mouth just beside it or tease at Sadie's opening. Sadie cried out in frustration, arching and feeding herself to Maxine. Her voice rose and fell as Maxine slid her tongue down over Sadie's clit and plunged it deep into her blossoming pussy. Maxine could feel Sadie's body pulsing around her tongue as she thrust it deep inside her again and again.

"Oh, Max, fuck me, give it to me, aahh!" Sadie was whimpering now, sweat surfacing on her pink flushed skin. Her body moved on the waterbed in a rhythm of desire, the two women connected, mouth-to-cunt, between Sadie's wide open legs. Maxine's dark curls fell around her face, her breasts hanging deliciously as she tasted Sadie's sweat juices. Her body, too, was slick with sweat and hungry for release. She could feel her clit pounding against the smooth fabric of her satin pants and it drove her to a faster pace. Tongue emerging from Sadie's tight hole, Maxine licked three of her long, well-trimmed fingers, moaning uncontrollably in anticipation of penetrating this incredible female form before her.

"God, Sadie, you're gorgeous. And I gotta be inside, gotta get inside you and fill you and fuck you with my fingers. Will you let me, huh? C'mon, say yes, say 'yes, Max, I want you to fuck me,' you gotta say it," she teased in a rough whisper, her voice getting hoarse and throaty from the pot, her passion, and their laughter before this.

"Yes, Max, I want you to fuck me," Sadie said without missing a beat. "Damn, I want you to fuck me so bad, please, please fuck me," Sadie begged without a trace of shame or humility. She seemed almost on the edge of mad tears for wanting it so bad. Maxine was entranced by Sadie's intensity, her deep level of engagement and concentration. Every time Maxine even just barely caressed her skin, no matter where, she received a response from Sadie. The two women seemed to be connected by fine electrical filament with a current that travelled between them at their points of contact, that bridged the gap between the spaces left open.

Maxine slid one, two, then three fingers deep into Sadie's opening sex, hearing the woman groan as she took Maxine inside her.

"Oh, fuck me, Max, fuck me fast and hard, yeah, like that, aahh! yeah, fuck me…." Sadie's voice was full of effort and excitement.

Maxine's wet fingers slid in and out and deeper and deeper into Sadie, seeking out the heart of her need. She finger-fucked her with increasing speed, leaning over to place her mouth at last on the woman's raging clit. The feel of it beneath Maxine's tongue was astounding, full and hard and beating out the passion that travelled the length of Sadie's body, down down down, pushing wildly at the barrier of her clit, seeking release.

Maxine built the pace, faster, faster, thrusting harder into Sadie as the woman rode her back, forcing her body down hard onto Maxine's long fingers and crying out with near hysterical desire. Maxine flicked her tongue faster and faster in response, concentrating on the perfect light but firm touch. Sadie's body gave immediate gratification for her efforts and, as the two women glowed with sweat and excitement, Sadie's hands went into tight fists and she held her breath. Maxine fucked Sadie fast and deep, her tongue riding Sadie closer and closer to the edge until Maxine felt Sadie's entire body tense, a low rumble escaping from deep in Sadie's throat.

"Oh, shit, Max, fuck me!"

Sadie's voice was almost a scream, it was so forceful. Maxine stayed on her, using one hand now to hold Sadie's ass aloft, the other pumping away inside her as Maxine's tongue did a frenzied dance on Sadie's clit. Sadie reached up behind her and pressed both hands against the wooden frame of the huge waterbed, trying to steady herself on the waves—the waves of the waterbed beneath her raging body, and the waves of pleasure that now ripped through her, contracting her cunt around Maxine's strong hand and blasting up through Sadie's abdomen and belly. Up and up went the flame of passion, up through her chest and out to the tips of her hard nipples, until it roared up into her head and slammed back down to her clit and out and out into Maxine's talented mouth. There was a blast of a scream as Sadie's body let loose in a raining orgasm that made her arch and buck and grab the headboard. The pleasure was excruciating in its exquisiteness and Sadie reached out, lowering her hands to grab a clump of Maxine's hair in her grip, trying to stop her as the intensity shook her to the bone.

Sadie's orgasm fanned out again and again, rippling and racing through her body as Maxine continued to move inside her contracting sex, tongue still teasing gently on the blonde's exposed and sensitive clit. Sadie let go of Maxine's hair, slipping back into the grip of orgasm. Maxine's own body was wet, coating the smooth insides of her thighs where her wetness flowed out, slippery inside her satin hip-huggers. The fire of her need roared up around her as she felt Sadie's body clamp around her fingers—contract and let go, contract and let go—so fast and furious at first, then slower, slower waves, kissing her hand, loving her fingers, honoring her good fuck.

Before the last contractions of pleasure ended, Maxine slid out on the wave of one, out of the soft, tight, sexy cave. Sadie's body seemed to breath with both disappointment and satisfaction. Sadie sighed, breathing hard.

"Mmm, I hate to let you go," she whispered hoarsely to Maxine. "I really do."

In reply, Maxine ran her tongue ever so gently over Sadie's clit, sending shivers through the woman. Then Maxine ran a finger down beneath Sadie's shining crimson cunt and down between her asscheeks, teasing at her tight hole, continuing to ever so passively urge Sadie's clit back to interest with her tongue.

It worked.

After a moment, Maxine felt the pressure build again in Sadie's body, felt the slippery tip of her finger slide easily into Sadie's tight asshole. Sadie's cries as Maxine entered her were like a million fingers on her own skin, and Maxine groaned in reply, her mouth beginning again to move more quickly, though still extremely gentle, teasing Sadie's already engorged clit. Maxine purred with pleasure as she felt the incredible mystery and thrill of the female form as Sadie's clit reloaded quickly, as if fed from the sensations in her ass as Maxine fucked her hole, teasing her with two long, slippery fingers, Sadie and the waterbed moving with Maxine's strokes.

"Oh, God, yeah, oh, Max!" Sadie sucked in her breath as she plummeted through the veil of barely holding back, riding into her second orgasm, body fluttering and pounding and dancing with pleasure as her ass beat with the contractions of her body's release.

Sadie cried out wildly then, the pleasure on her overstimulated clit now bordering on painful, the sensation too intense. She bucked and tried to shake free, but Maxine wouldn't let up; wouldn't let up until she felt Sadie, once more, flutter and beat in her hands, under the swift, gentle flicking of her tongue; felt Sadie's body give its last release of energy and passion.

Sadie was almost whimpering by then, her body shining with sweat. Maxine kissed the woman's exhausted clit, sending more shivers through her lover. Then she crawled up onto Sadie's body, crazy with need.

"Come on now, come on and touch me," Maxine said hoarsely, her beautiful eyes half-closed, flying on the high of alcohol, weed, and passion.

Sadie, breathing heavily beneath her, could barely move, her body throbbing with the aftermath of her pleasure. But the energy of the woman's body against her, as Maxine threw off her own top now, offering her naked torso to Sadie, seemed to flow right into Sadie's exhausted frame, revitalizing her, and she ran her hands over the beautiful sides of Maxine's fit body, running her open palms over the tips of Maxine's perky tits, the buds hardening under her touch.

"Taste me, eat me, c'mon, let me feed you, Sadie," Maxine begged.

Sadie peeled off Maxine's satin pants quickly, noting no underclothes beneath. Instead, the dark brown curls of Maxine's pubic hair emerged to greet Sadie's gaze. In a surge of ravenous desire for this delicacy before her, Sadie opened her mouth, pulling Maxine in close, onto her knees over Sadie's face. Maxine held on to the wooden bedframe and rode Sadie's energetic tongue, groaning and breathing hard, her entire body tight sinew and muscles as Sadie fucked her with her tongue, sucked her off hard as Maxine instructed. Sadie worked her with a passion, mouth and tongue a symphony of cooperation that built the pressure deep inside Maxine. Sadie's body seemed to ache in response, willing Maxine to the edge and beyond.

She didn't have to wait long.

With a groan that started in her toes, Maxine gripped the bedframe from her position on her knees and hung her head down, eyes shut tight, dark hair wild around her face, her hat long gone. She pumped her naked ass in a frenzy, feeding Sadie her throbbing clit and cunt as every nerve in her body exploded, racing from all corners to the very tip of her swollen pulsing button, the pressure blasting out and into Sadie's mouth as Maxine came.

The waterbed beneath them was a stormy, crazy sea that rippled and waved below them like a living thing. Sadie continued to work the woman as Maxine had done to her, holding on and sucking out every drop of pleasure from Maxine's body, forcing the woman to cry out, as she wished her to. Maxine finally obliged and Sadie made one last sweet, soft pass over Maxine's clit as the woman knelt above her, legs shaking. Then Sadie's hands were caressing the soft skin on either side of Maxine's slit, loving it, sliding around back and caressing Maxine's asscheeks, allowing the woman slowly to slide down and off her face and back onto the waterbed.

They folded into each other, into one gorgeous naked body of shining, breathing flesh, panted as they held each other, stroking and exploring, hearts beating close as the waves beneath and inside them slowly subsided, but the memory of them lingering. The two women entwined their legs and kissed deeply, hands in each other's hair, the heat of their spent bodies keeping them warm, pulling each other in closer.

"Promise you won't tell," Sadie whispered then in a breathy, contented voice.

"Mm, baby, I do promise," Maxine responded, urging Sadie's mouth back to hers, lingering there to explore further.

As the kiss wound down, Maxine reached absently for the tip of the comforter that still clung to the edge of the bed. She managed to locate it and pulled the cover up over both of them. Together they sank into the warmth of the waterbed, of the comforter, and into the ocean of their deep contentment.

# 4. Spirits

In the room directly across from the psychedelic lamp-shade, Lydia found herself sitting on the edge of her bed, but the room itself was an entirely different place. A dim lamp burned on an oak bedside table and her boxes were nowhere to be found; in fact the room was completely transformed. There was a beautiful antique-looking roll-top desk, a huge wardrobe closet, and many other things she had never seen before. As she looked around a little stunned, she heard music nearby, some-where in the house, outside the bedroom door.

She wasn't alone.

Voices and laughter eased in through the walls, which were painted a pale yellow, the ceiling white.

Incredible paintings filled the walls, most of them women of one sort or another. In fact, the only things that appeared to remain the same or similar were the lace curtains on the windows, gently billowing in the warm night breeze, and her nightshirt.

Lydia looked around, then slipped off the edge of the big bed. The door to her room, this room, was closed. She walked on thick, soft carpet across to the door and opened it. Wall lamps burned in the hallway, marking each of the six rooms, including her own. Lydia noted an unusual lamp burning directly across from her room.

From the other side of the closed door right next to it, sounds of pleasure and passion wafted out and around the upstairs balcony walkway. Neither voice sounded as if it belonged to a man and Lydia smiled. She stepped out tentatively into the hall, walking across to the railing that wrapped around the entire upstairs walkway. The space in the middle was open and Lydia looked down over the railing. She gasped. Downstairs, a huge, elegant, all-out festive party was in full swing. Women wandered between the dining room and living room, some heading down the hallway. They were laughing, talking, some that she couldn't see from her post singing fervently with raucous piano rag music playing. Others were kissing, making out with a gusto, some softly, sweetly. Still others were putting luscious foods from a huge dining room table below onto small china plates. It looked as if every chandelier in the house was lit and the place smelled of wonderful baked goods, fresh coffee, and a very spiked hot apple cider. It perked in a large warmed container just below Lydia on the dining room table. She inhaled as the aroma wafted up to greet her.

The house all but breathed a heartbeat of sexual desire and seduction. Sexual tension filled the air.

"Damn," she said aloud in wonder. "Where the hell am I?"

"Twelve-eighty-two Ruby Street," a voice answered her.

Lydia whirled around. A few paces away, a woman in brown bell bottoms and a tight beige T-shirt that hugged the curves of an incredibly nice body stood leaning on the railing. She was a temptation, indeed: firm stomach, her hair straight and golden brown, shiny. She had a great smile.

"Hi, I'm Kelsey," she said. "Did you just get here?"

"Did I just…? Uh, well, yes, I guess so," Lydia said, fumbling to make sense of the woman's question.

"Hey, great. I was just getting ready to take a shower, would you like to join me?" she asked as casually as if she had just asked Lydia if she wanted coffee.

"Um, a shower?" Lydia balked. Her mind raced. "You mean, with you?" she asked.

"Sure," Kelsey answered.

Lydia smiled. "Why not?" She thought quickly. "But first you have to answer a few questions."

"Like what?" Kelsey asked, face interested, her full attention on Lydia.

"Like what year is it?" she asked.

"Beats me," Kelsey said. "I've lived here since 1973. I should be asking you that question, I think."

"That's a long time. Twenty-three years," Lydia said, looking down as she calculated. "How old are you?" she asked, glancing back up at the woman.

"Twenty-three years? Wow, really?" Kelsey's voice was full of amazement and she paused for a minute, reflecting. Lydia watched her. Kelsey spoke again.

"How old?" she repeated. "As old as the day I moved in, we all are. Maybe a warm shower will make you feel better, help you to understand better," she added, changing the subject.

"Better understand what? I live here, too. Well, not here exactly, but…," Lydia said matter-of-factly, trying to make sense.

"Sure you do," Kelsey said. "We all live here, but it's different than *your* here. It's a one-way ticket to our house from yours, but it's a helluva ride." She winked playfully. "So how 'bout that shower?" Her pretty face was expectant.

Lydia agreed to join her.

"Great," was Kelsey's reply. "And there are so many other women to meet once we're…cleaned up and presentable." She smiled at Lydia. Her eyes were an incredible shade of light brown, almost gold, with long lashes and dark eyebrows that accentuated a beautiful nose and pink mouth.

Lydia smiled, too.

"Come on," Kelsey said then. "This is my place right here." The door to the room next to Lydia's was open—the door to Kelsey's room—and the two women went inside. Lydia closed the door behind them.

"Oh, this is great," Kelsey said grinning, lifting off her tight T-shirt, turning back to face Lydia as she pulled it over her head. Lydia couldn't take her eyes off of the woman's naked torso as she raised her arms, the woman's luscious tits jiggling slightly as her face emerged again, the shirt in her hand now. Then she leaned down and, in a single motion, opened the zipper of her brown pants and was out of them in an instant, standing before Lydia in lavender bikini panties that hugged her sexy hips. She ran a hand through her hair and smiled.

"Now it's your turn," Kelsey purred, standing comfortably in her nakedness, anticipation in her eyes.

Lydia's eyes were caught by the sight before her. Obediently, she slipped her hands down to reach for the bottom edges of her nightshirt and remove it. As she pulled it over her head, before she could see again, hands caressed her sides, sending shivers down her spine. The hands quickly made their way to her breasts and Lydia couldn't help but sigh and arch her back a little as Kelsey's warm, wet mouth wrapped itself around one hard nipple, sucking and teasing it with her tongue. Lydia finally got the shirt up over her head and dropped it to the floor beside her. Kelsey's head was bent to its task and Lydia ran her hands tentatively through the woman's incredibly soft hair. She could feel Kelsey sigh, the sensation from her mouth like a cat's purr humming on Lydia's tit.

Kelsey's hands were wandering on Lydia's body, pulling her in closer. Lydia wanted nothing more than to put her tongue on Kelsey's body, let her hands explore this incredible creature, but the woman was kissing Lydia's stomach now, her mouth hungrily and enthusiastically making its way down, down, to the soft curls of hair between Lydia's legs. A flush of desire ran through Lydia and she stepped her firm legs a little wider apart, opening for the woman, welcoming her mouth.

"Ooohh, God, yeah, mmmmm," Lydia's voice was a moan of pleasure as Kelsey's tongue darted in to take a taste of Lydia's soft mound. It had been so long since anyone at all had touched her, that initial moment of contact was like a jolt of electricity that turned on all the switches that had been far too long neglected in what she thought would be a permanent off position.

"Mmmmm," Kelsey moaned, her face buried between Lydia's flexing thighs as Lydia gave herself to the woman.

Kelsey was good, her tongue a fast and furious but gentle teaser. Lydia felt her sex swell and open for Kelsey and she was overcome with a wildness that pushed at her control. Her legs were like jelly as the pleasure moved in waves through her, and Lydia fell carefully down onto her knees, her mouth finding Kelsey's, feeding on her sweet lips like a starved animal.

Kelsey fed back, their kiss becoming a frenzy of desire. Lydia pushed the woman gently back onto the thick carpet of the bedroom, laying her naked body on top of Kelsey's, the woman moving and undulating beneath her. Animal sounds escaped from their mouths as they kissed and Lydia raised her hips up off Kelsey as she felt the woman trying to slide her lavender panties down and off. Successful, Kelsey tossed them aside quickly and wrapped her arms around Lydia, pulling her down on top of her. Lydia's legs opened and she slid one leg up between Kelsey's open thighs. Her mound made contact with Kelsey's and the two of them became frantic, thrusting against each other, feeling the explosive pleasure of their clits meeting.

Lydia could feel her body building toward a release. She wanted to do everything at once with this woman: be inside her and taste her and kiss her like this and more, slip her throbbing clit back into the warm sweet cavern of Kelsey's mouth. Their tits pressed against each other and Lydia moved her body over Kelsey, the woman dancing beneath her. Lydia moved to kiss Kelsey's neck, the woman raising her chin to let Lydia in closer. She moved her body in a way that found an even sweeter contact with Lydia's now-pounding clit and Lydia threw her head back, eyes closed, mouth open in a wave of pleasure as she and Kelsey rode each other.

And as the waves came more quickly, insistently, their bodies now slippery with sweat, Lydia cried out, feeling the sweet rush of all the blood in her body racing up to her head as she hung on the edge. And suddenly, as if she were falling into a white nothingness, her head seeming to explode with light, Lydia's body rose to meet her release, but instead she fell, fell, fell through her consciousness, through the white-hot heat of their sex, out of Kelsey's room, away and away from the contact of this woman's impassioned body until she passed out of Kelsey's world altogether.

# 5. The House

Lydia gasped for breath and sat up with a jolt, her body
drenched with sweat. She tugged down the nightshirt
that had wrapped itself up around her neck and looked
around in a panic, bleary-eyed, not able to focus
completely. What happened? Where was Kelsey? Lydia's
body throbbed, on the edge of release and reaching still,
but for something that was no longer there. This was
plainly her room again, just as she'd left it: boxes everywhere. Rays of bright sunlight flooded the room through
the half-open shutters. She squinted and pushed back
the covers in a flurry, looking underneath them, desperately searching for the woman. But Lydia was alone.

She groaned heavily, realizing it had all been a

dream, and fell back onto the moist sheets of the big bed, sliding her hands down over her fevered body. Wild with need, she reached one hand down to meet the slippery wetness between her legs. But just before she made contact, a buzzer rang, then rang again, a long, insistent sound.

She froze, listening. The buzzing came again and she sat up, pushing her hair out of her face. By the third ring she realized it was the front door.

"Oh, shit!" she said aloud. "What time is it? What fucking day is it?" Gauging from the angle of sunlight, whatever day it was, it was definitely well on its way, not just beginning.

The buzzer rang again and Lydia jumped quickly out of bed. Standing in her nightshirt, disheveled, she went to the window and hung her head out. A serviceman stood on her porch, reaching for the doorbell again.

"Hi!" she hollered down to him. "Hi, I'll be right down." She watched for a minute longer to make sure he looked up, that he had heard her. He did look up and she waved. He waved back, a man maybe in his early fifties, baseball cap on his head, wire-framed glasses on his face.

"I'll be right down," she hollered again.

He nodded, stepping back away from the doorbell. Lydia's eyes noted the truck in the driveway that said GAS AND ELECTRIC on it.

"Yay," she said, the word hanging in the air as she moved away from the window. Her head felt so fuzzy and she wanted nothing more than to go back to sleep, rejoin Kelsey on the floor—of the room next door! Maybe it wasn't a dream!

Quickly, she slipped off her nightshirt and pulled on a pair of jeans and a tank top. After making an insanely fast pit stop in the bathroom, running a brush through her rumpled hair and putting her wallet in her pants pocket, Lydia went to leave the room.

She opened the bedroom door. As she stepped out into the hallway, she couldn't help but look down over the railing, mesmerized, half expecting to see the remains of the party from the night before. She let out her breath in a little huff as her eyes took in the half-empty rooms below, her familiar things placed here and there. No lights were on anywhere.

Lydia faltered for a moment, knowing the serviceman was waiting at the door. But instead, she quickly turned right, sticking her head in the open doorway of the room next door to hers. It was empty except for a few boxes. Lace curtains, similar to the ones in her bedroom, hung on the windows, perfectly still.

Lydia stood staring at the empty room for a moment, her mind recreating their sex, the heat of Kelsey's incredible naked body. Lydia's clit throbbed between her legs and she groaned in frustration.

But her clit would have to wait.

Turning back toward her bedroom door, she took a big breath and let it out slowly, trying to calm the wildness she knew must be lingering in her eyes. Quickly she descended the stairs, again half expecting to find the chandeliers lit and the place full of furniture.

Moving across the hardwood floors through the empty dining room and into the living room, Lydia opened the heavy wood and glass-inlaid door, smiling out through the shiny modern metal screen door.

"Hi, sorry to take so long getting down here. I'm afraid I overslept this morning," she said by way of greeting.

"No problem," the serviceman said, "I was just getting ready to leave, though, thought maybe you changed your mind. Then I noticed a vehicle in the garage, thought I should just try a little longer."

He said garage like "gayrodge" and for some reason Lydia wondered if it was a weird insinuation because the rest of his speech seemed perfectly flat. She shook her head, obviously feeling a little paranoid out here in the sticks.

"Glad you did," she told him firmly. "I'd have hated to have gone through another night without electricity." Lydia opened the screen door and stepped out onto the porch. Her porch, she corrected herself and smiled even wider. The day was alive with color and birdsong and warmth, the air smelling of trees and wildflowers.

"I need to start at the switch box," the man said. "It'll need some new adapters; place's been vacant a long time and in the meantime we all upgraded to new wiring and all."

"Oh," Lydia said. "Hm. I'm afraid I'm not sure where the boxes are just yet."

"I can show you that," he said. "I been here before."

There was a strange way about him, about the things he was saying, though they seemed so benign, just information. Still, she couldn't put a finger on it. He seemed friendly enough, but there seemed to be some inside joke she wasn't getting.

"Come on in, then," she told him, watching him closely. He tipped his baseball cap, picked up his tool-boxes, and stepped inside.

"Yep, been a while," he said, standing just inside the living room and looking around. "Nothing much ever changes here."

"When was the last time you were here?" Lydia asked.

"Oh, round about fifteen years ago or so. Can't remember the gal's name, the last one who did herself in out here."

"Excuse me?" Lydia inquired.

He seemed lost in thought for a moment, but stirred when she spoke.

"What? Oh, you don't know the story? You know anything about this place you bought?" he asked.

"Not much, just that it was really cheap and escrow shot through so fast I hardly had time to say yes before it was mine."

She smiled. He didn't.

"Hm. Yeah, I bet them realtors were glad to see you." He looked around again. "Switch box is in the kitchen, behind the pantry."

Lydia learned a lot about the house's wiring in the next hour or so: where the electrical outlets were and which ones worked; which ones were too old to work and how to use the switch box. She learned that his name was Mr. Langford and that he was a patient man. He showed her the upgrades to the wiring he was making and gave her some tips on fire prevention.

By the time he was finished, Lydia knew a great deal about the foundation, the house itself, and all of its gas, electric, and lots of structural information. But after that initial exchange on the porch and on the landing, Mr. Langford refused to answer her questions about his previous comments or anything having to do with who lived here over the years at all.

"That'll do ya," he said, picking up his toolboxes and making his way to the front door, waiting for her to open it for him. "Company'll bill ya and you can pay it off in four installments. If you have any problems, call this number." He put down one toolbox and took a card out of his shirt pocket. DARDEN LANGFORD, SERVICE DEPT. it said.

"Thanks Mr. Langford," Lydia told him. "I appreciate your time and patience getting me up to speed on everything."

"No problem," he offered, lifting up the other toolbox again.

"Where can I get some information about the history of this place, do you know?" she asked quickly, shielding her eyes from the sun as she stepped out onto the porch, watching him slowly descend the few steps that led down to the walk. It was a last-ditch effort of sorts. He didn't turn around, but his words travelled well enough over his shoulder and back to her.

"Wouldn't bother askin' anyone in town," he said. "But there's the old library, up the road by the market on Main. Not much new books, but lots of old ones. And old Jenny Barlow's eccentric enough to chat about this place. Make sure you tell her you just moved in here; she'll have more to say than you might like to hear." He moved down to the walkway towards the driveway. "But I wouldn't believe everything she tells ya."

Then he was hoisting both toolboxes up into the back of his truck, shutting the tailgate, and moving around to open the cab door and slide up onto the seat. The engine started, the cab door shut, and his hand popped out in a brief wave, more like a salute. Lydia waved back, standing in her jeans and tank top, barefoot on the porch. Then the vehicle moved down the drive, blinker announcing a right turn, and Darden Langford and his truck drove off down the main road toward the edge of town.

Lydia stood on the porch after he had pulled away, listening to the birds and the stillness. It was a perfect day. Just perfect. Except for the loneliness that seeped in as her body reached out for the touch of a woman who Lydia could not reach, a phantom in her dreams. No one waited inside for her. But she could feel her body anticipating, wanting.

Quickly she stepped back inside the house, closing the door. The world outside seemed to disappear, the heavy curtains in the living room and dining room creating a wall between herself and those beyond it. Lydia didn't feel compelled to open them. Instead, she ascended the staircase and peered into each empty room. Her painting supplies and easel were all set up in the one room against the far wall. Sunshine filled the space and a large empty canvas waited for her. Painting what was in her imagination for years had been enough, she realized, standing on the threshold, not entering the room. But it wasn't enough anymore. She wanted contact. She wanted everything her body longed for.

Lydia moved down the hall and entered her bedroom, searching for a particular box. Finding it, she reached in and withdrew a smaller black box, taking it over to the bed. Lydia sat down and removed the lid. Inside were sex toys: a large magic wand vibrator, dildos in a variety of sizes, wrist and ankle restraints, a butt plug, a couple of blindfolds, an old bottle of lube, a gag....

"I thought I'd never open this box again," Lydia said quietly aloud. She felt her body respond to the toys, images of SM play long past wafting out of the box like old breath filling her again. She tried to remember what it had been about Cheri that had stopped her from wanting; from wanting in the deep, intense, and aggressive way that had always been hers; a fire that had propelled her through her life.

Until Cheri choked it.

Until Lydia had let her, shamed into silence, even in her mind.

Until now.

She reached for a long cream-colored dildo that had once been her favorite, and a gold coin condom that was still tightly closed, brand new. Opening the coin, she slipped the condom over the phallus, her mind filling with memories of the view of the party in her dream the night before, and of Kelsey. Hungers she had long denied herself surfaced again, her flesh recalling the feel of the whip and the force of orgasms blasting through her.

A light sweat reappeared on her skin and Lydia quickly undressed, leaving her jeans and tank top in a little pile on the floor by the bed. Kneeling on the bed, the covers pushed to the edge, Lydia closed her eyes and remembered the feel of Kelsey's mouth on her pussy, the way it probed her, seeking entrance. She placed the dildo base firmly on the bed and straddled the long shaft that begged to be mounted. Feeling the wetness flow again between her open legs, Lydia reached down and placed the tip against her slippery opening, groaning with pleasure as she lowered herself onto the dildo, filling and filling her cunt with the sensation of fullness and satisfaction.

Lydia raised and lowered her body again and again, pumping the tool inside her. Then, reaching quickly into the box, she withdrew the vibrator, pushing the on switch with her thumb and smiling in surprise when the still-live batteries kicked the head into action. Her hand hummed with the strength of its vibration and Lydia moaned as the head made contact with her hard, sensitive clit. Waves of pleasure shivered through her and Lydia's firm thighs flexed with effort as she fucked the dildo, pressing the sweet wildly humming vibrator against her sex, plunging down hard and harder onto the long shaft and bucking forward as her clit and sex exploded with orgasm. She cried out, her face a frenzied display of passion and release as her cunt sucked the dildo, contracting and pounding against it.

Lydia lowered herself all the way down to the base of the dildo, filling herself to the hilt, keeping the vibrator travelling up and down the length of her clit and around it, pumping the orgasm through her body and out out out the tip of her clit again and again. She whimpered with the overwhelming sensations, the tension free at last after being denied much longer than just the hour or so since she had awakened from her dream. The years unfolded like a banner behind her now and she let it go, let it go with the breaths she exhaled, breathing in what she had lost, and aching like mad for more.

Lydia spent the early part of the afternoon cleaning up the house, unpacking and arranging what little she had. She had come across her collection of what she called her sex music, having tucked it all away for the last year or so. After setting up her stereo first thing, she slipped in an old favorite. The throaty singer's voice filled the place as she cranked up the volume.

"Every time I try to move I find myself fallin'...deep into the wreckage I go, where the sighs have turned to howlin'..."

Lydia sang along at the top of her lungs. "So touch me here, with the power of pain, with the power of a hunger that has no name! You gotta be strong to get to me, 'cause nobody weak could ever reach me, reach me. And honey that's sex...in the deep forgotten..."

The unpacking process went faster than she'd expected, the walls of the house shaking with the intensity of the blaring music as she worked. Lydia felt rejuvenated as she broke down the empty boxes and put them out back by the trash cans. As she walked back inside through the kitchen, the tape ended. The house rang with the quiet aftermath; everything was in its place for now, though it wasn't much.

She wanted to know more about this house, all the stories that Mr. Langford had refused to tell, and why. He had said Jenny Barlow at the library might talk. Lydia decided to find out.

The town library was a charming weathered old brick building with half-dead ivy crawling up its sides. As Darden had said, Jenny Barlow, indeed, was old herself, but she wore it well. Her hair was dyed a pleasant shade of soft blonde, pulled back in a French twist at the nape of her neck. Fine lines wrinkled her face, but her blue eyes danced with life. She greeted Lydia with a smile.

"Yes, may I help you?" she inquired of Lydia, her voice a perfect hushed library pitch as she sat casually behind a wooden desk. An old computer squatted on the desktop.

The place definitely needed renovation, and a new shipment of updated computers, Lydia thought. "Are you Jenny Barlow?" she asked, standing beside the desk.

"The same," she said. "Ms. Barlow is what I prefer. What can I do for you?"

Lydia noted Ms. Barlow's dress was a perfect 1940s-era replica that fit neatly against the old woman's petite figure. She kept herself well, make-up applied lightly and obviously quite adeptly, every hair in its casual yet perfect place. Her nails were perfectly groomed, as well, painted a pale shade of pearly pink, her hands resting demurely on the top of a very thick old book as she waited for Lydia's reply.

"A pleasure," Lydia said, smiling stupidly but sweetly. There was something about older women, especially fashionable and well-maintained older women like Ms. Barlow, that completely undid her. Of course, after today she wasn't so sure there wasn't a woman on the face of the earth that she *wouldn't* be undone by—or undressed by! Lydia blushed furiously, afraid her face would betray her thoughts. She cleared her throat and continued.

"I, uh, well, Darden, Mr. Langford, told me I should look you up. He said you might have some information for me."

"Yes?" Ms. Barlow's eyebrows were lifted in expectation now, eyes lively. Her smile brightened. "Ah, well, Mr. Langford is a very nice man. What is it you need information about then?"

"I just moved into the house up on Ruby: 1282."

Ms. Barlow's face went very pale and her smile faded.

"I, well, Mr. Langford asked didn't I know anything about the place and I don't. But I would like to get more information about it and he said you might be able to help me. Are you all right?" Lydia asked.

Ms. Barlow's eyes were clouded as if she were lost in thought, far away. "I see. Yes, I'm fine. My, it took fifteen years this time." Her voice was a thoughtful whisper.

Lydia remained silent, hoping the woman would continue after leaving such a loaded comment hanging in the air. When she didn't, Lydia shifted her weight and cleared her throat again. "What do you mean?" she asked. "Why has the place been vacant so long?"

"You don't know anything about the house, nothing at all?" Ms. Barlow asked, surprised.

Lydia recalled her dream last night, but kept silent about it, not wanting to come off sounding like a nutcase. "Just that escrow closed in record time and the real estate agent seemed elated that I wanted it."

"You haven't met anyone there then?" she asked.

Lydia faltered. She knew she was a terrible liar. "No," she stammered anyway.

"Ever heard of Sarah Rondelle?" Ms. Barlow looked back at Lydia curiously, watching her closely.

"No, I'm afraid not." Lydia was relieved to have a true answer to give.

"Ah, well, Sarah was quite the up-and-coming item in the early 1940s fashion scene." And just as Mr. Langford had suspected, Jenny Barlow started to talk.

"Her husband was an extremely jealous man; took a job out here, which was just the sticks then, nothing more than a settlement really. He made her leave the cities behind—and her lover, I might add—and in those days, well, she didn't believe she could take care of herself. No woman did, you know."

"What happened to her?" Lydia asked.

"She died one night, sleeping in that house of yours, not even thirty yet. She wasn't the first one either, or the last. First one was found dead in 1910, looking like a sleeping angel in her bed."

Ms. Barlow stood up then and took Lydia over to some old books and journals. She pulled out old documents about the house and the town and the history of both and handed them to Lydia. She was a bottomless font of knowledge about the place. Once she got started, she wouldn't be stopped. When the library closed thirty minutes after Lydia arrived, Ms. Barlow invited her to have some coffee and sit in the little kitchen at the back of the old library building. They sat at a little round table. Lydia took a big sip of coffee as Ms. Barlow continued.

"Kelsey was the last one to live there; 1975 was the year, I think," she said and Lydia almost spat out her coffee all over the table and Ms. Barlow.

"What did you say?" she asked after gulping quickly, her face a pale display.

"I said Kelsey, Kelsey Norton. She was a pretty girl, moved in in 1975; a wandering wild soul who had inherited some money from an especially wealthy aunt of hers. I met her, very nice person. And she had this really beautiful shiny brown hair that always caught the sun and shimmered, making her whole face just shine. Are you all right dear?" Ms. Barlow asked as she glanced at Lydia.

Lydia had put her cup down and was coughing into a napkin, pretending it was the coffee that was making her cough. "Oh, yeah, fine, I just swallowed wrong, that's all. Hot coffee, the wrong pipe, you know." She tried to smile and laugh it off, but Ms. Barlow saw right through it. She paused for a moment, studying her.

"Well," she continued slowly, watching Lydia. "You really should be careful. Very careful," she said pointedly.

"Right," Lydia replied, her voice a little strained from coughing. "Maybe I should let it cool a little longer. Go on, though, I'm listening."

"Where was I?" Ms. Barlow asked after a moment.

"Kelsey," Lydia managed to choke out, clearing her throat and regaining her composure.

"Well, it wasn't more than a couple of months before she was found dead, the house empty, everything in its place. We looked up her relatives, but they hadn't spoken with her. No one had and no one did, never knew what happened exactly. That made at least a dozen women missing in the lifespan of the house, and who knew how many more that no one heard about?"

"When was the house built?" Lydia asked.

"Turn of the century, by a very wealthy, very wild and, well, unconventional young lady whose extremely well-off parents both died from influenza, or some such illness way back when. Left her everything. She didn't have any brothers or sisters."

Ms. Barlow sipped her coffee, thoughtful.

"She built the house herself the year after they died, had a large circle cleared out in the middle of that forest that still fans out behind the house. At that time hers was the only place for at least twenty-five miles north or south. Hardly anyone had automobiles yet, just horses and buggies, carriages still."

"Why did she do it?" Lydia asked. "I mean, why did she sink her money into putting up a house in such an isolated place in the woods?"

Ms. Barlow looked down and smoothed the lap of her skirt, then looked back up at Lydia, who sat with her elbows propped up on the table, chin resting in the tops of her hands.

"There were and still are, many rumors about this girl, Moira. She was thirty-one when her parents died, no brothers or sisters and not promised to anyone—and not interested in bein', I might add. She was known to have quite a temper but she was very bright, loved books. Hard to get along with, though, is how people described her sometimes, wild, passionate. She cooked okay, loved riding horses, but she didn't like lacy things, or even dolls when she was a child. She was always telling her mother she wanted a brother to play with, but from what I heard her mother had some complications after Moira's birth and couldn't have any more children."

Lydia nodded in understanding.

"Her father was quite a hunter, but he never would let her go out with him, though she begged him. According to some, he had a hard time handling her temper, too. But he loved her something fierce. That much, everyone knew."

Lydia smiled. She sounded great.

"Well, Moira—Miss Zane—certainly wasn't alone, not hardly. There were rumors of great, lavish parties at her place—your place. She'd hire female house servants to help throw the parties and they had to swear to secrecy. Anyone who joined her staff had to sign papers that swore them to silence."

Ms. Barlow looked out the small window beside the table. It looked out into a little clearing with benches situated here and there. The sun was beginning to set.

"Thing was," she continued, "no one ever saw any male guests come and go, and she never hired any men to tend the house or serve her guests. Some very, well, *dashing* women I'd guess you'd call them, but no men."

Ms. Barlow blushed. "Do you know what I mean by 'dashing'?" she asked, looking Lydia straight in the eyes.

Lydia looked back at her, stunned, remembering the

all-female party downstairs, and Kelsey, the old look of everything in the house. She understood completely now and nodded dumbly.

"Yes, I think I do," she said quietly.

"I thought you might," Ms. Barlow replied, pausing for a moment. "Thing was, Moira was found dead, see, in the same bed you more than likely inherited with the house like everyone else."

Lydia flashed back to her bedroom this afternoon, kneeling on the bed, overwhelmed with desire. She shivered.

"No one in town would ever buy any of the stuff from inside the house each time there was an auction after each death. Anyway, she and Constance—a stunning girl who was very into the fashions of the time—they were found dead together, both of them in that bed, naked as babies. Constance's daddy was very wealthy and he had a fit when the police found the two women in Moira's bed together, not only naked but dead as nails. And an autopsy didn't turn up anything but a heart attack. For no apparent reason. Why, they weren't even well into their thirties yet!"

"The same bed? The four-poster in the upstairs bedroom?" Lydia asked, swallowing hard.

"Yep, the same," Ms. Barlow confirmed. "And those other women, too. Some pretty and all of them *understanding*, if you know what I mean; like you I think, most of them. And who knew about the others?" Ms. Barlow winked and finished off her coffee.

Lydia's mind was reeling, images of a dozen beautiful dead women lying in the same bed she had slept in last night. Images of what they might have done together, in that bed, joined the ranks of her thoughts. Her body responded, imagination running rampant. A mixture of horror and fascination.

"Well, gotta get home to my kids and feed the husband," Ms. Barlow said, interrupting Lydia's daydreaming. "It's the road I chose and I drive it every day regardless of whether I feel like it or not." Ms. Barlow smiled at Lydia and picked up their empty coffee mugs from the table as she stood up.

At the front of the library a few minutes later, Ms. Barlow unlocked the front door to let Lydia out. Lydia moved through the doorway, arms full of books and journals, and out into the approaching night, turning back to wave good-bye with her fingertips, the rest lost under the books.

"Good-bye," Ms. Barlow said, waving too, her face looking happy but concerned. "You be careful now. You're a nice girl."

"Thank you, thanks for everything," Lydia called back. "I learned a lot." She smiled and turned away from the library door, walking down the steps toward her car.

By the time Lydia pulled into the garage at 1282 Ruby Street, a full moon was beginning to rise through the trees, the stars pushing their way out through the thick blanket of sky. Somewhere way up in the high trees behind the looming figure of the two-story plantation-style house, a hoot owl hooted right on cue, as if announcing her return.

Lydia wasn't so sure she wanted to sleep in the bed again that night. She paced the floor in the bedroom dressed in her bathrobe and slippers, glancing at the bed that she had covered with her comforter. She decided to situate herself in the comfortable chair she'd brought into the room from downstairs, putting the floor lamp by it, making a nice cozy reading area. She sat there flipping through the journals, feeling drowsy, enjoying the sounds of the rural night. The books were dry, containing a lot of census information, specific building stats on the house, and dates of sale, etc. Lydia yawned, her mind wandering back to her dream the night before.

"So," she said aloud to the room, not so sure it was empty at this point, even though her eyes saw an empty room. "What's it gonna be tonight?" she asked the house. There was no reply of course, but Lydia suddenly felt a wave of sensation pass through her, desire surfacing again. The herstory of the house seemed to echo in her ears and she could swear she heard laughing, music....

"Ho," she huffed, closing the books and piling them on the little table next to the chair.

"What I need is telephone service," she said, thinking of at least ten people she would like to have called tonight. Lydia had contacted the phone company from the library after they hadn't shown up at the house today. Turned out they'd forgotten her and couldn't get out to her place until the day after tomorrow. Actually, Ms. Barlow said it was tough to get anyone out to that old house; lots of rumors, she said. So, two more days without a phone. And not one lesbian bar or women's coffeehouse or gay anything for miles and miles around. What was a girl supposed to do way out here in the middle of fucking nowhere?

"Well, shit, I *live* in lesbian central!" she laughed out loud, her mind filling with thoughts of the lavish wild parties that had taken place here. Ms. Barlow was a great storyteller. Lydia wanted more than anything to go to one of those parties, try out her rekindled passions.

She stood up and wandered out into the hall, hitting the light switch that lit up the upstairs walkway. Leaning on the railing outside her bedroom door, she looked down into the dark dining room below. She half expected to find a party going on as in her "dream." Of course, it was just a dark dining room. She glanced over at her art studio room, concerned that for some reason she hadn't been feeling like painting, which was the whole reason she'd moved out here in the first place. Instead, she felt restless, as though she was waiting for something. She had tried the TV earlier in the night, just to bring some familiarity to her surroundings other than the hick radio stations, but way out in this rural little town there were very few choices (other than bad talk shows and sitcom reruns). Instead, a relaxation tape played quietly on the tape deck in the bedroom, a gift for her birthday a couple of years back. From Cheri.

Suddenly, Lydia couldn't stand the music anymore, realized she hated it actually. She turned and walked briskly across the bedroom floor to the tape deck that sat on the bedside table, stabbing the stop button and ejecting the tape. Then, very methodically, she pinched the tape inside the cassette and ever so carefully began to pull it out of its case, unraveling the horrible recording, wiping out the tape forever. Lydia smiled; she'd never done that—wrecked something that Cheri had given her, just for the hell of it.

It felt great.

Lydia spent the next hour blasting the cassette tapes from her old private sex collection while she sat on the thick carpeted floor and unraveled every relaxation tape that Cheri had ever given her until not one more tape, not one more memory, remained alive.

"Here's to my reawakening," Lydia said, reaching for the beer she'd brought up from the kitchen. It was starting to get warm, but she toasted her freedom anyway. "Fuck you and your little relaxation tapes, stale window-closed air, and uptight ass. I'm here to reclaim myself. Come and get me, girls. I'm on the make again." Lydia laughed and threw the dead tapes into the trash can, where they landed with a satisfying clatter.

"What the hell, I'm not afraid of you," she said to the bed and anyone who might be in it that she couldn't see. Then she turned and went into the bathroom, switched on the light and looked at herself in the mirror. Her face was flushed and her eyes looked tired, but definitely alive. She smiled at herself, reaching for her toothbrush. She brushed her teeth, her hair, washed her face. And then, just for the hell of it, she took the washcloth and washed her privates, too.

"Hey," she said to herself in the mirror, "you never know. Ghosts—if there really are such things—might like a clean pussy, too."

Then she switched off the light in the bathroom and crossed the cleared floor to the bed. Only a few boxes remained in the room, pushed up against the far wall by the walk-in closet. The place was looking pretty good. She glanced at the clock: 11:59. Sighing, she slid in between the sheets and pulled up the covers, enjoying the warm softness of the cotton on her skin. Yes, she was a little bit weirded out about dead people being found in this bed, but it was so comfortable. It was still strange to sleep alone, but she wasn't so sure she was alone really. Lydia smiled at the thought, imagining Kelsey. But it was Moira Zane who stayed in her thoughts tonight. Lydia wondered what she had been like to be with….

Closing her eyes, Lydia's mind wandered off, thinking of all the women who had lived in this house, but especially of Moira Zane. She would have loved to meet her, certain she would have liked to play as Lydia did: a little dangerously, spending every ounce of passion at each encounter.

With a subtle shift, the sights and sounds of the party in her dreams the night before slowly seeped in. It

was almost as if, as she closed her eyes, falling off to
sleep, as if the house lights came on, the music slowly
grew from a hint to a wild song, and the house itself
wrapped its walls around her, shimmering as the
present gave way to the past, locking every door in her
mind but the one that led her back to the house of spirits.

# 6. The Second Coming

Knocking. Someone was knocking at a door. Her door. Lydia opened her eyes to the dark bedroom. Light flooded in under the bedroom door, music sizzled through the house, igniting the warm night with festive laughing and singing, songs with swing beats and improvisational passages.

The knocking came again.

Quickly, Lydia sat up, mumbling, "Yes, yes, I'm coming." She slipped her body out from under the warm covers, sliding her feet into slippers, and wrapping her bathrobe around her fit frame and nightshirt. Was it daytime? Nighttime? Was there someone knocking downstairs, or here at her bedroom door? What if it was a burglar?

These thoughts and others caught in her brain, her body way ahead of her sleepy head. It propelled her forward, eyes half-closed, to the door. Carefully, she opened the door just a crack. Lydia stood, dumbfounded, staring at a gorgeous woman on the other side of the threshold. Her hair was shiny and straight, pulled back in a swooping, loose bun, wisps of fine hair escaping, framing her beautiful heart-shaped face. She wore a slinky, shimmery, pleated gown with a 1920s design. The gown was sleeveless, exposing soft, smooth shoulders, and a long, graceful neck.

"Hello," the woman said, smiling a seductive mixture of casual nonchalance and hungry huntress. "We've been waiting for you to come downstairs, so are you coming or not?"

"Oh, uh," Lydia stammered, rubbing her sleepy eyes. This was odd, she was awake, but was she?

"Well, c'mon, we don't have all night now," the woman said impatiently, casually running one open-palmed hand over her chest, cupping one breast, leaving her hand there. The motion pulled Lydia's eyes down to the woman's torso. The thin, nearly sheer fabric of her dress hugged the woman's incredible form: the slight soft curve of her belly, the slope of her full, pointed breasts. The woman wore no bra, or panties from what Lydia could tell from the well-fitted skirt that hugged her sexy hips.

Lydia's body responded, the nipples of her own firm chest hardening beneath her nightshirt and robe. She sighed unconsciously.

"Come downstairs," the woman said seductively. "I know you want to."

The woman's voice was a purr, a coercion so intense Lydia couldn't help but lean in toward her, moving ever so slightly around the door.

"I brought some things for you to choose from; you obviously can't go to a party dressed like that. Let me in and I'll do you up right. But you have to ask me in," she added.

Lydia thought for a moment. Past and present collided. She glanced around the room: It was hers, as she had left it when she went to sleep. But here was this woman, and the party outside her door. A time warp, but with a twist?

"Come in," Lydia said, opening the door a little further to allow the woman to pass into her room.

The smile on the woman's face was beautiful and excited. She seemed extremely pleased to enter Lydia's room. She sort of sashayed into the room, seemingly relieved and letting out a little breath of surprise. "Yes, a very nice room, too," she said to Lydia. "If a little sparse."

Lydia couldn't help but laugh at the woman's brutally honest assessment. She liked her electric energy.

"Well, I had no idea you were coming or I would have, you know, bought some more furniture," Lydia chuckled. But her chuckles trailed off as she watched the woman in the slinky gown begin unhooking the back of her dress. The dress slid off the woman's smooth glowing shoulders, ending up in a soft pile at her feet.

She stood naked before Lydia except for her slip-on heels.

"I need a little research done," she said. "Would you be so kind as to…assist me?"

Lydia stared, face glowing with pleasure. Damn, she was fine, all curves and angles and points of seduction. The woman stepped her feet apart a bit wider, opening the space between her thighs, her clit peeking out as the lips of her sex opened, soft pubic hair beckoning. She displayed herself with abandon, chin up, eyes clear and intense…and hungry.

"Come here," she demanded.

How could Lydia say no? Enraptured, she turned and walked toward the woman who stood at the edge of the thick, soft rug a few paces away. She left the door open, pulled to move in the woman's direction.

"Kneel," the woman said, almost in a whisper.

*Absolutely*, Lydia's mind replied without question.

She knelt in front her.

"Take off your robe," she instructed, and Lydia opened the sash, letting the robe fall to the floor around her kneeling figure. Her nightshirt was an extra large over-sized T-shirt that fit her more like a knee-length sporty nightgown. For some reason, the woman didn't ask her to remove this. The thought barely crossed Lydia's mind because the next moment she felt a hand gently on her head, indicating with a light nudge where her services were requested exactly.

At that moment there was absolutely nothing Lydia

wanted to do more than dive into the beautiful river opening to her from between this woman's incredible soft-skinned thighs. It was as if she'd waited her entire life to get to this very task.

The woman took a half-step closer and Lydia's mouth met the sweet flesh of the woman's mound. Her tongue emerged of its own accord, seeking out the soft flesh, and when the woman moaned softly—her body settling in against Lydia's gently probing tongue, legs opening just a little wider to accept all that Lydia had to give her—the room began to spin. Lydia could feel her heart beating in her ears, the rush of the ocean of her blood pumping, as if all her senses were suddenly super-powered, ears receiving the rustle of wild night animals, tree leaves, and needles shimmering in the light breeze, the sigh of the woman's breath from above her as the woman's hands played in Lydia's hair, coaxing.

The woman's body began to thrust gently against Lydia's now more swiftly moving tongue, with rhythmic pelvic thrusts, feeding herself to Lydia. The woman's musk was like an aphrodisiac to Lydia, making her want more and more of the sweet nectar that coated her tongue, her lips. She dove her tongue deep into the woman's slit, opening her, fucking her. The woman responded with a deep groan, lowering herself ever so slightly onto the peak of Lydia's tongue, up and down, fucking Lydia back.

Lydia slipped out then, danced on the woman's clit, up the sides of her flowering opening, feeling the electric pulses flash just beneath the surface of sensitive, tender skin under her touch. And then the woman was losing control, tugging on Lydia's locks and feeding herself more ravenously to Lydia's devouring mouth as her pleasure mounted.

"Oh, yes, mmm, ah…more," the woman chanted from above, the words falling like leaves in an autumn wind, spiraling down to coat Lydia with the woman's pleasure. Lydia's mouth licked and sucked and gently flicked the woman's clit, riding her now as the woman rode her back, the two of them connected at the point of the woman's pulsing swollen bud. Faster and faster the woman rode her, Lydia responding with quick light movements, teasing out the pleasure, calling out the release from deep inside the woman's naked, glowing body.

And then there was a sort of scream that filled the room, a high-pitched moan and cry. A wild shudder ran through the woman, forcing her hips to thrust and thrust again into Lydia's wildly working mouth. Lydia sucked in the hard throbbing button of the woman's clit and worked the contractions of her orgasm, touching every spot she could reach with the hot wet cavern of her mouth, the soft flesh of her strong lips. The woman's breath came in shaky, punctuated inhalations and then she held it, riding, riding the wave of pleasure to its crashing, breaking, dispersing resolution.

Still between the woman's legs, the woman's long-fingered hands resting on Lydia's head, Lydia smiled, eyes closed, savoring the taste, the smell, the sensations of the woman's body, the sound of her labored breathing. She licked her lips and inhaled the joyous scent of sex and passion, feeling the tingling excitement of her body's own need, the deep pulsing of her cunt, calling out for attention.

"Well, you moved rather quickly, didn't you, Dawn?" a woman's voice said.

"Yes, I'd say so!" agreed a second, higher-pitched voice behind Lydia.

Lydia jumped and turned her head quickly, startled out of her reverie. It was like waking up a second time and yet she still seemed to be dreaming the same dream.

Two women were laughing, standing at the bedroom door, just outside it.

"How in the world did you get her to let you in? I really must hear this one!" the first voice said.

The words came from a thin, androgynous woman in dressed in a 1930s-era man's-style black smoking jacket and matching pants, white shirt, black men's shoes and, of all things, a monocle. It hung at the end of what appeared to be a black ribbon, sitting on the woman's flat chest like a medallion. Her hair was cut short, flat bangs cut straight across and then straight like a box on the sides. This framed a long handsome face with large eyes.

"Don't be a boor now, ask her to let us in, or come downstairs and join the party!" said the other woman with a little whoop of celebration as a period.

She was dressed in full flapper garb: red flapper dress with full fringe and matching fashionable headwrap, and very high-heeled shoes. She seemed absolutely and perfectly at home in her costume and tottering around on those shoes. Lydia was amazed, never one to be a master of very high-heeled maneuvering. The flapper's face was round and rosy, heavily and perfectly made-up and glowing with enthusiasm. Her bobbed hair bounced as she did.

"Come on, come on then!" she practically squeaked, hanging at the threshold, but obviously fairly bursting with wanting to come in. Lydia had no idea why she didn't just barge right in. She, herself, felt a little like a cat caught with a stranger's pet bird in its mouth, the bird wriggling now as the woman beside her quickly leaned over and pulled up her long, clingy gown, fiddling with the zipper that zipped up the back. Her soft, shiny hair was still in its place, just a wisp or two escaping in front of one ear.

"Oh, Zoe, do you always let Rose just drag you around the house like a puppy?" Dawn barked. "I thought everyone was cutting the cake in the dining room? What in the hell are you doing up here anyway?"

Her voice rose in pitch as she shot the question at Zoe. There was no malice in her words, really, just indignation laced with playful amusement. She didn't seem *too* upset about being discovered; rather pleased, actually. She leaned over and put out her hand to help Lydia up off the floor. Lydia accepted after a moment and stood next to her, looking at the women in the doorway.

"Miss Randall and I followed you up here, if you must know," Rose said as though revealing a secret. Zoe, Miss Randall, ignored her.

"So what is your name?" Zoe asked Lydia very formally, lifting her monocle to take a better look. Squinting from such a far distance, she lowered it again and waited expectantly.

"Uh," Lydia considered lying for some strange reason. "Lydia," she told them.

The woman next to Lydia turned and smiled, dreamy eyes sparkling. She put out her hand again with a mischievous grin on her pleasant face.

"I know. You can call me Dawn," she said. "Pleasure to meet you, Lydia," she added, emphasizing the word "pleasure."

Lydia had to laugh, her chuckle loosening the edge of the adrenaline rush that initially hit when the women first broke up their party. Dawn chuckled, too. She didn't seem to notice that the two women were hanging out at the door, still waiting there, listening, obviously expecting some sort of response to their questions and comments. Dawn ignored them, turning to face Lydia.

"Now, what I was saying earlier is that you can't go downstairs in just a big shirt," Dawn said, picking right up where she had left off, as if her own clothes hadn't come off at all and nothing had been exchanged between them.

"There are a few different choices in this box. I brought a variety so you can choose what you fancy. In clothes, that is…" She smiled again and winked, then turned and headed for the door. Just outside it, she tugged on a large box, scooting it into the bedroom.

"She didn't ask *you*, did she?" Dawn said to the two women as she moved past them and back into the bedroom. Rose rolled her eyes and stuck out her tongue in a quick little dart, like a child hiding the action from a parent. She looked at Zoe to see if she had seen, but Zoe was busy ignoring both of them, eyes on Lydia instead. The two women at the door seemed extremely interested in staying put at Lydia's bedroom door.

"Here," Dawn said with a grunt as she pushed the box up next to Lydia. Then she tugged open the top panels, exposing a colorful group of items inside. "Hurry up now and pick what you like. We'll need to comb out your hair and I'll help you get dressed, of course," she said.

"I'll be happy to help, too," Rose called in her lilting voice from the doorway. "Just ask me in, please."

"Don't do it," Dawn said under her breath to Lydia, who disregarded their bickering—she had some sense that inviting in the whole company wasn't a good idea anyway. Instead, she lifted out a wide array of garments, from a couple of different period suits in mannish styles to a variety of dresses spanning the decades in design, and everything in between. They felt like authentic antiques, some of them, the fabrics very different from modern cloth. There were even bell bottoms and a halter top, psychedelic style.

"Of course I had no idea what you might like, so there are a few options—I lifted a few things from everyone's wardrobes. And when you're dressed, we'll all join the party together," Dawn said, addressing the two women, as well.

"Looking forward to it," Zoe said, looking Lydia up and down as Dawn aggressively lifted her nightshirt over her head. It wasn't that Lydia *wanted* to get naked in front of these strangers, God knows, but things just seemed to unfold the way they did, more like happening *to* her, rather than her having any impact on the outcomes.

Sort of.

As she stood momentarily nude on the carpet, in her bedroom with these spirits, these ghosts from her dreams, it was as if everything that had ever made sense no longer came together quite so conclusively. She wasn't really so sure she was still asleep. Time warped and bent and she didn't *feel* asleep. And this, this place and these scenes that had made no sense except in the definition of dreams, began gradually to develop a meaning of its own—a life of its own.

She liked it here.

Lydia allowed the woman to fuss over her for about five minutes, long enough for the woman to coerce Lydia into letting her do her hair. But Lydia drew the line at choosing her clothes. The other two waited, incredibly patient, at the door, with Rose lending comments and suggestions at a continuous pace. She wasn't about to be turned away by anyone, obviously. Lydia realized that even if she wasn't invited in, Rose would make do with pushing her personality and her presence into the room, if not her physical body.

Not that she had a bad physical body, either. Energetic enthusiasm could be fun.

Lydia smiled at Rose as Dawn finished with her hair.

Rose smiled back and waved excitedly.


Outside, through the door across the open space from Lydia's, a woman emerged, head bowed, closing the door behind her and moving quickly around to the staircase, oblivious to the two women hovering at the doorway on the other side. She descended into a cacophony of music: 1920s jazz radiating from the living room and from the other side of the house, in the huge sunroom, Purple Haze guitars rocked and rolled the place. The two soundtracks met in the middle, creating a somewhat headache-inducing level of noise, at least in Elisabeth's opinion.

"God, I hate it when Kenya gets an urge to blast that stuff, it's just awful," she said. Elisabeth wore a long corseted turn-of-the-century dress with a big hat with plumes on it. She stood at the long dining room table, sampling some of the incredible array of foods. The woman beside her wore similar clothing, but her outfit was much smarter, tailored on masculine lines with a waistcoat, slacks, and double-buttoned vest, stiff-collared white shirt, man's black tie. She wore a flat boater hat on top of her head, thick wavy hair pulled back neatly and pinned up off her neck. Her face was smooth-skinned, ruddy-cheeked, with well-chiseled lips, nose, a lightly cleft chin, and light brown eyes.

"Oh, Elisabeth, you have to learn to love all of it, to roll with the times as they change. It can't be 1911 for you forever, you know. That's just the way it is. And besides, you'll need new partners one day...."

Elisabeth looked up at her and raised her eyebrows. "Will I now?" she asked sarcastically.

"...and they certainly won't be from your day and age," the woman finished.

"Hm, well, my dear Moira, I think I might not have exhausted *all* of my options just yet," Elisabeth said dryly, her eyes riveted on the woman just descending the staircase. "There's Kathy and, mmm mmm, look what's she got on tonight." Elisabeth was shaking her head in admiration. "I will be leaving you now," she tossed to Moira, checking to make sure her hat was situated correctly. "Have a lovely time, dear."

Elisabeth put down an empty glass she'd been holding and moved quickly across the room toward the living room, where Kathy was headed, too.

"Kathy, dear," Elisabeth called in her sexy voice. Kathy turned at the sound and as Elisabeth arrived at her location, Kathy's surprised mouth was covered by Elisabeth's. The kiss was long, languid, searching; experienced. When it ended, Elisabeth spoke.

"Would you like to spend some time with me tonight?" she asked intimately.

Kathy, who wore a flowery mini-skirt on her trim figure, long multicolored beads, a tight-fitting short-sleeved knit top with no bra, and platform shoes, eyed Elisabeth with surprise.

"Sure," she said, as if there were no question about it. "Very cool. I'm free tonight even."

"Good," Elisabeth said with a smile, placing her hand on Kathy's shoulder. "I do hope you're good with eye hooks," she added with a soft chuckle.

Kathy laughed, shaking her head and making her long bleached hair shimmer and dance. Her voice was husky from too many cigarettes.

"I'm worth the effort," Elisabeth added.

"I bet you are," Kathy responded, making an invisible trail with one finger, following the curve of Elisabeth's breasts, the tops of them spilling out above her corset, held aloft by her form-fitting long dress with a slew of eye hooks running down the back of it.

"I don't know you very well," Kathy said. "But I'd like to get to know you better. We're awfully…different."

Elisabeth sighed under the woman's touch. Moira was right: new partners were always a good idea—from any era. She especially liked the uninhibited girls from the sixties. Kathy would be fun, she was sure.

"Oh, not so different," she sighed, running her hands down the woman's smooth arms, taking both Kathy's hands and smiling knowingly. Kathy's face lit up with an idea.

"How 'bout we catch a dance in the sunroom?" Kathy asked enthusiastically, eyes taking in every curve of Elisabeth's body, her oval face, high cheekbones, a fine canvas of beauty and puckishness.

Elisabeth groaned under her breath at Kathy's suggestion: the sunroom meant Jimi Hendrix, acid rock. Elisabeth tried to understand the music, she really felt she tried, but it just seemed like screeching electrical feedback to her no matter what. And besides it gave her a headache.

But Kathy had said yes. Yes! So there, Moira! And her large round tits and firm ass were too much to let go so easily tonight; not to mention her wonderful blue eyes: huge, long-lashed, and dreamy. Ten years from now was a long time. Why wait for new partners when she could start right away? Elisabeth realized that, in this case, she'd have to compromise to get what she wanted.

"Okay," she told Kathy. "The sunroom it is."

Kathy smiled brightly and the two women moved across the dining room and down the short hallway to the sunroom at the end of the hall. Music blared in a wall of sound that met them at the door as Kathy graciously opened it for Elisabeth. Elisabeth took a deep breath and entered Kathy's world.

Moira watched them go. She smiled and chuckled at Elisabeth's way. She, herself, found it more difficult to bed just any woman. It had been just she and Constance for years; lord knew how many years at this point. But something antsy had begun growing inside Moira and she could feel herself pushing Constance away. It was all too obvious. And just the other day she'd felt a new presence, something wild and alive and seductive. Someone nearby that smelled and felt and hummed with a life-force that obsessed Moira.

She could not sleep the past two nights because of this. Something, someone, was coming.

As Moira let her thoughts roam, her eyes rested casually on two women across the table: Alice and Ruth were going at it on one of the high-backed chairs, Alice perched on Ruth's lap, facing her, wearing only a pink 1930s slip and bra set, no panties, her slim legs straddling Ruth's, slip hiked up around her hips.

*Yes, someone is, indeed, coming,* Moira mused, enjoying the scene. She lingered where she stood, watching unobtrusively.

The two dark-haired women moved together on the chair, undulating backs and buttocks, entwining arms, legs, their bodies rippling and shimmering as if on the motion of an outside force that moved them both as one. Their faces were a study in passion, hands all over each other, exploring soft, feminine shoulders; exploring female form, naked thighs against naked thighs, Alice's wide open as she straddled Ruth.

They kissed long and deep, Ruth's hands reaching around to release Alice's breasts from their captivity. As the clasps opened, the bra slid off Alice's glistening shoulders, glorious round tits tumbling out to meet Ruth's aggressive hands. Alice moaned as Ruth leaned down and flicked one of Alice's hard, puckered nipples with her tongue, one hand caressing the other.

"Oh, Ruth, yes, mmmm," she cried softly, arching her strong back and hooking her feet up under the chair for leverage, the better to ride her naked pussy against Ruth's, beneath her.

Ruth, herself wearing nothing more than a black one-piece slip and black stockings with garters, black hair falling around her face, sighed as Alice's hand ventured up underneath her slip, fingers caressing the sensitive skin of Ruth's soft inner thigh, reaching for more.

"Yeah?" Moira could hear Ruth teasing as she took the tips of Alice's firm tits between her fingers, squeezing and tugging, using them like reins to manipulate the woman on her lap; Alice riding now, moving with Ruth's lead, withdrawing her own hand from its seeking place, the sensations overwhelming her with desire. Her eyes closed as she savored the pleasure and pain.

"Oh, Ruth, ah! Oh yeah…," Alice was begging now. Her eyes opened and she looked Ruth earnestly in the eyes. "C'mon, c'mon and follow me," she whispered intensely.

Moira watched with amusement as Alice broke free of Ruth's wonderfully cruel fingers, silky tits bouncing as she slid her slippery self down over Ruth's sexy thighs and off her lap. Then she playfully crouched down at Ruth's feet and lifted the edge of the tablecloth.

"Down here," she whispered hard, motioning underneath the table. Her face was so intensely serious, flushed with arousal, eyes unfocused slightly as she rode their wave, that Ruth laughed delightedly.

"My, you are a hungry one tonight, my Alice," she

said, approval in her voice. She glanced around the room, not catching Moira's eyes. Apparently satisfied, Ruth shook her head then, beaming, and slid her own naked buttocks off the chair, crouching playfully beside her lover on the floor.

They kissed, partially hidden by the tablecloth. Ruth held Alice's bra in one hand, her own full slip pushed up around her hips, exposing her sweet round ass and tender thighs. Moira saw Alice take the opportunity to slide one hand up between them, watched Ruth's face change as the pleasure rushed through her under Alice's command, her body extending itself as she rolled over onto her back just a little, stretching out to welcome her lover.

Moira watched as the two women disappeared under the huge, long table, heavy breathing and soft moans following them. The tablecloth fell back into its perfect place, leaving no trace of their passage. She smiled, feeling a wave of desire for something she couldn't quite explain, letting out her breath in a little huff. Then she filled a small bowl with ruby grapes, turned, and headed up the stairs.

# 7.Trump

Back in Lydia's room, the dressing party was finishing up.

"Interesting choice," Dawn said to Lydia, barely disguising her distaste, as the two of them headed out of the bedroom. "Very…unique. As opposed to what I would have chosen for you, of course."

Lydia didn't bother to smile or respond to that one, her high-top Doc Marten boots making a nice firm satisfying sound of contact on the rug and then on the hardwood floors as she walked with Dawn toward the door, and the two waiting women. Dawn had fixed Lydia's long hair into a French braid, which wasn't Lydia's style at all. But it was pretty and Dawn was getting huffy about not being allowed to do anything to help her dress, so she let her do it.

"Doesn't really go with what you picked to wear," Dawn had told her as she'd watched, incredulous, as Lydia had chosen clothes from her own wardrobe: well-worn blue jeans with slits in both knees (and in various other strategic areas such as just below her butt on either side), worn with no underwear, lightly tanned skin peeking through, enticing (Dawn approved of that part). On top, braless, she wore a gold long-sleeved body-hugging scooped-neck top that ended just above her belly button, exposing it and a firm patch of stomach and trim waist (another aspect that pleased Dawn as she admired the sexy swell of Lydia's beautiful firm chest).

In her ears, she allowed Dawn to hang antique gold earrings with topaz in them that caught the light and glistened, accentuating Lydia's tan skin. Dawn had chosen the earrings to try and soften up what she called Lydia's "interesting" choice of attire.

"I really can't believe work boots came in as *de rigueur*," she said more than once. "Incredible."

"You can even wear them with dresses," Lydia told her, just to rile her. "Chiffon, gauzy dresses even," she added, getting a good chuckle out of the stupefied look on Dawn's face. "It's an acquired taste, of course," she told her. Dawn replied that it really must be.

"But you look fantastic in anything, of course," she added swiftly, picking up on Lydia's quickly growing irritation.

"Really?" Lydia responded, growing tired of Dawn's company.

"So what's next?" Lydia asked.

"This way, my dear," Zoe offered from the doorway.

Lydia and Dawn joined Zoe and Rose out in the hall, Lydia closing her door behind her. At the same time, a door to their right—to what was, in Lydia's time, her painting studio—opened. The woman wore a Marlene Dietrich-style trouser suit and tie, with a soft turned-up hat. Her blonde curls cascaded down like a golden waterfall, framing her stunning face.

"Wow, interesting outfit you have on there," she said to Lydia. Her eyes covered all bases on Lydia's body, then moved up to meet her eyes. She smiled, showing off fabulously stunning pearly whites. "Oh, my. Have you come to join us then, aye?" she asked, very interested.

"Oh, Grace, Lydia doesn't have a clue what you're talking about, so leave her alone," Dawn scolded, taking a step closer to Lydia; ownership close. Lydia moved a step away, shooting a give-me-a-break glance at Dawn and wrinkling her brow. Grace seemed to be used to Dawn and just ignored her.

"Well, Lydia, come join us in the poker room—all of you. We're having a rip-roaring time tonight and the stakes are out of this world!" She seemed a bit tipsy and obviously in a highly festive mood.

The mention of poker got Lydia's attention. Her face brightened. "Great!" she said, maybe a tad too enthusiastically. Zoe raised her monocle and studied Lydia for a moment.

"Trying to get rid of us already?" she asked. "And we've barely even had a chance to meet you."

Lydia looked at the thin, angular woman, so smartly dressed. Zoe was a dead ringer for Radclyffe Hall, Lydia mused. The thought made her smile.

"I just adore poker," she said in defense of her wish to play. "You two seem nice enough, though, it's not that."

Lydia could not believe she was actually defending herself, but she felt compelled to be as kind as possible. After all, they hadn't done anything to her to make her judge them badly. She just felt a little trapped in their stuffy group.

Rose howled at Lydia's response, her bubbly laughter filling the space all the way up to the ceiling above and floating back down over them. She could hardly catch her breath, she was laughing so hard. Everyone was mesmerized momentarily by the uniqueness of her particular laugh and the catchiness of it. Lydia giggled, too, against her will, as did Dawn and Grace. Zoe smiled and shook her head knowingly.

"Oh, that's a good one," Rose howled again. "Nice people, ha!" Her eyes were tearing up and she turned to Zoe beside her. She reached over and pulled a finely made leather man's-style purse from Zoe's side. Lydia hadn't noticed it there.

"Oh, yes, so nice. I'll show you nice," Rose giggled, and she opened the purse, reached in. Out came a pair of wrist restraints and a blindfold. "Very *very* nice!" she said, her laugh winding down now. "God, I *hate* nice women! Can't stand the breed!" she said, still smiling, cheeks bright from her laughter.

She let the items slip back into the bag, closed it, and laid it back against Zoe's side, where it hung from a long strap.

"And these are nice enough, too!" Rose agreed, lifting a riding crop and small whip from their resting places: hidden beneath Zoe's long conservative smoking jacket. Rose chuckled some more as she watched Lydia's eyebrows jump up in surprise. Then Lydia was laughing, too.

"Well, hell, what do I know?" she said. "All I do know is, really, that what I was trying to say is poker's a good thing, a fun thing that I like."

"Actually, I agree with Lydia," Zoe said, still smiling and leaning over then to scoop up Rose by the waist and kiss her deeply. Their bodies spoke a million messages of desire and understanding; these were obviously two seasoned lovers who knew each other well.

Rose's chuckles were halted by the kiss, leaving her, after, with a happy smile on her face. "I do so love this woman," she told the group, caught up momentarily in watching them. "Mmm mm."

Rose slipped her arm through Zoe's, her flapper fringe bouncing as she situated herself. "Well, then, shall we play a little poker with our new friend?" she offered.

Zoe nodded.

"Not me," Dawn said. "I hate poker—I always lose.

Always the mistress and never the bride, you know." She looked at Lydia. "I'll see you later, downstairs, though. I'll be waiting for you."

Dawn smiled seductively, standing model-like in her slinky Fortuny of Venice gown, shimmering with curve-clinging fashion and hopeful persuasion. Then she turned away, without giving Lydia a chance to respond.

"So go ahead then, just take her away from me," she tossed at Grace as she moved past her and continued around to the staircase. Grace ignored the comment.

"Oh, yes, I have to run a quick errand!" she said, instead, suddenly remembering that she had walked out of the room for a reason, previously. She was all smiles and goodness. "You just go on in and find yourselves some comfortable spots. I'll be right in to join you. Should be a nice display by now."

She winked and took off behind Dawn, turning in halfway to the stairs at the door with the psychedelic lampshade. She entered the room, leaving the door open, calling out very singsongy sweet: "Hellooo, my pets, are you ready for a feeding?" Lydia turned and looked questioningly at Rose and Zoe.

"Well, there's a blonde who's Grace's longtime pet, you might say," Rose explained. "And then there's Maxine, who loves to make trouble; can't keep her hands to herself, that one. It's sort of an ongoing saga."

She paused, then whispered the next part, leaning in toward Lydia, still on Zoe's arm. "She's got them both in there right now, completely bound in these leather sort of straitjackets and fully masked except for a hole where their mouths are. She feeds and waters them when she feels like and only lets them loose to go to the bathroom, and even then, she keeps them hooded and tied."

Lydia was intrigued—and impressed. Who knew just by looking at these women? Rose noticed the expression on Lydia's face and winked.

"Yeah, if you're smart, you'll never judge a book by its cover around here," she said mischievously. "There might just be more to it than you think." Rose patted Zoe's arm, her own still wrapped around it.

"Anyway, she gets to do this for two full days and the two days are almost up, so she's giving them the grueling hard-time treatment now. They've been standing for, oh, probably five hours straight already. I've seen worse, though, especially from Moira. Only the real lovers of hardcore punishment cross her. The rest of us know better."

Lydia nodded, aching inside to meet this particular woman. She felt as though she already knew her somehow and her mind was distracted by the thought, and the possibilities.

Grace's chipper voice rose and fell melodically in the background as Rose spoke, escaping in bits and pieces from the room across the way.

"Well, shall we enter, then?" Zoe suggested. "You're in the lead, Lydia."

True. Lydia stood in front of the door through which Grace had exited a few minutes before, Rose and Zoe just behind her. "Absolutely," Lydia replied, and she reached out for the crystal door handle, turning it and pushing the door open carefully. The energy of the others behind her made her step inside as soon as there was room; they followed her in immediately, right up behind her. Zoe shut the door after them.

Inside, in the middle of the expansive room with two chandeliers and luxurious thick carpet and embroidered drapes, a dozen women sat around a large round table, some wearing only bras and panties, others completely naked from the waist up, and a very select few still clothed almost completely. The lighting was atmospheric, the glittery chandeliers dimmed, but it was bright enough to see everyone clearly.

Lydia tried not to stare at the wonderful display of so many different types of women. Her eyes travelled around the table as casually as possible, but suddenly there seemed to be a flash of light in Lydia's head or some sort of a strange blinding illusion that appeared to illuminate one particular woman. Lydia could do nothing but stare helplessly. The woman at the table turned her head to look, too, as the party entered the room. She met Lydia's eyes directly. Laser beams between them. Connection. The woman rose quickly from her chair at the far side of the table, almost knocking down her chair in the process, as if propelled by the same force that had Lydia dazed. They stood staring at each other across the table.

Rose smiled and leaned over to Lydia.

"That's Moira Zane, she owns this place. And I think you have her attention," she whispered.

Lydia could not take her eyes off the woman; she could barely catch her breath, much less speak. Her legs felt weak and she felt her entire body pulled like metal to this magnet of a woman. It felt as if all the years of her life were falling into place behind her as she stood, mesmerized; as if she'd waited a lifetime for this very moment.

"Moira," Zoe said, "what a formal welcome. No need for that now." She glanced around the table at all the lovely bodies and uplifted faces that greeted them. "It's a pleasure to see everyone, as always."

A straggle of distracted greetings floated up from the eclectic blend of players, but all eyes were on Lydia. Their manner of dress, what remained of it, ranged from turn of the century to the mid-1970s. There were women of all varieties of nationalities and appearance. But Lydia hardly noticed them.

Instead, she stood, amazed and floored by the strength of her attraction, her world view narrowed to the point of contact between her gaze and Moira's. Her eyes missed the coupled women, sitting close together and fondling each other, some openly, some bringing pleasure discreetly to each other with hands under the table, but their faces flushed with the fever of their excitement. Others who were not matched up were flirting shamelessly or just presenting themselves in a seductive way as they perched in their chairs. All of them stopped what they were doing to take in this new visitor.

Rose nudged Zoe with her elbow, raising her eyebrows and indicating Lydia with her eyes.

"Oh, allow me to introduce Miss Lydia…Lydia…" Zoe looked over at Lydia who was still staring at Moira. It took a beat or two before she felt Zoe's eyes on her. She glanced at Zoe's expectant face.

"Oh, uh, Ryder, Lydia Ryder," Lydia offered, eyes back on Moira Zane.

"Yes, Miss Lydia Ryder," Zoe finished.

"Ms.," Lydia corrected.

"Excuse me?"

"Ms. not Miss. Men don't have to indicate if they're married or not, why should we?" she explained, as if saying it directly to Moira.

Pleasant amused laughter erupted in little pockets around the table, cut by a clear strong alto voice.

"How very true. Please, join us, *Ms.* Ryder. And welcome."

It was Moira. She had emerged from her dumbstruck state and was now pulling back the empty chair to her right—an invitation to Lydia—removing her hat in a gentle-womanly gesture. As she waited, she patted her thick, dark waves of hair casually into place with the hand that held her hat, looking a bit nervous.

Everyone at the table exchanged glances. This was a rare scene and there wasn't a soul who wasn't aware of it. One woman raised her eyeglasses, holding them by their single stem and peering up at Lydia. Lydia glanced around the table, suddenly aware of all the attention on her. She blushed furiously, unable to move.

"Well, go on," Rose whispered emphatically.

Lydia cleared her throat. "Thank you," she said to Moira—and everyone else around the table.

Her heavy Doc Martens on the thick carpet made a firm sound in the silent room as she made her way around the table. Lydia could barely stand the pressure of her heart in her chest, intensifying as she approached the woman. It was like two hot wires, having been cut, but finding contact again; a connection that was staggering in its intensity. Lydia swayed a little as she walked. When she arrived, she smiled at Moira, standing in front of her. Moira smiled back, hat still in her hand, standing tall and handsome in her white shirt, double-buttoned vest, and matching suit slacks. Her jacket hung on the chair behind her with a loose tie slung over it. Her face was amazing: deep brown eyes, full of confidence and a self-assured calmness, edged with an obvious but not rude passion.

"You just moved in," Moira said matter-of-factly.

Lydia looked at her for a moment, perplexed. "Actually, yes, yes, I did, two days ago," she said.

"I felt you arrive," Moira went on, half whispering, as if thinking out loud but her words were meant for Lydia's ears. "I wondered when we would meet. I've been up all night for two nights thanks to you. Are you hungry, would you like a bite to eat from downstairs?" she asked.

Lydia was completely charmed. And floored. Every

woman around the table was staring at Moira and her uncharacteristically nervous behavior. Then all eyes shifted to Lydia, waiting for her response.

"Uh…" Lydia glanced around the table at smiling, knowing faces. She raised her eyebrows as if to ask those present if they wouldn't mind if she just came and went like this.

"Feel free," someone responded in a heavily French-accented voice. Lydia looked toward the source. The words came from a woman sitting directly to her right. She was an incredible sight, this one. Lydia couldn't help but stare at such extravagance: The woman was fairly loaded down with black furs, all mounted complete with heads, teeth, and nails, and draped over her shoulders in a flood. Her long-skirted, long-sleeved, early 1900s dress could barely be seen beneath them and her face was only half visible under a large elegant black hat, heavily decorated with deep red roses. She wore her obviously very long hair pulled up in a large loose bun at the base of her long neck. The woman could have been straight out of some French turn-of-the-century fashion magazine, Lydia mused, staring and blinking in disbelief.

"Wow," Lydia said.

Constance smiled at Lydia, but it was somewhat pained and none too friendly, then shifted her gaze to Moira, puffing on her cigarette, an out-of-character modern Marlboro in a short but stylish gold holder. Moira looked back at her.

"Thank you for your consent, my dear Constance," Moira said to her, the corner of her mouth slipping up into a smile. "Here, take my cards. If you would be so kind as to play these for me…"

"What's in it for me?" Constance asked, felinelike, running a pink tongue swiftly over her red painted lips, barely disguising this as a casual move. She did not smile back at Moira.

"Wouldn't winning the pot tonight be enough? After all, if my cards win, you do take it all," Moira returned, an edge of sternness in her voice.

"If you can talk JJ into giving me another pack of these cigarettes, I would be completely content," Constance said. But seeing Moira's face slipping nearly into a look of disapproval, Constance changed her approach.

"*Mon dieu,* I'm just kidding. Go, have fun with your new toy, of course I will play your cards," Constance said, smiling from under her somewhat bonnetlike black hat, furs dripping off her slender arm as she held her cigarette aloft for a moment. She laughed lightly, turned her head, and looked up at Lydia, who stood beside her.

"Very interesting choice of costume," she said. The swell of Lydia's luscious breasts did not go unnoticed by Constance. She took in the scope of Lydia's body, the heavy boots and ripped jeans mixing sexy with tough; the beauty of her face and figure with a bad attitude. Lydia was quite content with her attire and didn't play into Constance's game.

"I'm Constance," the woman said by way of introduction. "I hope you'll join us for a game very soon."

She winked, looking about ready to pounce, but Lydia just said hello politely, adding that she looked forward to meeting everyone soon. That was only partly true. All she wanted at this moment, and for all time it felt like, was to get away with Moira. Alone.

As Lydia turned again toward Moira, the full force of her energy rushed through Lydia again, her body preparing itself for something she could not as yet envision, but could feel. Lydia realized that she had no interest in anything at all but being with this woman. For this chance, this union, she would do anything.

*Whoa, Lydia!* her brain suddenly screamed at her. *What are you doing? What are you saying? You don't even know this woman! And what do you mean, anything?*

Next to Lydia, Moira pushed her chair out of the way, pushing Lydia's out of the way, too, clearing a path for them to exit.

"Ladies, gentlewomen, and others," she said to everyone around the large table, nodding her head. The women around the table nodded back, smiling. An especially butch woman, handsome as hell in her tailored gray pinstripe suit, winked at Lydia and blew her a kiss. Lydia smiled subtly, but found herself looking away, something she would not usually have done.

Moira indicated for Lydia to lead and together they moved toward the door.

"Kelsey, I think it's your play," someone said at the table.

Lydia glanced back, surprised. Kelsey was, indeed, at the table, seated at the far right end wearing only her bra and panties. She smiled at Lydia, shrugging her shoulders good-naturedly as if to say, "Oh, well, we almost had it, didn't we?" Then she waved a quick little flip of her hand before turning back to play her next card. The woman next to her wrapped her arm around Kelsey's shoulder.

"You'd better win this one or you'll be the naked one tonight," the woman said to Kelsey, kissing her soft shoulder.

Lydia smiled. That was the last thing she heard before she walked out of the room, Moira closing the card room door behind them.

## 8. The Grand Tour

Lydia turned around to face Moira, let her lead the way down the hall, not sure where she wanted to go. As Lydia turned, she almost ran smack into Moira who was close behind her. Lydia jumped, but her cry of surprise was muffled by the softest, most incredible lips Lydia had ever felt. Moira's sweet mouth kissed hers firmly and with purpose. Lydia kissed her back strongly, hungrily, eyes closing, wanting nothing more than to take this woman back to her room.

That was an idea.

But before Lydia had a chance to suggest it, the kiss was over and Moira was already speaking.

"Mm, I feel like I know you already," she said to

Lydia. "Damn, excuse my forwardness, I hope you don't mind, but…"

"No, no, it's fine," Lydia replied. "I would have done it myself if you…"

"Ah, good," Moira smiled, her hat still in her hand. "I guess I don't need this for the moment." She turned and hung it on the doorknob. "Someone will bring it to my room," she added as Lydia watched her every move.

"Where is your room?" Lydia couldn't help but ask. Moira laughed.

"Have you even seen the house yet, my house?" she asked.

Lydia smiled, delighted with the question, the honest asking of it after having already covered the territory that Lydia had moved in just two days ago. "Well, I live in it, too, of course," she said kindly. "But then it looks a little different, in my time," she replied.

"Allow me to show you around then. Tonight is an especially good night for…sightseeing," she added, offering her arm to Lydia.

"Oh, God no, I'm not an arm person, really. But thanks," Lydia said, trying to be kind about it.

"Oh, sorry," Moira said, blushing and lowering her arm. "It's an old-time habit I haven't quite broken yet." She laughed nervously. "Why don't we just walk together then?" she suggested. Lydia smiled and nodded, following just a little behind as they moved around the upstairs landing, past the psychedelic lamp, to the right side of the expansive staircase.

Of course, Lydia didn't really want a tour. Her mind raced with other ideas. But how much more rude could she be than to say to this perfect stranger she'd just met, "No, thanks, I'd rather go get fucked by you in private somewhere!" Lydia shook her head, amused at her own state.

As they mounted the staircase, Moira turned and caught Lydia's eye. "By the way, I love your outfit," she said. "You look good enough to eat. Right down to the boots. Just wanted you to know."

The two women looked at each other and Lydia felt an ache inside her; a hunger and a desire so deep it seemed to come from some primal, animal place that she couldn't explain. Lydia opened her mouth to speak, but no words came out. The women looked at each other, both studying the curves of each other's lips, one step away from each other's mouths. Neither one moved. Moira was the first to take a breath.

"How about the short tour?" she asked, a little breathless. "Unless you see someplace you'd like to stop, of course."

"Exactly what I was thinking," Lydia said, leaning every so slightly toward the woman, but catching herself and regaining her composure for the moment. She watched Moira smile, eyes heavy with desire, a mirror of Lydia's. The woman regained her composure then, too, and she turned slowly back around, leading Lydia down the staircase.

Lydia noted, following closely behind, that Moira had

a really great ass, even in her conservative suit vest and slacks. She couldn't help it; the words just tumbled out.

"Great ass," she commented under her breath.

"Yours isn't bad either," Moira returned, without so much as a backward glance or missing a beat. "Especially where your pants are so strategically slit below the cheeks."

Moira stepped down onto the landing between the dining and living rooms, turning to meet Lydia's shocked face as she took the final step onto the landing right behind her. Lydia burst into surprised laughter and Moira couldn't help but join her; Lydia's face would have sent anyone watching into a fit of laughter, the surprise was so charming and open.

"Touché!" Lydia giggled.

"Yes, quite a match," Moira said, eyes sparkling. She ran a hand absently over her hair, checking that it was still in place somewhat, looking a little uncomfortable without her hat. "How about something to drink before we start?" she offered. Lydia accepted and they made their first stop at the lavish buffet table.

As Moira and Lydia poured themselves drinks, laughter and talking wafted in from the living room. They were alone in the dining room for the moment.

"So where is everyone?" she asked. "No one hungry tonight?"

Before Moira could answer, Lydia was greeted with a passionate moan of pleasure. Thinking it an awfully bold response for Moira instead, she looked for the source of the sexual eruption. But there was no one else here, just the two of them.

Not wanting to come off looking weird, Lydia dismissed it as a figment of her mind's wishful thinking, glancing up at Moira quickly to see if she looked like she'd heard something, too. If she had, she wasn't showing it: Moira was busy carefully pouring red wine from an exquisitely detailed pewter decanter, keeping it clear of the white linen tablecloth.

"They roam in and out," she said in answer to Lydia's question. "Must be something interesting going on in the living room. Would you like to take a look?"

Lydia looked back down at the display of foods. Her eyes lingered on the overflowing bowls of fresh tropical fruits and she thought about splitting open a plump ripe mango, sharing it with Moira by dribbling it on her naked form and licking the juice off Moira's beautiful skin. Unconsciously, she moaned under her breath. And like the call of the wild, a muffled cry of excitement responded to her from somewhere nearby.

"Oh, for shitsake," she mumbled.

"I'm sorry I didn't hear you," Moira said, turning away from the table to look at Lydia. "Did you say yes, you would like to join the others in the living room?"

"No, no, I'd rather not," she stammered, distracted, and thinking that stepping into a room full of women in this house somehow felt like saying yes, I'd love to walk into that den of wild carnivorous wolves who haven't seen fresh food in months.

"Good," Moira said. "Let me just open a new bottle of wine." Lydia watched Moira walk in her long stride and hard black shoes across the huge room to a table along the far wall where an amazing array of wines and various other spirits were set out. She smiled at Moira's walk and how her body looked as though it wanted to just burst out of her clothes. She imagined her dressed in Levi's, work boots, and a flimsy nothing of a man's tank top. Lydia was reminded of her mission when another moan floated into the room. She turned quickly back to the table.

The sound seemed to be coming from right where she was standing, but how could that be? Lydia looked back: Moira was intent on opening one of the bottles of wine. Lydia turned back. From that same nowhere and everywhere place, a hoarse, wildly impassioned, barely muffled voice forced out whispered words of persuasion: "Oh yeah, mmmmmmm, right there..." Then, from the living room, a waterfall of piano keys suddenly sounded and an obviously small, but very vocal, group of singers burst into a drunk and ridiculously funny rendition of "Oklahoma," piano at full tilt, drowning out the sighs and cries of pleasure.

Looking down, her face set in a determined look, Lydia had a very wild thought. She crouched down, leaning on one ripped denim knee, and carefully lifted the long tablecloth. Underneath the huge table, two completely naked dark-haired women were going at it in a frenzy, their clothes tossed around them: slips, bras, blouses. One was on her back, knees wide, while the other was plunging her entire petite fist into the woman's flowering sex, leaning down now in an impressive contortionist move to place her pink tongue on the hard bud of the woman's exposed clit. The one on her back went wild then, beautiful mouth opening but no sound escaping. She arched her back and her face was a tight knot of emotion. Her long hair was wild around her head. The woman ran her hands down over her smooth, hard-tipped breasts, sucking in her breath as the woman between her slim legs increased the pace and speed of her tongue.

It was like a white moonlit tent under the table, the women appearing to be bathed in moonlight. The image flashed Lydia back in her mind to when a girlfriend of hers had invited Lydia over to stay the night—a "sleepover."

That night, in the girl's bedroom, after they had obediently said their good-nights and turned off the lights, the moon had been full outside and they had left the curtains pulled back, moonlight flooding the bedroom. It was the middle of summer, still hot and muggy even at midnight, and they'd quickly slipped out of their nightgowns, eyes flicking repeatedly to glance at the closed bedroom door which had no lock on it. Kicking back the blanket, the two of them lay together in the girl's bed, covered only by a soft white sheet. Lydia remembered how their brand-new bodies had shone and blended together as they'd made love under the white linen, the moonlight shining through the fabric creating a glow inside their created tent; their "love tent" as they'd called it.

Lydia smiled, watching the women's frantic sex under the table, remembering her own dogged efforts not to cry out as she and her lover came under the sheet, as the pleasure had ignited their young impassioned bodies; hands over their own mouths, then nervously over each other's, sweat making their skin slick, their bodies sliding easily and urgently over each other, the soft cotton sheet sticking to them, outlining youthful curves and peaks, the sensual undulation of their movements.

"Hey," Moira said from her crouching position beside Lydia. Lydia jumped so hard she hit her head on the table, her cry rudely and suddenly interrupting the lovers' play.

"What the hell?" the one on her back said, closing her legs, the other woman's fist still inside her, both women's eyes aflame with passion, barely able to focus on anything around them.

"Oh, sorry!" Lydia stammered. "Please, continue! Sorry!"

Quickly she backed up, tripping all over herself and letting the tablecloth fall back into its original place. She forced herself up into a standing position, still moving away from the table. Moira was moving away from the table, too, her face filled with a huge grin.

"Holy shit, you scared the living shit out of me!"

Lydia threw out at Moira who was standing beside her now, still smiling broadly, close-mouthed.

"I bet I did, Ms. Peeping Tom," she said, chuckling. "Did you like what you saw?" she asked, eyebrows raising, her handsome face glowing with amusement, and more.

Lydia had to laugh, too, if a bit nervously, adrenaline pumping through her, her body feeling like a fireworks display. Then her face settled into a serious gaze and the words presented themselves of their own accord.

"Damn, I want you so bad," she said directly, blinking through an onslaught of desire.

Moira stepped forward and pressed her body against Lydia's, hands wrapping around her back, pulling her in. Lydia moved in against Moira, feeling the strength of their attraction pulsing through her like a drug, wanting more, much more. She ran her hands over Moira's broad shoulders, then slipped them around the woman's narrow waist, the cloth of her suit a little rough, unfamiliar, from another time and place. The feel of it fascinated Lydia and she took in all the smells that made up this incredible person.

Moira's hands explored Lydia's body, too, tentative palms open, caressing the curves of Lydia's ass beneath her jeans, fingertips sliding along the bare skin presented by the slit fabric. Lydia held her breath, caught up in the incredible sensation of the woman's touch on her ravenous skin. Moira completed the kiss then, Lydia returning the final meeting. Moira's hands played at Lydia's waist, between the edge of her snug shirt, under which she wore nothing, and the edge of her jeans that dipped just below her belly button.

"You are one sexy woman," Moira whispered hungrily into Lydia's ear, sliding the tips of her thumbs inside the front of the waist of Lydia's jeans, barely touching the soft, tan, sensitive skin of Lydia's stomach, dangerously close to hidden flesh.

"So then you don't want the tour?" Moira asked, pulling her face away to look into Lydia's, both women's faces flushed with passion. Lydia found breathing difficult, held by the waist of her pants in this woman's strong grip, smelling her cologne mixed with the intriguing smells of almost a century's time between them. Lydia's body prepared itself obediently, the heat increasing at wildfire's pace between her legs and straight up to her head.

"Show me your favorite place in the house," Lydia said a little hoarsely, dizzy with desire. "Take me there."

"My favorite place...," Moira repeated. "What if you don't like it?"

Lydia considered that. "I doubt I won't like it," she said. "I'm open to anything, and I hear you're a cruel mother," she added pointedly. "Just my type."

Moira's heart beat hard in her chest, anticipation and a flush of adrenaline showing all over her face and in her body language. "I see," she responded breathlessly. "If that's true, then by all means let's not waste precious time."

She pressed her lips against Lydia's again passionately, hands finding Lydia's incredible tits, boldly massaging them through her stretchy gold top, taking the woman in her grip. Lydia moaned and Moira couldn't help but lift the fabric and bend her mouth to suck at the hard knob of one tit, her mouth insistent, the other arm around Lydia. Lydia's legs melted beneath her, Moira's strong arm holding her up for a moment as her body responded in a rush of sensation.

"Mmmm, oh, yeah, c'mon, show me this place," she whispered passionately as Moira's teeth bit lightly at her nipple, pleasure erupting in a little wave beneath Lydia's warm flesh. Moira's face resurfaced as she slid Lydia's shirt back down over her hard-nippled globe, keeping her thumb working against the firm bud.

"Follow me," Moira said. Their eyes bored into each other's minds, bodies, feeding the fresh soil in the garden of their fantasies.

Moira took Lydia by the hand then, not waiting to see if she was into hand-holding or not, and led her quickly out of the room and down the hall, her hard black shoes and Lydia's boots pounding the thick carpet. A wave of clapping and hoots and hollers broke out in the living room as someone at the piano burst into another round of song, the notes following Lydia and Moira briefly down the hall, then hanging momentarily in mid-air before dissipating into the walls of the house.

## 9. On a Full-Moon Night

To her surprise, Lydia found Moira leading her to the small service room at the very back of the house with the windows that looked out on a well-kept backyard. But she didn't stop there. Instead, she continued to the back door, unlocking it and pushing it open. She held it wide as Lydia looked at her, then followed silently, her hand still in Moira's grip.

"This way," Moira said, her voice excited, firm. She motioned toward the gazebo that sat in the middle of the lawn, circled by tall trees that marked the edge of the forest. The wilderness seemed to press in on them, barely kept at bay, the tree branches illuminated by the silver white of the moon.

The grass beneath Lydia's boots was moist with dew. She looked up at the incredible sky, at the perfectly round full moon that beamed down on them like a spotlight, following their progress.

"Watch your step," Moira said when they arrived. Lydia looked down in time to mount the few steps up to the landing of the gazebo. Moira moved swiftly to the center of the platform. It was a large gazebo with two elegant wrought-iron benches placed in it. Moira ignored these, letting go of Lydia's hand now as she bent down and slipped a key into a lock that was barely discernible in the wooden gazebo floor. As she turned, she lifted her hand and a trap door raised its head ever so slightly. With both hands now, Moira pulled the door open, the hinges creaking, and laid it back against the floor.

Lydia peered in from the edge where she stood. Rough steps led down into a deep darkness, and her heart pounded out a warning, igniting her nerve endings, which all seemed to flash at once: *danger*.

But her body spoke a different language altogether, oblivious to everything but Moira's presence, and the need for her.

When Moira reached in to flip on a switch at the top of the stairs and light flooded the space below, there was no question in Lydia's mind that she would follow.

Standing at the base of the steep cement steps, Lydia looked around. The space was large and it looked like an old root cellar or wine cellar maybe, but the shelves were full of other items now; items that might have been for use with horses or dogs.

Or people.

She walked around slowly, looking on the shelves that lined most of the huge room: metal collars, cuffs, restraints, head coverings, metal bars with restraints at both ends, and the smell of leather everywhere. The leather items appeared to have their own separate place, all together on one wall. The place was amazingly clean and warm.

But it was the equipment that made Lydia stare.

"Are you ready?" Moira asked and Lydia turned away from her perusal of the shelves. She moaned at the sight before her.

Moira had removed her vest and now wore only the billowy-sleeved white poet-style shirt. It tied up the front and the ties were loose, the shirt partially open, exposing enticing cleavage held aloft by a white undergarment somewhat like a bra, but different. Her slacks had been replaced by snug-fitting jodhpurs complete with high shiny black riding boots. She held a crop in her hand.

"I'll keep in mind that this is our first time together. Discipline is key. You follow me, I'll give you what you need. You don't, we'll see if what you heard about me is true. And if I really am your type."

Moira had let her hair down and it fell to just above her waist, though it was still held back in a large band that kept it out of her face. And her face was changed, but the same; tougher, a sense of purpose apparent in her intense eyes, strong jaw, mixing with an incredible passion that filled the room, drawing Lydia in.

"God, you're beautiful," Lydia whispered.

Moira smiled. "You're kind," she said gently. "And I don't believe you really want what I have to give you. I am willing to give you whatever you want, rather than what I am sadistically inclined to want to do to you, myself."

"Oh, but I do want it, all of it. I want you to do everything to me that you hunger to do. I want everything. I'm your slave tonight, Moira Zane, and I'm giving myself to you willingly, I swear it," Lydia said, eyes narrowing. "Take it from me. I accept the consequences."

They looked at each other directly for a few moments. Apparently satisfied, and propelled by her own desire, Moira took Lydia by the arm and led her to a wooden pillory that sat on a short wooden platform on the far side of the room. It was open.

"Up," she commanded. "You are my stock now and you will need training, discipline. I'll need to see what you've got."

Lydia's body shook with both anticipation and fear. It was a fear that fascinated her, seduced her, made her breathing difficult, her body sweat. She gave herself completely to this place, to Moira, and stepped up onto the platform.

"Head and hands," Moira directed. "But first, turn this way."

Lydia turned obediently.

"Raise your arms."

Lydia raised them, her breasts moving up with the movement.

Moira pulled her shirt up over her head, leaving Lydia's torso naked, nipples hard and puckered from the chill of danger and the thrill of Moira's hands brushing them.

"Now, head and hands," she directed.

Lydia looked at the pillory, moved to it and laid her wrists into the two side indentations, then, with a little trepidation, she lowered her head, placing her neck above the center indentation. Moira stepped aside and pulled the second wooden piece down over her, the two pieces meeting securely, creating three holes through which her head and hands now stuck out. She was able to stand up almost straight, but the posture was not comfortable. Moira fastened a lock to the two metal loops that stuck out on the left side and Lydia was a captive.

Then Moira moved around behind her and slipped her hands down over Lydia's hips, running over her jeans to rub the fabric that covered her mound. Lydia sighed, her need rekindled like crazy. She concentrated on the feel of Moira's hands as they slid around back, gripping Lydia's asscheeks, fingers sliding up under the slitted denim to pinch her ass, the exposed skin there.

"Ow!" Lydia cried, doing a little jump of surprise. Then Moira's hands were back on her belly, slipping down into her jeans, fingernails running lightly over her pubic hair, no underwear to impede Moira's progress. When Moira's fingertips found Lydia's clit, Lydia groaned with pleasure.

"Oh, Moira, mmmmm yeah," Lydia whimpered from her post. She could not see a thing, secured in the pillory as she was, the wood blocking her view. Her long dark hair fell around her face, her ears on overdrive, trying to take over for her lacking sight.

Moira unbuttoned Lydia's jeans then and in a hot second they were down around her boots. Lydia was naked now, except for her boots and the pants piled up around them. Her clit throbbed as the pants passed it. She tried to move, but the wooden bars held her. From behind, she was all tan skin, creamy ass, and flexing back as she struggled ever so slightly. Her legs were parted for better balance.

It was Moira's turn to comment.

"You look like a virgin with that creamy skin of yours," she said. "Not a mark on you. I'm going to find out a little more about you."

Raising the crop in her hand, Moira found her mark the very first time, the cruel end meeting Lydia's flesh with a thwack! She jumped, but contained her voice, feeling the old rush of indignation surface from deep inside her. She set her jaw and Moira raised the crop again, delivering a series of painful, painstakingly placed blows to Lydia's asscheeks and thighs. When the new marks began to crisscross the old ones, Lydia could not bear the pressure, could not contain her voice any longer; her body sweating, shaking her head in frustration as it jutted out through the pillory, Lydia was crazy with the pain. As the crop found its mark yet again, she yelled, her voice propelled out of her by the force of the blow.

"That's enough!" she hollered. "Aaa, please, that's enough!"

Sweat dripped down her face.

"The word is 'morning.' " Moira said from behind her. "Use it and everything comes to a halt. But I'll be kind this time and oblige your request. You took this part well. Time to change tools. But don't even try to move."

Moira's voice was cruel, filled with an obvious fondness for her sadistic endeavors. Lydia smiled inside; she had hungered for a woman just like this. She was determined to please this woman. She would never say the word.

"Make me proud," Moira said, as if reading her mind. "I always reward those who make me proud. You'll see."

Lydia breathed hard, straining to hear what Moira was doing behind her. The whistle of the heavy whip flying through the air hit her ears at the same moment the whip's tongue lashed out against the smooth, tanned flesh of her upper back. She grunted, unable to control the reflex.

Moira had a strong arm and the whip pounded her flesh unmercifully. Lydia could feel her cunt swelling with the fever of her test, of proving herself worthy of this woman's respect and passion. Her back burned, light welts rising to greet her lover-to-be.

"I want you," Lydia begged. "I want you so much."

Her words were hushed, bursting with desire, but they made it to Moira's ears.

The whip cracked again, finding its mark across her shoulders, a delicious, excruciating pain. Lydia grunted and sucked in her breath, envisioning her prize, nipples hard as her breasts hung there, hands in fists where they stuck out through the holes, her body a pillar of burning, sizzling flesh.

"What do you want from me?" Moira prompted. "What do you want me to do to you?"

The whip was raised again and thwacked against Lydia's reddened flesh.

"Fuck me!" Lydia cried out. "Oh, God, please fuck me! Make me come! I wanna come so bad…." Lydia's voice was wild with need, hot with the endurance of this pain.

"But if I do that, you'll be mine forever. If you come, you can't return," she told Lydia, her voice extremely serious. "I mean it."

She held the whip at bay, approaching Lydia from behind. She took a latex glove out of the pocket of her jodhpurs and slipped it on her right hand. The only sounds were her own breathing, the slap of the latex as she pulled it snug, and Lydia's strained breaths, coming fast and furious as she gulped air, hanging from the pillory.

Moira stepped up behind her and slid the latex-gloved hand between Lydia's now rosy thighs, sliding a finger up along Lydia's slit, opening her cuntlips, wetting her finger in Lydia's honey.

Lydia sucked in her breath, moaning, opening to Moira.

"Did you hear what I said?" Moira asked the panting creature, a slave in her grip.

"Yes, yes," Lydia whimpered.

"Do you understand what I'm saying?" she asked pointedly, at the same time moving over Lydia's rock-hard clit, sending Lydia into a fit of sensation.

"Oh, God, yes," Lydia cried.

"Yes, what?" Moira urged, sliding her finger off of Lydia's sweet clit, dabbling in her juices. She stopped for a second, waiting for Lydia to answer.

Lydia could barely formulate a thought, so wild had she become with the need for a release of the pressure that throbbed beneath her skin.

"Yes, what?" Moira asked again.

"Yes, I understand," Lydia panted.

"What?"

"That if I come, I'm here with you forever," Lydia managed to say, the words sinking into her own mind at the same time. "Forever?"

"You move in with me, share my house. Attend the parties. Live with me, sweet Lydia." Moira bent her head and kissed the light welts on Lydia's back, kissed them with love and care. "I do so want you to stay," she whispered from deep in her chest, from deep in her heart. "We've only just begun to explore the possibilities together, you and I."

Lydia didn't answer, but looked out into the room, feeling Moira's hands seeking out the flesh of her sex once again.

"Oh, God," Lydia moaned, wanting nothing more than to get lost in this passion....

"I'll do everything I want, but make you come. That's your decision," Moira told her. Then she slid a finger deeply into Lydia's cunt, Lydia crying out with the sweet pleasure of it. A second finger made its way in and Lydia opened wider.

"You have a great ass," Moira said, eyes taking in Lydia's sweet, tight asshole. "Like a virgin's sweet cheeks. Am I right?"

Lydia clamped the muscles of her cunt around Moira's fingers in answer, unable to speak.

"I'll just have to see for myself."

And with that, Moira removed her fingers from the hot walls of Lydia's sex and pressed one shining, slick finger against Lydia's asshole. In her unprepared, relaxed state, Lydia's asshole opened in surprise and Moira's long finger penetrated her deeply.

"Aaaahhh shit!" Lydia cried out. "Fuck!"

Her ass throbbed with the violation, fighting but to no avail, against Moira's second digit. Moira pressed and opened Lydia from behind, sliding in deep, deeper, to the hilt of her hand, her fingers slippery with Lydia's own lube.

Lydia caught her breath, eyes wide. Moira's fingers awakened points of pleasure inside her she had never felt before. Her clit throbbed harder, demanding release.

If only she could reach down, herself, Lydia thought, and ease the pressure. *If only Moira would...*

Then Moira was parting her fingers, forcing Lydia's hole wide. Lydia grunted and shook her ass, unable to control her response. Then she felt a long tool force its way inside her, Moira's fingers giving way to it. It slid in and seemed to settle itself up inside her, the chilly feel of a base up against the outside of her hole.

She wanted more, wanted motion.

"Fuck me," she begged, "Oh, please fuck me."

She heard a cruel laugh escape from between Moira's lips. Then the woman was unlocking the padlock and opening the arm of the pillory. Lydia stood up fully, slowly, her back a shimmer of pain that traveled down her spine, ending at the throbbing point of her clit. Her ass was still filled with a long, firm, bulbous presence.

She longed to press it deeper inside, feel its pressure, feel Moira fucking her up the ass. Her body had adapted, and she wanted more.

Lydia stood there in her boots, pants still helplessly around her ankles. Moira moved around to her front side and knelt down to help her step out of the pants that held her ankles captive. Then Moira approached her, fastening a thick, wide, heavy black metal collar around Lydia's soft neck. The collar was actually two metal pieces that secured on either side with a metal slip pin. The two pieces on each end stuck out from Lydia's neck. Attached to the collar on either side were chains that fell to the floor, cold against her skin where they touched.

Moira did the same with Lydia's wrists and ankles,

leaving the butt plug in its place. Lydia clamped her muscles around it and felt a wave of pleasure rush through her. But her clit hungered for attention, forcing itself out and out, seeking the sweet touch of release that was not forthcoming.

Then Moira moved Lydia into the center of the room where she lowered chains from the ceiling. Reaching up, she secured the chains from the ceiling to those that hung off Lydia's restraints. In a moment, two chains traveled up on either side of Lydia's head, secured to hooks at the ends of her neck collar; her arms were held aloft, but not excruciatingly high, by two heavy chains secured to those in the ceiling. Her feet were forced apart and held that way by two chains secured to heavy hooks embedded in the floor.

Moira stood before her and Lydia moaned with desire. Moira's gorgeous tits were free beneath her flimsy cotton shirt, the fabric now clinging to her flesh from the sweat of her body. Lydia watched as the woman approached her and slid a newly gloved hand down between Lydia's legs, seeking out the hard bud of Lydia's clit.

"Oh, pleeeease," Lydia whimpered, clinging to the chains that held her, looking out at Moira's handsome face, Lydia's mouth wanting hers something fierce. Moira obliged and Lydia dove into her sweetness, their tongues making love in the connection between them. Lydia moaned, moving her hips against Moira's hand between her legs. The sensation began to build and Lydia held her breath, anticipating, savoring.

But that must have clued Moira in to Lydia's impending release, because she ended the kiss and removed her hand from its passion play; a soft chuckle bubbled up from Moira's throat.

"Ooh, you are so hot, Lydia, so very hot and throbbing, coating my fingers with your passion." Moira's voice was a tease in Lydia's ears. She grunted in frustration.

"You are one gorgeous woman," Moira said, stepping back to look at her. Lydia was a vision of lightly tanned skin, a creamy-skinned presence where her bathing suit bottoms would be in the sunlight. Her dark hair was wild around her face as she hung from the rafters. Her jewelry had been removed and only the soft welts on her back, buttocks, and thighs remained to decorate her body.

Moira turned away and reached for a bag up on a high shelf. She turned back to Lydia.

"If you can take all of these, all seventy-five, and you ask me to—no, beg me to—I will take you all the way and welcome you to my home, for the rest of our days," she told Lydia, her face serious, a hunger so deep Lydia felt as if she could fall into Moira's presence, dive in, become one with her in spirit.

Lydia blinked, her gaze a little foggy from the need that ached her through to her bones. Spirit. For the rest of our days... Eternity. She meant eternity, Lydia realized.

Well, there were worse places to spend eternity, she thought. And being without Moira was no longer an option, but something that would be unbearable.

"Yes," Lydia said, not knowing what was in the bag but clinging desperately to the need to have this woman intimately close, to take her inside and keep her there forever. "Yes," she repeated.

Moira smiled, face flushed with the energy between them.

She set the bag on the floor and withdrew a handful of large smooth wooden safety pins. Lydia smiled.

"I dare you," she said playfully, wanting the test more than anything; wanting to please this woman and win the prize of her forever.

It was deathly quiet in the chamber as Moira approached her, a clothespin in each hand. She opened both of them and their mouths approached Lydia's tits, wrapping around her nipples and closing down on them firmly.

Lydia hissed with pain as they held on tightly. She felt her sex melt, the pain like pleasure, both mixing into a brand-new color of sensation that coated her skin.

Moira fastened a circle of pins all around both of Lydia's tits until they looked like two flowers, like two suns, the rays reaching out from their hold on her flesh. Lydia was trying hard to control her breathing. Every now and then, Moira reached down and slid a finger up between Lydia's restrained legs, greeting her clit; revisiting Lydia's pleasure again and again, driving her crazy with the waves of desire that grew with each clothespin that bit her flesh and hung on for dear life.

"Aaaahhhh, shit," Lydia cried out as the thirtieth pin

was secured to her left arm, which hung overhead. They stuck out from her skin now on both arms and Lydia felt like a bird with wings of clothespins. She crowed, releasing pressure with her voice.

"Ha, man, can't you go any faster?" she asked, the grip of the earliest pins now growing excruciating, the nipples of her tits throbbing.

Moira smiled, but did not respond. She was caught up in the project, enjoying herself, methodically and carefully applying the pins in a specific pattern. She continued, counting as she secured each one.

"Thirty-one," she said, beginning a new row at the very top of Lydia's smooth thigh. Lydia's voice punctuated her counting. She grunted and Moira reached for the next clothespin. It found its place beside the other and snapped its jaws tightly closed, taking its own bite of skin to hold onto.

"Thirty-two," Moira said, voice intense.

Lydia breathed in ragged breaths, using the chains to help hold herself up, her body pounding, pulses building at each point of contact. And just when she thought she could not stand the feel of one more pin, Moira would reach down once again, slide up along Lydia's wet slit and explore her, tease her pussy into submission. And again, after a minute or two, Lydia allowed her to continue.

"Seventy-four," Moira whispered, leaving the clothespin extended from Lydia's belly.

"Fuck fuck *fuck!*" Lydia cried out, shaking her body,

trying to dissipate some of the pain, swearing out the frustration, the stinging, raging fire that covered her entire front now: arms, shoulders, tits, thighs, calves, stomach... The only part of her that remained untouched was her mound, the dark hair between her legs like a marker of the final target.

She shook her legs as best as she could, the flesh there sizzling now.

"Seventy-five!" Moira announced. "Good girl!"

The final pin held its place just beside Lydia's belly button. Sweat was pouring down Lydia's face, trickling down in twisting paths that made their way around the seventy-five pins that stuck out from Lydia's now rosy flesh in an incredibly beautiful design.

"Now!" Lydia roared. "For God's sake, Moira, please fuck me now. Please, please, take me, forever, yes, take me good..." Lydia's voice was a delirious order, insistent, close to madness with desire. The plug in her butt only served to intensify the need for release, the clothespins adding an excruciating level of pressure to her body.

"My pleasure," Moira said seriously. "Are you sure?" she added.

Moira stood directly in front of Lydia, leaning in to kiss her shining cheeks, run her fingers through Lydia's matted hair. She looked her deeply in the eyes and waited.

"Oh, yeah, I'm sure," Lydia said with her whole heart and body...and soul. "There is nowhere else I would rather be in this time or any other. And I need you, I need you, Moira, I need you so badly." Lydia's words were part plea, part vow.

"Then I take you as mine," Moira said in return. "And I give myself, right here, to you."

They kissed powerfully then, passing their lives to each other, Lydia feeling her heart racing in her chest at the same time she was feeling a part of herself falling, falling deeper....

Moira was behind her then, removing the butt plug and at the very same instant, inserting a longer, hand-held dildo back into Lydia's ass. As it plunged her depths, seeking her very heart, Lydia cried out with pleasure. Moira fucked her in the ass, slowly at first, in and out, long strokes, gripping the tool tightly, eyes shut, concentrating. Moira leaned her chest and face against Lydia's hot back, listening to the woman's heart, to her body's direction. She paced herself to Lydia's urgings and as Lydia's commands erupted more violently, Moira's thrusts increased in speed and she wrapped her arms around Lydia's waist, careful not to disturb any of the clothespins, reached down between Lydia's legs to flick and tease and delight the woman's ready clit. Pressed up against Lydia's naked body, her breasts hot and moist against Lydia's flesh, Moira fed her new lover from behind, fingers dancing on Lydia's clit. She felt Lydia's breathing become ragged, her breath pressing against Lydia's pressurized lungs as Moira worked her good, so good.

"Oh God, oh yeah, oh take me, Moira, yes...!" Lydia

said as she held her breath until the last possible second. Her ass was a passageway of stars going nova, blasting her control apart, shattering it as they travelled madly through her erupting body and out, out, out into Moira's open hand.

Lydia's body exploded into a million shards of light. She felt herself catapulted out into space on an over-whelming wave of orgasm and release that took her breath away. She threw back her head and, for a moment, there was no breathing at all. Her heart stopped. The traffic of blood in her veins halted like cars in grid-lock, in suspended animation.

In her bed, Lydia's body let out a long, slow sigh of satisfaction and did not take another breath.

In Moira's arms, time moved on on a different plane and Lydia gasped, gulping in air as her body contracted and expanded in intense orgasmic waves, the pleasure ripping through her as Moira thrust a final few strokes, sliding way up inside Lydia's shimmering, shining body to touch every pleasure nerve she could reach.

"Oh, Moira," Lydia breathed, trying to catch her breath, profoundly overwhelmed by the intensity of both the pleasure and delicious pain she had received, wanting desperately now to escape from the bite of the clothespins and of her bindings, to wrap her arms around the woman. "You really fucked me good, just like you promised," she whispered gratefully to Moira. Then Lydia bucked again and cried out, another wave of contractions fluttering through her as Moira's hand lingered between Lydia's shaky legs in answer. Behind her, Moira smiled, slowly removing the long dildo from the tight tunnel of Lydia's sweet, brave asshole. Lydia grunted and sucked in her breath, little lights flashing in her head. Moira rested her open palm on Lydia's mound, feeling the woman's clit shiver and pound a few last times, Lydia's honey coating her hand.

Then she set down the dildo and moved around to face Lydia as the woman hung, exhausted, from her bindings. Moira leaned in carefully and pressed her lips against Lydia's, tenderly, with feeling, Lydia's mouth returning all of this and more.

"Welcome home, my love," Moira whispered.

Faces close, lips touching, they both smiled then.

## Epilogue

On a fine spring day near the end of the twentieth century, a young dark-haired woman's body was found in a huge four-poster bed at 1282 Ruby Street. The coroner said it was a heart attack, but the cause remained unknown. However, the police noted in their report that she was smiling.

Just like all the others before her.

They wasted no time clearing out the place and shutting the house up tightly.

Empty again, except for the huge bed, the house waited, breathing with the life that continued endlessly between its walls, shifted in time and space. Rumors were that the house was haunted. No one came close enough to find out. But Faith Hanson hadn't heard a thing about it, having just arrived in town the day before. The realtors were thrilled when she took a tour of the place, asking how much they wanted for it.

They made her a great offer.

Escrow went through in record time.

# MASQUERADE BOOKS

## N. T. MORLEY

**THE LIMOUSINE**

$6.95/555-7

Brenda was enthralled with her roommate Kristi's illicit sex life: a never ending parade of men who satisfied Kristi's desire to be dominated. Brenda decides to embark on a trip into submission, beginning in the long, white limousine where Kristi first met the Master.

**THE CASTLE**

$6.95/530-1

Tess Roberts is held captive by a crew of disciplinarians intent on making all her dreams come true—even those she'd never admitted to herself. While anyone can arrange for a stay at the Castle, Tess proves herself one of the most gifted applicants yet....

**THE PARLOR**

$6.50/496-8

The mysterious John and Sarah ask Kathryn to be their slave—an idea that turns her on so much that she can't refuse! Little by little, Kathryn not only learns to serve, but comes to know the inner secrets of her keepers.

## J. A. GUERRA, ED.

**COME QUICKLY:**

**For Couples on the Go**

$6.50/461-5

The increasing pace of daily life is no reason to forgo a little carnal pleasure whenever the mood strikes. Here are over sixty of the hottest fantasies around—all designed especially for modern couples on a hectic schedule.

## ERICA BRONTE

**LUST, INC.**

$6.50/467-4

Explore the extremes of passion that lurk beneath even the most businesslike exteriors. Join in the sexy escapades of a group of professionals whose ideas of office decorum is like nothing you've ever encountered!

## VANESSA DURIÈS

**THE TIES THAT BIND**

$6.50/510-7

This chronicle of dominance and submission will keep you gasping with its vivid depictions of sensual abandon. At the hand of Masters Georges, Patrick, Pierre and others, this submissive seductress experiences pleasures she never knew existed.... One of modern erotica's best-selling accounts of real-life dominance and submission.

## M. S. VALENTINE

**THE GOVERNESS**

$6.95/562-X

Lovely Miss Hunnicut eagerly embarks upon a career as a governess, hoping to escape the memories of her broken engagement. Little does she know that Crawleigh Manor is far from the upstanding household it appears. Mr. Crawleigh, in particular, devotes himself to Miss Hunnicut's thorough defiling.

**ELYSIAN DAYS AND NIGHTS**

$6.95/536-0

From around the world, neglected young wives arrive at the Elysium Spa intent on receiving a little heavy-duty pampering. Luckily for them, the spa's proprietor is a true devotee of the female form—and has dedicated himself to the pure pleasure of every woman who steps foot across their threshold....

**THE CAPTIVITY OF CELIA**

$6.50/453-4

Celia's lover, Colin, is considered the prime suspect in a murder, forcing him to seek refuge with his cousin, Sir Jason Hardwicke. In exchange for Colin's safety, Jason demands Celia's unquestioning submission....

## AMANDA WARE

**BINDING CONTRACT**

$6.50/491-7

Louise was responsible for bringing many clients into Claremont's salon—so he was more than willing to have her miss a little work in order to pleasure one of his most important customers. But Eleanor Cavendish had her mind set on something more rigorous than a simple wash and set. Sexual slavery!

**BOUND TO THE PAST**

$6.50/452-6

Doing research in an old Tudor mansion, Anne finds herself aroused by James, a descendant of the property's owners. Together they uncover the perverse desires of the mansion's long-dead master—desires that bind Anne inexorably to the past—not to mention the bedpost!

## SACHI MIZUNO

**SHINJUKU NIGHTS**

$6.50/493-3

A tour through the lives and libidos of the seductive East. Sachi Mizuno weaves an intricate web of sensual desire, wherein many characters are ensnared and enraptured by the demands of their carnal natures.

# MASQUERADE BOOKS

## PASSION IN TOKYO
$6.50/454-2

Tokyo—one of Asia's most historic and seductive cities. Come behind the closed doors of its citizens, and witness the many pleasures that await. Lusty men and women from every stratum of society free themselves of all inhibitions.

·············································

### MARTINE GLOWINSKI
## POINT OF VIEW
$6.50/433-X

The story of one woman's extraordinary erotic awakening. With the assistance of her new, unexpectedly kinky lover, she discovers and explores her exhibitionist tendencies—until there is virtually nothing she won't do before the horny audiences her man arranges!

·············································

### RICHARD McGOWAN
## A HARLOT OF VENUS
$6.50/425-9

A highly fanciful, epic tale of lust on Mars! Cavortia—the most famous and sought-after courtesan in the cosmopolitan city of Venus—finds love and much more during her adventures with some cosmic characters.

·············································

### M. ORLANDO
## THE SLEEPING PALACE
$6.95/582-4

Another thrilling volume of erotic reveries from the author of *The Architecture of Desire*. *Maison Bizarre* is the scene of unspeakable erotic cruelty; the *Lust Akademie* holds captive only the most luscious students of the sensual arts; *Baden-Eros* is the luxurious retreat of one's nastiest dreams.

·············································

### CHET ROTHWELL
## KISS ME, KATHERINE
$5.95/410-0

Beautiful Katherine can hardly believe her luck. Not only is she married to the charming Nelson, she's free to live out all her erotic fantasies with other men. Katherine's desires are more than any one man can handle—and plenty of men wait to fulfill her needs!

·············································

### MARCO VASSI
## THE STONED APOCALYPSE
$5.95/401-1/Mass market

"Marco Vassi is our champion sexual energist."    —*VLS*

During his lifetime, Marco Vassi's reputation as a champion of sexual experimentation was worldwide. *The Stoned Apocalypse* is Vassi's autobiography; chronicling a cross-country trip on America's erotic byways, it offers a rare glimpse of a generation's sexual imagination.

## THE SALINE SOLUTION
$6.95/568-9/Mass market

"I've always read Marco's work with interest and I have the highest opinion not only of his talent but his intellectual boldness."
—Norman Mailer

During the Sexual Revolution, Vassi established himself as an explorer of an uncharted sexual landscape. He also distinguished himself as a novelist. Through the story of one couple's brief affair and the events that lead them to desperately reassess their lives, Vassi examines the dangers of intimacy in an age of extraordinary freedom.

·············································

### ROBIN WILDE
## TABITHA'S TEASE
$6.95/597-2

When poor Robin arrives at The Valentine Academy, he finds himself subject to the torturous teasing of Tabitha—the Academy's most notoriously domineering co-ed. But Tabitha is pledge-mistress of a secret sorority dedicated to enslaving young men. Robin finds himself the utterly helpless (and wildly excited) captive of Tabitha & Company's weird desires! A marathon of ticklish torture!

## TABITHA'S TICKLE
$6.50/468-2

Tabitha's back! The story of this vicious vixen didn't end with *Tabitha's Tease*. Once again, men fall under the spell of scrumptious co-eds and find themselves enslaved to demands and desires they never dreamed existed. Think it's a man's world? Guess again. With Tabitha around, no man gets what he wants until she's completely satisfied....

·············································

### ERICA BRONTE
## PIRATE'S SLAVE
$5.95/376-7

Lovely young Erica is stranded in a country where lust knows no bounds. Desperate to escape, she finds herself trading her firm, luscious body to any and all men willing and able to help her. Her adventure has its ups and downs, ins and outs—all to the pleasure of the increasingly lusty Erica!

·············································

### CHARLES G. WOOD
## HELLFIRE
$5.95/358-9

A vicious murderer is running amok in New York's sexual underground—and Nick O'Shay, a virile detective with the NYPD, plunges deep into the case. He soon becomes embroiled in an elusive world of fleshly extremes, hunting a madman seeking to purge America with fire and blood sacrifices.

# MASQUERADE BOOKS

## CHARISSE VAN DER LYN
### SEX ON THE NET
$5.95/399-6

Electrifying erotica from one of the Internet's hottest authors. Encounters of all kinds—straight, lesbian, dominant/submissive and all sorts of extreme passions—are explored in thrilling detail.

## STANLEY CARTEN
### NAUGHTY MESSAGE
$5.95/333-3

Wesley Arthur discovers a lascivious message on his answering machine. Aroused beyond his wildest dreams by the acts described, he becomes obsessed with tracking down the woman behind the seductive voice. His search takes him through strip clubs, sex parlors and no-tell motels—before finally leading him to his randy reward....

## AKBAR DEL PIOMBO
### THE FETISH CROWD
$6.95/556-5

A trilogy presented as a special volume guaranteed to appeal to the modern sophisticate. Separately, *Paula the Piqúose,* the infamous *Duke Cosimo,* and *The Double-Bellied Companion* are rightly considered masterpieces.

### A CRUMBLING FAÇADE
$4.95/3043-1

The return of that incorrigible rogue, Henry Pike, who continues his pursuit of sex, fair or otherwise, in the most elegant homes of the most debauched aristocrats. Ultimately, every woman succumbs to Pike's charms—and submits to his whims!

## CAROLE REMY
### FANTASY IMPROMPTU
$6.50/513-1

Kidnapped and held in a remote island retreat, Chantal finds herself catering to every sexual whim of the mysterious and arousing Bran. Bran is determined to bring Chantal to a full embracing of her sensual nature, even while revealing himself to be something far more than human....

### BEAUTY OF THE BEAST
$5.95/332-5

A shocking tell-all, written from the point-of-view of a prize-winning reporter. And what reporting she does! All the secrets of an uninhibited life are revealed.

## ANONYMOUS
### THE MISFORTUNES OF COLETTE
$7.95/564-6

The tale of one woman's erotic suffering at the hands of the sadistic man and woman who take her in hand. Beautiful Colette is passed from one tormentor to another, until it becomes clear that she is destined to find her greatest pleasures in punishment!

### SUBURBAN SOULS
$9.95/563-8/Trade paperback

Focusing on the May–December sexual relationship of nubile Lillian and the more experienced Jack, all three volumes of *Suburban Souls* now appear in one special edition—guaranteed to enrapture modern readers with its lurid detail.

### LOVE'S ILLUSION
$6.95/549-2

Elizabeth Renard yearned for the body of rich and successful Dan Harrington. Then she discovered Harrington's secret weakness: a need to be humiliated and punished. She makes him her slave, and together they commence a thrilling journey into depravity that leaves nothing to the imagination!

### NADIA
$5.95/267-1

Follow the delicious but neglected Nadia as she works to wring every drop of pleasure out of life—despite an unhappy marriage. A classic title providing a peek into the secret sexual lives of another time and place.

## TITIAN BERESFORD
### CHIDEWELL HOUSE AND OTHER STORIES
$6.95/554-9

What keeps Cecil a virtual, if willing, prisoner of Chidewell House? One man has been sent to investigate the sexy situation—and reports back with tales of such depravity that no expense is spared in attempting Cecil's rescue. But what man would possibly desire release from the breathtakingly corrupt Elizabeth?

### CINDERELLA
$6.50/500-X

Beresford triumphs again with this intoxicating tale, filled with castle dungeons and tightly corseted ladies-in-waiting, naughty viscounts and impossibly cruel masturbatrixes—nearly every conceivable method of erotic torture is explored and described in lush, vivid detail.

---

**BUY ANY 4 BOOKS & CHOOSE 1 ADDITIONAL BOOK, OF EQUAL OR LESSER VALUE, AS YOUR FREE GIFT**

# MASQUERADE BOOKS

## MARY LOVE

### ANGELA
$6.95/545-X

Angela's game is "look but don't touch," and she drives everyone mad with desire, dancing for their pleasure but never allowing a single caress. Soon her sensual spell is cast, and she's the only one who can break it!

### MASTERING MARY SUE
$5.95/351-1

Mary Sue is a rich nymphomaniac whose husband is determined to declare her mentally incompetent and gain control of her fortune. He brings her to a castle where, to Mary Sue's delight, she is unleashed for a veritable sex-fest!

## AMARANTHA KNIGHT
### The Darker Passions: CARMILLA
$6.95/578-6

A shockingly sensual reinterpretation of Sheridan LeFanu's notorious chiller. Captivated by the portrait of a beautiful woman, a young man finds himself becoming obsessed with her remarkable story. Little by little, he uncovers the many blasphemies and debaucheries with which the beauteous Laura filled her hours— even as a hungry, otherworldly presence began feasting upon her....

### The Darker Passions:
### THE PICTURE OF DORIAN GRAY
$6.50/342-2

A fabulously decadent tale of highly personal changes. One woman finds her most secret desires laid bare by a portrait far more revealing than she could have imagined. Soon she benefits from a skillful masquerade.

### THE DARKER PASSIONS READER
$6.50/432-1

The best moments from Knight's phenomenally popular Darker Passions series. Here are the most eerily erotic passages from her acclaimed sexual reworkings of *Dracula*, *Frankenstein*, *Dr. Jekyll & Mr. Hyde* and *The Fall of the House of Usher*.

### The Darker Passions:
### DR. JEKYLL AND MR. HYDE
$4.95/227-2

It is a story of incredible transformations. Explore the steamy possibilities of a tale where no one is quite who—or what—they seem. Victorian bedrooms explode with hidden demons!

### The Darker Passions: DRACULA
$5.95/326-0

"Well-written and imaginative...taking us through the sexual and sadistic scenes with details that keep us reading.... A classic in itself has been added to the shelves."     —*Divinity*

The infamous erotic revisioning of Bram Stoker's classic.

## THE PAUL LITTLE LIBRARY
### FIT FOR A KING/BEGINNER'S LUST
$8.95/571-9/Trade paperback

Two complete novels from this master of modern lust. Voluptuous and exquisite, she is a woman *Fit for a King*—but could she withstand the fantastic force of his carnality? *Beginner's Lust* pays off handsomely for a novice in the many ways of sensuality.

### SENTENCED TO SERVITUDE
$8.95/565-4/Trade paperback

A haughty young aristocrat learns what becomes of excessive pride when she is abducted and forced to submit to ordeals of sensual torment. Trained to accept her submissive state, the icy young woman soon melts under the heat of her owners....

### ROOMMATE'S SECRET
$8.95/557-3/Trade paperback

Here are the many exploits of one woman forced to make ends meet by the most ancient of methods. From the misery of early impoverishment to the delight of ill-gotten gains, Elda learns to rely on her considerable sensual talents.

### LOVE SLAVE/
### PECULIAR PASSIONS OF MEG
$8.95/529-8/Trade paperback

What does it take to acquire a willing *Love Slave* of one's own? What are the appetites that lurk within *Meg*? The notoriously depraved Paul Little spares no lascivious detail in these two relentless tales!

### CELESTE
$6.95/544-1

It's definitely all in the family for this female duo of sexual dynamics. While traveling through Europe, these two try everything and everyone on their horny holiday.

### ALL THE WAY
$6.95/509-3

Two excruciating novels from Paul Little in one hot volume! *Going All the Way* features an unhappy man who tries to purge himself of the memory of his lover with a series of quirky and uninhibited lovers. *Pushover* tells the story of a serial spanker and his celebrated exploits.

# MASQUERADE BOOKS

## THE END OF INNOCENCE
$6.95/546-8

The early days of Women's Emancipation are the setting for this story of very independent ladies. These women were willing to go to any lengths to fight for their sexual freedom, and willing to endure any punishment in their desire for total liberation.

## TUTORED IN LUST
$6.95/547-6

This tale of the initiation and instruction of a carnal college co-ed and her fellow students unlocks the sex secrets of the classroom.

## THE BEST OF PAUL LITTLE
$6.50/469-0

Known for his fantastic portrayals of punishment and pleasure, Little never fails to push readers over the edge of sensual excitement. His best scenes are here collected for the enjoyment of all erotic connoisseurs.

## CAPTIVE MAIDENS
$5.95/440-2

Three young women find themselves powerless against the debauched landowners of 1824 England. They are banished to a sex colony, and subjected to unspeakable perversions.

## THE PRISONER
$5.95/330-9

Judge Black has built a secret room below a penitentiary, where he sentences his female prisoners to hours of exhibition and torment while his friends watch. Judge Black's brand of rough justice keeps his captives on the brink of utter pleasure!

## TEARS OF THE INQUISITION
$4.95/146-2

A staggering account of pleasure and punishment. "There was a tickling inside her as her nervous system reminded her she was ready for sex. But before her was...the Inquisitor!"

## DOUBLE NOVEL
$6.95/86-6

*The Metamorphosis of Lisette Joyaux* tells the story of a young woman initiated into an incredible world world of lesbian lusts. *The Story of Monique* reveals the twisted sexual rituals that beckon the ripe and willing Monique.

## SLAVE ISLAND
$5.95/441-0

A leisure cruise is waylaid by Lord Henry Philbrock, a sadistic genius. The ship's passengers are kidnapped and spirited to his island prison, where the women are trained to accommodate the most bizarre sexual cravings of the rich and perverted.

## ALIZARIN LAKE
### CLARA
$6.95/548-4

The mysterious death of a beautiful woman leads her old boyfriend on a harrowing journey of discovery. His search uncovers a woman on a quest for deeper and more unusual sensations, each more shocking than the one before!

### SEX ON DOCTOR'S ORDERS
$5.95/402-X

Beth, a nubile young nurse, uses her considerable skills to further medical science by offering insatiable assistance in the gathering of important specimens. Soon she's involved everyone in her horny work.

### THE EROTIC ADVENTURES OF HARRY TEMPLE
$4.95/127-6

Harry Temple's memoirs chronicle his incredibly amorous adventures—from his initiation at the hands of insatiable sirens, through his stay at a house of hot repute, to his encounters with a chastity-belted nympho, and much more!

## JOHN NORMAN
### TARNSMAN OF GOR
$6.95/486-0

This controversial series returns! Tarl Cabot is transported to Gor. He must quickly accustom himself to the ways of this world, including the caste system which exalts some as Priest-Kings or Warriors, and debases others as slaves. The beginning of the mammoth epic which made Norman a household name among fans of both science fiction and dominance/submission.

### OUTLAW OF GOR
$6.95/487-9

Tarl Cabot returns to Gor, to reclaim both his woman and his role of Warrior. But upon arriving, he discovers that his name, his city and the names of those he loves have become unspeakable. Cabot has become an outlaw, and must discover his new purpose on this strange planet, where danger stalks the outcast, and even simple answers have their price....

### PRIEST-KINGS OF GOR
$6.95/488-7

Tarl Cabot searches for his lovely wife Talena. Does she live, or was she destroyed by the all-powerful Priest-Kings? Cabot is determined to find out—though no one who has approached the mountain stronghold of the Priest-Kings has ever returned alive....

# MASQUERADE BOOKS

## NOMADS OF GOR
$6.95/527-1

Cabot finds his way across Gor, pledged to serve the Priest-Kings in their quest for survival. Unfortunately for Cabot, his mission leads him to the savage Wagon People—nomads who may very well kill before surrendering any secrets....

## ASSASSIN OF GOR
$6.95/538-7

Here is the brutal caste system of Gor: from the Assassin Kuurus, on a mission of bloody vengeance, to Pleasure Slaves, trained in the ways of personal ecstasy. The Masters and slaves of Counter-Earth pursue and are pursued by all-too human passions...

## RAIDERS OF GOR
$6.95/558-1

Tarl Cabot descends into the depths of Port Kar—the most degenerate port city of the Counter-Earth. There, among pirates, and cut-throats, Cabot learns the ways of Kar, whose residents are renowned for the iron grip in which they hold their voluptuous slaves....

## SYDNEY ST. JAMES
### RIVE GAUCHE
$5.95/317-1

The Latin Quarter, Paris, circa 1920. Expatriate bohemians couple with abandon—before eventually abandoning their ambitions amidst the intoxicating temptations waiting to be indulged in every bedroom.

## DON WINSLOW
### SLAVE GIRLS OF ROME
$6.95/577-8

Never were women so relentlessly used as were ancient Rome's voluptuous slaves! With no choice but to serve their lustful masters, these captive beauties perform their duties with the passion and purpose of Venus herself.

### THE FALL OF THE ICE QUEEN
$6.50/520-4

Rahn the Conqueror chose a true beauty as his Consort. But the regal disregard with which she treated Rahn was not to be endured. It was decided that she would submit to his will—and as so many had learned, Rahn's depraved expectations have made his court infamous.

### PRIVATE PLEASURES
$6.50/504-2

Frantic voyeurs and licentious exhibitionists are here displayed in all their wanton glory—laid bare by the perverse eye of Don Winslow.

## THE INSATIABLE MISTRESS OF ROSEDALE
$6.50/494-1

Edward and Lady Penelope reside in Rosedale manor. While Edward is a connoisseur of sexual perversion, it is Lady Penelope whose mastery of complete sensual pleasure makes their home infamous. Indulging one another's bizarre whims is a way of life for this wicked couple....

## SECRETS OF CHEATEM MANOR
$6.50/434-8

Edward returns to his late father's estate, to find it being run by the majestic Lady Amanda. Edward can hardly believe his luck—Lady Amanda is assisted by her two beautiful daughters, Catherine and Prudence. What the randy young man soon comes to realize is the love of discipline that all three beauties share.

## KATERINA IN CHARGE
$5.95/409-7

When invited to a country retreat by a mysterious couple, two randy young ladies can hardly resist! Soon after they arrive, the imperious Katerina makes her desires known—and demands that they be fulfilled...

## THE MANY PLEASURES OF IRONWOOD
$5.95/310-4

Seven lovely young women are employed by The Ironwood Sportsmen's Club, where their natural talents in the sensual arts are put to creative use. Winslow explores he ins and outs of this small and exclusive club—with seven carefully selected sexual connoisseurs.

## CLAIRE'S GIRLS
$5.95/442-9

You knew when she walked by that she was something special. She was one of Claire's girls, a woman carefully dressed and groomed to fill a role, to capture a look, to fit an image crafted by the sophisticated proprietress of an exclusive escort agency. High-class whores blow the roof off!

## MARCUS VAN HELLER
### KIDNAP
$4.95/90-4

P.I. Harding is called in to investigate a mysterious kidnapping case involving the rich and powerful. Along the way he has the pleasure of "interrogating" an exotic dancer named Jeanne and a beautiful English reporter, as he finds himself enmeshed in the sleazy international underworld.

# MASQUERADE BOOKS

## ALEXANDER TROCCHI
### YOUNG ADAM
$4.95/63-7
Two British barge operators discover a girl drowned in the river Clyde. Her lover, a plumber, is arrested for her murder. But he is innocent. Joe, the barge assistant, knows that. As the plumber is tried and sentenced to hang, this knowledge lends poignancy to Joe's romances with the women along the river whom he will love then... well, read on.

## N. WHALLEN
### THE EDUCATION OF SITA MANSOOR
$6.95/567-0
On the eve of her wedding, lovely Sita Mansoor is tragically left without a bridegroom. Sita is now free to leave India for America, where she hopes to become educated in the ways of a more permissive society. She could never have imagined the wide variety of greedy tutors—both male and female—who would be waiting to take on so beautiful and hungry a pupil.

### TAU'TEVU
$6.50/426-7
Statuesque and beautiful Vivian learns to subject herself to the hand of a domineering man. He systematically helps her prove her own strength, and brings to life in her an unimagined sensual fire.

## ISADORA ALMAN
### ASK ISADORA
$4.95/61-0
Six years' worth of Isadora's syndicated columns on sex and relationships. Alman's been called a "hip Dr. Ruth," and a "sexy Dear Abby," based upon the wit of her advice. Today's world is more perplexing than ever—and Alman is just the expert to help untangle the most personal of knots.

## THE CLASSIC COLLECTION
### THE ENGLISH GOVERNESS
$5.95/373-2
When Lord Lovell's son was expelled from his prep school for masturbation, his father hired a very proper governess to tutor the boy—giving her strict instructions not to spare the rod to break him of his bad habits. Luckily, Harriet Marwood was addicted to domination.

### PROTESTS, PLEASURES, RAPTURES
$5.95/400-3
Invited for an allegedly quiet weekend at a country vicarage, a young woman is stunned to find herself surrounded by shocking acts of sexual sadism. Soon she begins to explore her own capacities for delicious sexual cruelty.

### THE YELLOW ROOM
$5.95/378-3
The "yellow room" holds the secrets of lust, lechery, and the lash. There, bare-bottomed, spread-eagled, and open to the world, demure Alice Darvell soon learns to love her lickings.

### SCHOOL DAYS IN PARIS
$5.95/325-2
Few Universities provide the profound and pleasurable lessons one learns in after-hours study— particularly if one is young and available, and lucky enough to have Paris as a playground. Here are all the randy pursuits of young adulthood.

### MAN WITH A MAID
$4.95/307-4
The adventures of Jack and Alice have delighted readers for eight decades! A classic of its genre, *Man with a Maid* tells a tale of desire, revenge, and submission.

## MASQUERADE READERS
### INTIMATE PLEASURES
$4.95/38-6
Indulge your most private penchants with this specially chosen selection. Try a tempting morsel of *The Prodigal Virgin* and *Eveline*, or the bizarre public displays of carnality in *The Gilded Lily* and *The Story of Monique*.

## CLASSIC EROTIC BIOGRAPHIES
### JENNIFER AGAIN
$4.95/220-5
The uncensored life of one of modern erotica's most popular heroines. Once again, the insatiable Jennifer seizes the day and extracts every last drop of sensual pleasure!

### JENNIFER #3
$5.95/292-2
The adventures of erotica's most daring heroine. Jennifer has a photographer's eye for details—particularly of the male variety! One by one, her subjects submit to her demands for pleasure.

### PAULINE
$4.95/129-2
From rural America to the royal court of Austria, Pauline follows her ever-growing sexual desires as she rises to the top of the Opera world. "I would never see them again. Why shouldn't I give myself to them that they might become more and more inspired to deeds of greater lust!"

# RHINOCEROS

## LEOPOLD VON SACHER-MASOCH
### VENUS IN FURS
$7.95/589-1

This classic 19th century novel is the first exploration of the dominant/submissive relationship in literature. The alliance of Severin and Wanda epitomizes Sacher-Masoch's obsession with a cruel goddess and the urges that drive the man held in her thrall. Exclusive to this edition are letters exchanged between Sacher-Masoch and Emilie Mataja—an aspiring writer he sought as the avatar of his desires.

## JOHN NORMAN
### IMAGINATIVE SEX
$7.95/561-1

The author of the controversial Gor novels unleashes his vision for an exciting sex life for all. *Imaginative Sex* outlines John Norman's philosophy on relations between the sexes, and presents fifty-three scenarios designed to reintroduce fantasy to the bedroom.

## KATHLEEN K.
### SWEET TALKERS
$6.95/516-6

"If you enjoy eavesdropping on explicit conversations about sex... this book is for you."
—*Spectator*

Kathleen K. ran a phone-sex company in the late 80s, and she opens up her diary for a peek at the life of a phone-sex operator. Transcripts of actual conversations are included.
Trade /$12.95/192-6

## THOMAS S. ROCHE
### DARK MATTER
$6.95/484-4

"*Dark Matter* is sure to please gender outlaws, bodymod junkies, goth vampires, boys who wish they were dykes, and anybody who's not to sure where the fine line should be drawn between pleasure and pain. It's a handful."—Pat Califia

"Here is the erotica of the cumming millennium.... You will be deliciously disturbed, but never disappointed."
—Poppy Z. Brite

### NOIROTICA 2
$7.95/584-0

Another volume of criminally seductive stories set in the murky terrain of the erotic and noir genres. Thomas Roche has gathered the darkest jewels from today's edgiest writers to create this provocative collection.

## NOIROTICA: An Anthology of Erotic Crime Stories (Ed.)
$6.95/390-2

A collection of darkly sexy tales, taking place at the crossroads of the crime and erotic genres. Here are some of today's finest writers, all of whom explore the murky and arousing terrain where desire runs irrevocably afoul of the law.

## AMELIA G, ED.
### BACKSTAGE PASSES:
### Rock n' Roll Erotica from the Pages of *Blue Blood* Magazine
$6.95/438-0

Amelia G, editor of the groundbreaking goth-sex journal *Blue Blood*, has brought together some of today's most irreverent writers, each of whom has outdone themselves with an edgy, antic tale of modern lust. Punks, metalheads, and grunge-trash roam these pages, and no one knows their ways better....

## ROMY ROSEN
### SPUNK
$6.95/492-5

Casey, a lovely model poised upon the verge of super-celebrity, falls for an insatiable young rock singer—not suspecting that his sexual appetite has led him to experiment with a dangerous new aphrodisiac. Soon, Casey becomes addicted to the drug, and her craving plunges her into a strange underworld, and into an alliance with a shadowy young man with secrets of his own....

## MOLLY WEATHERFIELD
### CARRIE'S STORY
$6.95/485-2

"I was stunned by how well it was written and how intensely foreign I found its sexual world.... And, since this is a world I don't frequent... I thoroughly enjoyed the National Geo tour."
—*bOING bOING*

"Hilarious and harrowing... just when you think things can't get any wilder, they do."
—*Black Sheets*

Weatherfield's bestselling examination of dominance and submission. "I had been Jonathan's slave for about a year when he told me he wanted to sell me at an auction...." Desire and depravity run rampant in this story of uncompromising mastery and irrevocable submission. A rare piece of erotica, that is both thoughtful and hot!

# MASQUERADE BOOKS

## GERI NETTICK
## WITH BETH ELLIOT
**MIRRORS: Portrait of
a Lesbian Transsexual**
$6.95/435-6
Born a male, Geri Nettick knew something just
didn't fit. Even after coming to terms with her
own gender dysphoria she still fought to be
accepted by the lesbian feminist community to
which she felt she belonged. A true story.

## DAVID MELTZER
**UNDER**
$6.95/290-6
The story of a 21st century sex professional
living at the bottom of the social heap. After
surgeries designed to increase his physical
allure, corrupt government forces drive the
cyber-gigolo underground—where even
more bizarre cultures await him.

**ORF**
$6.95/110-1
He is the ultimate hero—the idol of thou-
sands, the fevered dream of many more.
Every last drop of feeling is squeezed from a
modern-day troubadour and his lady love in
this psychedelic bacchanal.

## CYBERSEX CONSORTIUM
**CYBERSEX: The Perv's Guide to
Finding Sex on the Internet**
$6.95/471-2
You've heard the objections: cyberspace is
soaked with sex, mired in immorality. Okay—
so where is it!? Tracking down the good
stuff—the real good stuff—can waste an awful
lot of expensive time, and frequently leave you
high and dry. The Cybersex Consortium
presents an easy-to-use guide for those intrepid
adults who know what they want.

## LAURA ANTONIOU, ED.
**SOME WOMEN**
$7.95/573-5
Introduction by Pat Califia
"Makes the reader think about the wide range of SM experi-
ences, beyond the glamour of fiction and fantasy, or the
clever-clever prose of the perverati."          —SKIN TWO

Over forty essays written by women actively
involved in consensual dominance and submission. Professional mistresses, lifestyle leather-
dykes, whipmakers, titleholders—women from
every conceivable walk of life lay bare their true
feelings about issues as explosive as feminism,
abuse, pleasure and public image. An indispen-
sible volume for all interested or involved in this
increasingly visible community.

## NO OTHER TRIBUTE
$7.95/603-0
Tales of women kept in bondage to their
lovers by their deepest passions. Love pushes
these women beyond acceptable limits,
rendering them helpless to deny anything to
the men and women they adore.

## BY HER SUBDUED
$6.95/281-7
These tales all involve women in control—of
their lives, their loves, their men. So much in
control that they can remorselessly break rules
to become powerful goddesses of the men
who sacrifice all to worship at their feet.

## LAURA ANTONIOU
## ("Sara Adamson")
**THE TRAINER**
$6.95/249-3
The Marketplace Trilogy concludes with the
story of the trainers, and the desires and paths
that led them to become the ultimate figures
of authority.

## TRISTAN TAORMINO &
## DAVID AARON CLARK, EDS.
**RITUAL SEX**
$6.95/391-0
The many contributors to *Ritual Sex* know—
and demonstrate—that body and soul share
more common ground than society feels
comfortable acknowledging. From memoirs
of ecstatic revelation, to quests to reconcile
sex and spirit, *Ritual Sex* provides an unprece-
dented look at private life.

## TAMMY JO ECKHART
**AMAZONS: Erotic Explorations
of Ancient Myths**
$7.95/534-4
The Amazon—the fierce, independent woman
warrior—appears in the traditions of many
cultures, but never before has the full erotic
potential of this archetype been explored with
such imagination and energy. Powerful pleasures await anyone lucky enough to encounter
Eckhart's legendary spitfires.

**PUNISHMENT FOR THE CRIME**
$6.95/427-6
Peopled by characters of rare depth, these
stories explore the true meaning of dominance and submission. From an encounter
between two of society's most despised indi-
viduals, to the explorations of longtime
friends, these tales take you where few others
have ever dared....

# MASQUERADE BOOKS

## AMARANTHA KNIGHT, ED.
### SEDUCTIVE SPECTRES
$6.95/464-X

Breathtaking tours through the erotic supernatural via the imaginations of today's best writers. Never have ghostly encounters been so alluring, thanks to a cast of otherworldly characters well-acquainted with the pleasures of the flesh.

### SEX MACABRE
$6.95/392-9

Horror tales designed for dark and sexy nights—sure to make your skin crawl, and heart beat faster.

### FLESH FANTASTIC
$6.95/352-X

Humans have long toyed with the idea of "playing God": creating life from nothingness, bringing life to the inanimate. Now Amarantha Knight collects stories exploring not only the act of Creation, but the lust that follows.

## GARY BOWEN
### DIARY OF A VAMPIRE
$6.95/331-7

"Gifted with a darkly sensual vision and a fresh voice, [Bowen] is a writer to watch out for."    —Cecilia Tan

Rafael, a red-blooded male with an insatiable hunger for the same, is the perfect antidote to the effete malcontents haunting bookstores today. The emergence of a bold and brilliant vision, rooted in past and present.

## RENÉ MAIZEROY
### FLESHLY ATTRACTIONS
$6.95/299-X

Lucien was the son of the wantonly beautiful actress, Marie-Rose Hardanges. When she decides to let a "friend" introduce her son to the pleasures of love, Marie-Rose could not have foretold the excesses that would lead to her own ruin and that of her cherished son.

## JEAN STINE
### THRILL CITY
$6.95/411-9

Thrill City is the seat of the world's increasing depravity, and this classic novel transports you there with a vivid style you'd be hard pressed to ignore. No writer is better suited to describe the extremes of this modern Babylon.

### SEASON OF THE WITCH
$6.95/268-X

"A future in which it is technically possible to transfer the total mind...of a rapist killer into the brain dead but physically living body of his female victim. Remarkable for intense psychological technique. There is eroticism but it is necessary to mark the differences between the sexes and the subtle altering of a man into a woman."    —The Science Fiction Critic

## GRANT ANTREWS
### ROGUES GALLERY
$6.95/522-0

A stirring evocation of dominant/submissive love. Two doctors meet and slowly fall in love. Once Beth reveals her hidden desires to Jim, the two explore the forbidden acts that will come to define their distinctly exotic affair.

### MY DARLING DOMINATRIX
$7.95/566-2

When a man and a woman fall in love, it's supposed to be simple, uncomplicated, easy—unless that woman happens to be a dominatrix. This highly praised and unpretentious love story captures the richness and depth of this very special kind of love without leering or smirking.

### SUBMISSIONS
$6.95/207-8

Antrews portrays the very special elements of the dominant/submissive relationship with restraint—this time with the story of a lonely man, a winning lottery ticket, and a demanding dominatrix.

## JOHN WARREN
### THE TORQUEMADA KILLER
$6.95/367-8

Detective Eva Hernandez gets her first "big case": a string of murders taking place within New York's SM community. Eva assembles the evidence, revealing a picture of a world misunderstood and under attack—and gradually comes to face her own hidden longings.

### THE LOVING DOMINANT
$6.95/218-3

Everything you need to know about an infamous sexual variation—and an unspoken type of love. Warren, a longtime player, guides readers through the forbidden realm of leathersex—and reveals the too-often hidden basis of the D/S relationship: care, trust and love.

# MASQUERADE BOOKS

## DAVID AARON CLARK
### SISTER RADIANCE
$6.95/215-9
A meditation on love, sex, and death. The vicissitudes of lust and romance are examined against a backdrop of urban decay in this testament to the allure of the forbidden.
### THE WET FOREVER
$6.95/117-9
The story of Janus and Madchen—a small-time hood and a beautiful sex worker on the run—examines themes of loyalty, sacrifice, redemption and obsession amidst Manhattan's sex parlors and underground S/M clubs. A contemporary adult thriller.

## MICHAEL PERKINS
### EVIL COMPANIONS
$6.95/3067-9
*Evil Companions* has been hailed as "a frightening classic." A young couple explores the nether reaches of the erotic unconscious in a confrontation with the extremes of passion.
### THE SECRET RECORD:
### Modern Erotic Literature
$6.95/3039-3
Michael Perkins surveys the field with authority and unique insight. Updated and revised to include the latest trends, tastes, and developments in this misunderstood genre.
### AN ANTHOLOGY OF CLASSIC ANONYMOUS EROTIC WRITING
$6.95/140-3
The very best passages from the world's most enduring erotic writing. "Anonymous" is one of the most infamous bylines in publishing history—and these steamy excerpts show why!

## HELEN HENLEY
### ENTER WITH TRUMPETS
$6.95/197-7
Helen Henley was told that women just don't write about sex—much less the taboos she was so interested in exploring. So Henley did it alone, flying in the face of "tradition" by writing this touching tale of arousal and devotion in one couple's kinky relationship.

## ALICE JOANOU
### BLACK TONGUE
$6.95/258-2
"Joanou has created a series of sumptuous, brooding, dark visions of sexual obsession, and is undoubtedly a name to look out for in the future."
—*Redeemer*

Exploring lust at its most florid and unsparing, *Black Tongue* is a trove of baroque fantasies—each redolent of forbidden passions.

### TOURNIQUET
$6.95/3060-1
A heady collection of stories and effusions from the pen of one our most dazzling young writers. Strange tales abound in this complex and riveting series of meditations on desire.
### CANNIBAL FLOWER
$4.95/72-6
"She is waiting in her darkened bedroom, as she has waited throughout history, to seduce the men who are foolish enough to be blinded by her irresistible charms.... She is the goddess of sexuality, and *Cannibal Flower* is her haunting siren song."
—Michael Perkins

## LIESEL KULIG
### LOVE IN WARTIME
$6.95/3044-X
Madeleine knew that the handsome SS officer was a dangerous man, but she was just a cabaret singer in Nazi-occupied Paris, trying to survive in a perilous time. When Josef fell in love with her, he discovered that a beautiful woman can sometimes be as dangerous as any warrior.

## SAMUEL R. DELANY
### THE MAD MAN
$8.99/408-9/Mass market
"Reads like a pornographic reflection of Peter Ackroyd's *Chatterton* or A. S. Byatt's *Possession*.... Delany develops an insightful dichotomy between [his protagonist]'s two worlds: the one of cerebral philosophy and dry academia, the other of heedless, 'impersonal' obsessive sexual extremism. When these worlds finally collide...the novel achieves a surprisingly satisfying resolution...."
—*Publishers Weekly*

Graduate student John Marr researches the life of Timothy Hasler: a philosopher whose career was cut tragically short over a decade earlier. On another front, Marr finds himself increasingly drawn toward shocking, depraved sexual entanglements with the homeless men of his neighborhood, until it begins to seem that Hasler's death might hold some key to his own life as a gay man in the age of AIDS.

## PHILIP JOSÉ FARMER
### A FEAST UNKNOWN
$6.95/276-0
"Sprawling, brawling, shocking, suspenseful, hilarious..."
—Theodore Sturgeon
Farmer's supreme anti-hero returns. Slowly, Lord Grandrith—armed with the belief that he is the son of Jack the Ripper—tells the story of his remarkable and unbridled life. His story begins with his discovery of the secret of immortality—and progresses to encompass the furthest extremes of human behavior.

# MASQUERADE BOOKS

**FLESH**
$6.95/303-1
Stagg explored the galaxies for 800 years, and could only hope that he would be welcomed home by an adoring—or at least appreciative—public. Upon his return, the hero Stagg is made the centerpiece of an incredible public ritual—one that will repeatedly, take him to the heights of ecstasy, and inexorably drag him toward the depths of hell.

## DANIEL VIAN
**ILLUSIONS**
$6.95/3074-1
International lust. Two tales of danger and desire in Berlin on the eve of WWII. From private homes to lurid cafés, passion is exposed in stark contrast to the brutal violence of the time, as desperate people explore their darkest sexual desires.

**PERSUASIONS**
$4.95/183-7
"The stockings are drawn tight by the suspender belt, tight enough to be stretched to the limit just above the middle part of her thighs, tight enough so that her calves glow through the sheer silk..." A double novel, including the classics *Adagio* and *Gabriela and the General*, this volume traces lust around the globe.

## ANDREI CODRESCU
**THE REPENTANCE OF LORRAINE**
$6.95/329-5
"One of our most prodigiously talented and magical writers."
—*NYT Book Review*

An aspiring writer, a professor's wife, a secretary, gold anklets, Maoists, Roman harlots—and more—swirl through this spicy tale of a harried quest for a mythic artifact. Written when the author was a young man, this lusty yarn was inspired by the heady days of the Sixties.

## TUPPY OWENS
**SENSATIONS**
$6.95/3081-4
Tuppy Owens tells the unexpurgated story of the making of *Sensations*—the first big-budget sex flick. Originally commissioned to appear in book form after the release of the film in 1975, *Sensations* is finally released. A rare peek behind the scenes of a porn-flick, from the genre's early, groundbreaking days.

## SOPHIE GALLEYMORE BIRD
**MANEATER**
$6.95/103-9
Through a bizarre act of creation, a man attains the "perfect" lover—by all appearances a beautiful, sensuous woman, but in reality something far darker. Once brought to life she will accept no mate, seeking instead the prey that will sate her hunger.

# BADBOY

## DAVID MAY
**MADRUGADA**
$6.95/574-3
Set in San Francisco's gay leather community, *Madrugada* follows the lives of a group of friends—and their many acquaintances—as they tangle with the thorny issues of love and lust. Uncompromising, mysterious, and arousing, David May weaves a complex web of relationships in a story cycle guaranteed to leave a lasting impression on any reader.

## PETER HEISTER
**ISLANDS OF DESIRE**
$6.95/480-1
Red-blooded lust on the wine-dark seas of classical Greece. Anacreon yearns to leave his small, isolated island and find adventure in one of the overseas kingdoms. Accompanied by some randy friends, Anacreon makes his dream come true—and discovers pleasures he never dreamed of!

## KITTY TSUI WRITING AS "ERIC NORTON"
**SPARKS FLY**
$6.95/551-4
The highest highs—and most wretched depths—of life as Eric Norton, a beautiful wanton living San Francisco's high life. *Sparks Fly* traces Norton's rise, fall, and resurrection, vividly marking the way with the personal affairs that give life meaning.

## BARRY ALEXANDER
**ALL THE RIGHT PLACES**
$6.95/482-8
Stories filled with hot studs in lust and love. From modern masters and slaves to medieval royals and their subjects, Alexander explores the mating rituals men have engaged in for centuries—all in the name of hidden desires...

**BUY ANY 4 BOOKS & CHOOSE 1 ADDITIONAL BOOK, OF EQUAL OR LESSER VALUE, AS YOUR FREE GIFT**

# MASQUERADE BOOKS

### MICHAEL FORD, ED.
**BUTCHBOYS:**
**Stories For Men Who Need It Bad**
$6.50/523-9

A big volume of tales dedicated to the rough-and-tumble type who can make a man weak at the knees. Some of today's best erotic writers explore the many possible variations on the age-old fantasy of the dominant man.

### WILLIAM J. MANN, ED.
**GRAVE PASSIONS:**
**Gay Tales of the Supernatural**
$6.50/405-4

A collection of the most chilling tales of passion currently being penned by today's most provocative gay writers. Unnatural transformations, otherworldly encounters, and deathless desires make for a collection sure to keep readers up late at night—for a variety of reasons!

### J. A. GUERRA, ED.
**COME QUICKLY:**
**For Boys on the Go**
$6.50/413-5

Here are over sixty of the hottest fantasies around—all designed to get you going in less time than it takes to dial 976. Julian Anthony Guerra, the editor behind the popular *Men at Work* and *Badboy Fantasies*, has put together this volume especially for you—a busy man on a modern schedule, who still appreciates a little old-fashioned action.

### JOHN PRESTON
**HUSTLING: A Gentleman's Guide to the Fine Art of Homosexual Prostitution**
$6.50/517-4

*"Fun and highly literary. What more could you expect form such an accomplished activist, author and editor?"*—Drummer

John Preston solicited the advice and opinions of "working boys" from across the country in his effort to produce the ultimate guide to the hustler's world. *Hustling* covers every practical aspect of the business, from clientele and payment options to "specialties," sidelines and drawbacks.
Trade $12.95/137-3
**MR. BENSON**
$4.95/3041-5

Jamie is an aimless young man lucky enough to encounter Mr. Benson. He is soon learns to accept this man as his master. Jamie's incredible adventures never fail to excite—especially when the going gets rough!

**TALES FROM THE DARK LORD**
$5.95/323-6

Twelve stunning works from the man *Lambda Book Report* called "the Dark Lord of gay erotica." The ritual of lust and surrender is explored in all its manifestations in this heart-stopping triumph of authority and vision.

**TALES FROM THE DARK LORD II**
$4.95/176-4
**THE ARENA**
$4.95/3083-0

Preston's take on the ultimate sex club. Men go there to abolish all limits. Only the author of *Mr. Benson* could have imagined so perfect an institution for the satisfaction of masculine desires.

**THE HEIR•THE KING**
$4.95/3048-2

Two complete novels in one special volume. *The Heir*, written in the lyric voice of the ancient myths, tells the story of a world where slaves and masters create a new sexual society. *The King* tells the story of a soldier who discovers his monarch's most secret desires.

**THE MISSION OF ALEX KANE**
**SWEET DREAMS**
$4.95/3062-8

It's the triumphant return of gay action hero Alex Kane! In *Sweet Dreams*, Alex travels to Boston where he takes on a street gang that stalks gay teenagers.

**GOLDEN YEARS**
$4.95/3069-5

When evil threatens the plans of a group of older gay men, Kane's got the muscle to take it head on. Along the way, he wins the support—and very specialized attentions—of a cowboy plucked right out of the Old West.

**DEADLY LIES**
$4.95/3076-8

Politics is a dirty business and the dirt becomes deadly when a smear campaign targets gay men. Who better to clean things up than Alex Kane!

**STOLEN MOMENTS**
$4.95/3098-9

Houston's evolving gay community is victimized by a malicious newspaper editor who is more than willing to sacrifice gays on the altar of circulation. He never counted on Alex Kane, fearless defender of gay dreams and desires.

**SECRET DANGER**
$4.95/111-X

Homophobia: a pernicious social ill not confined by America's borders. Alex Kane and the faithful Danny are called to a small European country, where a group of gay tourists is being held hostage by terrorists.

# MASQUERADE BOOKS

## LETHAL SILENCE
$4.95/125-X

Chicago becomes the scene of the right-wing's most noxious plan—facilitated by unholy political alliances. Alex and Danny head to the Windy City to battle the mercenaries who would squash gay men underfoot.

## MATT TOWNSEND
### SOLIDLY BUILT
$6.50/416-2

The tale of the relationship between Jeff, a young photographer, and Mark, the butch electrician hired to wire Jeff's new home. For Jeff, it's love at first sight; Mark, however, has more than a few hang-ups. Soon, both are forced to reevaluate their outlooks....

## JAY SHAFFER
### SHOOTERS
$5.95/284-1

No mere catalog of random acts, *Shooters* tells the stories of a variety of stunning men and the ways they connect in sexual and non-sexual ways. Shaffer always gets his man.

### ANIMAL HANDLERS
$4.95/264-7

In Shaffer's world, each and every man finally succumbs to the animal urges deep inside. And if there's any creature that promises a wild time, it's a beast who's been caged for far too long.

### FULL SERVICE
$4.95/150-0

No-nonsense guys bear down hard on each other as they work their way toward release in this finely detailed assortment of masculine fantasies.

## D. V. SADERO
### IN THE ALLEY
$4.95/144-6

Hardworking men—from cops to carpenters—bring their own special skills and impressive tools to the most satisfying job of all: capturing and breaking the male animal.

## SCOTT O'HARA
### DO-IT-YOURSELF PISTON POLISHING
$6.50/489-5

Longtime sex-pro Scott O'Hara draws upon his acute powers of seduction to lure you into a world of hard, horny men long overdue for a tune-up. Pretty soon, you'll pop your own hood for the servicing you know you need....

## SUTTER POWELL
### EXECUTIVE PRIVILEGES
$6.50/383-X

No matter how serious or sexy a predicament his characters find themselves in, Powell conveys the sheer exuberance of their encounters with a warm humor rarely seen in contemporary gay erotica.

## GARY BOWEN
### WESTERN TRAILS
$6.50/477-1

Some of gay literature's brightest stars tell the sexy truth about the many ways a rugged stud found to satisfy himself—and his buddy—in the Very Wild West.

### MAN HUNGRY
$5.95/374-0

A riveting collection of stories from one of gay erotica's new stars. Dipping into a variety of genres, Bowen crafts tales of lust unlike anything being published today.

## KYLE STONE
### THE HIDDEN SLAVE
$6.95/580-8

"This perceptive and finely-crafted work is a joy to discover. Kyle Stone's fiction belongs on the shelf of every serious fan of gay literature."
—Pat Califia

"Once again, Kyle Stone proves that imagination, ingenuity, and sheer intellectual bravado go a long way in making porn hot. This book turns us on and makes us think. Who could ask for anything more?"
—Michael Bronski

### HOT BAUDS 2
$6.50/479-8

Stone conducted another heated search through the world's randiest gay bulletin boards, resulting in one of the most scalding follow-ups ever published. Sexy, shameless, and eminently user-friendly.

### HOT BAUDS
$5.95/285-X

Stone combed cyberspace for the hottest fantasies of the world's horniest hackers. Stone has assembled the first collection of the raunchy erotica so many gay men surf the Net for.

### FIRE & ICE
$5.95/297-3

A collection of stories from the author of the infamous adventures of PB 500. Stone's characters always promise one thing: enough hot action to burn away your desire for anyone else....

# MASQUERADE BOOKS

## FANTASY BOARD
$4.95/212-4

Explore the future—through the intertwined lives of a collection of randy computer hackers. On the Lambda Gate BBS, every horny male is in search of virtual satisfaction!

## THE CITADEL
$4.95/198-5

The sequel to *PB 500*. Micah faces new challenges after entering the Citadel. Only his master knows what awaits—and whether Micah will again distinguish himself as the perfect instrument of pleasure....

## THE INITIATION OF PB 500
$4.95/141-1

He is a stranger on their planet, unschooled in their language, and ignorant of their customs. But this man, Micah—now known only by his number—will soon be trained in every detail of erotic service. He must prove himself worthy of the master who has chosen him....

## RITUALS
$4.95/168-3

Via a computer bulletin board, a young man finds himself drawn into sexual rites that transform him into the willing slave of a mysterious stranger. His former life is thrown off, and he learns to live for his Master's touch....

## ROBERT BAHR
### SEX SHOW
$4.95/225-6

Luscious dancing boys. Brazen, explicit acts. Take a seat, and get very comfortable, because the curtain's going up on a very special show no discriminating appetite can afford to miss.

## JASON FURY
### THE ROPE ABOVE, THE BED BELOW
$4.95/269-8

A vicious murderer is preying upon New York's go-go boys. In order to solve this mystery and save lives, each studly suspect must lay bare his soul—and more!

### ERIC'S BODY
$4.95/151-9

Fury's sexiest tales are collected in book form for the first time. Follow the irresistible Jason through sexual adventures unlike any you have ever read....

## LARS EIGHNER
### WHISPERED IN THE DARK
$5.95/286-8

A volume demonstrating Eighner's unique combination of strengths: poetic descriptive power, an unfailing ear for dialogue, and a finely tuned feeling for the nuances of male passion.

### AMERICAN PRELUDE
$4.95/170-5

Eighner is widely recognized as one of our best, most exciting gay writers. He is also one of gay erotica's true masters—and *American Prelude* shows why. Wonderfully written tales of all-American lust, peopled with red-blooded, oversexed studs.

## DAVID LAURENTS, ED.
### SOUTHERN COMFORT
$6.50/466-6

Editor David Laurents now unleashes a collection of tales focusing on the American South—stories reflecting not only Southern literary tradition, but the many sexy contributions the region has made to the iconography of the American Male.

### WANDERLUST:
#### Homoerotic Tales of Travel
$5.95/395-3

A volume dedicated to the special pleasures of faraway places—and the horny men who lie in wait for intrepid tourists. Celebrate the freedom of the open road, and the allure of men who stray from the beaten path....

### THE BADBOY BOOK OF EROTIC POETRY
$5.95/382-1

Erotic poetry has long been the problem child of the literary world—highly creative and provocative, but somehow too frank to be "art." *The Badboy Book of Erotic Poetry* restores eros to its place of honor in gay writing.

## AARON TRAVIS
### BIG SHOTS
$5.95/448-8

Two fierce tales in one electrifying volume. In *Beirut*, Travis tells the story of ultimate military power and erotic subjugation; *Kip*, Travis' hypersexed and sinister take on *film noir*, appears in unexpurgated form for the first time.

### EXPOSED
$4.95/126-8

A unique glimpse of the horny gay male in his natural environment! Cops, college jocks, ancient Romans—even Sherlock Holmes and his loyal Watson—cruise these pages, fresh from the pen of one of our hottest authors.

# MASQUERADE BOOKS

## CLAY CALDWELL & AARON TRAVIS
### TAG TEAM STUDS
$6.50/465-8

Wrestling will never seem the same, once you've made your way through this assortment of sweaty studs. But you'd better be wary—should one catch you off guard, you just might spend the night pinned to the mat....

## LARRY TOWNSEND
### LEATHER AD: M
$5.95/380-5

John's curious about what goes on between the leatherclad men he's fantasized about. He takes out a personal ad, and starts a journey of discovery that will leave no part of his life unchanged.

### LEATHER AD: S
$5.95/407-0

The tale continues—this time told from a Top's perspective. A simple ad generates many responses, and one man puts these studs through their paces....

## 1 800 906-HUNK

Hardcore phone action for real men. A scorching assembly of studs is waiting for your call—and eager to give you the headtrip of your life! Totally live, guaranteed one-on-one encounters. (Must be over 18.) No credit card needed. $3.98 per minute.

### BEWARE THE GOD WHO SMILES
$5.95/321-X

Two lusty young Americans are transported to ancient Egypt—where they are embroiled in warfare and taken as slaves by barbarians. The two finally discover that the key to escape lies within their own rampant libidos.

### 2069 TRILOGY
(This one-volume collection only $6.95)244-2

The early science-fiction trilogy in one volume! Set in the future, the 2069 Trilogy includes the tight plotting and shameless all-male sex action that established Townsend as one of erotica's masters.

### MIND MASTER
$4.95/209-4

Who better to explore the territory of erotic dominance than an author who helped define the genre—and knows that ultimate mastery always transcends the physical.

### THE LONG LEATHER CORD
$4.95/201-9

Chuck's stepfather never lacks money or male visitors with whom he enacts intense sexual rituals. As Chuck comes to terms with his own desires, he begins to unravel the mystery behind his stepfather's secret life.

### THE SCORPIUS EQUATION
$4.95/119-5

The story of a man caught between the demands of two galactic empires. Our randy hero must match wits—and more—with the incredible forces that rule his world.

### MAN SWORD
$4.95/188-8

The très gai tale of France's King Henri III, who encounters enough sexual schemers and politicos to alter one's picture of history forever!

### THE FAUSTUS CONTRACT
$4.95/167-5

Two attractive young men desperately need $1000. Will do anything. Travel OK. Danger OK. Call anytime... Two cocky young hustlers give more than they bargained for in this story of lust and its discontents.

### CHAINS
$4.95/158-6

Picking up street punks has always been risky, but here it sets off a string of events that must be read to be believed. Townsend at his grittiest.

### KISS OF LEATHER
$4.95/161-6

A look at the acts and attitudes of an earlier generation of gay leathermen, Kiss of Leather is full to bursting with gritty, raw action. Sensual pain and pleasure mix in this classic tale.

### RUN, LITTLE LEATHER BOY
$4.95/143-8

A chronic underachiever, Wayne seems to be going nowhere fast. He finds himself drawn to the masculine intensity of a dark and mysterious sexual underground, where he soon finds many goals worth pursuing....

### RUN NO MORE
$4.95/152-7

The sequel to Run, Little Leather Boy. This volume follows the further adventures of Townsend's leatherclad narrator as he travels every sexual byway available to the S/M male.

### THE SEXUAL ADVENTURES OF SHERLOCK HOLMES
$4.95/3097-0

A scandalously sexy take on this legendary sleuth. "A Study in Scarlet" is transformed to expose Mrs. Hudson as a man in drag, the Diogenes Club as an S/M arena, and clues only the redoubtable—and very horny—Sherlock Holmes could piece together.

### THE GAY ADVENTURES OF CAPTAIN GOOSE
$4.95/169-1

Jerome Gander is sentenced to serve aboard a ship manned by the most hardened, unrepentant criminals. In no time, Gander becomes well-versed in the ways of horny men at sea.

# MASQUERADE BOOKS

## DONALD VINING
### CABIN FEVER AND OTHER STORIES
$5.95/338-4

"Demonstrates the wisdom experience combined with insight and optimism can create." —*Bay Area Reporter*

Eighteen blistering stories in celebration of the most intimate of male bonding, reaffirming both love and lust in modern gay life.

## DEREK ADAMS
### MILES DIAMOND AND THE CASE OF THE CRETAN APOLLO
$6.95/381-3

Hired by a wealthy man to track a cheating lover, Miles finds himself involved in ways he could never have imagined! When the jealous Callahan threatens Diamond, Miles counters with a little undercover work—involving as many horny informants as he can get his hands on!

### PRISONER OF DESIRE
$6.50/439-9

Red-blooded, sweat-soaked excursions through the modern gay libido.

### THE MARK OF THE WOLF
$5.95/361-9

The past comes back to haunt one well-off stud, whose desires lead him into the arms of many men—and the midst of a mystery.

### MY DOUBLE LIFE
$5.95/314-7

Every man leads a double life, dividing his hours between the mundanities of the day and the pursuits of the night. Derek Adams shines a little light on the wicked things men do when no one's looking.

### HEAT WAVE
$4.95/159-4

Derek Adams sexy short stories are guaranteed to jump start any libido—and *Heatwave* contains his very best.

### MILES DIAMOND AND THE DEMON OF DEATH
$4.95/251-5

Miles always find himself in the stickiest situations—with any stud he meets! This adventure promises another carnal carnival.

### THE ADVENTURES OF MILES DIAMOND
$4.95/118-7

The debut of this popular gay gumshoe. "The Case of the Missing Twin" is packed with randy studs. Miles sets about uncovering all as he tracks down the delectable Daniel Travis.

## KELVIN BELIELE
### IF THE SHOE FITS
$4.95/223-X

An essential volume of tales exploring a world where randy boys can't help but do what comes naturally—as often as possible! Sweaty male bodies grapple in pleasure.

## JAMES MEDLEY
### THE REVOLUTIONARY & OTHER STORIES
$6.50/417-8

Billy, the son of the station chief of the American Embassy in Guatemala, is kidnapped and held for ransom. Frightened at first, Billy gradually develops an unimaginably close relationship with Juan, the revolutionary assigned to guard him.

### HUCK AND BILLY
$4.95/245-4

Young lust knows no bounds—and is often the hottest of one's life! Huck and Billy explore the desires that course through their bodies, determined to plumb the depths of passion.

## FLEDERMAUS
### FLEDERFICTION: STORIES OF MEN AND TORTURE
$5.95/355-4

Fifteen blistering paeans to men and their suffering. Unafraid of exploring the nether reaches of pain and pleasure, Fledermaus unleashes his most thrilling tales in this volume.

## VICTOR TERRY
### MASTERS
$6.50/418-6

A powerhouse volume of boot-wearing, whip-wielding, bone-crunching bruisers who've got what it takes to make a grown man grovel.

### SM/SD
$6.50/406-2

Set around a South Dakota town called Prairie, these tales offer evidence that the real rough stuff can still be found where men take what they want despite all rules.

### WHiPs
$4.95/254-X

Cruising for a hot man? You'd better be, because one way or another, these WHiPs—officers of the Wyoming Highway Patrol—are gonna pull you over for a little impromptu interrogation....

# MASQUERADE BOOKS

## MAX EXANDER
### DEEDS OF THE NIGHT:
### Tales of Eros and Passion
$5.95/348-1

MAXimum porn! Exander's a writer who's seen it all—and is more than happy to describe every inch of it in pulsating detail. A whirlwind tour of the hypermasculine libido.

### LEATHERSEX
$4.95/210-8

Hard-hitting tales from merciless Max. This time he focuses on the leather clad lust that draws together only the most willing and talented of tops and bottoms—for an all-out orgy of limitless surrender and control....

### MANSEX
$4.95/160-8

"Mark was the classic leatherman: a huge, dark stud in chaps, with a big black moustache, hairy chest and enormous muscles. Exactly the kind of men Todd liked—strong, hunky, masculine, ready to take control...."

## TOM CAFFREY
### TALES FROM THE MEN'S ROOM
$5.95/364-3

Male lust at its most elemental and arousing. If there's a lesson to be learned, it's that the Men's Room is less a place than a state of mind—one that every man finds himself in, day after day....

### HITTING HOME
$4.95/222-1

Titillating and compelling, the stories in Hitting Home make a strong case for there being only one thing on a man's mind.

## "BIG" BILL JACKSON
### EIGHTH WONDER
$4.95/200-0

"Big" Bill Jackson's always the randiest guy in town—no matter what town he's in. From the bright lights and back rooms of New York to the open fields and sweaty bods of a small Southern town, "Big" Bill always manages to cause a scene!

## TORSTEN BARRING
### GUY TRAYNOR
$6.50/414-3

Some call Guy Traynor a theatrical genius; others say he was a madman. All anyone knows for certain is that his productions were the result of blood, sweat and outrageous erotic torture!

### PRISONERS OF TORQUEMADA
$5.95/252-3

Another volume sure to push you over the edge. How cruel is the "therapy" practiced at Casa Torquemada? Barring is just the writer to evoke such steamy sexual malevolence.

### SHADOWMAN
$4.95/178-0

From spoiled aristocrats to randy youths sowing wild oats at the local picture show, Barring's imagination works overtime in these steamy vignettes of homolust—past, present and future.

### PETER THORNWELL
$4.95/149-7

Follow the exploits of Peter Thornwell as he goes from misspent youth to scandalous stardom, all thanks to an insatiable libido and love for the lash.

### THE SWITCH
$4.95/3061-X

Sometimes a man needs a good whipping, and The Switch certainly makes a case! Packed with hot studs and unrelenting passions, these stories established Barring as a writer to be watched.

## BERT McKENZIE
### FRINGE BENEFITS
$5.95/354-6

From the pen of a widely published short story writer comes a volume of highly immodest tales. Not afraid of getting down and dirty, McKenzie produces some of today's most visceral sextales.

## CHRISTOPHER MORGAN
### STEAM GAUGE
$6.50/473-9

This volume abounds in manly men doing what they do best—to, with, or for any hot stud who crosses their paths.

### THE SPORTSMEN
$5.95/385-6

A collection of super-hot stories dedicated to the all-American athlete. These writers know just the type of guys that make up every red-blooded male's starting line-up....

### MUSCLE BOUND
$4.95/3028-8

In the NYC bodybuilding scene, Tommy joins forces with sexy Will Rodriguez in a battle of wits and biceps at the hottest gym in town, where the weak are bound and crushed by iron-pumping gods.

# MASQUERADE BOOKS

## SONNY FORD
### REUNION IN FLORENCE
$4.95/3070-9
Follow Adrian and Tristan an a sexual odyssey that takes in all ports known to ancient man. From lustful turks to insatiable Mamluks, these two spread pleasure throughout the classical world!

## ROGER HARMAN
### FIRST PERSON
$4.95/179-9
Each story takes the form of a confessional—told by men who've got plenty to confess! From the "first time ever" to firsts of different kinds....

## J. A. GUERRA, ED.
### SLOW BURN
$4.95/3042-3
Welcome to the Body Shoppe! Torsos get lean and hard, pecs widen, and stomachs ripple in these sexy stories of the power and perils of physical perfection.

## DAVE KINNICK
### SORRY I ASKED
$4.95/3090-3
Unexpurgated interviews with gay porn's rank and file. Get personal with the men behind (and under) the "stars," and discover the hot truth about the porn business.

## SEAN MARTIN
### SCRAPBOOK
$4.95/224-8
From the creator of *Doc and Raider* comes this hot collection of life's horniest moments—all involving studs sure to set your pulse racing!

## CARO SOLES & STAN TAL, EDS.
### BIZARRE DREAMS
$4.95/187-X
An anthology of voices dedicated to exploring the dark side of human fantasy. Here are the most talented practitioners of "dark fantasy," the most forbidden sexual realm of all.

## MICHAEL LOWENTHAL, ED.
### THE BADBOY EROTIC LIBRARY
### Volume 1
$4.95/190-X
Excerpts from *A Secret Life, Imre, Sins of the Cities of the Plain, Teleny* and others demonstrate the gift for portraying sex between men that led to many of these titles being banned.

### THE BADBOY EROTIC LIBRARY
### Volume 2
$4.95/211-6
This time, selections are taken from *Mike and Me, Muscle Bound, Men at Work, Badboy Fantasies,* and *Slowburn.*

## ERIC BOYD
### MIKE AND ME
$5.95/419-4
Mike joined the gym squad to bulk up on muscle. Little did he know he'd be turning on every sexy muscle jock in Minnesota! Hard bodies collide in a series of horny workouts.
### MIKE AND THE MARINES
$6.50/497-6
Mike takes on America's most elite corps of studs! Join in on the never-ending sexual escapades of this singularly lustful platoon!

## ANONYMOUS
### A SECRET LIFE
$4.95/3017-2
Meet Master Charles: eighteen and quite innocent, until his arrival at the Sir Percival's Academy, where the lessons are supplemented with a crash course in pure sexual heat!
### SINS OF THE CITIES OF THE PLAIN
$5.95/322-8
indulge yourself in the scorching memoirs of young man-about-town Jack Saul. Jack's sinful escapades grow wilder with every chapter!
### IMRE
$4.95/3019-9
An extraordinary lost classic of obsession, gay erotic desire, and romance in a small European town on the eve of WWI.
### TELENY
$4.95/3020-2
Often attributed to Oscar Wilde. A young man dedicates himself to a succession of forbidden pleasures.
### THE SCARLET PANSY
$4.95/189-6
Randall Etrange travels the world in search of true love. Along the way, his journey becomes a sexual odyssey of truly epic proportions.

## PAT CALIFIA, ED.
### THE SEXPERT
$4.95/3034-2
From penis size to toy care, bar behavior to AIDS awareness, The Sexpert responds to real concerns with uncanny wisdom and a razor wit.

## ORDERING IS EASY

MC/VISA orders can be placed by calling our toll-free number
PHONE 800-375-2356/FAX 212-986-7355
HOURS M-F 9am—12am EDT Sat & Sun 12pm—8pm EDT
E-MAIL masqbks@aol.com
or mail this coupon to:
MASQUERADE DIRECT
**DEPT. BMRB97** 801 2ND AVE., NY, NY 10017

BUY ANY FOUR BOOKS AND CHOOSE ONE ADDITIONAL BOOK,
OF EQUAL OR LESSER VALUE, AS YOUR FREE GIFT

| QTY. | TITLE | NO. | PRICE |
|------|-------|-----|-------|
|      |       |     |       |
|      |       |     |       |
|      |       |     | **FREE** |
|      |       |     |       |
|      |       |     |       |

**DEPT. BMRB97** (please have this code
available when placing your order)

We never sell, give or trade any
customer's name.

| | |
|---|---|
| SUBTOTAL | |
| POSTAGE AND HANDLING | |
| TOTAL | |

In the U.S., please add $1.50 for the first book and 75¢ for each additional book; in Canada, add $2.00 for the first book
and $1.25 for each additional book. Foreign countries: add $4.00 for the first book and $2.00 for each additional book. No
C.O.D. orders. Please make all checks payable to Masquerade/Direct. Payable in U.S. currency only. NY state residents add
8.25% sales tax. Please allow 4–6 weeks for delivery. Payable in U.S. currency only.

NAME_____

ADDRESS_____

CITY_____ STATE _____ ZIP_____

TEL( )_____

E-MAIL _____
PAYMENT:  ☐ CHECK  ☐ MONEY ORDER  ☐ VISA  ☐ MC

CARD NO._____ EXP. DATE_____